IN ALL GOOD FAITH

Liza Nash Taylor

IN ALL
GOOD
FAITH

A Novel

BLACK STONE PUBLISHING

Printed in the United States of America

First edition: 2021
ISBN 978-1-9826-0397-7
Fiction / Historical / General

1 3 5 7 9 10 8 6 4 2

CIP data for this book is available
from the Library of Congress

Blackstone Publishing
31 Mistletoe Rd.
Ashland, OR 97520

www.BlackstonePublishing.com

For Annabel, William, and Thomas

Prologue
MAY MARSHALL

PARIS, FRANCE
APRIL 1926

The vaulted arcades of the Rue de Rivoli streamed with fashionable women in spring linen. Some wore neat cloches trimmed with silk camellias. Others resembled graceful birds, with wide hat brims floating like languorous wings. The counterparts of these fashionable Madams and Mademoiselles, the flâneurs of Paris, sported plumage of cream flannel or pastel seersucker suits. Leaning in to converse, the men's straw boaters touched—then stilled—the ladies' hat brims. In pairs, they perched shoulder to shoulder at tiny café tables or crossed the avenue to promenade in the Jardin des Tuileries. Like a crow among doves, one black-clad crone hurried by, shopping basket clutched to her bosom.

May Marshall stood in one of these arcades, below the entrance of number 228, the Hotel Meurice, unaware of the afternoon crowd flowing by. In sixteen months in Paris she had passed these mosaic-tiled steps, these glass-and-brass revolving doors dozens of times. Now, she clasped her handbag, counting silently: *Three steps up—one doorway, one vestibule, one lobby.*

Three steps, one doorway, one vestibule, one lobby, and he would be there.

Byrd.

Eight months had passed since they had last seen each other, on that sad August day when they traveled together from Paris to the American Military Cemetery in Château-Thierry. Their goodbye that day had been shadowed by the remembrance of Byrd's brother, and the grave they had sought and found, among those of 2,200 soldiers. They had parted with so much unsaid, with so much doubt and confusion. Byrd returned to Virginia and May remained in Paris, determined to honor a pledge to her loyal friend, Rocky, to help him open his first hair salon. She threw herself into the work, learning the business as they went along, building Rocky's clientele while rebuilding her own confidence.

Four months later the salon was a raging success. Returning to the house after closing one night, May had let herself in, looking forward to a bath. Crossing the hall to the stairs, she stopped. A stack of mail lay on the entry table. On top, a green envelope with American stamps. Later she would remember the sequence of emotions—first, hopefulness. She took a step closer to the table. Her name, written with a black fountain pen. The right-slanting, choppy cursive.

A letter from Byrd.

In a matter of seconds hopefulness bloomed into elation. Her breath caught, pausing the moment. She didn't know what she hoped to find. There were degrees of happy and well. *Happy* and *well* were relative, as in, *I'm happy and well, doing splendidly without you.* No. *Fine* would be acceptable. *I'm fine and alive.* She wondered, in that moment, if she might prefer to read, *I'm miserably unhappy, and cannot live without you?*

Inside the envelope were six scrawled pages stuck into a banal Christmas card illustrated with a Scottie dog holding a wrapped package in its paws. She had held her breath to the bottom of the first page, afraid to read on, afraid of what she might learn. Over the past months, she had, in her mind, composed her own letter, refining it over and over, hesitant to put pen to paper, to be the first to open communication, unsure if communication was even wanted.

His letter told of his new law office off Court Square in Charlottesville, *C. Byrd Craig, Esq.*; of Thanksgiving with his parents, of dove hunting in Bath County with his father. It was as if Byrd were in the room with her—the bedroom where she was living in Paris in her friend Rocky's house, with its grand, robin's-egg blue paneling and tall windows over-looking the Parc Monceau.

May had perched on the windowsill, holding the paper to her face, then touching the lines of ink, wanting to race through the pages. The early winter light turned blue outside and she forced herself to read slowly, to savor each word. He wrote matter-of-factly of his divorce being final-ized, of the awkward explanations made to friends and colleagues—that his wife of ten months had run away with an older, former lover and no one's heart had broken over it. He was living in a cottage in Keswick, on his parent's property. She read Byrd's words and knew that she still loved him.

The next three letters, in response to hers, grew more open, more con-fidential, with more of the ease she and Byrd had enjoyed all of those years ago, growing up as neighbors. It was what he wrote about Keswick that pulled at her heart; the vixen and three cubs with a den in the front field, the four new foals at his father's farm, his parents' annual Christmas party. She could picture it all—the hayfields and pastures between his family house and hers, bisected with lines of panel fencing, the deep green of the Southwest Mountains, the call-and-answer shrieks of red-tailed hawks, hunting in mated pairs.

Home. She had run from there and ended up here, in Paris. So many risks, so many mistakes. With each exchange of letters, the idea of return-ing home grew more appealing, and more so with the letters her father sent to her, with their own reconciliation and his news of Keswick Farm and the market.

Then, in early June; Byrd's telegram. Did she want him to come to her?

Eight days later, here she was, standing on a street in Paris, studying the tile design of the hotel entrance with more attention than it deserved. May squared her shoulders and took the first step.

After three days together in Paris, they were engaged. Rocky helped Byrd to choose a ring at a shop in the Place Vendôme—a sapphire with diamond baguettes. Next, a stop at Western Union to send the fait accompli telegrams to her father and Byrd's parents. Then, a blissful month alone together in a quiet stone house that belonged to one of Rocky's clients, in the wine region, near Beaune. They had explored the French countryside, the vineyards, the old châteaux, and the village markets, sleeping late and dining at nine as the summer sun went down. The pungent aroma of chestnut blossoms wafted through the air.

On the steamship to New York, they hesitated to discuss what people back in Virginia might say. They decided to marry at the county courthouse, as quietly and privately as possible, as soon as they could get a license. They made plans for Byrd's law practice and May tried to calm her nerves at the thought of seeing her father for the first time in almost two years. She steeled herself for the reaction of Byrd's parents and what those reactions might churn up for her. It was as if she were back at college, arriving with her scholarship only to become aware of all of the things she was *not*—not from Richmond society, *not* a debutante, *not* the virginal, sweet-tempered, future Garden Club president Byrd's mother probably hoped for.

May was returning home to Keswick, determined to begin afresh, to take her place as Byrd's partner and a woman with a head for business. Things were going to be different this time.

Part I
THREADBARE

"How many threadbare souls are to be found under silken cloaks and gowns!"

Dictionary of Burning Words of Brilliant Writers
Thomas Brooks, 1895

One
MAY

The apprehensiveness that kept May Craig from sleeping well followed her into the kitchen. The smell of percolating coffee was repellent; she was already jittery. Next, a frying pan of cooling bacon grease made her wonder, *How on earth could anyone think of breakfast?* (Rhetorical: her dear, thoughtful husband Byrd had, and was feeding the children.)

At work, the morning at Keswick Market progressed with no surprises, yet May continued to be plagued by a feeling of being displaced in her own body. Her awareness of time was amplified, as were her senses. Now it was almost eleven fifteen, and there was that glass canister on the market counter—pickled pig's feet, floating in brown-tinged vinegar. Their fatty pallor brought bile to her throat. She ran a hand over the back of her neck, pushing the ragged ends of her dark hair from her collar and wishing she'd made the time for a haircut.

Her alertness was a form of preparation—an anticipatory defense. *Showdown at noon.* Twelve thirty, actually. The phrase played in her head like a radio melodrama. Some people, she mused, are genuinely good at confrontation. Her lawyer husband, for instance. Every day, he engaged in it, by choice. May avoided confrontation, as a rule. Today she had an appointment with it.

The oak counter where she stood had a shallow trough worn across the width of the wood—the result of eighty years' worth of money and goods passing back and forth. Heavy glass canisters of dill pickles and beet-pink eggs were lined up beside the cash register. Smaller canisters held penny candy, and a curved glass case displayed the homemade sweets produced in the market kitchen. The telephone began to jangle, pulling May from her reverie. She lifted the earpiece and said, "Good morning, Keswick Market."

"May? Hazel Brownlow. How's your daddy getting on?"

"You're nice to ask, Mrs. Brownlow. Still not back at work. He got his cast off, but his back still acts up. I'll tell him you asked."

"And how's that darling boy? Saw him at the Post Office last week. I declare, he's getting so big, and those blond curls . . . just as handsome as his daddy. How old is he now?"

May's brow relaxed as her thoughts shifted to her son. "Almost five. And Sister is six months."

"Land sakes, they grow too fast! Listen, Sugar, I'm starting my fruit-cakes. I need a few things."

May half-listened, watching the clock, scribbling on a pad. She read the list back, then said, "Blue will drop this by, right after closing. Yes, ma'am. You're welcome. We appreciate your business." As she hung up, she thought, *At least the Brownlows pay their bill.*

May lifted the glass bell from a footed stand to cut a block of pecan fudge, wrapping it in waxed paper before weighing it in the zinc tub of the hanging scales. *Sweets*, she thought, *people will still indulge in a little sweet.* Going down the list, she filled the order, stacking items in a fruit crate. It crossed her mind to add a few things to the box, to see if Hazel Brownlow would go to the trouble of returning them to get her money back, or simply pay the bill and overlook the error. It was risky because if she were irritated enough, she might just quietly decide it was easier to drive to the Piggly Wiggly in Charlottesville instead.

On shelves behind the counter, neat rows of mason jars held the jams, preserves, conserves, and chutneys that Keswick Farm had always been known for. Each bore a black-and-white label, imprinted with a drawing of the farmhouse and the slogan: *Made with pride since*

1849. The words seemed a mockery. *Pride. Made with pride.* Jars filled with pride didn't pay the bills. Not unless they sold. May had tried to modernize, sewing fresh curtains for the front, installing an electric Coca-Cola cooler, stacking merchandise in pyramids, as she had seen in magazines. She gnawed on a hangnail as her gaze shifted. Above the front door, the Butter-Nut Coffee clock read eleven fifteen. She winced, shaking her thumb.

The bell above the front door tinkled as a blast of cold air swept in. May looked up, smiling reflexively, but her smile quickly faded. A hunched man in threadbare clothes clutched a limp tweed cap and shuffled toward her in shoes with no laces. "Howdy, ma'am," he said, bobbing his head. "You own this place? Wondering if you might have some work needs doing? Enough to get a fella a sandwich?" He tugged an earlobe, smiling in an apparently practiced way that managed to almost hide missing teeth. His nails were broken and black-rimmed, and reddish stubble covered his cheeks. Every day, more of these sad men showed up. Most went to the back door. The Keswick train depot had become a stopover for those heading south in search of harvesting work and warmer weather.

As May was about to reply, the canvas curtain covering the doorway behind her whipped open. Blue Harris scowled at the stranger. May said, "Blue, this gentleman is asking for work."

Blue flapped his hand toward the front door, saying, "Didn't I tell you to get on?" He assumed a habitual stance, thumbs hooked behind his suspenders, rocking on his heels. He said to May, "Just shooed him from the back door, and here he comes, right 'round the front, bold as brass."

The man's eyebrows raised in an expression of subservient hopefulness. She had seen it before, on a hundred different faces. "Ma'am," he said, quietly, "I can do whatever job he does, for half the wages." He inched closer until she could have reached out and touched his frayed sleeve. "Honest, I can."

May's stomach fluttered. The man's clothes put off an odor that stuck in her throat like a tiny fish bone. She walked to where Blue stood, passing the sales slip over the counter to him. "Here's an order for Mrs. Brownlow." To the man she said, "We're not hiring, and even if we were, this place couldn't function without Mister Harris. He's run this market for years." The man's mouth turned down, caught out. May and Blue exchanged looks. Blue nodded once. May said, "Hold on." She wrapped a wedge of cheese with a handful of soda crackers. "Take this. And good luck to you."

The man bobbed his head, looking May in the eye, and then Blue. He sighed, saying, "I 'pologize, ma'am, mister. Used to be, I'd never say nothing like that. I was a brake man on the C&O. A good-paying railroad job. Nowadays I'd dig ditches, only there's no ditches to be dug. I been looking for a job for two years." He dipped his head, licking his cracked lips, and whispered, "Much obliged to you both. Very kind." He plucked up the packet and backed slowly toward the door, clutching the food to his chest, his eyes shifting warily as if May might snatch it back. As the door swung shut, he called, "God bless, ma'am. Sorry again."

May wiped the cheese knife as Blue turned back through the curtain, shaking his head. She followed him to the kitchen, passing the storage pantry and converted storeroom where he lived. On the big cast iron stove, a round-bottomed copper kettle steamed. May leaned over it, inhaling sweet aromas of melted sugar and molasses with a pungent hint of vinegar.

Blue's forehead furrowed as he sifted cream of tartar into his palm then sprinkled it into the pot while May stirred. He said, "Hobos have got this place marked, May. I found their signs, chalked on the wall next to the back door. I don't know how to read those marks, but I reckon it says, *'Step right up, here—the nice lady will feed you.'* What do you s'pose that mark looks like? Hmmm?" With an air of authority, he took the wooden spoon from May. He scraped the inside of the kettle then tapped the spoon against the rim of a teacup filled with water. A long, glossy strand dripped into the cup, forming a blob in the bottom. For an instant, Blue studied it, then put the cup aside and began cutting chunks of butter into the bubbling mixture while May measured out baking soda.

The butter floated and melted as Blue continued, "I'm just saying, you're taking food out of your own family's mouths to give to them who might not be willing to hit a lick of work."

May said, "You sound like Daddy. What if *you* didn't have a job or a place to live? There are five million people in this country out of work. You heard that poor man. '*There by the grace of God . . .*'"

"You can't feed the world and your own family too. That's all I'm saying." Blue removed the heavy pan from the heat, then opened a small brown bottle and tipped it, pouring carefully without measuring. A waft of vanilla saturated the air, mellowing instantly as it melded with the other ingredients to form the singularly sweet aroma of Blue's Velvet Molasses Taffy. May spread butter over the marble slab that covered half of the work table, then Blue poured out the hot, thick liquid. As it spread and began to cool, May used a spatula to fold the edges inward while Blue rubbed butter over his calloused brown hands. He began to roll and stretch the candy as if it were cool to the touch. Since her childhood she had watched this process dozens of times and every time May had tried to help with this step, her palms and fingers blistered. They worked in tandem, with an ease that comes with years of familiarity and mutual trust. As he worked the taffy, pulling and looping the strands, it thickened, changing from syrupy deep brown into a glossy, pale tan that was almost pearlescent. Timing was everything. Once it cooled completely, it became too brittle to work.

May laid out three sheets of waxed paper and glanced again at the time. "I told Daddy I'd pick him up at 11:40. Sorry to leave you short-handed. If things go well today, maybe we *can* hire a clerk."

With an expert twist of his wrist, Blue spun a coil of warm taffy into a rope of uniform thickness and draped it gently onto the paper. May stood poised with a buttered knife to score the rope into individual pieces. It was, by necessity, work soon finished. Blue wiped his hands, and said, "You did tell Byrd what you're up to?"

May said, brightly, "Mrs. Brownlow's order is boxed up. She asked if you'd make her a double batch of candied orange peel and drop it by before Christmas."

Blue cocked his head. "You didn't tell him. May, I swear." He rubbed a palm over the back of his neck. "This is some risky business here."

"I'm going to make it work. *We're* going to make it work. I've got to run."

Outside, frost shimmered on the faded black paint of the old Stude-baker. May opened the driver's door and tossed a bundle of envelopes and a ledger across the seat, along with her hat. She tucked her coat beneath her legs, wincing at the cold leather. Shifting into second gear, she pulled around the market then turned left, onto Route 22. She was grateful to be alone—if even for a few minutes.

Times were hard all over, not only in Virginia. Drought, insects, and tree blight had decimated the orchards at Keswick Farm and threatened the closing of the canning operation that had operated since 1849. At the market the stack of unpaid credit slips from customers grew higher each month, and May asked her father, how could they deny milk to the children of neighbors? And he would answer that those very neigh-bors sent their children in for groceries because they were too ashamed to confront the debt they knew they would not pay. How—Henry Mar-shall asked—could they continue to feed the hungry wanderers who knocked at the back door? May would answer: those poor men might be out of work through no fault of their own. Then a cyclical argument would begin, where father and daughter inevitably ended up pressing the same, all-too-familiar points. It had become almost comical. In human-itarian terms, May knew she was right. From a practical standpoint, her father was. But he didn't have to face those poor men every day and see their shame. Shame was something that May Craig knew about. She had become adept at keeping it at bay.

It had been seven years since May had run from this place—from Kes-wick Farm and home, away from moonshining charges, away from Byrd Craig. She had run to New York, and then to Paris, with dreams of becom-ing a costume designer. *Shame.* Yes, May had a cabinet full of shameful memories—being expelled from Mary Baldwin College and the heartbreak that followed; the fibs that turned to lies as she told her father, and Byrd, and everyone at home that she was finding tremendous success in the the-aters of Paris, when in fact, she was nearly destitute. That was in 1925.

Now, in the winter of 1931, shame and destitution seemed to dom-inate the national news. Heartbreaking stories of lost savings, evictions, unemployment, and unrest were everywhere, not just in the cities, but here at home, in small, rural towns like Keswick, Virginia. And there were no signs that things were getting any better.

May rested her elbow on the window frame, pushing her too-long bangs off her forehead. *I should be optimistic, and grateful,* she thought. *God, what is wrong with me?*

Two
DORRIT

God? What is wrong with me?

Sometimes it was an invisible feather, a wisp skimming the back of her neck. Sometimes it was a spindle, winding tight inside her chest until she breathed like a cornered rabbit. And sometimes—the worst times—fear was a thing with teeth and claws. It rode on streetcars and hid in movie theaters. It came to church and sat down beside her.

On a Wednesday night in December, Dorrit Sykes was the cornered rabbit. She sat stiffly on a tufted velveteen cushion in a church pew in the Annex of the Mother Church of Christ, Scientist. Around her, Christian Science parishioners sat attentively, focused forward toward the altar. She breathed shallowly, silently reciting, *Our Father . . .* It was a familiar litany, though she found no comfort in the familiarity. She knew, as a practical person, that her fear was unfounded. She was doing something utterly normal. *Wednesday night is for church*, she told herself. *Church is a safe place.*

Who art in Heaven . . . Twelve long rows of pews between herself and the exit. How many people—maybe a hundred, maybe staring, maybe whispering to each other—*that poor Sykes family?* Maybe the others saw that she felt trapped, that her thoughts were not on the service at all, but were instead jumping erratically with imagined disaster, her mind whirling with memories she could not block. Around her, women fanned themselves with folded service programs; the church was overheated.

Dorrit had signed up for nursery duty, as she often did, as an avoidance of sitting through services. When she arrived there had been only one baby, and a volunteer already there, that horrid, bossy Mrs. Fleming. *Mrs. Phlegming*, Dorrit secretly called her. When a woman arrived with a second infant, Mrs. Fleming had reached for it, cooing in baby talk that she would manage *dest fine awone*, that Dorrit should go to the service. Then, patting the arm of the exhausted-looking new mother, Mrs. Fleming said—with a glance toward Dorrit—"You know, Cecelia, my own childbirths—all four—were truly divine transitions." She held up one index finger, her voice lilting, "One must free the mind of the illusion of pain. One must purify the thoughts. After my last, I got right up to make supper. Pot roast with pearl onions."

Dorrit thought of fleeing then, but the young mother had said, "Are you by yourself? I'll walk with you."

So, thus banished from the nursery, Dorrit had arrived just before the service started and had no choice but to take a seat in the second row. At least the other parishioners slid down to make room at the end of the pew. She wouldn't be trapped in the center. Small mercies.

Dorrit squeezed her eyes closed as a flush of heat spread over her cheeks and forehead. She hated those deep red stains, always so vivid against her usual pallor. Silently ordering herself to breathe, she opened her eyes and began her series of distractions—visually tracing the intricate stenciled designs bordering the walls—the burnished golds and reds and mossy greens in a pattern reminiscent of an oriental carpet. She devised names for the wall color, which was pinkish, and brownish—yet neither pink nor brown. She counted the tall pipes of the organ until they ran together, then studied the stained glass windows—the closest being a beatific Madonna swathed in cobalt blue, surrounded by pearly glass clouds. From the pulpit, ebullient parishioners delivered awed, grateful testimonies of healing. But she wasn't listening.

Hallowed be thy name. Dorrit had been raised in Boston and brought up to believe that pain and illness were illusions, as Christian Science founder Mary Baker Eddy proclaimed and parishioners like Mrs. Fleming espoused, signaling a defect in the spirit. When she had listened, on other Wednesday nights, from the safety of the back row, Dorrit experienced no inspiration, no reinforcement of faith. Instead, she was left with a resigned, disjointed sort of guilt—a feeling of failure that she herself had no testimony of healing to offer. Had she been passed over, for someone more deserving? Sometimes she could not help but wonder—if her nervous spells *were* miraculously cured, would that mean that someone else—someone with a worse affliction—might never be healed? Were healings some sort of holy ticket, with only so many issued? Were she and her family marked somehow as unworthy or undeserving, or worse—lacking in faith?

Second by second, minute by long minute, she willed herself to stay where she was. During the singing she stood, dutifully mouthing lyrics she knew by heart while discreetly inhaling the comforting mustiness of old paper and the leather binding of the hymnal, all the while wishing it were a Nancy Drew mystery instead, and she was safe, at home. During prayers, she pressed her palms together and studied the tail of her long, pale brown braid, then counted the tiny mosaic tiles of the floor, tapping her feet with silent agitation. The stitching of one sole of her scuffed brown shoes had worn away so that if she wiggled her toes just so, the split gaped like a fish's mouth.

Nancy Drew doesn't have holes in her shoes. She wears shined saddle oxfords. She probably has them in brown-and-white and black-and-white. New shoes cost $2.98.

Nancy Drew never has nerves.

They were the same age, she and Nancy. Sixteen. And yet, Nancy had her own automobile and two best friends. She traveled to exciting places and had adventures. Nancy Drew was fearless. *Our Father,* Dorrit recited again in a tiny whisper, *Who art in Heaven.* But it was starting. First, a heightened awareness of her skin. Less than an itch, more than a tingle. Every inch of skin on her body, all at once, heavy with dread. Then, the skittering thoughts. Her hands turned cold and seemed to disconnect from her body. Then, the pressure inside her ribcage, the squeezing; that feeling at the top of her throat, a drawstring pulling taut. *Hallowed be thy name.* Her eyes flicked from the altar to the side exit.

The Church of Christ, Scientist, had no proper minister. Services were led, as Mrs. Eddy decreed, by Jesus Christ and conducted by its members. So as the testimonies continued with one parishioner finishing a story of walking miles on an ankle he had sprained the previous day, another testifier took his place. The woman described the miraculous healing, through prayer, of a bunion on her left foot. When Dorrit had asked her mother about pain she was told to have faith, to pray that her thoughts would be changed—that her mind would cease to corrupt her body with weakness. But faith was hard.

Faith had not saved her mother.

When the service concluded, Dorrit sprang from her seat, her mouth dry, her back damp with perspiration. Outside, parishioners set off into the December night in pairs or family groups, fathers wrapping necks in mufflers; mothers stooping to adjust a child's mitten. She hurried alone through the church plaza, away from the tall granite columns and the 126-foot dome and spire of the Mother Church.

At the edge of the long reflecting pond, a pair of men in threadbare overcoats stood beneath a streetlight, bindles and bedrolls on the pavement beside them. One tipped his hat to Dorrit and she looked away, unable to accept his civility. If she gave him the change in her pocket, she would have to walk home, and all she wanted was to be at home. And there it was again, *guilt.* So many people in this city, hungry, without jobs or homes, sleeping on pavement in the winter wind. She turned back, but the men were walking away.

The skyline of Boston loomed gray, dotted with yellow-white windows, the air heavy with the promise of more snow. On Huntington Avenue, Dorrit waited for the Chestnut Hill Line trolley. The spell was not over, but it was waning. *Streetcar, bus, walk two blocks, three flights of stairs.* A loud, scraping noise caused her to turn. A weary-looking nag pulled a wide snowplow down the center of the street, led by a man with his head wrapped in a woolen muffler. Some entrepreneurial spirit had set up a line of fir trees on the sidewalk, with a brazier for warmth. A hand-lettered sign read: *Merry Christmas! Fresh trees!* The Sykeses would not have a tree. They never had. A long church service would be followed by a quiet Christmas day at home, intended to be spent in reflection.

At Copley Square, Dorrit changed to the bus, then walked the last blocks. Ahead, under a streetlight, she could see the darkened hulk of the Winchell School, and across the street, her own stoop, 23 Blossom Street in the west end of Boston. *Home. Safety.*

Inside, two shivering little boys sat side-by-side on the bottom step, hands clasped between their knees. They were dressed identically, in patched woolen knickers and frayed overcoats. Both had black hair and green eyes. "Colin, Fred," Dorrit said, "what are you doing down here? It's nearly eight thirty."

Fred, five, wiped his eyes. Colin Sullivan, two years older, said, "Quit your blubbering, Fred." To Dorrit, he said, through chattering teeth, "The baby lady's here. Da sent us out. Ma's hollering and now Fred's hungry."

Dorrit drew in a sharp breath. "The baby lady?"

"Ma sent Da to fetch her," Colin said. "We dinna get 'ny supper."

Dorrit took their cold, bare hands. "Well, come up with me. Let's see if we can't get you warmed up."

Colin and Fred lived on the second floor, rear, with their parents. Dorrit earned a nickel a day, watching the boys after she got home from school, while their mother worked late shift in a laundry. On the second-floor landing, Dorrit paused, listening. From down the hall, she heard raised voices. "Wait here." She knocked lightly on the Sullivans' door. Her breath steamed in the unheated hallway. There was shuffling, then the door opened. The boys' father squinted at Dorrit. She said, "I'll keep them upstairs. Hope it all goes . . . well."

Sullivan nodded once, blowing out a long breath. "Much obliged."

Dorrit unlocked the door of the Sykes' apartment, on the third floor, front. The boys stood in the doorway. "Come on then," she said. "Let's get you warm and then we'll have a story." Crossing the linoleum floor, she switched on gaslights, saying, brightly, "The snow's held off. I could have hung the wash outside after all." Tied from gas jet to gas jet, a wash line crossed the small kitchen, hung with union suits and trousers, and her own narrow dresses. The air was redolent with White Wizard soap flakes. *Wednesday, wash day.* Dorrit would not allow herself to imagine what might be happening in the apartment below. She wiped the boys' faces and hands and set them together on the parlor sofa, wrapped in a quilt. She gave each of them a slice of buttered bread and a glass of hot milk. The supper plates she had left for her father and brother were still in the cold oven; congealing beans and slices of fatty ham. *Wednesday, beans and ham.*

The Sykes' apartment consisted of four rooms. Beyond the kitchen were two small, connected bedrooms. The first she shared with her older brother, the second was her father's. In the parlor, two front windows looked down onto Blossom Street and offered a sliver view of the Charles River. On the sill, three red geraniums bloomed in a wooden cheese box. From the gray sidewalk below, muffled calls of newsboys hawking their last copies of late editions floated in, along with the odors of rubbish and low tide that tenaciously seeped through newspaper-chinked window frames to permeate brick and clapboard. Automobiles and carts rumbled past, clattering against the block paving of the street, splashing through puddles of slush. The rattle of a windowpane startled Fred, who was nodding off, his head held up by a small fist that still clutched a bread crust.

Dorrit took up the boy's cups, saying, "Listen to that wind! How about a little lie-down and a story? Just until your da comes for you."

Colin nodded, smiling. "Fred, wake up! I want to hear the rest of the story about the hidden treasure."

Three
MAY

A mile down the road, May pulled in at the Post Office and hurried inside, avoiding eye contact with the chatty postmistress. Usually, she tried to time her visits to Miss Spindle's lunch break, but today, apparently, was not a day for the avoidance of anything.

"Morning, Miss Spindle." May dropped the stack of monthly customer statements into the mail slot, hoping to convey through her purposeful gait that she had no time for conversation. Most of the envelopes were stamped in red ink: *Past Due*. Vaguely, she wondered how many of them might be paid this month, and how many would come back, folded inside sad letters describing temporary setbacks and failed crops, with requests for one more month's leniency.

"How do, May?" the postmistress called. "Where's my little buddy today?" Olive Spindle's acetate visor gave her face a green cast.

May pulled mail from her post office box. Miss Spindle said, "Don't run off, now. I've got a parcel for you. Actually, it's for little Hank." At the window, she tapped a green printed address label as she passed the carton across the counter. "From Miller & Rhoads, in Richmond! Goodness me, I thought Sybil Craig was the only one 'round here could afford to order anything from a department store these days. But of course, it's not *my* personal business. Not my personal business a-tall, and never let it be said that Olive Spindle is a busybody! You know, I can't recall the last time I went to Miller & Rhoads, but they always did have the *best* sponge cake, in the Tea Room? With the raspberry jam in the middle? And that woman who played the harp. What *was* her name? I used to take my Aunt Lydia there on Tuesday afternoons after she'd got her hair set. And did you hear about Mister Churchill?" She shook her head, not waiting for an answer. "Hit by an automobile, walking across Fifth Avenue in New York City! Cuts and bruises. Said it was his own fault! Did you know, they drive on the other side of the road over there in England? Said he looked the wrong way! You have a nice afternoon, and bring that darling boy to see Miss Spindle, you hear?"

Outside, as May opened her car door, a familiar truck pulled up, with a well-shined, empty horse trailer in tow. Painted identically across the side of the trailer and the door of the truck was *Chestnut Grove Thoroughbreds*, with its familiar horse-head motif surrounded by a wreath of chestnut boughs. A small, wiry horse trainer jumped out of the truck, tipping his hat. "Howdy, May."

"Where are you off to this morning, Rufus?"

"Mister Craig's sending Jack and me to Kentucky." He jerked his head toward his passenger and Jack tipped his hat. "Got word a couple hours ago. He says the missus bought a filly this morning. Wants us to leave right away to fetch her."

May's father-in-law, James Craig Sr., had not sold a horse in months, as far as she knew. He had not purchased one in almost a year. Maybe things were looking up. "Is Sybil coming back too?"

"Last I heard, she'll get here sometime Friday or Saturday, for the party."

May exhaled, realizing she had been holding her breath. *The Christmas party.* After Byrd's mother died in 1928, James had met his second wife, Sybil, at a horse show. Sybil Craig was a champion rider, competing all over the country and spending much of her time at her family's farm in Louisville. She preferred the company of horses to humans, and most of the humans she tolerated were dedicated horse people.

May said, "Hank was looking forward to seeing you this afternoon."

"Aw," Rufus said, "you tell him I owe him a lesson when I get back, okey-dokey?" With a small salute, he headed into the post office.

As May continued her drive down Route 22, she checked her watch again, thrumming her hand against the steering wheel. Silently, she ticked off a list of points to be made, trying to recall percentages and figures. Her stomach growled and still, she could not think of eating. She was oblivious to the scenery she passed. On the left, railroad tracks and telegraph poles paralleled the road. On the right, signs and stone gateposts identified properties that had passed from generation to generation. Long farm lanes wound through fields and past ponds, arriving finally at gracious houses situated to take advantage of the Southwest Mountain view. Now, in December, tall, browning grass swayed in the fields along the road. Across the mountains, bare trees mixed with evergreens. After two miles she turned right, at the fading white-and-green sign that read, *Keswick Farm.* Roiling the dust below, the car jolted down the rutted drive toward a large clapboard farmhouse with peeling white paint and a rusted, green metal roof.

May pulled into the circle in front of her father's house and cut the engine. She hurried up the front walk. Inside, she continued through the hall, calling, "Daddy? You ready?" From the parlor, a woeful baritone crooned from the radio, a song about hard times. The music stopped midnote when the radio snapped off.

She paused, peering through the glass panel in the kitchen door at her son, Hank, perched on the drainboard of the wide porcelain sink, laughing and splashing water with his feet. Standing nearby, Delphina had a dishtowel draped over her face so that only her graying hair was visible. Her long, thin brown hands poised, clawlike, and her voice growled from behind the towel, saying, "Swamp monster's coming to eat your toes, Hank Craig! You'd best not dangle them in the water!"

At the squeak of the opening door, the housekeeper snatched the towel from her face and began to wipe the counter. Hank continued to laugh, holding out his arms. "Mama!" he shouted.

Saying, "Hello, Delphina, hello, little man," May scooped him up, rocking him sideways as she smoothed his white-blond hair. He smelled like grass and fresh bread. "Where's your sister?"

Hank pointed to the corner of the kitchen where his baby sister, Elsie Lucille, sat in a playpen, chewing her fist. The baby was named after May's best friend, and for Byrd's mother. Hank seemed to take tremendous pride in defining himself as *bigger* and *older* and had called the baby "Sister" from the start.

May shucked off her coat and unbuttoned the top of her dress with one hand. As the baby nursed, May asked Hank about his morning. Outside, the sky was a uniform pale gray, threatening snow.

As the grandfather clock in the hallway chimed noon, May tucked the blanket around her now-sated daughter. Sister's eyes were closing, and her tiny lips were still puckered. *Such a good baby.* With a kiss to her forehead, May laid her gently in the playpen. *I hope you have sweet dreams.*

Hank said. "Mama, are we going home now?"

"Not yet, Sweetie. You and Sister are having lunch with Delphina. I'll pick you up after that."

"And then I get to ride Peanut!"

"Oh," May said, "Honey, Rufus had to go out of town. But I'll take you to see Peanut later, if you're a good boy."

She crossed the front hall. In the parlor, a single iron-framed bed had been moved from upstairs and now stood next to a window, flanked by the radio cabinet and a small table. May's father, Henry Marshall, had been bedridden on and off since one hot afternoon in August when he decided that a pint of applejack would improve his aim and he could surprise the groundhogs that burrowed beneath his barn by shooting them from the branches of a nearby ash tree. He had broken his right leg and injured his back. *Complete bed rest,* the doctor had decreed, *give things time.* The leg had healed, but slowly, and his back still flared up, making him unable to attend the daily running of the market or the canning operation at the farm. Sequestered at home, he rarely bothered to shave, gave himself the most perfunctory of sponge baths, and his gray hair stuck up stiffly from the back of his head. Today, he smelled of Bay Rum aftershave, his freshly combed hair bore track marks of a comb, and he wore a dark suit.

He reached to radio dial and lowered the volume. "You're late," he said, "I've been ready for an hour."

"I posted the bills." May passed him the market ledger and he grunted an assent, flipping the cover open. When would she stop hoping that her father might say *thank you*, or *you look tired, why don't you take a load off?* He accepted, with prickly dignity, the consequences of his foolish actions. She knew that his ill humor came from pain and frustration, but still, the past months had been a trial. Thank God, she thought, that Dennis and Delphina put up with him. Dennis, a young cousin of Blue's, had started at the farm as a teenager. He was the only person Henry had allowed to move him while he was laid up. Henry's housekeeper, Delphina, simply demanded Henry change his pajamas and eat what she prepared.

With a groan, Henry pushed himself to standing and leaned on his cane. May said, "Are you sure you don't want to use your chair? It's icy. The last thing we need is for you to slip and fall. Dennis can drive us."

"No way in hell am I going in there in a goddamned wheelchair. I'll be fine."

In the hall mirror, May tugged on her coat and applied lipstick. Appearances were important when dealing with the President of the Albemarle Bank & Trust Company.

Henry made his way outside slowly, taking the ice-slick steps gingerly before heaving himself into the car. May slid into the driver's side, balancing a small box on the seat between them, saying, "There's a blanket in the backseat."

"Quit coddling me, for chrissakes. Let's go."

On Main Street in Charlottesville, May pulled over in front of the Albemarle Bank building. Twin evergreen Christmas wreaths with big brass bells and red ribbons decorated the doors. Across the street, yet another store had closed, as had a photographer's studio. At the brick Methodist Church up the street, a line of men waited outside a side door, where a chalked sign on the sidewalk advertised a free lunch from noon until one o'clock. May held her father's door open as he pulled himself upright with a grimace. She plucked a hair from her coat sleeve. "Do I look all right?"

"Just fine, little gal."

She asked, "We're really doing this?"

Henry raised his brows, pulling his mouth to one side—the facial equivalent of a shrug. "They can only say no." May knew that his nonchalance was a front. For the past year, he had tried to avert the closing of the canning operation, but there was no one to run it after his injury, not to mention that repeat seasons of bad crops had left little to pick and process. Over the years the orchard had weathered hard seasons but never closed down, and though Henry didn't speak about it, the failure was taking a toll. Since his accident, May had watched him decline with the loss of mobility. He, whose days were spent chatting with customers and evenings drinking with friends, now suffered the slow poison of isolation, his days spent twirling the radio dial obsessively, hoping for better news. He patted her arm. "Now don't act nervous. We're operating in all good faith. It's fifty percent bluster with these folks."

May looked down, silently chastising herself. *Was* she operating in good faith? Her husband didn't know what she was doing and almost certainly would advise against the idea of borrowing money. *It's not time to take risks*, he would say, *we need to tighten our belts. It's lucky I've still got clients.* Since the stock crash of 1929, Byrd's legal practice had dried up to almost nothing, with those clients who could pay offering twenty-five cents a week—the price of a dozen eggs or a pound of butter—with payments stretching far into the future. Others tendered chickens, or honey, or even moonshine. Byrd did everything he could to take care of them all. It was the least she could do, to not add to his worries. So May didn't tell him about her nursing difficulties, or the baby's diaper rash, or that she was tired too. She didn't want to worry him with her concerns about her father.

A guard held open the bank door while May followed Henry inside. The chill white-and-gray expanse of glossy marble was relieved by potted ferns and the polished brass grilles of teller stations. The creaking of the heavy door echoed up into the vaulted ceiling, breaking a quiet so solemn as to be almost monastic. Henry made slow progress toward the desk of a pewter-haired secretary who sat sentry before two offices and the gaping steel door of the vault. The secretary, a one Miss B. Pugh, according to her name plaque, dropped her chin and peered over the top of her eyeglasses to address Henry. "Good morning. May I help you?"

May answered, "We have an appointment with Cecil Boxley."

"Have a seat. Mister Boxley will be with you shortly." Miss Pugh returned to her typewriter. May guided Henry toward a pair of chairs, while he muttered, pushing away her arm. Perching on slippery leather upholstery, she shut her eyes briefly, reviewing, silently, the points to be made:

1. The mortgage on Keswick Farm is nearly paid off.
2. The Marshalls have been clients of Albemarle Bank since 1859.
3. An expanded candy business could provide profit to cover loan payments.
4. Everybody likes candy.

Then she enumerated the points her father had warned her *not* to bring up:

1. The canning operation has been working at a loss.
2. Keswick Market is barely breaking even.

The single customer at the teller windows completed his transaction and his heels tapped across the floor toward the exit. As the guard tipped his hat and opened the door, a wiry man in a patched plaid overcoat entered, coattails flapping. Seeing Henry, he stopped and smiled. Hitching his shoulders, he raised an arm, calling out across the lobby, "Henry Marshall, you damned old cuss! Merry Christmas!" The greeting reverberated around the ceiling like a panicked, trapped bird, and Miss Pugh glared at Bose Shifflett. Since Henry's arrest seven years ago, and his subsequent retirement from the moonshine business, Bose had cornered the market, earning the nickname, "King of the Blue Ridge." His Bacon Hollow was now the largest site of illegal liquor production in the state. Bose strode toward them, one hand extended, reaching the other to slap Henry on the back. The center office door opened behind Miss Pugh and the President of the bank stood splay-legged in his shirt sleeves, watching the exchange with obvious interest. May busied herself with her handbag. Cecil Boxley looked to be in his midfifties, with salt-and-pepper hair plastered to his scalp in oily strings. He was a bold-faced, shiny-toothed man with an arrogant belly that began below his armpits, spreading beneath his starched white shirt like an overly risen bread loaf.

Bose Shifflett offered a salute, then moved on to the teller's windows as May and Henry were ushered into an office.

"Welcome, welcome," Boxley said. "Have a seat, Mrs. Craig. Nice to see you."

Following a further exchange of niceties, May took a big breath and laid out ledger sheets with projections for a small candy business. After a romantic description of Blue's mysterious gift with sugar, she opened the candy box and held it out to Mr. Boxley, wishing she had brought another to sweeten up Miss Pugh. Boxley's hand hovered over a meringue, then a pecan cluster, finally plucking out a cube of butterscotch. He listened with steepled fingers tapping against his chin, sucking wetly on the candy. After ten minutes May had completed her presentation and Boxley had consumed another butterscotch and two caramels. She sat back, hoping she projected perky, enthusiastic confidence through her smile, instead of the groveling, clammy anxiety she felt.

Boxley leaned his crossed arms on his desk, smiling condescendingly. "A second mortgage is mighty risky in the best of times, Henry. I had Miss Pugh pull your file this morning. Three of your payments were late last year. In fact, it might be time to think about closing the canning business. I can't imagine things are going too well."

May's hopes sank.

"You know," he continued, "it warms my heart to see you taking an interest in the family finances, Mrs. Craig. Truly, it does. Always glad to see a supportive wife, 'specially in these times. Byrd getting along all right?"

"Just fine," May said. Then, before she could stop herself, she blundered on. "Actually, Mister Boxley, Byrd is so busy, Daddy and I haven't really had a chance to catch him up on our plans. We were hoping to—to surprise him—with our expansion, you know? One less thing for him to worry about." She tilted her head, blinking up at him from beneath the brim of her cloche.

Boxley nodded slowly, his eyes darting to the candy box. "So . . . he is unaware that you are here today?" May nodded, concentrating on her clasped hands. Boxley continued, "In that case, I suggest you make an appointment with Miss Pugh. Be best if we gentlemen can sit down and have a proper chat."

While Boxley reached for a piece of divinity, May cut a pleading glance to Henry, who said, "Cecil, the Marshall family have been loyal to your bank. So have the Craigs. Lord knows, nobody likes the way things are going, but the day has come when that loyalty needs to be honored. Our canning operation's been running for over eighty years. But it's time to modernize, to adapt to the times.

"You know how bad crops have been—what with blight and drought and low prices—but we've got a viable alternative here—slow down the canning for a bit. This candy thing could take off. The way I see it, Cecil, you don't need to be sitting on another failed farm nobody wants to buy." Henry poked his finger on Boxley's desk.

May picked up where her father stopped. "Look at what's happening in Orange—right up the road. Mister Rubin put an advertisement in the *New York Times* for a place to host his mill, and he chose a tiny town in Virginia! I've spoken with him. The American Silk Mill provides two hundred local jobs, and he pays his employees forty dollars a month. Manufacturing's keeping that town alive, not agriculture. People want to work, Mister Boxley, not beg. We won't start on such a grand scale, of course."

Boxley said, "And that Rubin fella came down here with his own money." He shook his head sympathetically, laying a hand on his blotter as if it were a Bible, "Henry, I hear you, friend. I hear from five farmers every day in similar straits. Breaks my heart." He bit into a caramel, his words slightly garbled, "I was right sorry about Cy Waddell's laundry closing down. Reckon folks are doing their own washing at home nowadays."

May looked away, composing her face to hide her shock. She wondered if her father knew about this. Her Uncle Cy had run the laundry in town for as long as she could remember. What on earth would he do now? She forced herself to focus on what Boxley was saying. "But it's my job," he continued, "to keep this bank afloat. Frankly, you don't have the assets to support a loan of this size. And what, with you having a felony arrest, Henry—"

"He wasn't convicted," May interjected.

Boxley looked at her, as if remembering she was there. "And there was a warrant out for you for a time, Mrs. Craig, if I recall correctly. From what you've shown me today? I'm afraid we'll have to pass." He lowered his chin with dismissive finality. "'Preciate the candy. Miss Pugh will show you out. Have Byrd give me a call." He began to rise. "But come to think of it, I'll see him tomorrow evening, at H and H. You going to the meeting, Henry?"

May froze. Byrd absolutely could not hear of this plan from Cecil Boxley. He droned on, and May imagined snatching the candy box from his desk, shoving the pieces into her mouth as he watched, then hissing at him, *You can't have it all!*

On the drive home, May tapped the steering wheel in agitation, dread tickling the hairs on her neck. She would have no choice but to tell Byrd tonight. The exclusively male Hog & Hominy Club met monthly. Local landowners and businessmen gathered for supper, ostensibly to discuss agriculture and commerce. It was common knowledge, however, that in reality, they played poker and drank. If by some chance Byrd *did* see him there, and Boxley brought it up . . . She could telephone the banker—ask him to keep it quiet—not mention it to Byrd. No. That would be tantamount to admitting she was afraid of her husband knowing what she was trying to do. That sounded desperate. She would talk to Byrd when he came home, to try to head off a scene. He *might* be supportive. She banged her gloved hand against the steering wheel. *Who am I kidding? Why did I think for a minute that it would work?*

At the farm, she helped her father up the front steps. Inside, she pulled off her hat and asked, "Do you want to put on pajamas, Daddy? Can I get you a hot water bottle? A cup of tea?"

"No, no, and no. It felt good to put on a suit." Henry limped into the parlor. The radio switched on, then came the sound of scrambled channels as the dial turned. May followed and held her hands over the radiator briefly, staring out the window at the winter-brown front field. With a deep sigh, her father sank into his armchair, loosening his tie.

She reached to turn down the volume. "You know," she said, one hand idly rubbing the side of her neck, "I imagine your grandfather coming up with the idea to sell jams and jellies and opening the market. Who's to say it wasn't his wife's idea, or his sister's? Who is Cecil Boxley to tell me that my idea isn't worth anything?" She faced her father. "I helped my friend open his hair salon in Paris. We came up with the plan ourselves, and it worked. I miss that—the feeling of creating something from an idea. That meeting was a waste of time. Did you know about Uncle Cy?"

"Yup," Henry said. "He told me. Asked if he might work a few shifts in the market. 'Hell,' I told him, 'I can't even give my own daughter a salary.'" He rubbed his chin. "We could always go back to making moonshine." His voice dropped. "Least then I'd feel useful."

"Right," May said, her voice caustic, "that worked out so well the first time, didn't it?" Instantly, she regretted her sarcasm. "Sorry," she said, "I'm just so disappointed."

She left her father staring morosely at the radio. In the kitchen, Delphina was feeding chunks of raw meat through a hand-cranked grinder clamped to the edge of the countertop. She paused, putting a finger to her lips. Sister was sleeping in her playpen.

May whispered to Hank, "Go get your coat and say goodbye to Grandpa." She gave his shoulder a nudge.

Taking a ginger ale from the icebox, she popped the top, then took a long drink. Delphina said, "You want some lunch?"

"I'll get something at home, thanks."

"Hank's been talking about that pony all day. Why don't you take him? Sister just went down."

"You don't mind?"

"Go on."

Hank came barreling back through the swinging door, calling, "Grandpa gave me some peppermints. I saved one for Peanut." He dug into the pocket of his overalls, extracting a lint-covered candy. Delphina shushed him and he bobbed his head solemnly, then leaned toward her, whispering, "Got a peppermint in my other pocket too. I'll share with you."

Delphina dusted his shoulder in her version of a caress. "No, but thank you." She rubbed her jaw. "I've got a toothache. Reckon I've had too much of Blue's candy already."

May held Hank's hand as they walked to the car. Its sugar-sticky warmth pressed into hers, small and trusting. She resolved to enjoy this brief time alone with him—to try to put the meeting in the back of her mind. In a matter of hours, it would be the subject of unpleasant discussion.

Hank climbed in and immediately began shaking the wrapped parcel, saying, "Mama, what's in here?"

"Your godmother sent that, for you. It must be a Christmas present." He began to pull at the twine, bouncing on the seat. May turned left out of the Keswick Farm driveway. Half a mile down the road, toward Gordonsville, she turned left again, passing between a pair of stone pillars, each fronted by a white marble plaque and topped by a stone urn.

They passed through a mile-long allée of massive chestnut trees. Above, broken, bare limbs tangled like thick, ungraceful jackstraws, threatening to drop at any moment while below, fallen limbs grayed and rotted on the ground, surrounded by tufts of dead grass. In May's childhood, the allée had been a summertime oasis of shade. Now, it was eerily bare. Every one of the trees had fallen victim to the chestnut blight that came to America in 1905. In late April, four of the dead giants had toppled in a wind storm. As she neared the house, the drive was better maintained, bordered with rows of large, neatly pruned boxwood and gnarled old dogwoods.

Before they married, May Marshall and Byrd Craig grew up as neighbors. The Craigs' gracious family estate, Chestnut Grove, shared fences with the Marshalls' somewhat dilapidated Keswick Farm. As far as society was concerned, however, there might as well have been miles between them. While the Craigs had always been wealthy, May's family never had been, and her insistence upon helping at her father's country market had been a source of friction. Her mother-in-law had been emphatic—none of the Craig women had ever worked.

Byrd's mother had been one of the 'Richmond Byrds', and had expected her sons to marry young women she approved of. After her first-born, James Jr., was killed fighting in France in 1918, she pinned her hopes on Byrd. His first marriage, to the daughter of an English diplomat, had pleased his mother. His divorce, a mere four months later, had not. May had felt her mother-in-law's disappointment until the birth of Hank, six months before Lucille Craig died of cancer. In her final days, she doted on her grandson and seemed to regard Byrd as his own man, instead of a stand-in for her lost firstborn.

Now, James Sr. and his second wife, Sybil, lived in the main house, a stately brick Georgian revival with triple-sash windows and black-green shutters. A long, pillared portico defined the front. From that portico, a view of grassy hills rolled down to the front pond. In the distance, low mountains swelled in rounded contours of deep evergreen.

In double-fenced pastures, sleek, carefully bred horses in custom-made wool blankets grazed. The War had taken a toll on the thoroughbred busi-ness, but James kept on, sending horses to Kentucky and Saratoga each year for the shows and sales. After the War, he built his business again until the downturn in 1929, when the value of yachts, racehorses, exotic automobiles, and other toys of the very rich disintegrated. These days, the poor might have to choose between meat or shoes, the middle class might decide not to splurge on a jar of chutney from Keswick Farm, and those who had been able to afford them before thought twice about the pur-chase of a well-bred yearling from Chestnut Grove Thoroughbreds.

Passing the main house, May saw her father-in-law's big Packard out-side the garage. "Let's ask your Grandfar to supper," she said, thinking, *so I won't have to tell Byrd until later.* She continued around the pond toward a white clapboard cottage perched on the opposite bank, where she and Byrd lived. She pulled up to the cottage and cut the engine.

Hank shook the parcel, whining, "Please, can I open it now? Please?" May untied the twine, and he tore into the box and tissue paper. "Lookie, Mama!" He clapped his hands and pulled out a little red gingham shirt with white piping and pearly white snaps. Beneath the shirt was a brown felt cowboy hat with a tooled leather band. He pulled it on and May slid the lanyard up to his chin. "Bang, bang!" Hank made guns with his hands, pointing toward the sky. "Bang, bang!"

A small white card was tucked into the box. May read aloud, "Merry Christmas to my little cowpoke, with heaps of love and lots of kisses, Godmother Elsie." She smiled. "Isn't that just like your godmother, to do something so thoughtful?"

May gathered the wrappings and helped Hank from the car. He galloped up the walkway and stood waiting at the door, shouting back, "Hurry, Mama. I want to show Peanut my hat."

"Let me change clothes. Peanut is a good pony. He'll wait patiently, and so must you. And," she admonished, "a gentleman never wears his hat indoors."

In her bedroom May changed into dungarees, still mulling over the afternoon's meeting. Right now, she could manage working at the market while Delphina kept the children at her father's house on weekdays. She continued to ruminate as they walked across the field to the horse barn. Hank raced ahead to toss stones into the pond. As they approached the main house, a spotted English pointer scooted through a gap in the lattice below the side porch, wagging her tail, head low.

"Patsy!" Hank called. Bounding behind the dog were a pair of puppies. Hank ran to them, kneeling in the grass. They jumped up to lick his face as his new hat slipped to his back. The sun glinted on his curls and his laughter was contagious. The puppies, the last of a litter of eight, were fat as sausages. They squealed, tumbling over each other, and Hank squinted up at May. "Grandfar says I can have a puppy for my very own. Only just he says if my mama says all right. Please, can I have a puppy, Mama? This one's best." He stroked the ears of a white male with a black mask.

"Your daddy and I will talk about it. Now, I'll saddle Peanut, but you're going to have to brush him down, after." She continued toward the barn. Hank was still too small to ride alone, but he loved to be walked on a lead line.

"Yes, ma'am," Hank called, still busy with the puppies. Like his father, he adored horses and dogs.

The trainer had closed up the barn before leaving for Kentucky. From inside, she heard neighing and the reverberation of hooves against wood. As she pulled open the wide doors, the iron hinges creaked. She paused to swat away a cluster of flies. A shaft of sunlight flooded in, illuminating an aisle immaculately swept by horse grooms who knew that in these tough times they would do well to keep busy. The familiar tang of fresh hay and manure wafted out into the chill air. At the first stall, she stopped to soothe Byrd's hunter. The black gelding's eyes were wild. He pulled away, tossing his head, whinnying, frothing as if he had been galloping all morning. May continued down the aisle, greeting the horses. In a small stall at the end, Hank's Shetland pony stood in a corner. She crossed to the tack room, where the lead lines were kept. The door stuck and May shoved with her shoulder. When it gave, suddenly, she stumbled inside, tripping, scraping her hands on the rough cement as she landed. The hum of flies was more intense. The air was still and close—metallic.

Panting, she backed up, crablike, to the far wall. James Craig's legs were splayed in front of him like a fallen scarecrow. He was dressed in a black suit; the collar of his white shirt soaked dark. Flies crawled in his blackening blood, splattered on the wall behind him and puddled on the floor, where a pistol lay. May scrambled to her knees, gasping, unaware that her palms were bleeding and she had ripped one knee of her blue jeans. She pulled herself to standing, unable to take in what was before her. *So much blood.*

Hank called from the barn door, "Pea-nut? Pea-nut?" May stepped over the legs and backed out, pulling the door closed, one hand over her mouth. Beside the door, an envelope was tacked to the wall, with Byrd's name on it. Swallowing, she told herself to move. Maternal instinct commanded she shield her son. She took Hank's hand in her shaking one, firmly leading him into the sunlight. "Mama, your hand is awful cold," he said. "And look, you hurt it!"

May gulped air as she closed and latched the barn doors. She spoke rapidly, her voice growing higher, then shrill, "Peanut is sleeping. He's very sleepy right now and we have to let him have his nap. We're going to go find Dennis. You can show him your hat. Will you help Mama find him?"

"I want to see Peanut, Mama. You promised." Hank tugged her back toward the barn and stamped his foot.

May's vision dimmed and for an instant; stars exploded in front of her eyes. "Hank, listen to me. Mama needs you to help." She dropped his hand then ran to the fence and vomited over the side.

"Poor Mama." Hank crossed his hands over his belly. "Do you have a tummy ache?"

May wiped her mouth on her sleeve. "Yes, honey, a little bit."

She started toward the main house, then remembered that her mother-in-law was in Kentucky. In a fog, she got Hank into the car and drove back to Keswick Farm, barreling past the house, around the back, to the cannery building that stood at the edge of a field, a quarter-mile from the house.

"There Dennis is, Mama! There he is." Hank pointed to a slim young man, who looked up from stacking bushel baskets.

"Hank," May said, her voice now even, "Sweetheart. You wait here in this car. Do not move." She shook her finger at the solemn child.

"Dennis?" she called, running toward him. "Dennis. Oh *God.*" Her breath heaved as she leaned forward, her hands on her knees. Tipping his straw hat, Dennis frowned in apparent concern. May whispered, "It's Mister Craig. I found him, in the horse barn. He . . . he's shot himself in the head."

Dennis's eyebrows shot up as his mouth fell open. "Mister Craig?"

May continued, "Please. The grooms are away. There's no one else. I need for you to go over there, and . . . God, it's horrible. Byrd can't see him like that." She grasped his arm; her shoulders began to shake.

Dennis inclined his head solemnly toward the Studebaker.

"Yes," May said. "Drop us at the house. Take the car. I'll telephone Byrd, and I suppose I ought to call the police. Or a doctor. Oh God."

Dennis followed May back to the Studebaker and held open the passenger door for her. She stopped, confused. "Hank? Hank? Where did he go?"

The sound of giggling came from the back seat. Hank's head popped up from beneath a blanket on the floor. "Surprise!" he called. "I was hiding."

May rubbed her forehead while Hank held his new hat over the seat to show it to Dennis. In front of her father's house, Hank jumped out and ran inside, leaving the rear door open. As May pushed it closed, she caught Dennis's eye through the window, giving him a brief nod of silent gratitude.

Inside, she stood in the entry hall, attempting to gather herself. She told Hank to show his grandpa his presents. Her hand shook as she picked up the telephone and asked to be connected to her husband's office. He answered after the third ring, "Byrd Craig, here."

May drew in her breath. She had not thought of what she would say. How could she tell her husband what she had seen? She cupped the receiver, hoping her voice would not carry. "Oh, Byrd."

"What is it? You sound upset."

"You need to come home, right now."

Four
DORRIT

As the bells of Old North Church rang nine o'clock, Dorrit softly closed the door to her bedroom, where the boys lay in her single bed. She stretched her neck and shoulders, scrubbing her palms over her tired eyes. She was home, she was safe, and something was happening one floor down that she *would not* think about. She rolled up the drawings that were strewn across the kitchen table then wrestled open the drawer that held her father's papers—what he called his research—folders, old envelopes bulging with yellowed clippings, mechanical drawings sketched on the backs of letters or receipts. Gathering newspapers from around his chair, she added them to a tall stack beside the Hoosier cabinet. Sentences and paragraphs were underlined, with columns missing where he had clipped them for his files.

Voices carried from the hall with the shuffle of heavy boots. The doorknob rattled and her father entered, shaking snow from his jacket. The odor of boiled cabbage wafted in, along with angry fragments of German from across the hall. Roy Sykes put his toolbox down before pulling off his cap. He swiped at the cowlick on his forehead, but as it always did, a lock of dark hair fell into his eyes. Behind him, Dorrit's older brother Walt stomped the mat before slamming the door. Swiping a cuff below his nose he said, "I'm starved."

"Hush," Dorrit hissed, "the Sullivan boys are here. Hang your jacket over the radiator. You're dripping all over."

"Hello, Baby Doll." Roy grinned the gap-toothed grin that added to his air of an overgrown boy. "Sorry we're late, but we got in some good hours. Might bring in twenty-five dollars this week!" He passed Dorrit his cap, leaning to kiss the top of her head. Both she and her brother had his blue eyes, Walt's were bright, hers the color of a faded work shirt.

The tin cover of the breadbox clattered. Walt tore a chunk from the center of the loaf, filling his cheeks like a squirrel. "Any supper left?" He rooted in the icebox, sniffing the milk. His prominent Adam's apple bobbed as he upended the bottle and drained it. At eighteen, he was tall and gangly with big hands and a shiny face. "Ahhh . . ." He swiped his mouth with the back of his hand.

"You are a disgusting pig," Dorrit said.

"Oink, oink, oink," he snorted, using his finger to wipe cream from inside the top of the bottle. "You'd be hungry too if you hadda go from school to work."

"I do! I keep those boys every afternoon, and I sew, *and* I keep house. Who do you think washed your clothes today?"

"Bah. Sewing? That ain't work." He reached into the oven. "Pop? Supper? Ham and beans, again?"

Roy said, to Dorrit, "We had a frankfurter on the way home."

Walt forked food into his mouth. "Those brats better not be in my bed. Bet they got bedbugs."

"Their mother is in"—Dorrit's eyes flitted to her father—"her baby is coming." She searched his face for reassurance.

Roy turned away, patting his shirt pockets. "Going down the cellar for a bit." He paused in the open doorway.

Dorrit folded clothes into the laundry basket, watching him. "Pop, you have work tomorrow?"

"Ay-up. And I need a second pair of hands in the afternoon." A woman's wail rose from the floor below. He flinched. "Stay home, tonight, Walt," he said. "You've got school in the morning." The door closed behind him.

Walt waited five minutes, then took his jacket, grinning as he swiped at his damp hair. He said, over his shoulder as the door closed behind him, "I'm making tracks. Behave yourself, now, sis. Looks like you and your boys gonna have a rip-snorter of a night." He winked.

The latch clicked. Dorrit said, "And you have a big hunk of ham in your teeth."

Dorrit sank into her chair with one leg tucked beneath her. She inspected Fred's little overcoat then chose three matching buttons from a jarful. She threaded a needle and as she rolled a knot she gazed longingly at her mother's empty chair and the sewing basket that stood beside it. Two months had passed, and still, she could not bring herself to claim either as her own. On the work table between the chairs sat a pincushion shaped like a tomato, and a well-worn copy of the Christian Science spiritual text, *Science and Health with Key to the Scriptures*, written by the founder, Mary Baker Eddy. Dorrit stared at the pincushion as her free foot began to tap, faster and faster.

Dorrit's mother, Augusta, took in sewing and taught her daughter fine stitching from the age of six. With great patience on her mother's part, they had begun a change purse of green felt, to teach measuring and seam allowances. Next, at Dorrit's enthusiastic insistence, a calico apron taught gathers and pockets and an ambitious, if tortured, buttonhole. By the time she was nine, Dorrit could confidently roll a neat hem on organdy. At eleven, she could smock a batiste christening dress and embroider perfect French knots by the dozen. By the time she was fifteen, she sewed as well as any professional seamstress and helped her mother after school.

In the long afternoons, when Dorrit's foot would begin to jiggle, her mother would say she was having *growing pains*, though pain was not a word she used often. "Go on," Augusta would say, with a pat to Dorrit's shoulder, "Go walk off the fidgets," and Dorrit would go to the roof, if the weather was mild enough, and walk around the perimeter until she felt calm. If the weather was bad, she walked up and down the steps of their building. Sometimes, a few minutes was enough. Sometimes, it took an hour.

Another wail, more prolonged this time, echoed up the stairwell.

Crossing her arms Dorrit began to rock, transported back by memory, to a day in early October. She and her mother had been sitting in these chairs. Augusta pulled a thread taut and snipped it, then said, simply, "Come April, there'll be a baby."

Dorrit had tried for days to summon the courage to ask her mother questions, but she could not find the right words. She had wanted to research the birth process on her weekly trips to the Boston Public Library, but to do so she would have to request a reference book, and she wouldn't even know what to ask for. She knew, from furtive, horrified paging through the crude cartoon booklet her brother hid beneath his mattress, that her parents had done something together that seemed disgustingly intimate. When she had thought of it, she could scarcely look either of them in the face.

Augusta Sykes had been raised in Christian Science; her husband had joined the church at their marriage. Following Mrs. Eddy's teachings, neither Walt nor Dorrit had ever seen a doctor. When the first-grade teacher sent home a note suggesting medicine for Dorrit's sensitive stomach, the Sykeses sought healing and solace through prayer and the guidance of their church. When there was an illness, a church practitioner was called in to lead prayer. Hard times seemed to have deepened Augusta's religious zealousness. She never missed a church service, attending on Wednesday evenings as well as Sundays. Her graces before meals were effusive with gratitude for a roof over their head, and for bounty. As far as Dorrit could tell, there was no bounty. There was enough.

The windowpane rattled, and in the distance, a siren wailed, sending Dorrit deeper into memory so that she doubled over, her hands over her ears until the sound died out. Two weeks after Augusta's announcement. Mid-October. Dorrit could almost see her mother in her chair, the flashing needle pausing as she rocked forward, discreetly rubbing her lower back. Dorrit had watched from the corner of her eye, knowing she saw pain, and worry, and perhaps fear. *Why may we not speak of it?* she wondered, but she knew not to voice her questions.

Her mother suddenly sat up straight, grasping the embroidery hoop with both hands until it bowed. Removing the fabric, she folded it carefully before laying it on top of her basket. Dorrit leaned closer, saying softly, "Let me fix you something. You haven't eaten all day."

"You're a dear. I'm not hungry." A sharp inhale, a controlled exhale, then, "If you'll just fix a bite for your pop when he gets home? He'll be late tonight."

"I'll make you some tea?" Dorrit said, "Ma?" the word a question in itself. Augusta only nodded, reaching for her pincushion.

When the kettle boiled, Dorrit measured mint leaves into the teapot then poured the hot water, all the while watching her mother. Offering the steaming cup, Dorrit held the saucer until their eyes met. Augusta smiled weakly and took a tiny courtesy sip. "Just what I needed."

"It's almost five, Ma. What about testimony service?"

Augusta frowned. "Ah. Well. If I don't finish this dress for Mrs. Frazier . . . her party . . ."

"Let me help you. We can miss tonight."

"You signed up for nursery?"

Dorrit nodded. Augusta pushed herself up from her chair then leaned back, fists kneading the small of her back. Crossing the room, she paused in the doorway, gripping the frame, perspiration dotting her upper lip. "Going down the hall," she called over her shoulder. "If you signed up, they'll be depending on you."

"Yes'm," Dorrit said. When the door clicked behind Augusta, Dorrit swallowed, trying to dislodge the dry lump of dread that had formed in her throat. After ten minutes she began to wonder if she should check on her mother. It was improbable, at this hour of the afternoon, that both of the toilet closets on the floor were occupied. Usually, days were quiet in the building, with no one knocking to get in next. When Augusta returned and went into her bedroom and closed the door, Dorrit felt the first scratch of fear.

After a few minutes, she knocked softly. "Ma?" A soft moan. "Ma?" She pushed the door open. Augusta sat on the edge of her bed, clenched fists gripping the quilt. Dorrit noticed the pale, straining tendons and greenish veins on the backs of her mother's hands. Thirty-eight seemed far too old to be pregnant, and certainly too old to have done that revolting act. Dorrit took the hand her mother reached toward her and did not pull away when the ferocity of the grasp made her gasp. *Pain is to be borne with grace. It is but an illusion.* "What's wrong?" She pleaded, "Is it the baby?"

"Hush now," Augusta said, "Only a little sour stomach. When you go to testimony, I'd like for you to ask them to send a practitioner tomorrow."

"But what's happening? What can I do? I'm not going to the service and leaving you here."

"Nonsense. I'm going to rest for a bit." They looked at each other for a moment. "You'll be fine. If you get the fidgets, pray on it."

After the service, Dorrit had hurried home. When she saw her father's toolbox beside the door, she exhaled in relief. From the bedroom, she heard his voice. "Gussie, I . . . I . . . think we should call a doctor."

"No," Augusta said. "Pray. Call for a practitioner."

"But they won't *do* anything. You need a doctor to examine you. Please." Her father called, "Dorrit?"

Her mother was pale. Beneath the covers now, in her nightgown. She smiled, saying, "How was the service?"

Dorrit said, "I asked them to send a practitioner, in the morning. Mrs. Fleming asked if you'd like for her to come and read."

Augusta plucked at the quilt edge. "Things don't . . . things don't feel quite right. We need to pray, Dorrit. Pray with us. Pain is an illusion. A trick of the mind." She inhaled through her nose, looking up with the pleading eyes of a wounded animal. She whispered, "Pain is an illusion. Mrs. Eddy says it is so. Pray with me. Such a good girl. My Dorrit."

Dorrit's voice quavered. "You're going to be fine, Ma."

Roy eyed the front room. Dorrit patted her mother's hand then followed him out. She said, "Where is Walt?"

"Went to a friend's, to study. Don't know which one." Roy dug into his pocket then poured coins into Dorrit's palm. "Something's wrong with your mother. I don't know; she might be losing the baby. Go," he whispered. "Call the midwife, Mrs. Holcomb, on Boylston. Hurry." A moan issued from the bedroom.

"I'll be right back." Gasping, panicky, Dorrit held the coins tightly as she ran down the stairs and pushed out the front door. Heavy rain had begun. Olivetti's Newsstand was closed, dark, as was Coughlin's Bakery. Why was there no one on the street she could ask for help? She ran on, breathlessly reciting the Lord's Prayer, past the barber and the grocery and the shut-down diner, to the phone box at the end of the block.

Our Father . . . Cars passed, sending plumes of dirty water over the curb. *Who art in Heaven* . . . With wet, shaking fingers, she dropped a nickel into the slot and stood holding the earpiece. *Hallowed be Thy name.* The operator came on. *Thy kingdom come* . . . Dorrit asked for Mrs. Holcomb, on Boylston Street. No, she told the operator, she did not know the name of Mr. Holcomb, but it was an emergency. The line rang and rang. *Thy will be done, on earth as it is in Heaven.*

Finally, a gruff voice, "What?"

"Mister Holcomb? This is Dorrit Sykes. On Blossom Street?"

He said, "Guess you're wanting Dot."

"Yes, sir. My father told me to call. There's a problem, I think." Dorrit wrapped the telephone cord around her finger.

"She's at Hull Street, with twins. You'd best call for an ambulance. Blossom Street, you said? Closest is Mass General. If you can't pay, there's Haymarket Relief Hospital."

"Yes, sir. Thank you, sir." Dorrit hung up and dropped another nickel into the slot.

She prayed all the way back. In her mother's room, her father knelt beside the bed, hands clasped. "Ma," Dorrit wiped her wet hands on her skirt, her breath heaving. "Help is coming." She stroked her mother's shoulder gently, hating to wake her. As she lifted the edge of the quilt, the fabric resisted, stuck to the bottom sheet by a viscous slick of red-black. It had spread, staining the underside of the quilt brown, seeping, paler, to the edges of the mattress. Dorrit gasped, her chest constricted as her hands stiffened, instantly cold. She dropped the coverlet. Augusta's eyelids fluttered open. Dorrit said, "Ma?" Her mother licked pale lips; her breath a whisper. Dorrit leaned closer. "Ma? I don't think there should be so much . . ." *So much blood.*

"God is merciful." Augusta's eyes shone. "Pray."

Fear is a thing with teeth and claws. Her mother was carried out on a stretcher, weakly whispering protests, calling for prayers, begging to stay. Dorrit had stood like a statue, trying to slow her heart, trying to breathe, trying to grasp what was happening as her father, ashen-faced, said he would get word to her as soon as there was news.

When Roy Sykes returned home at dawn, Dorrit and Walt were at the table, Walt asleep on his crossed arms. *Ectopic gestation*, her father explained. It sounded like a foreign language. Nothing to be done, he explained, a baby growing outside the womb, something ruptured. If she had come in sooner, they could have operated.

They could have saved her.

Later, on that terrible day in October, Dorrit had Walt take her best dress to be dyed black, while she sewed mourning bands on her father and brother's coat sleeves with small, perfect stitches. Images flashed in her mind, of her mother crying out to stay home, to pray, to have faith. Dorrit stared without focus at the empty chair, her needle poised midstitch, knowing she had disobeyed her mother's final wish, knowing she had doubted.

Five
MAY

From the quiet hallway, May listened to the hum of the radio in her father's room, and his low voice, speaking to Hank. She pressed the back of her hand over her mouth as if somehow, she might contain within herself the horror she had seen. Crossing the hall, the tap of her boot heels on the wide pine boards sounded unnaturally loud. Gripping the newel post, she sank slowly to sit on the stairs, rubbing her hands over her knees as if she were wiping something away. Grit abraded her palms and she inspected the scratches. There was no pain; her hands were icy, bloodless.

She had to tell Byrd. Crossing her arms, she began to rock. Which words to use? Inside her pocket, the envelope crinkled as she moved. How could she offer comfort when she so needed it herself? How was it possible, that none of them had seen the desperation? Byrd would ask. She would have no answers. There were no answers. Dread, like voracious, frigid vines, twined up her legs, encircling her arms before it cinched her ribs tight, constricting her breath. It continued, wrapping her neck, choking her. The vines held fast, anchoring her in indecision, preventing a deep breath. The longer she sat, the tighter they became. And Byrd would be home in—how much time had passed since she'd hung up the telephone? Minutes? The grandfather clock chimed three. The resonating vibrato was a call to action. From the kitchen, she heard the baby cry once, then Delphina, soothing her. May slapped her hands against her thighs, then pushed herself to stand. There was one person who could help her.

In the kitchen, Delphina leaned over, tucking a blanket around the baby. She put a finger to her lips, then motioned May to follow her into the pantry. May had never understood—and somehow knew not to question—how it was that Delphina sensed her distress. Since the little-girl nightmares had begun after May's mother left, Delphina knew of crises without being told.

After May explained what had happened, Delphina went into action. She took Hank to feed the chickens, promising him cake at her cottage. May drank glass after glass of water. The baby slept on. The sound of Byrd's car speeding up the drive was almost a relief. Brakes squealed. A car door slammed. Closing the door to her father's room, she continued outside and waited, squeezing her damp hands together. Her husband's handsome face wore an expression of concern as he hurried up the walkway.

"What's wrong?" he asked, holding May at arm's length. "What happened to your hands? You're hurt." Without speaking, she took his hand, silently passing her love into his.

"I'm fine." She led him inside and up the stairs, then into a quiet bedroom. "I have to tell you something awful," she said. "You should sit down."

Byrd's eyes did not leave hers as he sat on the edge of the bed. "Tell me." He took off his hat and wiped his forehead. "Where are the children?"

May perched beside him. His hand was so warm—so alive—in her cold ones. She took a deep breath. "Your father . . . Your father is dead. I don't know how else to say it."

"What?"

May's voice was quiet. She was surprised at how calm she sounded; her words seemed empty of emotion. It was as if she were hearing someone else speak while her own thoughts spun ahead, to the pain and desperation that might drive a man to choose to die alone. "I found him, in the horse barn. He shot himself."

Byrd put his head in his hands and rubbed his face. When he looked up, his blue eyes were dark with shock and pain. "He shot . . . No. He wouldn't. He would never . . ."

"He left this, for you." She held out the envelope.

He shook his head, leaning forward, elbows on his knees. His shoulders sagged. "Where is Hank?"

"With Delphina. Sister is asleep."

"Did he . . . see?" May shook her head, still offering the envelope. Byrd let out a whoosh of breath and sat up straighter, regarding the envelope as if she were holding a snake. In a quiet monotone he asked, "Will you . . . ?"

The tearing paper sounded harsh and abrupt when everything felt as if it ought to whisper. May's hands fumbled, shaking slightly. Inside was a smaller envelope, addressed to Sybil. Taking a deep breath, she unfolded the sheet of familiar stationery.

December 16, 1931

My dear son,

I am sorry. Sorry for whoever finds this, and sorry that your father is so cowardly. I cannot bear to face the world as such a miserable failure.

You know that I had many investments and that the horse business has not been kind to us for several years. I did not tell you that I had mortgaged the farm and invested unwisely in several prospects in hopes of turning our fortunes around. I kept thinking that things would right themselves, and you would not need to know.

I am not brave enough to tell you that I have lost everything. Within a few days, the bank will take possession of the farm and horses. I am a ruined man. I leave nothing behind for you and your dear family.

I cannot ask you to understand. I have been proud and foolish. Now I leave you with nothing but

All my love,

Father

May rubbed Byrd's back as his shoulders began to shake. Nothing she could do would ease this raw pain. She, too, needed to process the shock of the letter—the sinking realization that Byrd's father, and his inheritance—the house, the horses, the farm—were lost. That Cecil Boxley had to have known those things when he met with her.

"I should tell Sybil." Byrd took out his handkerchief and blew his nose. In a baffled voice he said, "I don't know her sister's telephone number," as if finding a telephone number was insurmountably difficult.

"I'll call her," May said, grasping at this small, helpful task she might perform. "Maybe you ought to lie down. Would you like to be alone?" She stroked his wavy blond hair, so like his son's. He gasped once, clinging to her, and she held him tighter. "We'll get through this," she said. "We will." She flushed as anger blossomed—a defensive, almost childish desire to shield him, to wail: *This isn't fair! How could you do this to Byrd, to us? How could you leave him to bear it all?*

Byrd insisted on telephoning his stepmother, but she was not in. While he was on the phone, May told her father what had happened. From the parlor, she could hear Byrd speak to the undertaker, then the minister at the Episcopal Church. She sat beside her own father and did something she rarely did; she took his hand and held it tight. Silently, he returned the pressure of her grasp, his gaze directed outside. He and James Craig had been in different social circles, but they had hunted together every fall and been cordial neighbors. Byrd came in, pale and stooped. "I need to go over there," he said, "to talk to the staff."

"I'm sorry, son," Henry said. "Little gal, bring in that bottle from the pantry."

May poured out two tumblers of apple brandy. The smell turned her stomach. From the kitchen, she could hear Delphina sorting pots while Hank chattered. May thought, *Alice is probably starting dinner at Chestnut Grove, right now. She doesn't know yet. She doesn't know that she will be out of a job. So will the grooms, and the gardener, and the maid.*

Byrd took a big swallow from his glass. "I called the funeral home. Mister Hill is on his way. The minister will come by in the morning to talk about the service. I need to talk to Sybil. I need to go over there, to show

Mister Hill where . . . where Dad is." He stared into his brandy, looking dazed. "The party, we'll need to cancel . . ."

"What did you tell them?" May said, "Because maybe you should say that . . . that he was cleaning his gun."

Byrd frowned, swirling the brandy in the glass. "There's no way to cover this up, May. I've got to go over there."

"No." She put her hand on his arm. "I'll tell the staff. You stay here, in case Sybil calls." She squeezed his shoulder.

Driving down the farm lane toward Route 22, May began a list in her head. Making it gave her a small sense of control. *This* would happen, then *this*, then somehow, things would start to make sense. *Sybil must come home. The funeral. A reception. Cancel the Christmas party. The staff. Is there money for severance? Where will they go? Where will we go?* It would crush Byrd to lose his family home. *Hank's never lost anyone before. Will they take his pony?* As she turned in at the farm drive, she added a final item to her list:

Must tell Byrd about Cecil Boxley.

At Chestnut Grove, Dennis stood, arms crossed like a sentry, outside the barn as the undertaker's hearse backed up to the doors. May got out of the car and motioned to him, turning her back to the barn with a shudder. She could tell by his expression that he had been inside. "Dennis," she said, "I'm sorry. Thank you for doing this." She had asked a terrible favor, and he had acquiesced, unflinchingly. They shared an intimacy in what they both had seen, and May hoped that no one else, save the undertaker, would have to endure that memory. She rubbed her arms, looking him in the eye. "I don't know what I would have done without your help. Thank you."

"He was a good man." Dennis cocked his head toward the main house. The Craigs' maid and gardener stood on the porch with the cook, who was wringing her apron in her hands. "They came over once the hearse got here. I didn't let them go inside. Reckon you need to say something."

"You go on back now. Tomorrow will be a busy day."

As May neared the porch, Patsy and her puppies came out to greet her. *More mouths to feed.* Before her stood a line of expectant, worried faces, all waiting for her to explain.

Six
MAY

By the time May returned to Keswick Farm, the sun was low; diluted yellow light streamed through the windowpanes, casting patterns on the floor. In the kitchen, Delphina put down the dish she was drying, saying, "May, Chérie, you've got to sit down and eat something."

May rubbed her forehead. "There's so much to do."

Delphina pressed May's shoulders, forcing her into a chair. She held out a plate of biscuits in a manner that was not an offer, but a command. "Tell me what needs to be done," she said. "Is there a day for the funeral?"

"Not yet." May broke a biscuit. "Sybil is on her way back, and the minister is going to call. I told the grooms and servants to come over here tomorrow. We'll have to make room for them, at least temporarily. And where will *we* live? Do you think they'll really sell the farm? Who would buy a thoroughbred farm now?"

Delphina wiped her hands on her apron. "Listen to me. That doesn't have to be decided right now. Nobody's going to have to leave there tomorrow. Now, you've got to take care of yourself. I made up the beds upstairs. You and Byrd and Hank will stay here."

"Where are they?" May said.

Delphina jerked her chin upward. "Byrd told Hank—just that his granddaddy died, and Hank was crying. Byrd went to lie down with him in your old room."

"Good." May pushed herself up from the table.

"Go on, now," Delphina insisted, "I want to see you finish that biscuit, then get yourself upstairs and have a bath. You've got to be worn out." It was a relief, May thought, being told what to do.

The house was eerily quiet. She walked softly through the hall and up the stairs, then eased open the door to peek into her childhood bedroom. At the squeak of the hinges, Byrd glanced toward her with a finger to his lips. Sorrow had settled heavily into his face. He rubbed the bridge of his nose and closed his eyes. Hank lay, flush-faced and tearstained, sleeping in Byrd's arms. She pulled the door closed.

In the big bathroom in the center of the hall, she ran the water hot to wash her stinging hands, then turned on the tap to fill the claw-footed tub. The water ran rusty for a few minutes. When it was almost full, she pulled off her clothes, then eased herself in. Submerging her head, she let sweat and dust float from her skin.

Raising her left leg, she traced the purpling bruise on her knee. As she soaped herself, her eyes followed the tiles up the wall to where the wallpaper started, then traced the vine pattern to where it met the ceiling, peeling back in a scroll, revealing a brown stain. It was in this bathtub that May had once tried to take her own life, after being expelled from college, after being caught with a young man at a hotel. In her hopelessness, she swallowed pills with gin, wanting only to slip beneath the surface, into oblivion. At the time, no one suspected that she might attempt such a thing and after her failure, no one had known, until she confessed it to Byrd.

She *knew* that feeling, the utter desperation James Craig must have felt. Shame was an evil motivator and May nearly died of it—she had wanted to die. After, she had felt a different sort of shame, at her shallowness in believing that life held so little value—that one selfish, dishonest cad had enough control over her emotions to inspire her to give up. She shuddered, chastising herself for being morbid when it was time for practicality. Her own feelings could wait. Lathering her hair, she considered her dresses. She would need something black.

She dried herself and finger-combed her hair. Wrapped in a towel, she tiptoed into the hall, listening. No sound came from the room where Hank and Byrd were. Hopefully, they were both sleeping. Carrying her clothes, she opened the door of the room that had been her mother's. At her father's decree, this bedroom had remained closed since Helen Marshall's departure eighteen years ago.

May supposed that she and Byrd would sleep in this room now. That seemed most sensible. She would make new curtains and rearrange the furniture and bring a rug from Chestnut Grove. It might be enough— enough to exorcise her mother's presence. *If ever a room needed to be purged of a bad spirit*, May thought, *it's this one*.

She raised the brittle roller shade. The window resisted at first, then with a creak and a thump of sash weights, it rose a few inches. Outside, shadows were lengthening. A mockingbird called. Life went on. The lace curtains began to ruffle, dissipating a long-established mustiness. The air was cold; May's damp skin tingled. The initial shock was wearing off; her abraded palms stung. She was able to think past the horror of finding James Craig, to the man himself. He had taken her sledding, and to horse shows when she and Byrd and Jimmy were children. He had given Hank his pony. *He must have been in such despair, but we didn't see it.* Leaning on the sill, she inhaled deeply, wishing she had a cigarette.

They would have to begin again.

But first, there were things that must be finished.

The latch clicked behind her, and Byrd leaned against the closed door, his shoulders slumped. His hair hung over his forehead; his creased shirt was untucked. Without speaking, he strode across the room. May put her arms around his neck; his cheek against hers. The familiar scents of skin and hair tonic brought her back to the present as his hands moved down her back, grasping, his cufflinks pressing against her skin.

He kissed her, his fingers tangling her wet hair. Dropping her towel, she backed up until she pressed against the side of the high bed. Byrd lifted her to the edge of the mattress. Lowering his head, he rested it between her breasts. She raised his chin to kiss him and he pushed her gently back on the bed as she pulled at his clothes. Wordless anguish radiated from them both as they made love.

Afterward, a peculiar exhaustion settled over May, like a heavy scrim of black lace. She knew that Byrd felt it too. They could see through it and move—albeit with the ponderous clumsiness of grief—but she understood that all would be through a veil until the passage of time wore sorrow into translucence, then, much later, a wisp of its former oppressive presence.

Their bodies cooled; still, they were silent. May studied the grayed net-lace canopy above them. *We've pushed the bad spirits from this room ourselves.* More lists formed in her mind: *paint, crib, mattresses to the bunkhouse.* Byrd's eyelashes fluttered on her chest. He was probably making his own lists. From across the hall, the patter of footfall sounded and, as parents of young children have done for centuries, she and Byrd froze, wishing they had locked the door. He pushed himself up. May added to her list: *Find door keys.*

Byrd buckled his belt, then glanced around, frowning. "This was your mother's room, wasn't it? It looks like Miss Havisham lives here."

"It's our room, now."

From the landing, Hank called plaintively, "Mama?"

Byrd said, "Your father told me he met with the bank officer today."

"I was there too. Boxley knew about the foreclosure. He had to."

"And I was at my desk when Dad . . ." He shook his head. "Doesn't it seem like . . . like we should have felt some sort of intuition? I've wracked my brain, and I can't think of anything."

"Don't think about that now," May said, "don't." Her words turned to soothing sounds.

Seven
MAY

Three days later, May stood in the same room. She knelt to knot Hank's navy-blue sailor tie as he fidgeted, asking her, "What'll happen to Peanut, Mama?" He frowned. "I haven't seed him for days and days and days." She smoothed his collar then tugged the tie into place. Instead of wearing his new sailor suit to his grandfather's Christmas party, he was wearing it to a funeral.

"Peanut will move over here to Grandpa's, with us. And so will Patsy's boy puppy. You'll have to think of a name for him."

"What will happen to Patsy?"

"Sybil will take her and the girl puppy back to Kentucky to live." May tried to add a lilt to her voice.

"Will Santa Claus find me here?"

"He will. This is our family place now. Come sit." Hank sat on the dressing table seat, and May parted and combed his damp hair, renewing her determination to keep Keswick Farm going, to give her father something to work for—something to *live* for. There needed to be a home place for her children, and for *their* children. That loss, she knew, was what was so difficult for Byrd. His older brother would have inherited Chestnut Grove, had he not been killed in the War. Jimmy Craig had been groomed for it from an early age. Byrd wanted to be a lawyer, not a horse breeder. After Jimmy died, Byrd embraced his newfound responsibility, understanding that it was his duty to keep the place up. Well, that didn't matter now, did it?

When she looked up, Byrd stood in the doorway, neat in his dark blue suit, his hair slicked back severely. He looked dignified, May thought, and so handsome, despite the pallor of grief.

"We ready?" he asked, then came to tousle Hank's hair.

"I don't want to wear a sailor suit, Daddy."

May and Byrd locked eyes over Hank's head. Volumes passed between them, of sorrow, of dread, and, like a halo around those emotions, love.

"Buddy, go on downstairs and help Grandpa with his necktie." Hank took off, clattering down the stairs.

May leaned against her husband, knowing that if she let down her guard now, she would not get through this day. And he needed her strength. Over his shoulder, she saw their reflection in the glass of the dressing table. His broad back, her hands at his neck. She moved out of his embrace and put a hand to each side of his face. "We're going to be all right. Things *will* get better. They will. That's hard to see right now, but as hard as you work, we'll get along."

"May, listen to me for a minute. About work . . . The day it happened, when you called to tell me, I had just gotten off a call from Washington. I'd been talking with a fellow from my law class, who works at the Federal Trade Commission. Last week I applied for a job there."

"Washington?"

"I was going to tell you, that night. I'm going for an interview. If I get it, I'll come home on weekends. It's less than three hours on the train."

May's hand went to her throat. "I didn't know things were so bad."

"The only lawyers making money are doing foreclosures and bankruptcies. This will be temporary. I'm sorry. It's the best solution I can come up with, to take care of you all. And that's the most important thing to me. You and the kids. I'm doing my best to be responsible."

May blinked and blew out a long breath. It seemed impossible to envision this life Byrd was talking about. She said, "We're partners, aren't we? If we have to do this for a while, we will. I have faith in us, as partners."

"Any regrets?" He held her gaze. "Though now might not be the best time . . ."

"Never. There's no one—and I mean *no* one—I'd rather go through bad times with." May pulled back, grasping his hands in hers, holding his gaze. "When I think about how reckless I was, in New York and Paris—I felt so lucky to have been given another chance. We were meant to go through life together. The good and the bad."

From the hall below, Henry called, "May? Byrd? The car's here."

Byrd drove the Packard that had been his father's, with Henry beside him in the front. Hank sat between May and Sybil in the back. Sybil's taut face was inscrutable behind a black hat and veil and she kept her gaze trained out the window, clasping her handbag with rigid, black-gloved fingers. Hank tugged at May's sleeve. "Is Grandfar really inside a box, Mama? Does he have on his pajamas?"

"Hush, now," May said, "remember, you promised to behave like a big boy today."

When Sybil spoke, only her mouth was visible below her veil. "For God's sake, this is not the place for a child."

Byrd spoke up. "I wanted him to come. He should be allowed to say goodbye to his grandfather."

Hank looked up at Sybil and whispered, "I'm naming my puppy Bandit. What's yours called?"

At Grace Episcopal Church, the hearse was parked beside the front doors. Henry refused help, pulling himself from the car, leaning on his cane. Byrd held Sybil's door as she stepped out, checking the seams of her black stockings. May reached back for Hank's hand as he scooted across the seat. He broke away to stand behind his grandfather. May's Uncle Cy approached, shyly bobbing his head, blinking repeatedly, as if he did not know what to say. He bent down to whisper to Henry. Sybil continued into the church, not waiting for anyone. She had flown back from Kentucky the night before and, while Byrd explained her newly diminished situation, she emptied several tumblers of Kentucky bourbon and asked about her trainer and her show horses, making it clear that what she had owned before her marriage would remain in her name. When May tried to take her hand, Sybil stood up and threw the heavy crystal glass into the fireplace, then crossed her arms over her chest, announcing that she would return to Kentucky after the funeral.

Cars were arriving, along with a few horse-drawn wagons. Byrd took May's arm. "You go on in and sit with your dad. I want to wait for the pallbearers."

"I'd rather wait with you. There's Elsie's car." May stifled the urge to wave as her friend's butter-yellow roadster pulled in. The car bumped over the loose stones that defined the parking area, jolting to a stop, inches from a granite obelisk.

Byrd said, "I can't believe Archie lets her drive." Elsie Nelson had been May's roommate at Mary Baldwin College and remained her best friend, even though they lived a hundred miles apart. While Elsie donned a dramatically large black hat with iridescent dark feathers, her husband Archie made his way around the back of the car to her door, his familiar limp a result of childhood polio. He opened the driver's side door for Elsie, and she started across the parking lot with arms outstretched, fur coat flapping, a jet cigarette holder clamped in her teeth. She embraced Byrd, then May, kissing them exuberantly in turn, as her husband shook Byrd's hand and patted his back.

"Terrible news, terrible news," Archie said, shaking his head. Archie seldom spoke, unlike his wife, whose throaty voice and booming laugh tended to dominate most occasions.

Elsie held Byrd's forearms. "Oh, Gawd, honey," she said, "just the saddest thing. Honestly. I was telling Arch on the way over; your dad was such a prince of a fellow." When Elsie wrapped May in a bear hug, the taut, sapping stress of the past days wavered. Her friend had held her up before and would do so again, she knew. Guiltily, she counted the hours until the day was over—the procession to the grave site, the reception at the Keswick Hunt Club. Byrd had designated his father's stock of bootleg liquor for the occasion. Then, tomorrow, there would begin the emptying of Chestnut Grove; the awful disassembling of a family place. May took a deep breath, pushing back from Elsie. It was far too early to give in to despair.

Elsie took May's arm, leading her, saying, "You'll come down to Richmond for luncheon, soon. I'll take you to the Palm Court at the Jefferson, and we'll have one of those lunches that last until cocktail time. You look like you need it. You holding up?"

May kept her gaze fixed ahead, slightly out of focus, as if Elsie was her guide. She sighed. "How do you do it, Elsie?"

"Do what?"

"How do you stay so optimistic? I feel so helpless."

"Aw, sugar pie, I have hot and cold running help. I could never manage all that you do."

Inside, they separated. The church was nearly full. May squeezed her eyes shut for a moment, desperate to recall names she ought to remember. Cy took her arm. The still air smelled of beeswax and lilies, the lily scent seeming to bubble up from the floor like tar. May and her uncle made their way slowly up the aisle, pausing for handshakes or grave nods of greeting from neighbors. Hank seemed absorbed in the solemnity, sitting quietly on the front pew next to his grandfather. May took her place beside him, reaching across to squeeze Byrd's hand when he sat to join them. She focused on the stained glass windows above the altar—the saturated hues of amethyst and grass-green and ruby, the shading of the individual pieces, the meticulous detail. Everyone rose silently, as James Craig's coffin was borne in. May dipped her head as the acolyte carrying the cross passed and moved up the two steps to the chancel. Byrd stared ahead, stiff and controlled, as the minister began the service. A tear escaped and she brushed it away. Pressing her nails into her palms, her gloves prevented the sharp, distracting pain she sought. Tilting her chin up, she studied the vaulted ceiling, then read the stone wall plaques, placed at intervals between the windows. Several bore the names of ancestral Craig benefactors. The largest, most elaborate crypt in the churchyard also bore the name. Relief flitted through her mind, that the Craigs were not buried in a plot at their home, as her family was at Keswick Farm. At least the graves of the ancestors would not be auctioned off to the highest bidder.

Eight
DORRIT

The funeral of Augusta Sykes was small and simple, and as Christian Science proscribed, it was held in the Sykes's home.

Dorrit resented the sad, assuming eyes of parishioners; their sympathetic shoulder pats proffered with murmured bromides and quotations from Mrs. Eddy. She suspected that she and her family were being judged, for not relying on prayer. Dorrit wanted to shout, *You didn't see what was happening; you weren't here! I'm not sure God was here either!* But she stayed silent. After five days, Roy returned to work, Dorrit to school. Walt began staying out nights and refused to go to church.

Now, four months later, Dorrit still missed her mother in every part of every day. Twice, she visited the grave. Once before the headstone, once after. No comfort was forthcoming from the mound of earth or the plain granite slab. Her mother's memory rested in the empty chair and the sewing basket, with its threaded needles and half-darned socks. Dorrit understood now that her mother had been the glue that held the family together.

Without being aware of doing so, Dorrit had begun to shape her days around her mother's memory. *Washday on Wednesday, ironing on Thursday.* On Saturdays, she walked up Blossom Street to catch the streetcar on Cambridge Street. From there she rode to Beacon Hill, where she delivered

sewing to the houses of the wealthy. Most of Augusta's clients had continued to supply work and it seemed she was doing more mending, with fewer
new dresses to be hemmed or altered. Dorrit had heard her father speak
about the financial crash, but with no investments to lose, the Sykeses had
gone on as before, while half of the businesses on Blossom Street had shut-
tered in the past year. Fortunately, her father continued to have steady work
and for several weeks had been in Cambridge, tending machinery at the
New England Confectionery Company. Like Dorrit's mending, repairing
factory engines and machines was cheaper than replacing them.

On a gray February Saturday, Dorrit rinsed the breakfast plates while
Walt slouched against the drainboard, wiping them ineffectively. "Wish
we had a radio," he said, sullenly.

"I'd rather have a telephone."

Walt lowered his voice. "Dor? You think Pop's got a screw loose?" She
followed his gaze to where their father bent over his plans with both hands
in his hair, pulling it straight up. From behind, it appeared as if he were
trying to lift himself from his chair.

"No more than anybody else, I s'pose," she said.

"But whoever heard of an electric mousetrap?"

"Pop says it's a modern innovation. He says somebody else already
patented one, only it's different from his. It might make us rich." Her
father seemed not to hear them.

Dorrit opened the brown leatherette ledger she took with her each
week. The handwriting still squeezed at her heart, almost like hearing a
beloved voice unexpectedly, then turning to find no one there. Columns,
neatly scored and filled with Augusta's careful script listing client, job,
hours, supplies. A separate page listed weekly payments made on the treadle sewing machine, purchased over a period of two years. Her mother
had been so proud to make the final payment.

Dorrit put the ledger into her satchel. Library books went in next, then
her pincushion, tape measure, and blue marking pencil, along with her
mother's sewing shears in their red morocco leather case, with "Sears, Roe-
buck & Co." embossed in gold letters. Finally, the sewing work she would
return, carefully folded in tissue paper that she would iron and reuse.

Outside, the air had that particular winter clarity that precedes snow. Within minutes, tiny, frozen pellets began to fall, pinging softly against tree branches and bouncing off windshields, eddying into miniature crystalline dunes. By the time Dorrit reached Beacon Hill, the sidewalks were nearly covered. A pair of girls Dorrit's age strolled toward her on the opposite side of the street, one wearing a fur coat, with ice skates slung over her shoulder. With their heads together, the girls seemed to be telling secrets. Dorrit imagined herself walking between them, arms linked, like Nancy Drew with Bess and George. But these girls were braver than she was. Ice skating seemed to have so many possibilities for humiliation. Plus, there were the skates themselves, to buy or rent.

In front of Mrs. Frazier's brownstone, the chauffeur brushed snow from a large dark-blue Packard. He tipped his cap to Dorrit. "Morning, miss."

"Good morning, Mister Mitchell." The girls' singsong voices were still audible, calling out rhymes from down the street. Dorrit climbed the slippery granite steps. She peered through the door glass, her breath steaming as she straightened her hat. She rang the bell and waited, cold seeping into her leg bones.

Through the glass, she watched the gray-uniformed maid approach. Dorrit knew she was Irish, and that her name was Connie, but despite a year of seeing each other every other Saturday, Connie maintained an air of disdainful superiority. "Mrs. Frazier's expecting me," Dorrit said, without preamble. "I got her tea dress finished."

The maid narrowed her eyes as she opened the door fully. Dorrit stepped up, into the warm hallway. "Wait." Connie pronounced the "t" as if she were spitting a seed from her teeth. For another few minutes, Dorrit shifted her satchel from hand to hand before Connie stuck her head from a doorway down the hall, lifting her chin as she said, "Go on up, then." Dorrit took a deep breath. Twenty-two steps, then sixteen more, to reach the third floor. Although it was one room wide, the townhouse had five stories.

"Mrs. Frazier?" Dorrit called, from the top of the final flight.

"Come on in!" The bedroom was a confection. A ruffled, quilted satin spread covered the bed and the canopy was hung with lace that Mrs. Frazier once said was made by nuns in Belgium. A coal fire blazed in the grate, while on an apricot velvet chaise lounge, the lady herself sprawled in dishabille, one hand holding a novel while the other languidly explored a pink box of chocolates. Below, pleated paper doilies were scattered on the carpet. Mrs. Frazier licked her index finger, then stuck a doily between the pages. She sighed deeply and laid the book on her bosom. "Oh, my dear girl. Forgive me." She pushed herself to sitting. "Where *has* this day gone? I was with William the Conqueror, I'm afraid. Have you read Mrs. Heyer's latest?" She held up the novel, and Dorrit shook her head. "I must say," she continued, "I don't think *The Conqueror* can hold a candle to her *Simon the Coldheart*, but it does grip one. Have a sweet. Mister Frazier sent these for Valentine's Day." She held out the candy box. A few pieces were upside-down, oozing from wounds inflicted by Mrs. Frazier in her quest to identify the fillings inside.

Dorrit chose a piece with sprinkles of coconut. "Thank you, ma'am."

Mrs. Frazier put the box down and held out a tattered lace pillow. Her voice went up an octave. "Darling Boo-boo had his way with this widdle pillow slip, I'm afwaid. Twy to mend it, would you?" At the sound of his name, a panting, beribboned Pekingese stuck his head out from his gilded bed, which was modeled after a pagoda. His eyes bulged in a way that made Dorrit think of someone being strangled.

"Who's Mother's naughty boy, Dowwit, hmmm?" Mrs. Frazier resumed her normal tone. "Well, thank *God* you're here. We have a bit of an emergency." She jerked her head toward a velvet gown that hung in front of the armoire. On a chair nearby, several evening dresses lay heaped, next to a stack of magazines and an overflowing ashtray. When she stood, Mrs. Frazier's broad back was reflected in the oval of the large mirror of her dressing table, where hairpins lay strewn amidst spilled face powder. She continued, "I've got a party tonight, and I bought this dress a month ago. I went to try it on this morning only I couldn't get the damned zipper up! I can't possibly get anything else in time. I told Earl—Mister Frazier—I'd get something blue, you know, to go with my sapphires? It's the perfect shade, don't you think? Only it won't zip."

Bertha Frazier was a kind woman and always gave Dorrit an extra nickel for the streetcar or else had her chauffeur drive her to the library when they were finished. She was also stout, so each time Dorrit met with her, she knew to take new measurements. Dorrit said, "Well, ma'am, let's have a look."

Mrs. Frazier said, "Your mother was such a marvel with her needle." Dorrit looked down.

"You must miss her terribly."

"Yes, ma'am."

Mrs. Frazier shrugged out of her kimono, letting it fall to the floor. She resembled a trussed turkey, bound into a one-piece undergarment that seemed to have an infinite number of seams, laces, and straps. Dorrit savored her chocolate, pretending to be absorbed in the magazines on the floor. *Silver Screen* and an open copy of *Screenland*. With her foot, she slid it toward her. One page had photographs of the English Princesses, Elizabeth and Margaret, now aged five and one, in matching smocked dresses. On the other page, in an advertisement for hosiery, a coy-looking young woman perched sideways on a stone wall, her knees drawn up. Mrs. Frazier huffed, then stepped into the dress, pulling it over the jutting shelf of her bosom. A gap of an inch prevented the zipper from closing. "See?" She said, peevishly, "You try." She drew in her breath as Dorrit tugged. The fabric pulled taut, seams almost groaning with the strain of trying to contain Mrs. Frazier. She exhaled in a whoosh. "Oh, it's no use. I've got so damned fat. Did you know I used to be on the stage, in New York? I was in the Ziegfeld Follies in '23, Dorrit. Oh, I had such legs then!" She clucked, looking over her shoulder at her plump calves in the mirror. "Mister Frazier was wild for me. I could have had my pick of gents, let me tell you."

Dorrit puzzled out the problem, focusing on the wide taffeta sash that spanned, unbecomingly, the girth of Mrs. Frazier's hips. She had observed, watching her mother with her sewing clients, that tact was a significant part of their stock-in-trade.

"But then," Mrs. Frazier flashed the large diamond on her left hand, "he got down on his knee. A girl certainly couldn't turn *this* down. Even if it did mean giving up my career. Ah, well." She arched an eyebrow. "Maybe if I wear my white fox stole . . ."

Dorrit had heard the story before, about the Follies and the ring. She had no response to offer, and really, none was expected. The intimacy between seamstress and client was a one-way street. "I have an idea," she said. She folded open the magazine, pointing to the advertisement. "If we take the sash apart, I could make up a placket to run down the back and take out the zipper. A placket would give you two inches. We could close it up with little bows, like the ones in this picture."

"Oh, Dorrit, you are a clever girl. I despise that sash, anyway. Here, sit." Mrs. Frazier pushed everything from the chair to the floor, patting the seat. "You get comfy and get to work."

A clever girl. Dorrit flushed. Nancy Drew was clever. Dorrit said, "But I have other clients." Technically, this was true. She did have one other client to see today. Really, she hoped to spend the afternoon at the library.

"Phooey. This is an emergency. I'll give you a little luncheon, and you'll whip this up, and that's that."

Dorrit considered. Would Connie have to *serve* the little luncheon to her? Downstairs, at the kitchen table, Dorrit measured and cut the taffeta and stitched it to the velvet. Connie sullenly prepared a plain chicken sandwich, plopping the plate on the table beside Dorrit, then left the kitchen without a word. A little after two o'clock, with Mrs. Frazier exclaiming with happiness, Dorrit folded the lace pillowslip and put it in her satchel, along with Mrs. Frazier's library books.

"Here you go, you little darling," Mrs. Frazier pressed money into Dorrit's palm, then closed up the box of chocolates and held them out. "You *must* take these, and next time you see me, I'll be a size slimmer. I'll live on boiled eggs and grapefruit, starting tomorrow. You'll have to take everything in. Won't that be wonderful? Happy Valentine's Day, dear!"

At the Boston Public Library, the car idled while Dorrit gathered her things. Mitchell hurried around to open the door for her. "Let me carry those books?" he asked. "It's icy out there."

"No, thank you," Dorrit said, "I'll be fine. Thank you for the ride."

"Sorry about Mrs. Sykes. She was a lovely woman. Always a kind word."

Mrs. Frazier had said something nice too. Something was shifting,

Dorrit realized, from grief to warm memory. After four months, she had reached a point where she could hear this and not cry. "Thank you," she said, and her smile was genuine. When he tipped his hat, she pondered again if Mitchell was his first or last name. She had never found the nerve to ask.

She walked slowly up the broad stone steps, through the bronze doors, and into the odors of damp woolen overcoats and musty dry heat. In the golden-hued marble lobby, she paid silent homage to the majestic pair of lions flanking the stair landing. Above, on the vaulted ceiling, she read off the names of American authors and scholars, worked in mosaic tile. Past the main desk, to the left, was the elevator. What a luxury, to not have to climb those beautiful steps.

In the cavernous reading room, Dorrit left the books at the return desk. She used one of the small yellow pencils to record the titles of the books she wanted: *From the Tower Window, Simon the Coldheart,* and the newest Nancy Drew, *The Bungalow Mystery.*

From the Tower Window was volume five in a set of anthologies for children, called *My Book House.* For as long as Dorrit could remember, her mother had brought her to the library on Saturdays, after visiting her sewing clients. *Saturday: Sewing clients, library.* They read all twelve of the *My Book House* volumes. Dorrit would be embarrassed to admit that she chose the book for herself now, but the familiar stories of princesses and fairies reminded her of her mother. If asked, Dorrit would have denied vehemently that fairytales and mythical creatures still held her in thrall. If asked, she was prepared to say that she intended to read the book to the little Sullivan boys. So far, no one had asked. The book she most looked forward to was *The Bungalow Mystery* by Carolyn Keene. Nancy Drew, a high school graduate at sixteen, had lost her mother too. Only, unlike Dorrit, Nancy had no chores to do and no siblings to pester her. She had a housekeeper and drove around with her friends, finding clues and solving mysteries. Nancy Drew was brave and wealthy and popular. Her life was never dull or lonely—it was perfect.

In the Abbey Room, next door, several people sat in rows of wooden chairs, waiting for books. Dorrit passed her request to a clerk at an open window then took a chair. As a rule, silence was kept in the Abbey Room, but the sounds of footsteps and subdued conversations echoed from the grand staircase. Time here was to be savored. The walls were paneled in dark, glossy oak, and above, richly colored gilded murals surrounded the room, depicting scenes from·the life of Sir Galahad. Of all King Arthur's knights, Galahad was the only one pure enough to receive the Holy Grail. She studied his face in each of the panels and each week, she found him perfectly handsome and gallant.

A librarian she recognized held up one of Dorrit's books, whispering, "Sykes?" Dorrit slid from her seat and went to the window. "Here you go, miss," the young man said. He glanced at her card, peering through the tops of his glasses. "One of these . . . uh, *Simon the Coldheart* by Georgette Heyer—out for repair. Maybe try back next week?"

Dorrit thanked him and hefted the stack. She exhaled a deep sigh, silently debating returning to the crowded reading room or going home, to Walt and her father. Instead, she climbed the central stairs to the soaring, skylit stone gallery on the third floor. John Singer Sargent's massive murals, *The Triumph of Religion* filled the walls in sixteen panels, from the stone balustrades up twenty-six feet to the vaults of the ceiling. Brass wall plaques chronicled how the series took the artist twenty-nine years, painting the sections in England, traveling with them to Boston for four installation phases, and how he died before completing the final panel.

Dorrit had paced this gallery many times, never tiring of finding new bits of texture in a prophet's gown or an undiscovered glass jewel in an angel's halo. Scenes featured Egyptians worshiping their gods, the Assyrians before Christ, Judaism, and Christianity. For Dorrit, each face brought faith to life, suffused with emotion—regret, ecstasy, grief. Sitting on a stone bench, she wrote in her notebook:

February 13, 1932—So many ways humans have worshiped and suffered. So much faith, directed to versions of God. Different forms, different rules, different rituals. It's like Mr. Sargent is asking, 'who's to say that one way is right?'

Dorrit paused, wondering where Christian Science fit in all of this. She wrote:

How could a church that preaches love and worships a merciful God expect anyone to watch someone die? Are doctors liars? Mr. Sargent chose this subject himself. He could have spent 29 whole years working on anything. And he chose religion.

Back at home, Dorrit pulled herself up the stairs, her books and work bag dragging from her left arm. From behind a door on the first floor, a radio played orchestral music. A raised voice carried down the staircase. Raised voices were not unusual at 23 Blossom Street, and halfway to the second floor, Dorrit knew who was shouting.

Inside the apartment, Walt stood in front of the sink, his breath heaving as he held a dishtowel to his mouth. His face was red, the pimples darker exclamations. Roy sat, tapping a white envelope against the edge of the table.

"What's the matter?" Dorrit dropped her satchel.

"Police brought your brother home this afternoon, for fighting." Her father waved an envelope. "And this arrived today. Apparently, he's not going to graduate in June."

Walt removed the towel, revealing a split lip. "I'm already the oldest in the class. No way I'm gonna repeat. And I won't be your lackey, neither. I can get work at the docks. I can't stand it here." He ran his hands through his hair, pulling it in a mannerism exactly like his father. "Crammed in here like sardines—no privacy—and that stinking baby downstairs, howling all the time."

Roy said, "You know I want us to make a business together. *Sykes & Son*—has a good ring, doesn't it? You'll never amount to nothing if you don't finish your schooling."

Walt pushed away from the sink. Half-laughing, he said, "So's that *your* excuse? Is it, Pop? Did you even finish fourth grade?"

Roy blinked. "When I was eleven, my father died in a factory fire. You know that. Me and my brother had no choice but to work. Bobby and

me, we were going to be the *Sykes Brothers*. Then he died in the War. If
you're determined to throw away this opportunity to better yourself, then
you're coming to work with me. My roof, my rules." He stabbed the ta-
bletop with his finger. "You got that? And you'll be going to church with
us tomorrow."

"No."

They stared at each other. "Maybe," Walt said, "if you'd finished
school, you'd be smart enough to get that Christian Science is baloney!"
Then he said, succinctly, quietly, "You and your stupid religion. You let
Ma die." He strode to the door, grabbing his jacket without stopping, calling over his shoulder, "And nobody's ever gonna buy your stinking electric
mousetrap!"

Roy's ears went back, but he did not speak. When the door slammed
behind Walt, Dorrit wanted to embrace her father, or reach for his hand,
but she didn't. They barely touched anymore. Her mother would have
said something placating to assuage both father and son. If her mother
had been here, Walt might not have failed. With a fresh welling of grief,
Dorrit understood how disconnected the family had become. Walt was
right, though; most likely, nobody would ever pay her father for his inventions. *But we all need something*, she thought, *something to call our own;
something to dream about.*

Nine
MAY

May belted her bathrobe in a hasty knot as she crossed the upstairs hall. Creeping past her father's bedroom, she was relieved to hear gentle snoring, anticipating a few moments of much-needed privacy downstairs. Diplomacy was key—she had learned over the past two months—in the negotiations of a shared house. When her father's back flared up and he slept in the parlor, the radio would be playing at dawn. It was his house, and his radio, and May had adapted. First, to the combined household, and then, only a few weeks later, to Byrd working in Washington. They had sold his car, and he stayed the week in a rented room in a house in Georgetown.

In the children's room, Sister lay in her crib, eyes wide, shaking her little fists at the sight of her mother. Hank slept on his stomach, arms and legs at all angles. The puppy, curled at the foot of the bed, thumped his tail submissively as if to say, *I know I'm not allowed*, and May let him stay. She scooped Sister up, hushing her, then opened her robe to nurse as she sat in the rocking chair beside the window. It was not yet seven o'clock. Outside, the grass sparkled with frost, and robins hopped along the frozen ground.

She shifted the baby, wondering if the day would stay clear. Today was important. She would wear her blue wool suit. It wasn't terribly up to date, but it was in good shape and she had lost the baby weight. Elsie, of course, would have on the latest style—probably something she had ordered from

Paris. May looked forward to seeing her friend—to girl talk, and luncheon at the Jefferson Hotel. It would be like the old days, before the crash.

She changed the baby's diaper then tiptoed down the stairs, hoping that Hank would sleep longer. The puppy ran ahead, waiting at the back door. In the kitchen, coffee grounds trailed across the counter and the pot steamed on the stove, but Delphina was nowhere in sight. May opened the back door and the puppy bounded down the steps, lifting his leg on the nearest boxwood bush while looking back to her for approval.

"Good boy, Bandit." She stepped out onto the porch, breathing in the fresh, cold air.

"Ain't too soon to train him to hunt."

May started, hugging Sister to her chest. At the end of the porch, her uncle Cy leaned against a railing, balancing a coffee cup. With his yellowed gray beard and wooly eyebrows, he looked like a scrawny, scuffed Santa Claus in his plaid overcoat with a red union suit showing beneath. He wore one gray sock and one blue—orphan socks, he always called them, singles left behind at Waddell's Laundry.

"Uncle Cy?" May tugged her robe, holding it closed.

"Morning!" he scratched beneath his chin, nodding and squinting. "What time's breakfast?"

"Seven-thirty?"

"Ain't had a proper breakfast since I can recall. Maybe Henry's right, I ought to find a good woman." He frowned slightly, then chuckled. "Hope you don't mind I fixed a pot of coffee. Can't get the old plumbing going in the morning without it, if you know what I mean."

"I didn't know you'd be . . . joining us. For breakfast, I mean."

"Ah. Yeah, well. I got in right late last night. You was already upstairs. Surprised you didn't hear me come in." He rubbed his neck, looking toward the mountains. His voice dropped. "Sorry about that. Henry told me he'd ask you." He looked down at Bandit, who now leaned against his knee. "*Damn* that Cecil Boxley." He sounded defeated. "It's not enough that he foreclosed on the laundry. Last evening, while I was out at my card game, he padlocked the place. Every damned thing I own's in the apartment. Had to climb through the back window like a common burglar." He paused. "What's a fella supposed to do? Men out of work; women taking in laundry now for pennies—else folks are buying their own e-lectric washing machines. You know, I had to let go ten people. Ten! Some of 'em been working for me for twenty years or more. And all I can tell 'em is, 'Sorry, friend, I'm in the boat with you,' only that's cold comfort to a widow woman with five children to feed." His shoulders drooped and he stared into his cup. "But listen, I won't get underfoot around here. Truth of the matter is, I got nowhere else to go. You know that downtown, there's men getting theirselves arrested just to spend a few weeks in the jail and get fed?"

May compressed her lips. Irritation and sympathy walked ten paces and had a duel. How would this work? There was one bathtub in the house, upstairs. *But,* she silently chastised herself, *it isn't my house.* What had her father offered, or promised? She said, "I'm sorry. Where did you sleep?"

"In the parlor."

Across the yard, a screened door whined and slapped closed. Delphina came from her cottage, humming as she knotted an apron behind her. Bandit ran toward her, tail wagging, crouching to play. Delphina flipped her hands. When she spotted Cy, she stopped, hands on her hips. May felt like she had just been caught doing something very naughty.

May left Sister in the playpen in the kitchen and went upstairs, happy to close herself in the bathroom. She hung her skirt on the towel rod to steam out the creases. Leaning toward the mirror, she trimmed her bangs with nail scissors. If she wore a hat, the fact that she needed a haircut might not show. After her bath, she sat at her dressing table to put on rouge and lipstick. She took her nicest handbag from the closet shelf—one she had bought in Paris in 1925. The tan kid leather was still buttery soft. Back downstairs at eight thirty, she checked Sister's diaper and supply of formula then whispered to Delphina, "I'm going by the market. Need anything?"

"I'm making a meatloaf for supper. Get a can of beets. Better make it two."

In the parlor, Hank was in his pajamas, setting up a checkerboard, placing the pieces with intense concentration. She kissed the crown of his head. "I think it's going to snow. I'll be back before it gets dark."

"Grandpa says if I win checkers *two* times," he held up two fingers, "he'll give me a penny."

A lurid newscast began on the radio. A woman named Winnie Ruth Judd had recently been given the death sentence for the murders of two female friends after a jealous falling out over a shared suitor. She had transported one victim's dismembered body by train, in luggage. Hank listened attentively, while May tried to catch her father's eye, miming *turn that off!*

Hank crowed, "It's The Trunk Murdewer, Grandpa!"

Outside, the Studebaker roared to life. Passing the front windows, May could see her uncle inside, buttoning his shirt. By the time she reached the end of the driveway tiny, icy snowflakes were falling. A glorious elation, almost to the point of giddiness settled over her. She stifled the urge to hoot, *No diapers, no waiting on customers, no Uncle Cy in the parlor! Free for a whole day!* Passing the stone pillars at the entrance to Chestnut Grove, she noticed that one of the biggest trees had fallen across the long driveway, near the road. She smiled to herself. It would be difficult for Mr. Boxley to show the property if no one could get to it.

A few minutes later, she pulled in behind the Keswick Market. As she pushed open the kitchen door, growling started inside. Blue had recently adopted a small stray, and he hushed the dog, then said, "Woo-hoo. You look mighty nice this morning, May."

May stepped inside the warm kitchen. The aroma of caramelized sugar and roasted pecans already permeated the air, making her mouth water. The dog had retreated to its nest of gunny sacks in a corner, her eyes tracking every movement. "Now, look here," Blue said, motioning May toward the work table, "I ordered these nice cartons and fancy paper cups." He opened a glossy white box, displaying a dozen pieces of candy, nestled in small pleated cups. There were two stacks of identical boxes, each tied with blue-and-white twine. Blue ducked his head with uncharacteristic bashfulness. "What do you think? The boxes cost three cents apiece, but they look real high-class. Leastways, I think so."

"Blue, what a wonderful idea. They look so professional!" They smiled at each other.

Blue began to stack boxes carefully into a fruit crate. "These ought to travel fine in the trunk. Don't leave them up front near the heater."

"I have appointments at ten thirty and eleven o'clock. I should be back by late afternoon, hopefully with some good news." The dog began pawing the door, barking furiously at something outside. Her tail stood straight up, except where it bent over at the top like the crook of a candy cane.

A ragged man with a pack on his back stood outside, smiling hopefully. Blue held the dog's collar. Seeing May, the man doffed his cap as she opened the door. "Top of the morning, ma'am." He eyed the snarling mutt.

May thought of her uncle, who was probably tucking into a second stack of hotcakes right about now. "Morning," she said. "You look like you could use something to eat."

At exactly ten thirty, May presented herself at the purchasing department of Richmond's largest department store. She was asked to wait and sat primly, legs crossed at the ankle, holding a folder, hoping she appeared cool and professional with her freshly mimeographed order form and price list. After posing for ten minutes, she began to thumb the pages of a woman's magazine. Most of the advertisements promoted economy: *Grape Nuts: Big in energy but oh so little in cost! 7¢ for a he-man's breakfast! . . . Campbell's Soup provides so much real substantial nourishment, tastes so good and is so delightfully convenient! Especially beneficial to children! . . . If your child "Eats Poorly," try nutritious, economical Ovaltine! Mail in coupon below for a trial package!*

She sat up straighter, suddenly inspired, and began to scribble in tiny print on the back of a discarded business card:

Nuts- peanuts? Pecans?
Raisins/dried cherries
Sugar- meringue? Marshmallow inside?
Chocolate (cocoa-expensive)
Caramel? Mix with marshmallow?

She tapped her pencil, thinking. What if she and Blue could invent a candy bar that might nourish a person for a whole day? Could they do that? And might they be able to mass-produce them? They would need large quantities of ingredients. They would need wholesale accounts, storage space, a larger workspace. They could buy ingredients locally, supporting area farms—farmers, and their wives—people she knew, who had fallen on hard times just as Keswick Farm had. And she would hire local people—local women—to work. She began to write again:

Local:
Nuts-pecans, peanuts
Fruit/berries (seasonal)
Honey
Mint/sassafras?
Eggs (meringue) 29¢/doz.
Butter 28¢/lb.
Cream

She paused, tapping the pencil again. *This could be big.*

The buyer at Miller & Rhoads accepted a sample box, then placed an order for a dozen more, asking if May might come up with some sort of seasonal packaging later on.

Buoyant, May moved on, and at noon on the dot, a white-jacketed waiter pulled a gilded chair away from a small round table. May thanked him and sat down. Around the Palm Court of the Jefferson Hotel, lush tropical plants flourished, and the ceiling was a dome of intricate stained glass. The scent of moss and loam mixed with cigar smoke. May unfolded her linen napkin and laid it in her lap. Looking down, she allowed herself a big, private grin, then assembled her features as she removed her gloves. She had just taken orders from Miller & Rhoads and the head chef here, at the Jefferson. He bought the boxes she had on the spot, ordering ten more for the following week.

When May pulled out a cigarette, the attentive waiter hurried to place a silver ashtray in front of her and light a match. Up close, she noticed his white jacket; the edges of the collar were frayed. Even the majestic Jefferson Hotel showed the strain of the downturn. Only three other tables were occupied, when only a few years ago, a reservation would have been required a week in advance. But the hotel was still beautiful, the linens still crisp, the flatware well-polished. May lined up her forks and glanced at her wrist-watch. Of course, Elsie would be late. It was only a matter of *how* late.

Twenty minutes later Elsie breezed in, clad head to toe in an arresting shade of peacock blue. Her arms extended as she crossed the room, and the long feathers of her blue hat dipped and swayed. She called out, "There you are! *Gawd*, it's good to see you. Give Elsie a hug this very minute!" After they embraced and the waiter seated Elsie, May reached across the table to run a finger over the bright suede of her friend's gloves. May's own powder blue suit faded in comparison to Elsie's vividness. "These are beautiful. Where did get them?"

"Montaldo's. You don't think they're a bit too . . . blue? And that re-minds me," she dug into her large handbag, removing a flat, wrapped package. "A little late Valentine gift for my favorite godson. How is that precious boy?" She passed the package to May then fitted a fresh cigarette into her holder. The waiter hurried over to light it.

"He's a handful. He's been acting out since Byrd started in Washing-ton. I think he's jealous of Little Elsie. It's been hard."

"It's always something, isn't it? Look at this." Elsie continued to dig in her bag, then unfolded a handbill and read, "*The Virginia Board of Health suggests that all children and infants between the ages of twelve months and thirteen years be injected with the diphtheria toxoid. Public nurses will be coming through your neighborhood on Wednesday, February 24th.*" She passed it across the table, saying, "Have you had something like this in Keswick?"

"Not a printed notice, but I did get Dr. Sawyer to give them the shots when I took Sister in for an earache."

"Honestly, though, diphtheria is the least of my worries. It's more likely that the little monsters will kill each *other*. But I suppose I ought to get them vaccinated. Only I absolutely hate to see those little *faces* when they see that needle—so shocked and scared. I'll have Nanny take them."

May toyed with her knife, trying to quash her niggling envy. Elsie had a cook and a nanny, and a gardener, and a summer house on a river, and a rack of new dresses every season. Her life had always been that way. Yet, somehow, it never came between the two of them. Despite her blustery manner, Elsie was always generous and sensitive, steering their conversations to a middle ground.

May sighed, relishing the final bite of Crab Louis. As they sat over coffee, she peeked at her watch. "I've got to go. Delphina's been watching the children all day. I've just about got Sister weaned. Honestly, nursing makes me feel so tied down. Here, I brought you a little something. Happy belated Valentine's."

Elsie opened the white box and popped a piece of candy into her mouth. She closed her eyes; her face took on an expression of bliss. "*Gawd*, honey! What do you put in these things?" She smacked her lips. "It's pure heaven! *Dee-vine*, simply divine."

"Blue calls those 'Fluffy Ruffles'—it's a meringue, with pecans and vanilla."

"Oh, I must have another teensy one. I'm going to hide these when I get home, if I don't eat them all on the way. The monsters are not getting *near* these. I might let Archie have one if he's good. *Mm.* Really heavenly, darling. Just this little-bitty one more. You're absolutely ruining my slimming regimen."

"I'm glad you like them." The waiter refilled their cups and May leaned across the table to whisper, "Can you keep a secret?"

Elsie looked up at the ceiling for a brief moment, the tapped an index finger against her lips. "Usually not. I mean, one always *says* one can, with all the best intentions, but in reality, I'm dreadful about it. Especially with Arch. So do tell, at your peril. I'm all ears and you *must* tell me now, of course. I'm over here simply *dying* of expectation." She puffed on her cigarette holder, resting her fingers on her chest.

"Well, I've cooked up a little scheme, you might say. Byrd hasn't a clue, but I'll tell him when it all works out. This morning, I had a meeting at Miller & Rhoads, then I met with the chef here. I'm going to sell this candy." May tapped the box top. "Since business is so terrible lately, we've shut down the orchard production, because of that wind storm, and the tree blight, and the drought last summer, and don't even get me started on the early frost this year."

"Not to worry."

"Anyway, Blue and I figured out that the highest profit item we have in the market is . . . well, just guess."

"Pig's knuckles?"

"*Candy*. We sell out of everything he makes. Divinity, caramels, meringues—everything. Customers come from Somerset, and Gordonsville, and even Harrisonburg to buy it. They certainly don't come to shop for groceries, what with the Piggly Wiggly about putting us out of business. We're going into the candy business! We'll start small, of course, but I got my first real orders today. I can't wait to tell Daddy." May bounced in her seat. She pulled a magazine from her bag and held it out. "I even made an order form. And look at this. The buyer from Miller & Rhoads gave it to me. *The Confectioner's Gazette*. I was looking through it while I was waiting for you. It tells where to get *everything*—dyes, machines, and all sizes of paper doilies." May leaned forward. "And you know, the price of milk has never been lower."

"How utterly thrilling."

"The only problem might be the heat. Delivering in summer could be a problem. But we'll work that out."

Elsie's eyebrows rose as she nodded. "How marvelously creative of you, my dear girl. It's a splendid idea! Quite original. I can probably get you in to see someone at the Commonwealth Club, and you can sign me up for a regular shipment."

Driving home from Richmond, May's imagination blossomed with scenarios of a burgeoning candy empire; of telling Byrd that he could move home again and reopen his office—hearing him tell her how clever she was, how her simple little idea was the answer to all of their problems. By the time she passed Goochland, she glowed with anticipated esteem. In Gordonsville she stopped to get gasoline, thinking that perhaps a year from now they might have a new car. Blue might be able to buy the little house he'd been talking about. Really, it was a bit overwhelming. She put her hand over her mouth to cover the silly grin she could not suppress. After the attendant polished the windshield, she followed him inside the station. She paid for a ginger ale and he popped off the top, then wrapped it in a paper napkin and passed it to her. She raised it, in silent salute to her success, then took a long sip. Handbills were posted around the door. One day, they might be advertisements for her all-day candy bar. Cradling the bottle to her chest, she held out her other palm, absently accepting her change.

A fresh-looking bill was tacked up on the left side of the door. As she read the headlines, she drew in her breath. Slowly, without shifting her gaze, she set the bottle on the counter, then moved closer.

PUBLIC SALE

CHESTNUT GROVE FARM

ABSOLUTE AUCTION

Friday, May 13, 1932
on the premises.

Commencing at 10 o'clock.

RT. 22, ALBEMARLE COUNTY, KESWICK, VIRGINIA
529 acres- including a fine brick residence, twenty-stall horse barn, and six outbuildings. 1500 feet of state road frontage. Two ponds. Extra good well of water -a driven well which never fails. Equipment, including: John Deere tractor, 1 hay rake, 2 mowing machines, 1 hay wagon. Also saddles, bridles, and other items too numerous to mention. Free lunch at noon. Terms: $100 and under, cash. 10% Of the purchase price to be paid when the farm is bid off to the highest bidder, balance and final settlement to be made on or before 60 days from date of sale. Terms available.

FRANK HALL, *AUCTIONEER.*

CECIL BOXLEY,
Albemarle Bank & Trust Company, Agent
Charlottesville, Virginia Telephone Preston 5232

May tore down the flyer and hurried outside, leaving the ginger ale fizzing on the counter. Alone in the car, she read the print again. She wanted I to ball up the notice, to toss it away and drive off. But even if she did, the *event*—she refused to call it an auction—would still take place. Folding the paper carefully, she slid it into her purse, feeling sick and ashamed because she hoped someone else would tell Byrd before she had to do it.

Continuing home, more handbills fluttered from telephone poles and fences; one was even tacked outside the Keswick Post Office. *As if*, May thought, bitterly, *some malignant spirit wanted to be sure I noticed. God forbid I should enjoy an afternoon on my own. A few hours of real hopefulness. God forbid.*

At Keswick Farm, she pulled in, then sat in the driveway, reluctant to go inside. Her day had turned into a bad joke. She gathered her things, couching what she would say to her father—*Well, I've got some good news, and I've got some bad news, which do you want to hear first?*

Inside, she heard the radio snap off as she closed the front door.

"Well?" her father asked, expectantly. "Tell me how it went."

May sank into a chair beside him, silently holding out the handbill. Her full breasts ached. As Henry read, his eyebrows shot up. He whistled quietly. "Well." He was silent for a moment. "I suppose we all knew this would happen."

Early Friday evening, May drove with Hank to the Keswick Depot. Byrd's train was ten minutes late, and they sat in the warmth of the car until they heard the whistle blow. When Byrd stepped onto the platform and saw them, his face lit. He scooped Hank up and kissed May.

Hank insisted on carrying his father's bag and he struggled along in front of them, the bag banging against his legs. At the bottom of the stairs, Byrd stopped and took off his hat. He ran his fingers through his hair as he read one of the handbills for the auction, posted on the side of the building. May laid a hand on his arm. He had taken the news well, when she had spoken to him on the telephone on Wednesday. She said,

"I'm sorry. They're posted all around. And, well—you're going to see it—they've put up a big sign, at the entrance gates."

Byrd looked down, saying, "I'd just as soon not talk about it if you don't mind."

The whistle blew as the train left the station, and the three of them walked around the platform. Standing well away from the tracks, they watched the last car recede to the west. Hank tugged Byrd's hand and together they walked to the now-empty track. As Byrd watched, Hank crouched down, searching the gravel embankment. "Here it is!" he cried, triumphantly. "It's a good one!" He held up a penny, now a flattened oval of copper. "It got smashed good, Daddy. See, Mama?'

"Very nice," May said, not even looking. "Let's get home."

Byrd held the car door and Hank scooted in to sit between them on the front seat of the Studebaker. Byrd's voice was cheerful when he said, "Sure is good to be home." He glanced at his watch. "Sorry you had to wait for the train."

"We're so glad you're here. I went to Richmond this week," May ventured, "and I took orders from two places, for our candy. I was so nervous! And I had lunch with Elsie."

"How was she?"

"Fine." May had hoped for more response. Well, he'd see, when she got that big order from Miller & Rhoads. She said, "Delphina's cooking pork chops."

"Oh. Did your father not tell you? We're going to a Hog and Hominy meeting tonight. We'll have supper there."

"But you just got home!"

"Yeah, Daddy," Hank said. "You only got home."

Byrd said, "Henry has his heart set on going. I told him I'd take him."

"Let Uncle Cy drive him. You've been gone all week." May knew she sounded petulant, but she was disappointed.

"I haven't been to a meeting since before Dad died. I think I should go. It's at Castle Hill. We shouldn't be late."

Ten
DORRIT

A week after the fight, Walt left school and started working at the docks, vowing he would move out as soon as he found a place. Soon after that, Dorrit found a map in his pocket while doing laundry—a penciled route that started at the piers, along with a handbill for a burlesque show in Scollay Square. She suspected her brother worked for a bootlegger, but she did not ask. Some nights, she woke to the sharp reek of church-forbidden illegal liquor, with Walt banging into furniture, cursing under his breath. Roy either slept through his son's nocturnal bumbling or, Dorrit suspected, simply chose not to deal with the situation. Dorrit was torn between a desire to try to mend things between them for her mother's sake and a wish that Walt would leave them in peace. Her father spent more and more time in the basement; his increasing obsession with his inventions worried her.

By March, Walt often stayed away overnight, returning home smelling sour, his clothes crusted with salt, and at the beginning of April he left with no goodbyes, only a note saying he was joining the Merchant Marine. When the Sullivan family left soon after, disappearing in the night, they owed Dorrit babysitting money and the landlord months in back rent. Dorrit worried about the little boys, and baby Shevaun, as the world followed the terrible search for the toddler son of Charles and Anne Lindbergh, abducted from his crib in their home. She forgave the Sullivans the lost wages. It was the leaving without saying goodbye that left her sad.

Now the Sykes family was two. Along with smelly socks and passing pinches, the tension Walt created was gone, but its shadow remained like soot stains on the wall, spelling out in large letters the great question of faith. Had the Church failed them? Or, as Dorrit wondered in moments of weakness, had God failed them? Walt had given up, turned his back, and Dorrit did not know what to believe anymore.

Although she never spoke of it with her father, she suspected that he also doubted. She sat beside him in church, feeling dwarfed in the cavernous Sanctuary, with its three-story-high pipe organ and pews to seat 3,000 parishioners in tiers of balconies. She had to concede that no matter how much she prayed, she had not been able to change her thoughts. Cramps still came every month; her spells did not cease, nor the obsessive remembering or the panic-filled projections of what terrible things *might* happen. Though no one at church had said anything directly, she wondered—was it real, or her imagination—the judgment, the cold glances, the whispers of *hospital, ambulance?*

On Dorrit's seventeenth birthday in April, Mrs. Coughlin sent up a caramel cake from her bakery. Alone at the table, at six o'clock, Dorrit lit a single candle. "See, Ma," she whispered, "I get to make a wish." In the newspaper on the table, something caught her eye:

Boston Public Library—Part time, book maintenance and repair. Experience in bookbinding desired. Apply in person, at the per . . .

Dorrit blew out the candle. The newspaper page had a hole where her father had cut something out. She searched for a date, then folded it and put it in her pocket. As she washed the dishes, she pondered whether this was a sign, maybe a sign from her mother; this job, seeing it at this particular moment. She smiled to herself. Maybe she could start when school finished for the summer. She wondered if sewing skills and a love of books might be considered experience, and how many hours they might want. Maybe the job could be done in the evenings, from home.

Dorrit returned to the table with a composition book. It had been Walt's for school, but he had used only three pages. After tearing those out, she wrote in large letters in the center of the new page:

> *Dorrit Marie Sykes,*
> *23 Blossom Street, Boston, Massachusetts.*
> *PRIVATE, DO NOT READ.*
> *If found, please return.*

Nancy Drew, in her latest adventure, had found a mysterious secret diary, written in Swedish. Dorrit had written a letter to Carolyn Keene, in care of her publisher, agonizing over whether the author might be *Mrs.* or *Miss*, to ask how she went about her research. One character, Felix Raybolt, had made himself rich by swindling inventors out of their patents. Her father might want to know. She also asked Miss/Mrs. Keene how she found the time to write two books in one year.

Dorrit considered copying the idea of the secret diary by using a code, but with Walt gone, there was no one to find it, no one to tease her. She drew curlicues around the corners of the page then, smoothing the blank whiteness, began to write.

Friday, April 15, 1932
> *Today I am seventeen years of age, and will begin a new notebook.*

Goals for seventeenth year:
> *1. Save for an electric sewing machine (50¢/wk./50 weeks =$24.95)*
> *2. Make friends*

She paused, the pencil hovering over the paper. Item number two was, in fact, a sort of code. A long, unwritten list of goals preceded its being achieved. She had tried going to the movies once, when she was fifteen. After she balked at the show with a live wrestling bear, Walt had chosen "Little Caesar" and they had to sit in the middle of a row, joining 2,198 other patrons at the huge Majestic Theater. She had told Walt she needed to sit on the end. She hated the gangsters and their guns, and when she ran out in the middle of the film, feeling sick, the usher wouldn't let her back in without her ticket stub.

Dorrit pondered her two goals. Surely, she could think of something else. She wanted to write: *a real job, maybe at the library.* Every day, she saw lines of men outside employment agencies and church soup kitchens, holding empty buckets. But still, the advertisement for the library job was a hopeful sign.

The next morning, Dorrit packed her satchel as she did every Saturday. Her father sat at the table, wearing gray trousers with a pajama top. It was not unusual for him to forget to finish dressing. He would wander through the apartment, buttoning his shirt, then exclaim, "YES!" and hurry to the table to scribble something.

"How about fish chowder tonight?" Dorrit said, "Promise me you won't spend the day down in the cellar? Pop? Please remember to eat something." He nodded without looking up.

As she pulled on a sweater, she said, "Maybe I should stop at Ferguson's now, and get them to deliver? There's nothing here but those smashed chocolate bars."

"I'll manage. You go on." He scratched his head and looked up. "Did you eat?"

"I'm fine. You might want to put a shirt on." Her father's eyebrows rose, and he plucked at his pajama top with a sheepish expression.

Dorrit bought an egg roll from Mrs. Coughlin and ate it on the streetcar. She called on sewing clients and by the time she knocked at the door of Mrs. Frazier's townhouse, it was one thirty. Dorrit waited, steeling herself for *The Contempt of Connie,* idly thinking it might be a good title for a novel. She knocked again, but no one came. The shiny automobile was not at the curb and Dorrit began to think that she had wasted a nickel getting here. She went around to the alley behind the house then down the back stairs. At the kitchen door, she peered through the window. No sign of the maid or the cook. She knocked on the glass.

A rattle and clatter from above made Dorrit look up. A window sash rose, and Mrs. Frazier stuck her head out. Her hair was in pin curls wrapped in netting, and the head of her Pekinese appeared beside her. She called down, "Come on up, hon."

Cautiously, Dorrit pushed open the door and stepped into the kitchen. First, she noticed the odor—a mixture of old bacon grease, coffee grounds, and spoiled milk. She expected the cook or Connie to sweep in, commanding she wipe her feet, but the stove was cold, the sink filled with unwashed pots and dirty teacups. Stacked dishes lined the countertop. Dorrit wondered if someone had died.

Upstairs, she rapped lightly on the bedroom door. The dog barked as the door swung open. Mrs. Frazier took her cigarette holder from her mouth, blowing a long stream of smoke. "How do?" she said in a monotone. The room was, if possible, even more in disarray than it had been when Dorrit last visited two weeks ago. A half-full bottle of whiskey sat on the mantel with a tumbler.

"I've got your kitchen curtains finished, ma'am," Dorrit said. "Maybe Connie and I could hang them for you?"

"S'pose you're wondering where she is." Mrs. Frazier plopped down on the side of her unmade bed. She tossed a lacy pillow and caught it. "Connie's gone. Cook too. And Mitchell. No sense having a chauffeur if there's no car, is there?" She flapped her hand toward the door. "Mister Frazier says we just have to 'make do' till things start to look up."

Dorrit couldn't think of anything to say. Mrs. Frazier continued, "I can pay you, not to worry." She rummaged in a handbag and handed Dorrit two dollars, saying, "I had something else . . . what was it? Ah. My green dress. The beaded one." She sat up, scratching beneath her chin, surveying the room. "Where the hell . . . ? Look around, would you? The lining split. Not that I'll be going to any swanky parties any time soon." She snorted mirthlessly, patting her hairnet. Her voice changed from flat to shrill. "Can't even go to the hairdresser anymore, he tells me. We're ruined, he tells me. But does he come home from New York? Oh, no. He's still got his apartment and, I suspect, his little chippy to keep him company." Her voice dropped to a whisper. "I wonder if she'll stick around now. Now that he's lost everything." She leaned forward, elbows on her knees, pulling at her lower lip. "Life is not a romance novel, Dorrit."

Mrs. Frazier looked old; used up, though Dorrit knew that she was not yet forty. Her shoulders sagged, her breasts falling heavily in the cups of her satin slip. Without her usual girdle and heavily boned brassiere, she looked as if she might continue to collapse, ending up in a puddle on the carpet.

"Ma'am?" Dorrit reached among the underclothes and laddered stockings, and held up the dress, "I'm not sure this can be fixed. But I'll certainly try."

Mrs. Frazier continued to stare at the carpet. At the foot of the bed, the dog shredded a sock. "Keep it. I don't really care."

When the long ash fell from her cigarette holder, Dorrit brushed it away then said, softly, "Is there anything else this week, ma'am? Any books you want me to return?"

Mrs. Frazier bit her lip and shook her head. "This will be our last visit, I'm afraid."

Downstairs, Dorrit had a final look around, then let herself out of the kitchen door. She would miss riding in the big, warm, leather-smelling car. Mitchell had always been so pleasant, and he would sometimes drive her home. Twice he even stopped at the grocery on the way, so she did not have to carry the heavy bags on the streetcar. What had become of Mitchell? Of Connie? How many people were hiring chauffeurs and maids these days? What would become of Mrs. Frazier?

Continuing up Beacon Street, large budding trees cast lacy webs of shade. Spring had come to the city. Dorrit thought about sitting in the park, by the pond, but Saturdays were for the library, and she had never had an overdue book, not once. And there was that advertisement . . .

At the Boston Public Library, Dorrit paused in the vestibule to check that her sweater was buttoned straight. At the information desk, a young man looked up. "May I help you?"

Dorrit smiled, and said, "I wanted to ask about the advertisement? For a book repair person? Do you know what the hours are?"

"Sorry, I wouldn't know about the hours. Repairs are done in a different building." The young man inclined his head to the left. "But see that line over there? That's just to get the *application*. They've had more than a hundred, so far. The office ran out of printed forms." He shook his head. "Heard there was a professor from Harvard applying, even. Times like these, folks'll take anything that pays, I guess."

"Oh," Dorrit said, glancing up at the clock. "I suppose I could wait for a little while."

"Don't waste your time, miss. New library policy, I'm afraid: Hire the men, so's they can take care of their families. It's not official, mind you, and you didn't hear it from me," he pointed to himself and lowered his voice, "but that's how things are."

"I see. Thank you." And there, in the space of a few sentences, her aspirations deflated like a balloon. The loss of Mrs. Frazier began to sink in, and Dorrit backed away, clutching her bag to her chest like a shield. Climbing the stairs to Bates Hall, she regarded the majestic marble lions—both reclining males, huge paws overhanging their plinths, forever looking across the stairs at each other, as if the paltry humans passing below were unworthy of notice.

At the entrance of the reading room, Dorrit stood on tiptoe to see over the rows of tables. As usual on a Saturday afternoon, there were no vacant chairs. A man rose, closing a thick volume. As he gathered his belongings, Dorrit moved quickly to stand close by, politely waiting to claim his place. Sitting close to other patrons here had never been a problem for her; most everyone ignored each other. As she sat, the others at the table either gave her a cursory glance or none at all. Reaching to switch on the green-shaded lamp, she read the spine of the book the man had left: *The Modern Home Physician-Illustrated*-Wise & Co.

Eyeing her tablemates, Dorrit pulled the book closer. With a thrill of the illicit, she flipped to the index, the weight of seven hundred pages shifting heavily from her right hand to her left. Holding her breath, she scanned listings and found *cramps, p.187*. There were descriptions of leg cramps and stomach cramps, but not monthly cramps. Maybe they weren't real. Maybe her mother had been right. She looked up *monthly*, finding an entry for *monthly sickness, p.479,* which referred her to *menstruation, p.464.* She read: "*A period may be preceded and accompanied by a feeling of fullness in the lower part of the abdomen and by a feeling of lassitude. Sometimes there is definite pain, or dysmenorrhea.*"

Dysmenorrhea? Dorrit grimaced, thinking, *What a horrible-sounding word.* She flipped to a new page in her notebook and, checking again that no one was watching, wrote it down, flushing with vindication. *Dysmenorrhea. Definite pain.*

Further down the alphabetized page, below *Menstruation*, she stopped at *Mental Disease*, a subject allotted three pages of small print. She read *Causative Role of Heredity*, then copied out: *State of bodily health, poverty, bad sanitary conditions increase incidence.* The next paragraph made her stop and check around her again.

Sex is another important factor. To mate with a member of the opposite sex is the natural destiny of the sexually mature individual, and the frustration of this design may occasion mental disorder. The incidence of insanity is considerably greater among the unmarried . . . Insanity is also more common among those who have been widowed . . . at puberty the body comes under the strong influence of the secretions of the sex glands . . .

Here Dorrit paused, her face heating again. What was a *sex gland,* and when was a person *sexually mature? Mental Disease* continued, with dementia, paranoia, neurasthenia, and institutional treatment. She stopped again and wrote: *Anxiety neurosis, p.466. A constant state of nervous apprehension. Forms of psychoneurosis—hysteria, anxiety hysteria, see Neurosis, p.503.*

Flipping through quickly, holding her breath, she paused, distracted by lurid photographs of parasites and blistered rashes. She read on, no longer caring who was watching. Ten minutes later she had formed her diagnosis: *anxiety neurosis,* which, according to the editor—the aptly named Doctor Wise—required psychotherapy. *See Freudism; Obsession.*

When she had read these entries, she looked up, amazed to see that it was nearly four o'clock. She wrote, then underlined: *Entirely mental. If this is true, then perhaps anxiety neurosis can be cured by praying to change one's thoughts!* She frowned, tapping the end of her pencil. She *had* prayed, a lot. She flipped to the last page of her notebook. Over time, she had been compiling a list, in tiny block letters:

MIDDLE OF PEW
CROWDED BUS/STREETCAR
MOVIE THEATER
SCHOOL ASSEMBLY

The fidgets had a name, and she wrote it at the head of her list:

ANXIETY

According to Dr. Wise, Anxiety was real, and she wasn't the only person who had it. Those bits about sex were just confusing, but here, *here* was real information she could use. She gathered her call slip and went to the Abbey Room to turn it in, pondering, as she sat waiting for her books, where a person could discreetly ask about psychoanalysis, and how much it might cost.

She was about to sit down to wait when something occurred to her. She hurried back to the reading room, reclaiming her seat. She swallowed, and with determination, continued. Here was information. It was best to know.

Ectopic Gestation, p.244. "The ovum develops for a time but eventually, at some time between the sixth and twelfth weeks of pregnancy as a rule, there is abortion or a rupture of the tube. There is usually then such considerable bleeding as to constitute an immediate threat to the life of the woman . . . The only treatment is by operation, but if this is timely, the woman's life will almost certainly be saved; if rupture or bleeding has been allowed to occur, however, the prospects of success are very uncertain.

The book closed with a thud. Dorrit stared into space. *It happened exactly like that. "The woman's life will almost certainly be saved."* How could one book change so much? Dorrit believed what she had read. Her mother could have been saved with an operation. The baby, it seemed, would not.

What kind of church allowed God to take people away?

Dorrit rose slowly and returned to the Abbey Room. Her stack of books waited at the pickup window. Brightly printed covers, and page after page of fiction. All fiction.

Eleven
MAY

The morning of May 13 was clear and warm. Spring, in its full regalia, had settled in Virginia. In clashing shades of pink and red, dogwood and redbud trees bloomed in exuberant profusion with bright azaleas below. The orchards of Keswick Farm were a riot of white and pink, the fruit blossoms laden with bees.

Henry Marshall sat in the passenger seat of the farm truck, dressed in a somber black suit more appropriate for a funeral than for a celebration of spring. May slid in next to him and donned her sunglasses. Her uncle took the driver's seat. Henry pulled his hat down and brushed the shiny, worn lapels of his jacket, muttering, ". . . get there early . . . right up front. Look that goddamned Cecil Boxley right in the eye."

Cy nodded, starting the ignition. "Me too, Henry. Me too."

The greening mountains in the distance and the fragrance of blooming viburnum went unnoticed by May, sandwiched as she was between the two men. Her intention for this day was to observe and report, filtering events and delivering news to Byrd as gently as possible. These months of grief, of loss, of change and separation had unsettled their foundation as a couple, and as a family. Now he was only home two days a week. As much as May loved her children, she felt the strain of those other five days, when she had to be the sole parent—judge, guard, nurse, comforter.

She took, with gratitude, what help she could from Delphina, and from her father. Yes, Byrd was making sacrifices for them—living in a rented room, spending hours on the train each week, with one phone call on Wednesdays. At home she sensed his discomfort, feeling like an interloper in his father-in-law's house, not quite knowing where to settle himself. Like Byrd, May knew they were the lucky ones, to *have* a house, even if it lacked privacy.

The ache she felt when Chestnut Grove was packed up was visceral. Each painting and chair was connected to her husband. The Craig family heirlooms were stored carefully in the empty cow barn at Keswick Farm; the mahogany sideboard now covered in a horse blanket, the gilt-framed landscapes stacked in the rafters. The Keswick farmhouse had simpler, wide pine-board mantels and tongue-and-groove wainscoting; the furniture waxed but well worn, with only a few ornate pieces May's mother had brought from New Orleans. In the parlor, they made room for Byrd's father's desk and a portrait of his grandfather. His shaving mirror was carried upstairs.

The glory of the morning seemed, to May, a stage setting. The setup for a fairy tale that would end, in an unseen twist of fate, a tragedy. This would be goodbye to Chestnut Grove. Byrd had not come home for the auction, maintaining that he didn't wish to talk about it. May had been surprised by his stoic resolve.

The evening before, she had sat up late, watching Hank sleep while she rocked Sister, reluctant to lay her in the crib. At eleven months, she was healthy and good-natured and trying to walk. Afternoon reports on the radio had announced the terrible discovery of the remains of Charles and Anne Lindbergh's twenty-month-old son, only a few miles from their home. The kidnapping was so senseless; the death so cruel. May stroked her daughter's silken hair, her heart breaking for the Lindberghs. They would have done anything, paid with all that they had to have their baby back.

Byrd, May knew, would have sacrificed Chestnut Grove willingly if it meant his father would still be alive. They could have worked together to salvage the business or started over with something new, learning to do with less. But the shame had been too powerful for James Craig. And now he was in his grave; his farm, empty. Today, it would go to the highest bidder.

Miss Spindle had told May a rumor, that there were two real estate developers coming to the auction—one from Richmond, one from Washington. She asked her father about it, but he had been reserved, saying only, "We'll see what happens, little gal. We'll have to wait and see." She had not returned to the house or their cottage since they had been emptied. Sybil had settled in Kentucky, and that seemed to suit everyone. Occasionally, Byrd rode across the fields from Keswick Farm to Chestnut Grove, leading Hank on his pony. Hank came home telling her that *his daddy said* they would move back one day. May could not bring herself to correct him, or to challenge Byrd.

At the turn-in to the Chestnut Grove drive, a sign stood close to the road. Ten feet tall and bordered in red, it proclaimed in large black letters: FARM AUCTION! with a plot map below. Every time she passed it, May gritted her teeth. Someone had cleared the fallen chestnut trunk that blocked the mile-long driveway. She said, "Think there'll be a big crowd, Daddy?"

"No telling. No telling." Henry rested his chin on his fist, rubbing his thumb over his jaw absently. Cy held the steering wheel with both hands, blinking, his focus straight ahead. Passing the ghostly chestnuts, no automobiles or trucks were visible until they neared the house, where three black cars were parked in the pasture. On newly mown grass, farm machinery was displayed, with saddles and bridles draped along the fence. With a pang, May recognized Byrd's hunting saddle. On the wide front porch of the house, two men were setting up a platform with a podium while, beneath a big oak in the side yard, picnic tables and benches were lined up. It was nine fifteen.

Cy drove off to park, leaving May and Henry in front of the house. He leaned on his cane as they made their way up the brick walkway. Behind her shield of dark glasses, May's gaze flitted from point to point. On the first floor, one shutter hung crookedly. James Craig would have had that fixed. The spring weeds between the bricks of the walkway would have been pulled, and the boxwood border would have been trimmed into perfect globes. At one end of the porch, Cecil Boxley stood with two men in gray suits, deep in conversation.

"Riiight over there," Henry said, speaking quietly. "We're going to stand right in the bastard's line of sight."

May said, "Let me find you a chair."

"No way in hell. I don't care if I have to spend the next month flat on my back. You might want to wait in the truck, little gal. Doubt there'll be any other ladies here."

"No way in hell," May said. "I want to see it myself." They grinned at each other.

A recent model, deep-red convertible pulled up and a man in a gray seersucker suit with a straw boater got out and ambled up the walk, hands in his pockets. He held up a hand in greeting to the men on the porch. Boxley's clerk tipped his hat to May, before handing Henry a mimeographed list of items. He did not offer one to her. The man in the boater stood across the lawn, close to the auctioneer, but away from Henry and May. Henry asked the clerk, "That fella. Heard he's in real estate?"

The clerk nodded toward the man in the boater. "Yup. Least somebody's making some money on these old places."

By nine forty-five, only one other truck had arrived. Painted on the side of the door in clumsy, hand-executed lettering, was, *Oak Lane Farm, Hereford Cattle, Lexington, Va.* Lexington was over three hours away. A man got out, spit a stream of tobacco juice, then started down the line of equipment. Hitching the knees of his overalls, he squatted, inspecting tractor tires, then came to stand on the lawn, tipping his hat to May before he paged through a copy of the list, making notations with a pencil.

At ten o'clock on the dot, the auctioneer stepped up to the platform and introduced himself. As he recited the terms of sale, Boxley stood with his clerk. Both had their arms crossed, both looked annoyed. May leaned over to whisper in Henry's ear, "There's hardly anyone here. The man in the suit must be a developer. What's going on?"

Henry looked toward the drive, smiling slowly, his eyes crinkling at the corners. Rust-colored dust plumes rose between the chestnut trees, moving toward the house from the road as a line of trucks and cars streamed toward them. The auctioneer stopped speaking and looked to Cecil Boxley as the automobiles pulled in and parked. A horse and wagon pulled up the rear. May recognized neighbors and market customers; farmers and landowners from Charlottesville and Albemarle County. Without a word of greeting to each other, thirty or forty unsmiling men assembled into lines. Each of the new arrivals held a pitchfork or a rake, prongs up. Facing the auctioneer, they flanked the man in the boater, the nearest not quite touching him. The scents of cut hay and fresh sweat rose from the crowd—an honest, clean, country smell.

May stayed in front beside Henry, afraid to speak and afraid to leave. Goosebumps ran down her arms and her mouth went dry. She watched her father. Around her, men shifted from foot to foot. The auctioneer mopped his forehead and tugged an earlobe. With a sidelong glance at Cecil Boxley, he began with item number one. He described the age and condition of a John Deere hay rake, then said, "Thirty dollars, folks. A fair price. Who'll bid thirty?" No one raised a hand or called back. The auctioneer shuffled his papers, saying, "Twenty, then. I can see this crowd is looking for bargains. Okeydokey, here's a good one, gents. Twenty dollars for the hay rake."

Silence. He went down to ten.

Vernon Twyman, who lived five miles up the road at Cobham, called out, "Two cents." His voice sounded more declarative than hopeful.

"Gen-tle-men," the auctioneer said, bouncing his palms downward, "we all know the value of a good hay rake, don't we? And this one barely three years old. Now, let's hear a fair offer."

The only farmer without a pitchfork, who had been the first to arrive, called, "I'll bid two dollars!" The crowd surged around him, silently.

The big man beside him leaned close, and said, loudly enough for everyone to hear, "Bid's right high, don't you think, friend?"

There were no further bids. The auctioneer banged his gavel. "Sold!"

The farmer from Lexington did not place another bid. The men with pitchforks stood shoulder to shoulder, bidding in turn. No one placed a second bid and the man in the boater bid on nothing as item by item went for five cents, eight cents, ten cents. The custom-made horse buggy with red ostrich-skin seats went for twenty cents, to a man from Charlottesville who owned no horses and lived in town. May watched it all, her fear of disaster and violence giving way to a rising hopefulness.

At eleven thirty the auctioneer wiped his forehead wearily and looked over his shoulder at Cecil Boxley, whose face was red and shiny. When a dark green truck pulled up to park behind the picnic tables, everyone waited in expectant silence. The doors opened, and two women in aprons emerged, chattering, pulling out baskets with cloth covers. They began to arrange food on the tables.

The auctioneer clasped the lapels of his suit, rocking back on his heels. He called out, "Now, friends, we come to the final item on your list. Five hundred twenty-nine acres of the love-li-est farmland in the state of Virginia." He held out both arms, all-encompassing, saying, "This gracious home, of gen-u-ine Virginia-made brick, built in 1820." His index finger poked the air. "Never need to paint it, no siree. And let me assure you, it has modern plumbing and central heat." He removed his hat and swung it in an arc. "Up there's as fine a horse barn as I've ever seen. Three tenant houses and an equipment shed with a new tin roof. Who'll start us off at twenty thousand dollars?"

Vernon Twyman leaned over, whispering something to the man in the boater, who frowned and fidgeted. The women setting out food stopped to watch. Cecil Boxley leaned forward. Seconds ticked by. In the crushing silence, a crow flew overhead, cawing.

From the back of the crowd, came the call, "Two. Dollars."

May gripped her father's arm, afraid to turn around. *Byrd is here? Byrd is here.* Like a platoon of soldiers, the assembled neighbors continued to face forward.

The farmer from Lexington piped up, "I'll give ten!" then, "Hey!" as the crowd silently compacted around him. May waited, afraid to breathe. Her fingers began to tingle.

"Eleven," Byrd said, making his way forward through the crowd.

The auctioneer again looked to Cecil Boxley, then raised his palms and shrugged.

"No further offers?" He leaned over his podium, scanning the crowd. "Going once. Going twice. Sold, to the man in the Panama hat, for eleven dollars." The gavel rang in the silence. May stood frozen, as the men with pitchforks moved around her to line up in front of the folding table that served as a makeshift desk, pulling out worn billfolds and pocket change.

Stunned, May watched it all. For weeks, she had mentally bolstered herself—to be strong, for Byrd, to appear dignified. She'd been thinking of how she might describe the day to him. But he was *here*. Her thoughts were in tumult, and as she tried to sort them, something unanticipated dawned. Around the edges of her consciousness, a pale triumph, a pride in the loyalty of her community welled up. James Craig would have approved. Byrd was surrounded by neighbors, slapping his back while shoving "paid" receipts into his hand, returning almost every piece of equipment to him.

May's expression stiffened with another sudden realization: *This whole thing was planned. And no one bothered to tell me about it.* She tried to tell herself that her irritation at being left out was childish. But why had Byrd not told her? Did he not trust her? May crossed her arms and looked at her father. Why had *he* not said anything? She knew her question to be rhetorical, but she asked it anyway. "You knew about this, didn't you?" Henry rubbed his fingers over his mouth to hide a smile as they watched Cecil Boxley push through and stride to his car, only to discover that his tires were flat. He yelled at his clerk, who ran to fetch his own car. In the time it took for the clerk to drive out of sight with the apoplectic Boxley, May realized that she was more than irritated. How would they possibly pay the taxes? How could they keep this place up?

And now, Byrd was apparently avoiding her. Henry said, "Fried chicken smells good. Let's get some." May walked beside him to a spot beneath the oak tree. Her father sank to sit on a wrought iron garden bench. With Boxley gone the gathering took on the tenor of a picnic.

Byrd broke away from the crowd and started toward her. She busied herself with getting her father a plate of food, using him as cover, racking her brain for a clever, biting remark. But those sorts of retorts always came to her after the fact. Invariably, she found that sudden anger or confrontation left her speechless. It was so frustrating, to not be able to defend herself with arrows tipped in sarcasm. Approaching her, Byrd's expression radiated triumph, with a very slight tinge of sheepishness. May stood beside her father, keeping the plate in front of her, shooting her husband a look of unambiguous anger. Byrd grasped Henry's outstretched hand, covering it with both of his. He looked from Henry to her. A tentative smile twitched at his mouth.

May raised her chin, saying, evenly, "Why didn't you tell me?"

"I'm sorry." Like a naughty, recalcitrant schoolboy who was not actually sorry in the least, Byrd dropped his head again in momentary capitulation. "We weren't sure it would work. If Boxley had gotten wind of it, he'd have put a reserve on the property, so that it wouldn't sell for under a specific price. We planned it all at the Hog & Hominy meeting. They've been doing this out in the Midwest. Bunch of farmers almost strung up a judge out there for foreclosing on farms."

May nodded and said, "Cecil Boxley looked furious." What she did not say was, *I am furious that you didn't tell me this was going to happen.*

Henry flipped his hand dismissively and chuckled. "Yeah, well. After we left home, I had Dennis drop off a letter at the bank. As of this morning, my account is closed, except for the mortgage. As long as I make the payments on time, Boxley can't do a thing to us. And y'all have your accounts at Virginia National anyway."

Vernon Twyman strolled over and raised his straw hat toward May. From the bib pocket of his faded overalls, he pulled a flat flask. "Sweeten your lemonade, May?"

She shook her head and he poured some into Henry's cup. Their voices faded as she shifted her focus inward, frowning as more and more questions popped up. She flushed with humiliation, as if she'd been left out of a joke.

Henry held his cup in salute, saying, "Thanks, neighbor." Vernon nodded slowly. His gaze met May's, and her anger shifted without diminishing.

Byrd looked down. "Thank you, Vern," he said, quietly.

"Yes." May echoed, "Thank you." Her emotions were having a tug of war, anger versus gratitude, with a puddle of mud in the middle. Either way, things were going to get dirty.

"Aw, shoot," Vern said. "Wouldn't be good for anybody, to lose this place. Y'all would've done the same for me." He arced an arm, encompassing the crowd. "We all feel that way." May handed the plate to her father, then shook Vern's hand with both of hers. Turning away from Byrd, she went from man to man until she had looked each one in the eye and thanked him. By the time she finished circulating among the bidders, Cy had brought the truck up to the oak tree.

Henry looked tired. "Cy's going to take me home," he said. "You coming with me or with Byrd, May?"

"I'll stay, Daddy. I'll see you at home. Don't tell Hank, all right?" She couldn't keep sarcasm from her voice when she said, "I'm sure Byrd wants to surprise him."

Byrd came to stand beside May and put his arm around her. She did not lean into him. He led her to the front door of the house and pulled a familiar heavy brass key from his pocket. The door screeched on dry hinges, the sound echoing up into the tall ceilings of the wide entry hall. The grandfather clock and oriental rugs and portraits were gone, but the mural landscape wallpaper was still there. Light filtered through the leaded sidelights of the back-hall door, reflecting off the brass chandelier and wide floorboards. The house was warm, the air close. Crossing the bare dining room, their steps echoed, overly loud. Neither remarked on the recently dead starling that lay in the fireplace, among black cinders. They continued, unspeaking, through the downstairs, finishing, finally, on the upstairs portico. At midday, the mountains were vividly shaded emerald against the yellow-green of pastures.

Byrd said, "I needed to do this for Hank. Forgive me?"

"You deceived me." When he tried to take both of May's hands in his, she crossed her arms over her chest.

He rubbed her shoulders instead, saying, "You can't imagine how much I wanted to tell you."

May took a small step back, shifting out of his reach. She met his eyes. "This is a decision we should have made *together*. We'll have to keep this place up. Did you think about how we're going to manage that, with you away all week? I can't take on any more than I have now, Byrd. I mean, it's all very heroic, getting it back this way, but you're not being at all realistic. You haven't thought this through." Her voice dropped and she looked away, toward the mountains. "What if both farms fail? Did you think about that?"

Byrd leaned back against the railing, speaking to May's profile. "Calm down. Calm down for a minute and listen, all right? Actually, there's a second part to this plan."

"Oh, really?" May sputtered, "And when am I supposed to find out about *that*?"

He held out his hands, tamping his palms. "Just listen, please?" He held up an index finger. "To be fair, I have to credit to your uncle for this part."

"I hope it involves him finding another place to live."

Byrd stabbed the air. "Well, exactly!" He said, "It does ex*actly* that. See, Cy had the idea of turning Keswick Farm into a rooming house. He could run it, and we could all move over here—put your dad on the first floor, and there's room for Delphina and Dennis."

May looked at him and held up one hand: *Stop talking, right this minute, or I will slap you.* "Did you ask my father about this?"

"When Cy brought it up, we agreed to take one thing at a time—at least, that's what he suggested. But think about it for a minute."

May set her jaw, flushed with indignation. "I don't *need* to think about it. I absolutely will not ask my father to leave his home. I cannot be*lieve* you would even consider it."

"May, honey, we have to think about the future. Things are going to turn around. It might take a couple of years, but they will."

"My father might not have a couple of years. The answer is no."

"Why can't you be happy about this? What if some developer had bought it? How would your father feel about looking out the window and seeing fifty flimsy little houses next door?" Byrd sighed and pushed his hair back off his forehead. He put his hand over hers. "Look," he said, "I'm sorry you're upset. What can I do to make things right?"

"You should have asked me first."

Part II
MENDING

"A man who leaves home to mend himself and others is a philosopher; but he who goes from country to country, guided by the blind impulse of curiosity, is a vagabond."

Oliver Goldsmith,
The Citizen of the World,
1760–1761, Letter VII

Twelve
DORRIT

Following the revelations of Dr. Wise's handbook, Dorrit determined that she would cure herself of anxiety. Using the list she had made in her notebook—things that for her, brought on panic—yet most people considered normal—she began by raising her hand in school, briefly making herself the center of attention as she answered the teacher's question. Her palms sweated in anticipation, but she managed it, then savored the brief glow of knowing she had answered correctly. Next, she imagined herself sitting calmly in the middle of a full pew at church, not feeling trapped. Then, she did it. During the service, she concentrated on the prayers and readings, forcing herself to stay in the present. Afterward, she was exhausted.

Dorrit wondered what her mother might have said about her efforts. She pondered what she might have asked, if she might have been bolder or more challenging, had she known that their time together would run out. The hours alone in the apartment echoed with Augusta's memory. Dorrit's solitary prayers felt wrong to her, and she wondered if she was being selfish, praying for calm, praying to feel lighthearted and happy; to enjoy normal things, instead of praying for the starving or destitute?

Like Dorrit, Roy seemed to find the apartment oppressive with memory, and after Walt left, he began taking jobs that kept him out of town for days, returning unshaven and unbathed. Instead of attending church, he spent Wednesday evenings at the VFW hall with other veterans, playing cards and listening to the radio. He came home telling her about the upcoming summer Olympic Games, to be held in Los Angeles. He began to follow the Red Sox season. He followed the tragic search for the Lindbergh baby, and in the third week of May, he followed Amelia Earhart's daring transoceanic flight. At the same time, he began to follow the story of a group of eight veterans who had left Oregon on May 8, intent upon marching to Washington to demand early payment of their war bonuses from President Hoover. They vowed they would not wait until 1945, when payment was promised. They were in dire straits, and it was *their* money, after all. Mr. Hoover needed to hand it over now, while it was urgently needed. Christening themselves the 'Bonus Expeditionary Force,' the men were making their way across the country by rail, automobile, and on foot, gaining both followers and momentum along the way.

Roy returned from the VFW hall one night in late May, more excited than Dorrit had seen him in a long while. He announced that he planned to join the march to Washington and camp out on President Hoover's lawn at the White House with the other veterans. He said that if enough showed up, the legislators would have to give in. He read from a clipping: "*A dollar for every day served, and a dollar-twenty-five for every day served abroad.*"

To Dorrit, it sounded too good to be true, and yet there it was, in the newspaper. She said, "How long will you be gone, Pop?"

"I figure, one day down, one day back . . . ten days? You'll be all right, won't you? You do fine when I'm working out of town. And think about it. I could come back with a thousand dollars . . ."

Dorrit imagined the photographs she had seen of the White House and Capitol turning from black and white to vivid color—verdant green grass and blue sky. She said, "I want to go with you."

She would. She would see the capital and the monuments she had learned about. School was out for summer, and when would she have another chance? Her father assured her that there were toilets on the train, that they would be sitting together in a row of only two seats. There would be windows that could be opened, and a person could stand by the door if they needed air. What Dorrit did not ask, but dearly wanted to know was this: *But what about people who need to run away? People who get the fidgets?*

Anxiety. She corrected herself. *It has a name.*

Six days later, Dorrit settled a wicker basket on her hip and made her way up the stairs to the roof of 23 Blossom Street. Pushing open the door, she inhaled the tang of warm tar, blistering in the heat of early June. Late afternoon sun threw chimneys and surrounding roofs into shadow, and she left the basket beneath the clothesline. Close by, in the wire pigeon hutch that belonged to a man on the fifth floor, shuffling and scratching noises accompanied the simmering murmur of ten birds. She stuck her fingers through the wire, cooing as she dropped breadcrumbs. The birds bobbed, watching her with bright orange-and-black eyes. "I'm going away for ten days," she told them. "Pop says we'll come back with some money. So just maybe, we'll move to a real house. Maybe even with a garden. I bet you all would like to have a garden to live in, wouldn't you? I sure would." Dorrit rolled up the paper bag slowly then waggled her fingers through the cage wires. "Bye now, Snow White, and Gray Lady, and Princess. Don't forget me, you hear? I'll be back before you know it."

This was her safe space—these stairs, this roof, this building. This was home. Within this big city that she had been so afraid to explore, she had her own small world—home, church, the library. And yet, even in those places she knew so well, she had fears. If she left, there would be far more unknowns, more chances for panic. Her fears might travel with her.

Dorrit pulled laundry from the line and as she stacked it in her basket, she mused over what her father described as a great adventure—a patriotic lark. Maybe, like Nancy Drew, she would uncover a mystery or encounter a fascinating stranger with a story to tell. She hitched the basket to her hip and, at the door, looked back at the birds again. They were safe, and they were caged. She would make a change. Or else she would spend the rest of her life in a world that seemed to grow smaller and sadder every day.

Back in the apartment, she set up the ironing board beside the open window. The scent of starched, laundered cotton mixed with the pleasant, green pungency of geraniums. Bent over a stack of papers, her father shifted a ruler, making small marks on a page.

"What are you working on?" she asked.

"Hinge, for the bottom tray of the trap. Works on a special spring." Without looking up he said, "Go down and ask Bridie if she'll collect our mail while we're gone."

"You go, Pop," Dorrit said, sprinkling a shirt with water. "I've got to finish the ironing."

"But she likes you."

Dorrit set the iron upright, looking at her father. "We'll be back in ten days?"

Roy began to sort his files and plans. His voice was light. "Soon as Congress votes, and they give me my check."

Downstairs, Mrs. Coughlin bustled about her bakery, her hair and eyelashes dusted with flour. The yeasty scent of warm bread still wafted from the big ovens. "Well, pet," she said, in her brogue, "your pa tells me you'll be leaving in the morning. Let me give you a loaf for your supper." She expertly rolled a seven-cent loaf in brown paper, tying it with twine. "Have a hermit." She handed Dorrit a molasses cookie and wiped her hands on her apron.

"Thank you, Mrs. Coughlin," Dorrit said. "Pop was wondering if you might not mind collecting our mail. I'd hate to miss a letter from Walt, and Pop's waiting to hear about his mousetrap. He was hoping he might telephone you, to see if the letter's come? He says we'll be back in ten days, only he says that if the trap design sells, we might go on to Ohio, to the actual factory. Have you ever been to Ohio?"

Mrs. Coughlin shook her head. "I haven't. But of course, pet, of course you can ring me anytime. I'd be happy to hear that you're all right. And I hope you have a safe journey and your pa gets his bonus from Mister Hoover."

"Pop says he'll buy a truck and start a delivery business. He says fish, but maybe he could deliver bread for you too."

Mrs. Coughlin's wide face split into a grin. "Mother a God! That's a nice thought, only I don't think folks'll be wanting a raisin loaf that's been sitting with a string of cod, do you? It's hard enough to sell them anyway. Who'll I save the crumbs for, now? Those pigeons have got spoilt. Now, then, you be sure to stop in to say goodbye in the morning."

Back in the apartment, Dorrit rolled quilts and blankets into bedrolls as her father instructed, then wrapped them in the oilcloth from the kitchen table. Into her sewing satchel, she packed a small cooking pan with two forks and two knives. Her father insisted on taking his toolbox because, he said, he could make money fixing cars along the way. In the small cardboard suitcase that had been Augusta's, Dorrit packed her best dress, her nightgown, her shears, and a sewing kit. On a whim, she packed Mrs. Frazier's beaded dress, then her Nancy Drew library book. She was re-reading *The Secret at Shadow Ranch*. She had first read it shortly after her mother's death and realized she didn't remember it very well. Nancy Drew took trains all the time. When she traveled to Cliffwood mansion in River Heights to investigate thefts in *The Hidden Staircase*, Nancy's father loaned her a revolver to protect herself. Dorrit knew, from *The Mystery at Lilac Inn*, to keep her possessions close while traveling, lest they be stolen like that foolish Mrs. Jane Willoughby's jewels, from her handbag.

Roy held up two yellowed pages, a triumphant look on his face. "Found my discharge papers and my bonus certificate! The Watertown boys said we need to bring them along." He began to stack his files in a fruit crate. "Going to lock these up in the boiler room. Can't be too careful. Somebody might break in if they know we're gone and try to steal my plans." Dorrit thought it unlikely but she did not say so. Of course, there had been that case in *The Clue in the Diary*, where the patents were stolen.

This bonus money, she thought, would be her father's holy grail—the answer to all problems, a promise of a better life. As she packed, she imagined her father shaking hands with President Hoover as he accepted a thousand-dollar bill. Or maybe it would be ten hundred-dollar bills instead. Dorrit wondered if the thousand-dollar bill was actually larger in size than the hundred. She had never seen either one.

Dorrit warmed a can of beans and toasted soda bread. When the pot was bubbling, she broke three eggs into the beans, leaving them to poach. Roy returned from the cellar in high spirits. "When we're on the road, I'll show you how we cooked in the army. Sometimes they couldn't stop to set up the mess wagon, so we'd cook over an open fire. Wait till you see what an outdoorsman your old pop is." He went to the closet and pulled out his olive-green army uniform and brushed off the shoulders. "Fourteen years old, but I reckon I can still fit into it. The fellows are saying that they're going to wear their uniforms. Suppose I ought to go along. Press the trousers for me, would you, Baby Doll?" Roy tugged at his hair, then went through the apartment opening drawers and cabinets, muttering to himself. They ate in silence, with Roy occasionally jotting something on a paper beside his plate. When he went back to the basement, Dorrit pulled her notebook from the bottom of her work basket. She turned to a fresh page and wrote in large block letters:

THE TRAVELS AND ADVENTURES
of
MISS DORRIT MARIE SYKES, age 17
Featuring her account of the
BONUS EXPEDITIONARY FORCES MARCH, June 1932

June 6, 1932
Spent day packing for departure on the morrow. We shall meet up with a group of veterans marching from Watertown at 0900, sharp. Pop says there are 8,000 men in Washington DC already. Yesterday we visited Ma's grave. We have not been to church for weeks, but I

have been reading 'Science and Health' sometimes, at night. In the
back is a church directory list. There is a Christian Science Church in
Washington, at 1770 Euclid Street, N.W.

She put down her pencil. It all sounded rather too formal, she thought, and it lacked import. A travel diary should be colorful. She resolved to try to write in the style of Miss Keene and maybe even send her account off to a magazine or something when they returned to Boston. Later, she lay in bed, wondering if they would be sleeping under the stars soon, and if there would be other young people on the March, and if she might make any friends. She slept fitfully, dreaming of a line of handsome young soldiers with faces like Sir Galahad, in neatly pressed uniforms, tipping their hats as she passed. She dreamed of President Hoover, holding out a basket of money and thanking her father for serving his country.

Dorrit woke to find her father shaving, whistling "The Battle Hymn of the Republic" as he tapped his razor on the enamel washbasin. As she put on a pot of oats, lists ran through her head like chants: things to pack; notes—one to stick to their mailbox, telling the mailman to take their mail to the bakery, and one to leave on the door, in case Walt came home.

While Dorrit sliced bread, Roy came out of the bedroom, buttoning up his uniform jacket. Aside from a few moth holes, it looked neat and fit him well. He said, "We'll meet the Watertown VFW fellows on the Common. We'll all start marching from there. You all packed?" her father asked.

"Pop, you got train tickets, didn't you?"

Her father brushed off a sleeve. "Well . . . we got to talking last week, and there's boys from Watertown going together. We can save the price of the tickets!"

Dorrit's hands turned cold.

On the Boston Common, they waited on a bench beside the statue of George Washington. Roy checked his watch and wiped perspiration from his brow. At ten thirty he made a round to the other statues. Dorrit pulled out her notebook and pencil.

June 7, 1932

Pop and I left at 0800. Mrs. Coughlin gave us a paper sack of raisin buns, which she knows are my particular favorite. She hugged me and cried, then I got flour all over my dress, and that made her laugh then cry some more and she shook Pop's hand and wished us well. The morning is hot already and poor Pop looks very warm in his wool uniform. I am glad I have my wide-brimmed hat and a book to read. Pop has his toolbox and our valise, with a bedroll on his back and I am carrying my sewing satchel. We look like a couple of gypsies. Right now, I am not anxious. I am just sitting in the park. We are going to have an adventure.

12:00—So far, nothing exciting has happened. I have eaten two raisin buns. Now it is noontime and we have been waiting to meet up with the eight men from Watertown. I am thirsty and Pop is fussing because the man at the newsagent shop told him that the Watertown group left yesterday! Pop is quite beside himself and tugging at his hair because he got the date wrong. Now he says we will go on the train to catch up with them. I am so relieved!

At two o'clock, Dorrit and Roy disembarked from the streetcar at South Street Station. Soldiers and railroad guards with rifles patrolled the tracks. A conductor told Roy they were there to keep the Bonus Expeditionary marchers from riding the rails to Washington without proper tickets. All along the East Coast corridor, trains were being patrolled to keep more marchers from coming. Roy checked each of the tracks and the waiting areas, but there appeared to be no other veterans heading south.

Dorrit was hot and thirsty, and the ladies' room at the station was dirty. She said, "Can't we just buy a ticket? We'll find the Watertowners when we get there."

In the petulant voice of a child not invited to a party, Roy said, "But I wanted to go with our own boys, Baby Doll." Dorrit felt sorry for him in his dejection. He was determined, she knew, as determined to have an adventure along the way as he was to reach Washington. A train ride would be too easy. "So," he said, "we'll walk to Washington if we have to." Dorrit sat on a bench. He squatted beside her and swung his pack off his back. She crossed her arms, shaking her head. Roy blew out his breath and said, in a matter-of-fact voice, "Now then, here's how we'll do this. You'll stand at the side of the road, and I'll stand behind you."

"You *said* we would take the train. I want to go home. You can go without me."

"Listen, we have to adapt to our circumstances, like a good soldier on the battlefield, understand? And you can be real helpful here. All you need to do is to look all sad and pitiful—like you're hungry. We should catch a ride south in no time."

"I want to go home," Dorrit said. That tickle, at the back of her neck. She tamped down the urge to run.

Roy pulled a scrolled paper from his toolbox. Unrolling it, he pointed to each of the words as he read:

Veteran needs BONUS to feed his little girl.
Mr. Hoover, here we come!

Dorrit flushed. Heat replaced the cold fingers around her throat. "Criminy, Pop. I'm not a little girl!" She looked around to see if anyone was watching.

His ears went back. "We're using our resources, like I told you, to help us get where we need to go. Think about it. A *thousand* dollars. We got to get there before the vote. This is the way you can help." He put a hand on her shoulder. "You want to help, don't you? I can't leave you here on your own." Dorrit didn't know what to think. Her father seemed so determined. She was afraid to say no.

"Listen," Roy licked his lips. "When I left you and Walt and your ma and went to fight for our country, I didn't know what would happen. All of us vets served our country. We're *owed* that bonus. Nobody knew how bad things would get these past few years. Nobody could've predicted that all these men, vets included, wouldn't be able to find an honest day's work. Times have changed, and the President needs to work with us, not against us."

So they stood together on the southbound side of the road. The asphalt shimmered in the heat and each time a car passed, a cloud of dust blew up from the roadside. Nancy Drew would have her own car, of course. And a suitcase full of stylish traveling suits. She wouldn't be standing here trying to keep the dust off of her dress. After a while Dorrit gave up. She gave up on trying to keep her dress clean and she gave up on going home. Then she thought of every sad thing she could. She arranged her face in a way that she hoped showed all of the sadness she could conjure. After a few minutes, she worked herself into a genuine funk. She wanted to sit on the ground there by the road and howl.

It was after four o'clock when a car pulled over. It was a rusty black jalopy with white words painted across the back: "Washington or Bust!" and, "Bonuses for Veterans NOW!" On top, a water-stained mattress balanced, tied with a frayed rope. Wire had been run around the sides, with a zinc basin and frying pans and a lantern attached. These banged against the sides, leaving scratches and dents. Inside the car were two men, wearing parts of army uniforms. They hopped out and the driver offered a small salute and said, "Howdy folks! I'm Charlie. This is Bert."

The man called Bert had small round eyeglasses and wore a black derby hat and an army jacket that was too tight. He shook Roy's hand formally. "Delighted to make your acquaintance." He bowed slightly to Dorrit and tipped his derby.

Roy gave Dorrit a wink as he pumped Bert's hand, saying, "You got room for us? We'd sure appreciate a ride."

Charlie nodded. "Bert here doesn't drive, don't you know, so if you can take a turn at the wheel, we'd be happy to have you along. I been driving since New Hampshire." Charlie wore overalls under his uniform jacket and had brush-cut blond hair and freckles.

Inside the car, Dorrit was wedged against the back door with their belongings stacked on the seat between her father and herself. She breathed shallowly. Even with the windows down, the men smelled of camphor and old sweat. They talked about where they had served and the progress of the March. Her father spoke animatedly, telling the others that he could fix the ticking in the engine. He talked about the Watertowners and as they drove past the men hitchhiking south in twos and threes, Roy searched faces, calling out to ask if anyone had seen John Fahey and his men, but Dorrit figured they were well ahead. She had grown used to the smells and felt grateful to have a ride, even if it was closed in and hot. The car bounced along, pots clanging dully against the sides. Her eyes began to close.

When she woke it was almost dark and the car was bumping over a dirt road, clanging, as if to herald their arrival. At the edge of a wood a grouping of rough tents surrounded a circle of stones, where a large pot hung over a fire. Dorrit was thirsty; her back stuck to the car seat with sweat. Bert and Charlie waved as they neared, and Charlie pulled to a stop beneath a large willow and cut the engine. The car spit and convulsed, as if in capitulation, before shuddering to a halt.

After everyone exchanged friendly greetings, Roy began to make a tent, stringing a rope between the willow and a nearby sapling. After he pulled taut a complicated-looking knot, he grinned with obvious pride, looking back over his shoulder at Dorrit, where she sat on the running board of Charlie's car, watching, fanning her face with her hat and swatting the occasional mosquito. She had never imagined that her father knew how to do such a thing. Charlie and Bert set up their own tent, then hauled the mattress inside. Everyone took places around the fire, some bringing wood they had gathered. A big woman tended the steaming kettle, and those who had something to add offered it up. Roy proffered their loaf of bread, now squashed on one side. Without slowing her stirring, the big lady accepted it with a civil, "Thank you kindly."

Three small children chased each other, with the woman tending the fire chastising them to stay away. "Git on, you varmints! You'll get scalded."

Dorrit said, "Ma'am? I'd be happy to help, if anything needs peeling or whatever."

The woman whipped around as one of the boys tugged at her apron string. "Barney! I told you!"

Dorrit smiled at the child and said, "I know a story about a little boy who lived in the woods. He found buried treasure there." The child stopped, a finger crooked in his mouth. His brother stopped, too, and stood swaying from side to side. Dorrit said, "Get your sister and come sit with me over by that automobile. I'll tell you about it."

The cook smiled, and nodded, arcing her spoon to shepherd her brood. "Git! Go listen to a story."

The aromas of fire and cooking made Dorrit's stomach rumble. She supposed everyone was hungry, but all ten campers followed the lead of the cook, remaining aloof yet polite, observing some sort of camp etiquette Dorrit did not yet understand. The men hunkered around the fire circle, some with uniform jackets unbuttoned and suspenders hanging, others stripped to undershirts with military identification tags glinting silver on their chests. They seemed to be trying to top each other's stories of how many men they had shot or how many bullets they had dodged. When a man lifted his shirt to show a bayonet scar, Dorrit looked away. Besides Margaret, who cooked, there was only one other woman—a young mother, who stayed in her tent with a crying baby.

When Margaret announced that the stew was done, everyone lined up, holding tin cups and plates. She gestured first to a young man Dorrit had taken for a teenager. Shyly, he held out two plates, then retreated to the tent where the mother and baby were. Everyone else settled around the fire, balancing plates on knees, tucking bandannas into collars. Dorrit sat beside her father. On her plate, chunks of salted pork steamed with white beans and carrots and potatoes. She wanted to bolt it down, but it was too hot. She said a silent grace.

After supper she asked Margaret where they were from. "Kansas," Margaret said. "Been on the road for five days already. My mister's feeling poorly. Tuberculosis. If we get the bonus, we'll head to Arizona. Hope we beat this next one!" She rubbed a wide palm over her bulging belly. "Seems like everybody's problems are going to be solved by the bonus. Seems almost too good to be true, don't it?"

A man called Frank brought out a harmonica and, despite the heat, the men stayed by the dying fire. When Margaret went around the circle pouring coffee, Roy held out his mug, shooting a sidelong glance toward Dorrit. In that instant, she understood that they had left Christian Science behind. Her father held the cup to his nose, inhaling steam, then took a sip. Dorrit wasn't sure if she felt disappointed in him or not. He seemed happier than he had in months. She understood that he would want to fit in, that he would want to avoid explaining to people he'd just met that he didn't drink coffee, because his version of Christianity found it a sin. Explanations such as these always conveyed, on some level, tacit disapproval of those who did indulge. She understood that he was choosing to avoid the skeptical looks that came when Christian Science was mentioned. Margaret left the coffee pot on a warm stone, disappearing into the darkness beyond the circle with her brood.

The men seemed unaware of Dorrit. When Frank played "On Top of Old Smoky," some sang along in a sad, slow cadence that made her sleepy. Bert passed around a mason jar and Dorrit followed with her eyes, a little scandalized, certain it was liquor. Who would want to drink something that smelled so bad? And what was the point? She remembered the drunken burglars from *The Secret of the Old Clock*. Liquor was not only an intoxicant, but an *illegal* intoxicant besides. They could *all* be arrested if the police came, and it was only the first night. When the jar circled around again, Roy leaned over and told Dorrit to go to bed.

Venturing into the shadows beyond the firelight, she found a secluded place in the bushes and pulled up her dress. She hated the furtive, rushed squatting, recalling the mountain lion Nancy Drew had encountered while camping. Inside the tarp the tent was airless and hot, the sheltering cover, she realized, was also a screen preventing awareness of what was outside, what might be lurking, or sniffing, or spying. Switching on the flashlight, distorted shadows mimicked her as she unrolled the quilts then unlaced her shoes and gingerly peeled off her cotton stockings. They had worn through at the heels, leaving blisters. With a mason jar full of creek water, she washed herself, feeling only slightly cleaner than before. A deep fatigue came over her as she lay down in her dress. It was too dark now to darn stockings or to write in her notebook. The men's songs were soldier's songs now—rowdier, louder, and when her father's voice joined in, she felt a separation from him. Here was a version of Roy Sykes that was not her pop. He was a soldier once. Mosquitos buzzed around Dorrit's ears and she startled, in that half-sleeping way of falling into a dream.

Thirteen
DORRIT

In the morning, Dorrit's legs ached. She sat up stiffly, scratching a mosquito bite on her neck, and cocked her head. No clatter of carts on the street, no calls of newsboys, no slamming of doors up and down the hall, no rattle or backfire of automobiles. Instead, she heard the music of the creek, accented by bird calls. She smelled the smoldering fire site and the mossy sharpness of the earth. Outside, most of the tents were gone. Charlie and Bert tied the mattress on the car as Roy worked on the engine, banging something with a wrench. Dorrit rolled and tied the quilts while her father talked about spark plugs and pistons.

Sitting on the running board, she inspected the holes in her stockings. Bert leaned against the side of the car, scratching his stubbled chin as he watched Roy. "A most exceptional talent," he said, "the aptitude for mechanical things. Never been gifted that way myself."

"Nah, he sure ain't," Charlie said, shoving Bert's shoulder. "Bert here was a big-shot pro-fessor, don't you know? Cain't you tell by the fancy way he talks?"

"Really?" Dorrit asked, considering him with a fresh aspect. The men she had seen so far, she only thought of collectively, as marchers. But each had a history.

Before Bert could answer, Charlie piped up, "This here's Doctor Bertram Harold Purvis, of Dartmouth College."

"Formerly," Bert said, holding up an index finger.

"What did you teach?" Dorrit asked.

"English Literature," Bert said, "Are you familiar with Dickens's *Little Dorrit?*"

"I'm named for her! I liked *Oliver Twist.*"

Roy put the hood down and rubbed his hands on his trousers, then dusted them together with apparent satisfaction. Now they weren't begging a ride anymore. He took a turn driving, and Dorrit sat in the back again, with Bert. She was more at ease now. These men were not strangers. She listened as the men talked about how they would spend their bonuses and she forgot to be afraid. It all sounded glorious, and she was proud of her father for fixing the car, and for having the gumption to march. She liked this version of her father, she decided. They would buy a truck, and he would work every day, and not be so distracted by his trap. Maybe they could move. Maybe she could have a canary. As the miles passed, the men's continued chatter began to run together, and the metallic thuds of pans became rhythmic. It occurred to Dorrit that—being a person who spent much time alone—she found it a strain to talk and listen for so long with no respite of solitude. She made lists in her head of what she might plant in a garden, attempting an alphabetical list of flowers, then birds, then sewing stitches while she watched the scenery. At times she realized she was praying without memorized lines, but with silent, conversational questions and observations.

Nearing Washington on the third day, traffic became heavier with more and more cars like Charlie's, some steaming on the roadside as men stood around them, scratching their heads. There were more hand-lettered signs and a steady stream of tired-looking veterans on foot. When they passed the road sign announcing that they were leaving Maryland and entering the District of Columbia, everyone in the car cheered. Dorrit sat forward in anticipation, watching for street signs. She was the first to point out Pennsylvania Avenue. They continued, following the parade of slow-moving cars as bored-looking soldiers waved them on.

When they passed a partially demolished office building which was now, apparently, occupied by marchers, the car went quiet. This was not the mowed lawn with shade trees and orderly rows of canvas tents Dorrit had envisioned. The front of the building was gone, but the windows in the rear were intact—some with blinds hanging crookedly, some still with curtains—which was so odd. Exposed stairways zigzagged up the floors, dividing the building into three sections. As they got closer, she smelled piled garbage and smoking fire circles. The odor of latrines wafted in with the heat, along with flies. Inside, campers had strung tarps or blankets on ropes, dividing the offices so that the building resembled a sloppy beehive. A group of boys in grubby clothes sat on the raw edge of the second floor, swinging their legs, tossing something down to try to hit a tin can on the ground. A spiral-tailed dog with ribs showing nosed the rubbish, and the boys threw pebbles at it until it yelped, looking around, not knowing where the rocks had come from. It slunk off, tail between its legs. Dorrit could hear the boy's mean-spirited laughter—a sort boys of that age should not know about yet. Around the base of the building, automobiles had parked haphazardly, some with veteran's slogans painted on the sides. Charlie stopped and leaned out the window to speak to a soldier, then nodded and drove on, saying, "That private says the stink is on account of these folks have been using the toilets in that building, with the water shut off. Some of 'em been here for months, he says." He shook his head, "He said if we go on a ways, there's a campsite with proper army latrines and water, along the Anacostia River."

Along the river's edge, cattails waved and mallards paddled in pairs and rested on the shore, reminding Dorrit of the Public Garden at home. Boston and Blossom Street took on soft edges in her memory, contrasting with her first, hard-edged impressions of this unknown place.

Leaving the paved road, the car jostled slowly through the motley patchwork of the camp. Heat shimmered from scrap metal shack rooves and tents were pitched at odd angles, wherever anyone decided to plop them. Some shacks were simply rooves on sticks, covered with cardboard or tarpaper, and one flew an American flag. A wooden crate that might have held a grand piano stood open-ended, the stenciled, THIS END UP reading sideways. Inside, cooking pots and bedding were visible. Men lounged alone or in groups, some lying on the grass. Several stood on crutches or had rolled, empty sleeves or eye patches; some wore medals pinned to undershirts or overalls. Veterans waved as the car passed, and everyone seemed hopeful and happy to see each other. Despite the men's uniforms, the camp lacked the order and sameness of a military outpost, resembling more a collection of little boys' backyard forts and tree houses. Dorrit looked in vain for women and children, her apprehension growing as they continued. Roy and the men talked excitedly. Farther down the riverbank, Charlie stopped at what appeared to be the outskirts of the camp, saying, "Looks like as good a spot as any."

Dorrit got out of the back seat, her legs stiff. She had looked for a bathroom as they drove through camp but not seen one. Roy stretched his arms over his head and smiled. He said, "Baby Doll, you stay here while we go find supplies. The army's supposed to be giving out cots and rations somewhere."

Sitting alone on the running board, Dorrit tried to reconcile her expectations. Nancy Drew wouldn't be caught dead here. After a few minutes a growing sense of urgency caused her to wonder if she could duck behind the car. But anyone might come along. They had parked near a large oak tree and a shack made from egg boxes with fading red print. She could find this tree again. She set off down the single street that had been plowed haphazardly between the tents and shacks. Garbage cans overflowed, and in a rustling of tin cans, a brown rat foraged. Farther up the row was a square green tent with *Women's Sanitary Unit* stenciled on the side flap. Cautiously, Dorrit pulled aside the canvas. There were real toilet seats in cubicles and four galvanized metal sinks stood in a row. Two big water tanks supplied a pair of shower stalls, with rubberized curtains. The heat intensified the sharp smells of bleach and lime, irritating her eyes. As pungent as it was, it could not cover the odor of human waste and damp. Even though the tent was cooler than outside, no one would want to stay any longer than necessary.

The men's sanitary tent across the way was larger, and farther up the line, someone had set up a small trading post. Sacks of potatoes and cornmeal hung from metal poles, out of the reach of vermin. On the ground, a stack of iron frying pans nested inside each other and zinc wash-tubs were stacked beside boxes of soap flakes and army blankets and shiny oilcloth tarps.

Returning to Charlie's car, Dorrit studied how the men had set up their camps. In a few places, metal army cots were stacked into makeshift bunk beds, right out in the open, with tarps covering the tops. Someone had woven a sort of screen of twigs around his ground-level pallet and as she passed, rings of cigarette smoke rose from inside, expanding in the sunlight. A hand-lettered sign was affixed to the upper bunk: *HOTEL CHICAGO, $15.00 & up.* Propped against a Model T Ford was a sign: *War is hell, but loafing is worse.*

At the car, Roy was waiting, pacing. "Where'd you get to? I found us a real lucky spot, come on." He took their bundles and led her to a shack near a small tree. The roof and door were of corrugated metal. The walls were made of boxes and odd-sized pieces of plywood nailed to posts. "See?" he said. "How lucky are we? Me and the boys were walking past, and the man here was packing up. Said he had a crop to get in so he couldn't stay. The boys told me to take it, on account of you being along. It's a good sign, Baby Doll. Yes sirree, a good sign." He rubbed his palms together.

Dorrit's shoulders fell. "We're only staying until the vote, right, Pop?"

"Right. Now, I'm going to buy a bucket and get us some water. We tried to get cots, but they ran out weeks ago. You get settled in, all righty?" He bustled around, tapping the roof at a rusty spot.

While Roy went for water, Dorrit gathered the trash the former occupant had left and carried it outside to a can. Beside the can was a fruit crate that might serve as a table. In the shack, she hung her father's pack on a nail then unrolled their oilcloth over the dead grass.

Stepping outside to dust off her hands, Dorrit stopped to watch a quartet of geese gliding low over the water. A young woman crouched among the reeds at the riverbank, singing quietly as she scrubbed clothes against a washboard. Seeing Dorrit, she raised one thin arm, shading her eyes, smiling quickly before closing her lips over protruding upper teeth.

Standing, she tugged self-consciously at the neckline of her faded dress, and Dorrit could see she was barely more than a girl. She spoke slowly, with a deep Southern drawl. "Howdy-do? I'm Nellie."

"Hello. I'm Dorrit. Dorrit Sykes. We just got here from Boston. Where're you from?"

Nellie returned to her washing. "Montezuma, Georgia. Been here since the end of May—me and my family. Came on a Southern Railway boxcar. My husband Sam was a sharecropper, like his daddy and his daddy's daddy. Last fall the place got bought up by a big canning company—peaches, mostly. The pay for shares went so low we couldn't buy no seed corn." She lifted her chin in the direction of the camp. "Evathing we own's here, in that shack." Nellie said she was nineteen, but too many lines crossed her forehead for one so young. The shirt she washed looked like a rag, and her dress was made from a flour sack. She said, "Where's your husband?"

Dorrit squatted to rinse her hands. "Oh, I'm not . . . I'm with my father."

"Your ma here?"

Dorrit shook her head, unwilling to share her story, unable to imagine her mother in this setting. *In this place*, she realized, *no one knows my past. Only what I choose to tell.*

Dorrit told Nellie that they would use the bonus to buy a Chevrolet truck, with the doors painted to say, "Mr. R. Sykes," and then her father would drive her around to her sewing ladies. When Nellie did not reply, it occurred to Dorrit that perhaps she sounded boastful instead of optimistic. She held out her hand. Wordlessly, Nellie passed pieces of clothing to her. There wasn't one that wasn't full of holes and stains, and there seemed to be no soap. One by one, Dorrit wrung them out and shook them flat before stacking them in the carton that served as a laundry basket.

"Nellie?" Dorrit said, "Tell me what you and Sam will do with his bonus."

Nellie seemed to have a habit of sucking her lower lip. "If'n it comes, reckon we'll head back to Montezuma. My people's there. S'pose we could buy a little patch of ground of our own; start up a little farm. I'd fancy a place by a creek. Nothing I like better than to soak my feet in a cold creek." She leaned over her washboard, hiding a secret sort of smile, as if she were embarrassed to have told Dorrit her dream. At Nellie's shack, they hung the wash on a cord strung between two saplings. "Reckon we'll be neighbors for a piece," Nellie said. "You're welcome to borry my washboard, any time need be." There was a tone of shy pride in her voice. She had something to offer, even if was only the use of a washboard.

"Thank you," Dorrit said. "That's awfully kind."

Inside, Nellie put down her washing and raised her chin toward an older woman, sitting on the edge of an army cot, smoking a corncob pipe. "That's Sam's ma."

The woman rocked, swinging one tanned leg as a man's shoe flopped on and off her heel. Her cheeks were sunken, and gray-streaked blond showed beneath her kerchief. The mother rose and shuffled outside without a word. On the cot was a fruit crate, and Dorrit was startled to hear whimpering.

Nellie said, "This here's Flora Mary. My boy Claude's with Sam."

The crate was lined with newspapers, and the baby lay diagonally, apparently having grown too large to fit in the box lengthwise. When Dorrit lifted her, the odor of wet diaper and velvet baby skin dropped her heart in her chest, remembering little Shevaun Sullivan. She jiggled the baby against her shoulder. "She's a pretty baby," Dorrit said. "I'd be happy to help with her. Looks to me like you've got your hands full."

"They's not a lot of womenfolk nor little 'uns in this camp. But truth be told, we're glad to be here. We was down to eating wild greens. Leastways here, my boy gets some food. Set a piece with me," Nellie said, as she lowered herself to a box and unbuttoned the top of her dress. When Dorrit passed the baby to her, it began to root frantically, sucking wetly as Nellie gazed out, her fist beneath her chin. Dorrit didn't know where to sit. Sitting on the bed of someone she had just met seemed far too familiar. She settled herself on a piece of cardboard on the ground, embarrassed to witness Nellie's bare breast and bony chest. This was not the same as pinning a dress on a woman wearing a slip and girdle. This was far more primitive; more intimate. When Nellie switched the baby to her other side a strand of thin dark hair fell into her face and she did not bother to move it. Her hair was parted in the middle, pulled into a tight knot the size of a walnut. Everything about Nellie was slight, but she had about her an air of sinewy resilience. Her hands were thick-skinned and freckled, her fingers nubby. Dorrit rose and excused herself, saying she needed to meet her father, telling Nellie she would come by the next morning.

The shack was as neatly arranged as Dorrit had left it, save that Roy's toolbox was not there and his uniform jacket hung on a nail beside the door. She stroked the rough wool of a sleeve, examining the stripes. Who had sewn them there? The fabric smelled of mildew and woodsmoke. She inspected each of the buttons to see that they were securely sewn, then checked the pocket linings for holes. Inside the breast pocket she found a photograph of her parents, taken on their wedding day. Her father wore a silly grin. Augusta appeared more subdued and a bit hopeful, Dorrit decided, as she ran her finger over her mother's smooth young face. She returned the photograph, buttoning the pocket closed. *Life*, she mused, *isn't very predictable, is it? Who knows where anybody will end up?* For the time being, there was nothing else to be done. She sat gingerly on the crate, then began to write in her notebook.

As the long days of waiting passed, the pages filled.

June 10

Today we arrived in Washington! The place we are camping is called Camp Marks and the area is Anacostia Flats. (Really, 'flats' is only a nicer word for a swamp.) There are mosquitoes and it smells. There is the low-tide smell to begin with, plus the stink of people who need baths, and the latrines. Pop said that the front line used to smell the same.

I'm glad I brought my notebook because it is a good way to pass the time. As I write this, the sun is going down. I can hear frogs at the river. I never knew frogs could be so noisy, but then I have never slept out of doors before this trip. The insects are bothersome and it is hot inside our shack because of the metal roof. But it should cool down at night. I think this will be an adventure. We have a flashlight and Pop says he will get a lantern. He says that when he gets his bonus we will ride the train back to Boston in style and eat in the dining car and maybe he will even buy me a dress from a shop in Washington. I have seen a cardinal, a blue jay, several doves and goldfinches, and some ducks. I made a friend today. She is nothing like Bess Marvin or George Fayne (Nancy Drew's best friends). Her name is Nellie and she is nineteen. Her husband is called Sam, but I have not met him yet. Her little boy is three. His name is Claude.

June 13

Last night was very scary. Pop told me what he was going to do, but still, I hated sleeping here alone. Three hundred men marched around the Capitol Building all night long. This morning when he got back he was worn out. He told me that the government people turned on the water sprinklers around the Capitol and will keep them on day and night, to keep people from pitching tents or sleeping there on the grass. Pop said that a bunch of children were playing in the water, like it was a park. I'd like to be able to do that. He has gone to sleep, so I will leave him here and go to Nellie's. Every day there are big meetings and marching. They seem to say the same things, over and over. I have stayed away from the crowds.

June 15

A congressman from Tennessee, Mr. Eslick, dropped dead while pleading for the passage of the bonus bill! Some of the veterans who were awarded the Distinguished Service Cross were invited to view the body.

June 17
10:00 a.m.

Well, so far, we have been here for one week. Pop waits in line in the mornings to get our rations then spends his days marching with the other men or listening to speeches. There are lots of speeches. I have been keeping our shack tidy and helping Nellie with little Flora Mary during the day. I take my sewing things over there and I've tried to patch some of their clothes. I've been reading my Nancy Drew to them. (I don't believe that Nellie can read). The phantom horse at Shadow Ranch gives us all the willies. Nellie's little boy has nits, but Pop and I have not got any yet, and we have been checking our heads every night. The army has been spraying for mosquitos, but they seem to get into our shack no matter how tight we try to shut it up. I don't know if I'll ever get used to that whining buzz around my ears.

More people come every day. The food is all donated. There is not much of it, and the cardboard parts of our shack are peeling. Pop is having a great time. A few times a day, soldiers on motorcycles (some with sidecars) drive through the camp, looking over everything. Yesterday I saw Mr. Pelham Glassford, who is the head of the Washington Police, on his blue motorcycle. All the men were cheering. Mostly, it's dusty and hot and there is mostly nothing to do. I have started to cut Mrs. Frazier's green evening dress into rectangles to make change purses from it. I gave one to Nellie yesterday. She cried and kissed my cheek and said she never owned anything so pretty before.

All around camp today there is an air of excitement. Congress voted for the bonus payments, and tonight the Senators will vote. Today Pop is marching on the Capitol steps. I will spend the day at Nellie's. I have finished reading "The Secret of Shadow Ranch." I wish I had another book, or at least a newspaper or a radio. It seems like it takes forever for us to hear the news in camp.

10:35 p.m.

Tonight the Senate voted and Pop says only 28 of 96 senators voted to give the bonuses early. When they announced the no vote, the veterans all sang "America," and it was like the whole world was singing it. Mr. Waters, who is in charge of all the marchers, made an announcement that it was only a temporary setback, and we should all stay until the senators change their minds. Pop was telling me this but he looked confused, like his feelings were hurt. I felt so sorry for him, because I know he never really thought about what would happen if they said no. He just thought he needed to wait for his money. He is awful down and out. I can't think of anything to do to cheer him up. He laid down on his bedroll and faced the wall. But I know he is not sleeping. I don't want to ask him any more tonight.

June 18

   Today I was very excited to see that the Salvation Army has set up a big tent here at camp. It is called "The Hut" and they have checkerboards, and letter-writing paper, and a lending library with magazines! Today I found a copy of "The Secret of Red Gate Farm" and "The Hidden Staircase"! Nellie will be so excited. (I have already read both of them myself but I will not spoil the mystery for Nellie. She loves Nancy Drew. I showed the Salvation Army lady (they are called Salvation Sallies) that one of the books has some water stains because when I return it, I do not want her to think I was careless. She said that they are so busy no one would notice, and that gave me an idea. I offered to help arrange the children's books. While I was doing that, some little ones came in. I started reading them a story, and afterward, the Sallie (her name is actually Sally!) asked me if I would do story time again. I said yes.

   Mr. Glassford has sent the military bands to play music at Fort Myer (that is one of the other camps). Pop says they're trying to make folks feel homesick. Twice they've sent airplanes over to drop printed flyers, asking us all to go home. Pop says the VA is offering cheap train tickets and rations to men who will leave. He says the police don't know what to do with 20,000 people, camping all over. They can't arrest them all. I have never seen 20,000 people in one place before. Now I know what it looks like.

June 19

   Today is Sunday. The Salvation Sallies held services in their tent. Sally invited me and asked if I'd like to become a soldier of Christ, and take the Soldier's Covenant. I asked what that involves, because it sounds serious. She said their mission is to 'preach the gospel of Jesus Christ and to meet human needs in His name without discrimination'. I like the sound of that, I must say. I asked Pop if he wanted to go, but he did not. I did not want to go alone.

In the afternoon, about 3,000 Bonus Expeditionary Force men met in front of the Capitol. A line of police were there to keep the veterans from coming up the steps. Pop said that five men broke the line and got past the police and were arrested, but no one was hurt. The men are getting impatient, he says. There was a thunderstorm this afternoon. The rain was so loud on the roof! But we only have one leak. Pop has found some boards at the dump to patch our walls. Ma's suitcase got moldy and fell apart from the damp. It made me sad to throw it away. The rain makes the paths between the shacks and tents a slough of mud. It is hard to walk, and harder to keep the mud off of our things. I have only gone out to use the sanitary unit. Morale around camp is low. Tomorrow would have been Ma's birthday. I will not write about that. I wonder what she would have thought about this place.

June 21

The men stay on. Pop says there are 8,500 now. I think that many of them don't have anywhere else to go. Pop says we are staying. It is two weeks now since we left home. He says that if enough of us stay, they will have to vote again. He seems angry about it now. The men march in shifts. The women cook, and play cards, and try to wash their clothes in the river but there is not much soap. I have kept on sewing Mrs. Frazier's dress into purses and on each one I put one of the paste jewel buttons, and line them with crepe de chine from the under slip. They are pretty, if I do say so myself. I think I might be able to trade them for food. I have made three so far, then today I got a headache so had to stop. I am worried that my Boston library book will be overdue.

Fourteen
MAY

In the moments before May opened her eyes, her senses began to register the heat of mid-June. Her scalp prickled, sticky with perspiration, and her legs were pinned by a solid, warm weight, as was her left arm.

"Mama?" Hank whispered anxiously, "Are you sleeping?" He poked her right shoulder. Sister slept curled inside the arc of May's left arm and Bandit was draped across her shins, paws twitching in sleep. Hank's bright eyes blinked at her. "Do you think she was here?" He touched the red gap on his gums where a front tooth was missing.

"Shh." May nodded and kissed his forehead. The shoulder of her nightgown was sodden with what she already knew to be drool, and not her own. A cautious sniff confirmed: no obvious odor of diaper. *Small mercies.* Maybe she could slide from the bed before the baby woke and have a bath with the bathroom door open. Never mind the luxury of privacy. At least Uncle Cy had moved out. A week after the auction he moved to Chestnut Grove, to the main house. Two weeks later, it had quietly opened as a rooming house, and over the past three weeks, had filled with boarders. *Small mercies.*

A bath, that was all May wanted. *Clean hair!* Oh, to have clean hair.

"But Mama," Hank tugged the sleeve of her nightgown. "If I wasn't in my own bed, could she find me?"

May whispered, "Go look under your pillow." Hank's eyes widened and his voice was breathless. "But what if she's still *in my room?*"

"Quiet. Let Sister sleep. The tooth fairy can only fly at night."

"You promise?"

"Promise."

He slid off the side of the tall canopy bed. Bandit rose, stretching languidly with a protracted, vocal yawn before jumping down to follow. The running *slap-slap* of little-boy feet resonated down the hall and back again as May extracted her tingling arm, wiggling life into her fingers. Hank shook her leg, holding up a shiny nickel, smiling broadly. Then he frowned, squeezing the coin. "Mama," he asked, "what does the tooth fairy *do* with the teeth? Does she have a whole cave full of little children's teeths?"

What an unpleasant thought. Sister gurgled and began to stir. May pushed herself up to sitting, whispering, "Your daddy's coming home tomorrow night. Maybe he knows where the teeth go. And you'll sleep in your big boy bed."

May slid from the bed, pushing damp hair off her forehead before she picked up her now squirming daughter. The bedside clock read 6:15 a.m. A bath would have to wait.

Downstairs, the radio hummed, turned low. She let the dog out and put on a pot of coffee, then filled a baby bottle with milk. When Sister was happily ensconced in her playpen, May carried two cups of coffee to the parlor, saying, "Morning, Daddy. Did you sleep well?" Her father raised himself and she fluffed his pillows.

"Not so bad. I'll move back upstairs this weekend. About time we got this room back in order." May sat in the rocking chair. Henry switched off a news broadcast, saying, "They're talking about these dust storms, and the farmers out west. Everybody's heading to California, like that's gonna solve their problems. And all those poor vets, hanging on in DC. No jobs, and now no bonus. They're hunkering down, refusing to leave."

"Byrd told me last night on the phone, he sees them marching, just waiting for something to happen. He says, from what he hears around the Capitol, he doubts they'll change the vote."

Henry's cup clinked in its saucer. "Will he be on the six ten tomorrow night?"

"As far as I know."

"Cy's itching to show him around over there, you know."

"I don't know what to tell you. Byrd will see it when he's ready."

"He has to know how lucky he is, to get his homeplace back."

"He does—I'm sure he does. But it's still shameful to him—it makes him feel like he can't provide enough to take care of his family."

They were silent for a moment, with only the creak of the rocking chair. When Henry spoke again, his voice was resigned. "I certainly understand that. I do, indeed." He set his cup down and stared out the window.

May considered his profile. There was still a shadow of the handsome young man he had been. She said, "What if Byrd asks to see the market ledgers?"

"We'll show him. How was this week?"

"No better. But Blue has almost perfected the all-day candy bar. I'll bring one home tonight. I want to see what you think."

"Oh," Henry rubbed his abdomen, "don't make me try another one."

"But he's worked out the recipe. I can take samples around, and take orders."

"May," Her father's look was interrogatory. ". . . have you talked to Byrd about this yet?"

"I want to get the recipe just right, so he can taste one."

"Well, you ought to let him know what you're planning."

May grimaced at the irony of her father's words. "He hasn't shown the least bit of interest when I've brought it up before. And besides, it's *your* business. It's *our* business." She gestured to Henry then back to herself. "And Blue's too. We should get to make the decisions. Byrd doesn't know anything about running an orchard or a market, much less a candy business."

"That may be, but no good will come of hiding bad news. Business has never been worse."

May's sigh acknowledged the frustrating truth of her father's wisdom. But when had her father become so complacent? He lost faith, after that meeting with the banker. He gave up.

Henry gestured to the radio. "Turn that on, would you?"

On her way to the market May stopped at the Post Office, where Miss Spindle called excitedly from the counter, "Oh, May! You have a parcel, from Paris, France!" May thanked her, then took the package back to her car, knowing she was thwarting Miss Spindle's curiosity to know what it was.

At the market, Blue was waiting on someone up front. May went to the back room. Impatiently, she cut away the wrapping and sat at the table to read the letter inside.

June 1, Paris

Dear May,

I absolutely adored your last letter. You're becoming a confectioner! But then, you always were so good at reinventing yourself. I could tell, when you were helping me to plan the salon, that you had a head for business.

So, as you requested, I have twice been candy shopping at À la Mère de Famille. It's exactly as it was when you were here. Remember the wonderful sweet smells, when you walk in the door? Just the same! If I could turn that into perfume, I'd be rich as Rockefeller. I've befriended one of the vendeuses and she remembered my dear Philippe (he did love his bonbons and marrons glacés).

Here is what my sleuthing has uncovered:

The nougat you remember comes in two flavors: Almond with honey and apricots, and vanilla with cherries and pistachio nuts. I was able to find out, (through careful detective work), that they make their own pistachio paste and the recipe is a closely guarded secret. I am enclosing some of each flavor, although it will be stale by the time it reaches you.

I'm also enclosing two of my newest shades of lipstick and nail varnish. Did I tell you I'm coming out with a second line of cosmetics? Josephine Baker has come out with a suntanning stain, only it's streaky and oily. The white women over here think it's de rigueur to look like they've been on a desert island for a decade. Mine is called

'J'aime Soliel.' I'll send you some when we get the packaging done. Now, in return, you must send me some of your candy, or better yet, come to visit and deliver it yourself. You are missed here, and always welcome.

Much love, Rocky

May folded the pages.

Rocky. Dear Rocky. She could still picture him as he was when they met in 1924, at the New York Biltmore Hotel. He, an elevator operator, looking like Duke Ellington in a khaki uniform. After federal agents raided the farm and arrested her father for moonshining, May had fled to New York, avoiding a warrant for her own arrest. She had started out as a seamstress in the Biltmore laundry, and Rocky had shown her the ropes. He had ambition, and dreams, taking hairdressing courses at night. He encouraged May to dream, too, and together they signed on with the troupe of a new theater revue and sailed to Paris. May's aspirations of becoming a costume designer had not panned out, but Rocky found success and moved in with a French aristocrat named Philippe de Clermont, who had left him a mansion in Paris when he died. When May left Paris to come home and marry Byrd, Rocky encouraged her to follow her heart.

She opened each of the tubes of lipstick. The colors seemed overly vibrant, almost to the point of garishness—a deep plum called *Damson and Delilah*, and a vivid red with a bluish cast, called *Crimson as Sin*. May smiled to herself. All perfect for Paris, but woefully *outré* for Keswick, Virginia. Paris was an ocean and a lifetime away. *Crimson as Sin*, indeed.

Rocky had also included a tin of the violet-flower tea she loved. She held it to her nose and closed her eyes, lost for a moment in memories of having tea at Ladurée on Rue Royale, with the gilded cases of pastries and delicate pink porcelain cups. Finally, she inspected the gold-bordered, dark green candy box. As Rocky had predicted, the candy inside was somewhat dry. She could almost recall the aromas of the candy shop; it was an institution in Paris, run by the same family for generations.

When Blue came in, she cut the pieces of nougat in two, saying, "Taste these, while they're fresh—as fresh as they're going to be." He immediately began taking notes, then nibbling a bit more, and writing things down.

The following night at 6:05 p.m., May pulled up to the Keswick Depot. Hank bounced on the seat beside her. "Hurry Mama, I got to get my penny on the tracks!"

Holding his hand, she led him around the side of the building where, with a serious expression, he dug into the pockets of his overalls, extracting a coin. He laid it on the flat top rail of the track. May said, "Remember where you put it; right beside that lamp post, all right? Now let's go up to the platform. It's not safe to stay down here." The evening was humid; the air, still. May held Hank's hand and together they looked expectantly eastward, toward Orange, listening for the whistle. At six fifteen the ticket agent came out to say that the train was running late due to delays out of Washington. The news fueled May's anxiety. They sat on a bench and she picked up a newspaper someone had left. Passing the funny papers to Hank she studied photographs from Washington, of crowds of veterans on the Capitol steps, of the shantytown camps, now dubbed "Hoovervilles."

When May heard the train whistle, she folded the paper and smoothed her hair. Hank took her hand, tugging her toward the railing at the end of the platform, saying, "Mama, come down here so I can see the train go over my penny."

Byrd disembarked, looking hot and tired. He had loosened his necktie and his suit was rumpled. Hank ran toward him and Byrd knelt to scoop him up. May stood back, allowing them the moment, observing how much Hank resembled his father. Each Friday when she saw her husband, she never failed to have a skip in her heart—that small jolt of attraction that had not diminished. Byrd exclaimed over the lost tooth, and after the train departed the three of them walked hand in hand to the tracks. Hank squatted down, checking between the rough wood ties. With a whoop of triumph, he held up the flattened coin. "Lookie, Daddy! I found it." He rubbed it between his fingers. "It's still warm. See, Mama?" He ran ahead, toward the car.

Byrd pulled off his necktie and took May's hand as they followed behind. She leaned against his arm, saying, "I'm so glad to have you home. We've been listening to the news. I've been worried about you. What were you working on this week?"

"A group of Senators is proposing an antiforeclosure bill. I sure hope it passes." What he did not say, she knew, was that if the legislation had been in place earlier, his father would not have been so desperate. Just the week before, Byrd had come home jubilant over the passing of The Emergency Relief and Construction Act, which he had worked on. Hoover was due to sign it any day. "And how was your week?" he asked.

"Fine. When Hank's tooth came out, he seemed upset at first, so I asked him what was wrong. He said he needed all of his teeth." May laughed. "I explained that a new tooth would grow in after a little while, then he asked if the fairy would try to snatch out his big-boy teeth, because that must have happened to Uncle Cy. It was hard to keep a straight face."

"He was scared of that clown at the State Fair, remember? But he was only four. What else have I missed?"

"Well, someone tried to break into the market. Blue says they jimmied the kitchen door, but Taffy must've scared them away."

"Taffy? Who's Taffy? Why didn't you tell me this on Wednesday?"

"Sorry. Hank was right there, wanting to talk to you. I didn't want to frighten him. Remember that mutt Blue found? She's a fierce little thing. And look. See, over there?" May stopped, pointing to an opening in the trees that bordered the far side of the tracks. Two red bandannas were tied on low-hanging branches and hung like limp flags. "Blue says there's a hobo camp through there, with ten or twenty men. And yesterday, at the Post Office, Miss Spindle told me that somebody stole three of Walt Twyman's hens this week, right out of his henhouse."

"People are getting desperate. You should've seen the Bonus Marchers."

Byrd shook his head. "Some of them brought their wives and children, and some had been camping since May. I tell you, it makes me grateful to have a job and a roof over our heads."

Again, May sensed that a topic was being avoided. Byrd's brother had fought in France and been killed there, in 1918. She wondered, if Jimmy were alive, with no inheritance or job, might he be at the March right now? Allowing the subject to pass unremarked seemed insensitive, yet she knew that to bring Jimmy up might stir painful memories. She said, "Do you think they'll vote again?"

"I don't know. Hard to say if it would be a good thing or a bad thing. I mean, I know those vets need the money, but paying out 43,000 bonuses now would all but bankrupt the Treasury. There are thousands of people who aren't veterans who need assistance too. The opponents are saying we need some national form of relief, only Hoover says if that happens, no one will be inspired to even try to find a job."

"He seems so disconnected from the people he's supposed to serve and represent, doesn't he?" Byrd nodded, looking discouraged, and May tucked her thoughts away, wishing they could continue an adult conversation for more than a few minutes. The easy talks they used to have were now luxuries. There were no rules for this arrangement. Their restructured partnership went weekend to weekend. She felt sure there were topics that Byrd spared her, too—his fears and worries and the grief and loss he seldom spoke of.

Hank trotted up to take Byrd's other hand. "Daddy, wait for me!"

Byrd said, "Your mother tells me the tooth fairy paid you a visit."

Hank stopped and pointed out the red spot in his mouth, then said, "Will you take me to ride Peanut tomorrow? Mama says we maybe can go on a picnic on the mountain." He frowned, looking serious. "Only Sister ought to stay at home."

Byrd ruffled Hank's hair affectionately. "Sure, buddy."

May said, tentatively, "Dear, Sister's first birthday is Tuesday, remember? I thought we'd just have a little cake after dinner tomorrow. And there's something I'd like you to do with me, in the morning. It won't take more than an hour."

"Welcome, welcome!" Cy Waddell's voice echoed in the high-ceilinged hallway of Chestnut Grove. He fidgeted with apparent disquietude, standing inside the door of the house while its owner stood before him on the stoop. Byrd shook Cy's hand and May followed him inside. Although the rooming house had been running for three weeks, Byrd made excuses each weekend to avoid visiting. May had not wanted to press him, and they had not talked about it, aside from her initial reports of moving beds and finding mattresses and one discussion about how much Alice, the cook, should be paid in her new capacity in the kitchen. In the hallway, the floors gleamed as from a recent mopping and there was a vague odor of disinfectant. Small wooden plaques with stenciled numbers were now mounted on the doors. With a perfunctory knock, Cy led them into what had been the dining room. Three mismatched iron bedsteads were lined up along one wall and above, an elaborate crystal chandelier hung. Tassel-trimmed damask curtains still hung at the windows. Socks were draped to dry over the fire screen and on the opposite wall, various items of clothing and towels hung from picture hooks. The fifteen-foot high ceilings seemed cavernous. Other downstairs rooms had been partitioned off, now furnished with twin beds and a motley assortment of dressers, wardrobes, and chairs. Byrd's face was inscrutable.

"Now," Cy said, pointing out a chart tacked up beside the stairs, "All the tenants—we have twelve gentlemen now—only three beds empty—do a bit of work around the place; some planting the vegetable garden, some in the kitchen, or the laundry. Alice locks up the pantry at night, and I got a laundry system worked out, too, of course, only ain't any of 'em can use an iron worth a damn.

"I'll be honest, we've had a few bumps, but things are running like clockwork now—though I did have to show one fella the door on account of him getting drunk and falling down the front steps. Yep, they've got to follow the rules—no women, no alcohol, make their beds, and say grace before meals." Byrd nodded and Cy continued enthusiastically, "Couldn't hardly believe how May managed to get fifteen beds in a week. Dennis helped me bring them from the Madison Hotel. Can you get over it closing down? Been open long as I can recall, but you know how things is these days. Yes, sir. Poor devils, sleeping on the sidewalk and so many places out of business . . . Reckon I'm right lucky to land on my feet. Heh, heh. Anyway, Delphina and May mended all the sheets and towels so they're good as new. And you be sure to tell Hank what a good job he did, helping me stencil room numbers onto those little signs."

Byrd did not congratulate Cy or May for their resourcefulness, as she might have liked, but only nodded, frowning now and then as Cy babbled on. Upstairs, Cy introduced them to two tenants who were having cigarettes on the portico, explaining that he had forbidden smoking inside. In the upstairs bathroom, four razors lined the glass shelf above the sink. It occurred to May that she would hate to see four strange razors in her own bathroom. She would feel invaded. She imagined Byrd must feel the same, seeing his childhood home stripped now, housing a dozen strangers. Back downstairs, the tour continued. A long table on sawhorses was set up in the kitchen. Alice, who had cooked for the Craigs, smiled warmly when they came in, asking after the children. Byrd was quiet. May said, "Alice, Uncle Cy, thank you both for the tour. Byrd promised Hank he'd take him riding, so we'd best head on."

Byrd shook Cy's hand and said, "Looks like you're doing a fine job here, Cy. Tip-top."

Cy scratched beneath his chin. "I'll tell you what, I'm mighty grateful for a roof over my head and a job to do. I do 'preciate that. I aim to earn my keep."

Driving back to Keswick Farm, Byrd was silent. As they pulled in to park, May said, "Cy has worked hard over there." Her intuition told her that now was not the time to bring up the expansion of the candy business. Byrd's pride was smarting.

He shook his head. "The house will be ruined. Did you see how they're hanging dirty clothes all over the place?"

May did not answer, once again stifling what she really wanted to say.

What she was thinking was: *Would this have bothered you if it was happening at Keswick Farm instead? Because even though you haven't come out and said it, you think your home place is more important than mine because it's all you have left of your family. I understand that, but you made this decision on your own. You'll have to live with the consequences. Well, maybe I can make some decisions on my own, too, to do what I think is best, without asking you about it.*

Fifteen
DORRIT

Before Dorrit's first week in camp passed, the novelty had worn off. After the patriotic speeches and parades of The Fourth of July, Franklin Delano Roosevelt accepted the nomination of the Democratic Party on July 7. His stirring acceptance speech engendered new enthusiasm and strengthened resolve among the veterans.

> "I pledge you, I pledge myself, to a new deal for the American People. Let us all here assembled constitute ourselves prophets of a new order of competence and of courage. This is more than a political campaign; it is a call to arms. Give me your help, not to win votes alone, but to win in this crusade to restore America to its own people."

In Washington, veterans arrived full of enthusiasm and hope, and veterans departed discouraged and fatigued. The ration lines grew longer, and a summer cold made its way through the camp, shack by shack, and tent by tent.

Now, six weeks in, Dorrit felt only resignation.

On the morning of July 25, she awoke to a banging on the metal door of the shack. She rolled over, conscious of the hard ground beneath her.

She had not ceased missing her lumpy bed on Blossom Street. Roy went outside, and she heard him speaking with someone. When he came back, his face was grim. "What's happening, Pop?" she asked, pushing herself up.

Roy rubbed his palm over his stubbled cheek. "Police. They're going down the line, asking everybody to go back where we came from. The VA's offering a penny a mile toward train tickets." He sat down heavily on a crate, looking bewildered, and spoke into the air. "They're calling us tramps, in the newspaper. Nobody called us tramps in 1917 and 1918. Somebody's got to make something happen here." Dorrit rose and went to him, putting her hand on his shoulder. She did not tell him that she no longer nurtured hopes of a house and a canary. All she wanted was to go home.

"There's a rally at noon," Roy said. "I know you don't like crowds, but I want you there. It's important for the families to show up, for the government to see every single face." Dorrit swallowed. She had managed to avoid the larger gatherings—the crowds, shoulder to shoulder, shouting support while speakers went on and on until they were hoarse.

At noon, the beleaguered and bedraggled veterans, freshly insulted by the formalized request to withdraw, stood in sullen clumps, some holding dog-eared placards. Over the weeks they had settled into groups, by state, gathering under hand painted signs. Roy lifted Dorrit to stand on a low stone wall beside Nellie, who jostled a fussing Flora Mary against her chest. Sam stood on the sidewalk below with little Claude straddling his shoulders. Dorrit watched her father wind his way through the crowd, patting men on the back, nodding at others, stopping to stand with Charlie and a group from New England, near the front. The police commissioner, in his now-familiar khaki jodhpurs and well-polished black boots, began speaking through a megaphone, once again urging marchers to go home. When he paused, Charlie yelled back, "We ain't leaving, Glassford! We'll stay till '45!"

A murmur of uneasiness passed through the crowd. Dorrit stood on tiptoe watching, balancing with a hand on Sam's shoulder. With a red-faced roar, echoed by the veterans, Charlie hurled a brick toward the line of police. She watched her father's face contort as he hefted a stone, as if he absorbed the combined anger and hopelessness of the assembled men. As he pitched it forward, his uniform cap fell behind him. The veterans shouted, fists raised, as whistles shrilled. A black-uniformed line of police surged to meet them, billy clubs raised.

Dorrit called out, "Pop! No!" but her voice was lost in the fracas. All around her, people pressed close, and suddenly, she was nine years old again, lost in the parade crowd, her voice overwhelmed by horns and cheering. Her throat closed, her heart pounded. Nellie grasped her arm as she watched policemen surround her father and Charlie, pulling them away.

July 25

I was so scared today it made me dizzy. Here is what happened after the rally: Nellie and Sam walked me back to camp. On the way, I found a policeman and asked him what would happen to Pop. He said I should check the jails. Then I tried to telephone the police station, but they said Pop might not be processed yet, whatever that means. We have a little food left, but not much. Without a veteran's card, I can't get rations. And Pop has all of our money. Oh, I wish we had gone home after the vote!

A little while ago, Sam and Nellie came back to our shack. Sam said they are going home to Georgia. He gets a train ticket from the VA and the Red Cross is buying tickets for some of the women and children. Nellie started to cry and told me to stay with them until they leave, though there is hardly room in their shack for her family. I said no, that I needed to be where Pop could find me. I asked another policeman about Pop and he said I needed to ask the military police, only I haven't seen any. Tomorrow I might go to the Red Cross tent to ask if they can help me find him. I do not like staying here by myself.

July 28

As long as I have a light on I feel safe. Tonight is my fourth night alone. I need to write fast because the lantern is low on kerosene and the batteries in the flashlight are nearly gone. I have blocked off the door with a piece of wire and a board and placed my shears with Pop's heaviest wrench where I can reach them. My satchel is my pillow. Lumpy as it is, I am grateful for it on account of I don't believe I have ever been so tired in my whole life. I am hungry and the mosquitoes are terrible. The police came around today telling everyone to clear out, and they weren't so nice about it this time. I asked them about Pop but they said they couldn't help me. I thought he would be back by now. Most of the folks around our shack left this afternoon, but I need to wait till I find out where Pop is. I hope he is not hurt. The Salvation Army has taken their tent away. They will not be recruiting Dorrit Sykes.

Yesterday, I went to knock on the doors of some nice houses close by, but nobody would buy one of my beaded change purses. I believe that the people here in Washington are tired of us. One kind lady gave me a sandwich and a glass of milk. That got me through the day. She reminded me of Mrs. Frazier, and that made me homesick. Tomorrow I will go find General MacArthur myself, and ask him about Pop. The lamp is sputtering, so I had best turn it out.

The rattle of metal woke Dorrit. Alarm constricted her throat. Raising herself to her elbows, she reached for the flashlight and her father's wrench, calling, in a thin voice, "Pop? That you?" Sitting up, she switched on the light, looking around frantically, as if a back door might magically appear. "Pop?" this time, a pleading whisper. A strong smell of smoke hung in the air, along with another harsh, chemical odor. Clutching her nightgown, Dorrit peered out from the door, and her hand dropped to her side.

As far as she could see, Anacostia Flats was burning. In the distance, bands of soldiers resembled insects in their gas masks, their images wavering in the firelight, crisscrossed by the blaring white of searchlight beams. Wielding torches, they worked their way systematically down the lines of shacks and tents. Cardboard structures went up like fireworks. As Dorrit watched, a tent canvas flapped upward like flaming wings, then fluttered into bits of red ash. Army tanks crawled over the landscape, appearing and reappearing through columns of smoke. How long until the soldiers and tanks got to this shack?

Despite the heat, she trembled. The air burned her skin. The noise outside grew louder, nearer, as she struggled into a dress, unaware of the time or how long she had slept. Holding a handkerchief over her mouth and nose, she took a final glance around the shack. Taking up her satchel and her father's tools, she began walking carefully, looking out for live cinders and nails. Away from the bands of soldiers, away from the drifting, noxious brown smoke.

A shimmering, dirty-orange dawn illuminated the once-colorful printed cardboard walls of shacks, now faded after weeks of sun and rain. The familiar designs swirled and recombined as she watched. Around her were piles of rubbish, empty tin cans, scorched fire circles, and belongings abandoned in haste—a single man's shoe with a cracked sole, a baby carriage listing on one bent wheel, a stained mattress sprouting rusted springs. Where the sanitary units had been, metal frame poles outlined the standing porcelain toilets, lined up, incongruously, beside the water tanks, among the ashes. It was as if the world had ended, Dorrit thought, and she had missed the rapture. Her throat felt scorched; she began to sweat. From far away, soldiers shouted warnings: *Clear out! Move on!*

Flames rose from the camp in patches of orange while ash swirled in small funnels, mixing with dust then settling, like snow, into drifts. Dorrit stood, mesmerized by the hot snowflakes, falling from a July sky. Ahead, heat shimmered up from the ashes, and she continued onward, toward whatever God was planning to put in her path.

Sixteen
DORRIT

Fear is a thing with teeth and claws. It loomed close behind Dorrit as she walked away from the camp. It crouched behind her now as she wiped her burning eyes with her sleeve. She had a terrible, raw-throated thirst. She spit, then held her handkerchief over her streaming nose. By the time she reached a real paved street, the air was clearer and the sky was fully light. Setting down the toolbox, she sat on the curb, palms over her stinging eyes, rocking. It would not do to look back. Squinting, she peered down the street. A snub-nosed Army truck with thick wheels rumbled toward her. She pushed herself to stand, panic cutting through exhaustion.

But there was no place to hide.

Rummaging in her satchel, she clasped her sewing shears as the truck pulled alongside. The back end, she could see now, was canvas stretched over ribs, like a covered wagon. A soldier in a combat helmet leaned from the passenger side and said, "Little lady, we're taking stragglers to the Maryland line. Hop in back."

Dorrit stared up at him as if he were speaking a foreign language. He continued, "Gassed, huh?" He stepped out and when he reached for her arm she flinched away. "Come on, now," he said, cajolingly. "We've got orders. You can't stay here."

Beneath the canvas, men sat on long benches on either side. The idea of being shoved in among them froze Dorrit. One pulled down the bandanna covering his mouth and nose and called, "Greetings! My word, is that Miss Sykes?"

Dorrit recognized the professor's eyeglasses and his derby, but his voice came from a tunnel. When she tried to speak, only a croak came out. She swayed. The soldier caught her. "Whoa, there." He pushed her forward, and Bert pulled her up into the truck.

The man beside Bert scooted over to make room. His face was tanned, with white hair showing beneath the brim of the fedora he wore tilted back on his head. The professor guided Dorrit to sit and said, "Dynamite, this is Roy's girl. Give me your canteen." Dorrit sipped water, then the professor wet his bandanna and wiped Dorrit's eyes and face. "It's tear gas," he told her. "A noxious irritant of the worst sort. But I must say, quite efficacious. All of the camps are empty now." His voice became quiet, difficult to hear over the grinding of gears. "We're headed to the rail yard. My companion here is called Dynamite. He was a specialist in explosives, in the War, and the mines of Kentucky. He's rather hard of hearing." Bert spoke loudly, "Dynamite, this young lady belongs to Roy, from Boston. He was arrested, with Charlie." He turned back to Dorrit. His voice was soft and kind. "I heard what happened to your father." The man called Dynamite touched the brim of his hat.

Bert continued, "Listen, my dear, it isn't safe for you to be out here on your own. Come with us, at least as far as the rail yard. Perhaps we can find someone there, or at least a telephone, and try to find some information about your father." He cast a concerned glance to Dynamite, who nodded imperceptibly.

When they reached the rail yards, the three got out and the truck rumbled on. Dorrit did what Bert told her to do. Something in her had retreated, far inside. She only spoke when he asked her father's full name, and if she knew his serial number. When a military policeman approached carrying a rifle, Dorrit could hardly breathe. Bert spoke to the officer, standing tall and respectful, his hat in his hands. He then made telephone calls while Dorrit sat on a bench with her eyes closed. The stinging was not as bad. Bert returned, and after conferring with Dynamite, told her that her father was charged with assaulting a police officer and inciting a riot, and would be held until his trial. "Listen, missy," he said, "your father will be in for at least a month. Do you have any money?" Dorrit shook her head, trying to clear it. This was important; she needed to listen to what he was telling her.

"I sincerely wish we had funds to afford you a train ticket home, but we haven't. In all good conscience, I can't leave you here." Behind Bert, Dynamite scratched his head and twisted his mouth. Bert continued, "Now, my companion and I are heading south, with the intention of picking peaches in Georgia. The plan is to then work our way back north, in apple season. If you come with us, your father might be released by the time we return." At this, Dynamite leaned his head to the side, looking like he might interject, but Bert held up a finger. "If the idea of actually picking doesn't appeal, perhaps you could work as a sorter. The sorter sits on a stool and pulls out bruised fruit. You, my dear, could perform that task admirably, I should think." He smiled, but Dorrit did not respond. Dynamite nodded encouragingly.

Dorrit blinked, clutching her satchel, telling herself she must *think*. The address for the Church was in her notebook, but her eyes watered too much to read. *Euclid Street NW*, came to her, but where in the world was Euclid Street? Would anyone be at the Church at this time of day? The tools in her father's box were heavy. She had no money and no food. Her rational mind understood that she ought to leave this place, and there was little chance of her having a better offer than this one, from these kind men. "I don't want to slow you down," she said, finally. "But you're awfully kind. I'd be honored to travel with you gentlemen." Bert bowed, then held out his hand to help her stand.

Together they crossed over the tracks, where, behind a pair of abandoned boxcars, a rough camp had been set up. In the morning light, bedraggled men sat on folded army blankets, their hastily gathered belongings strewn around them, post-evacuation. As best she could tell, there were no women. Flames licked upward from an oil drum and a group stood around it, holding green sticks wrapped with biscuit dough above the rim, cooking what her father called a "doughboy." When Dynamite brought her a hunk of bread, she knew she ought to eat it, but swallowing the crust seemed impossible with her raw throat. She forced each mouthful down, chewing mechanically. "Thank you, sir," she said.

Dynamite slapped his knee. "Ha. Missy, I ain't been called 'sir' in a long, long while. Sounds right nice, but you can call me Dynamite." He opened his pack, then laid out his bedroll on a shaded spot of grass between two rusted flatbed cars. Bert sat on the ground, leaning back against a wheel, and pulled his pipe from his pocket. Dorrit sat close to him. The men talked over what they'd heard. A southbound freight train would be going through that afternoon at four thirty. Dynamite said he was going to look for supplies, and Dorrit squinted upward, studying the sky. Where would she be tomorrow afternoon, or the day after?

Bert shook out the small flame of his match, saying quietly, "You know, I have a niece about your age. You seem like a scrappy little thing, but you must be fatigued. Get some sleep. I'll be right here." Dorrit didn't answer but scooted down and arranged her satchel beneath her head. From the fireside, there were whoops and the sounds of a harmonica. Bert puffed his pipe, leaning back and stretching his legs out in front of him. The tobacco smelled of warm fruit. He said, "Do you know the story of *Little Dorrit?*" She shook her head. His voice was so gentle that she rolled over to face him, pillowing her fists beneath her cheek. A tear ran across her nose and dripped onto her wrist. Bert continued, "I was a great scholar of Charles Dickens, a long time ago. At least, it seems a long time." He blew out his breath, then altered his voice into that of a narrator. "So you see, in England, about a hundred years ago, there was a debtor's prison in the city of London, called the Marshalsea . . ." She focused on his comforting drone, and everything began to fade.

Dorrit started awake. She recognized the impatient clangor and huffing of a waiting train engine, its hot brakes shrieking. *A train.* She gasped, clenching her fists. *Only a train.*

Bert touched her shoulder. "Gather your things. If you need to . . . if you need to answer the call of nature, go back there." He waved toward one of the old boxcars. "There are no accommodations on the train. Meet us at the end of the line. Here, give me your bundle."

Dry-mouthed and woozy, Dorrit did as she was instructed then followed the train cars to the end, where Bert and Dynamite waited. Dynamite said, "Shouldn't be too crowded. Word is there'll be a couple of empty boxcars."

"How do you know that?" Dorrit asked, rubbing her swollen eyelids.

"Sympathetic engineers know folks are hoping for a ride," Bert said, "so they add a few empty cars. And sometimes, if fortune should shine upon us, the railroad detectives look the other way. They know we're down on our luck."

Dynamite helped her up into the boxcar and handed in the toolbox, saying, "This is a right heavy load for a little 'un."

Dorrit pulled the box close. "My pop's tools. He'd be upset if I left them behind."

As the train whistle blew, a dozen men scrambled aboard. Dorrit grasped the side of the door as the car lurched forward and swayed. Below, tracks clicked by. The train yard receded and hot air moved through the boxcar. She breathed it greedily, until the train gained speed and thick meal dust eddied upward from the floor, blowing into her irritated eyes, making her cough. Someone called, "Shut the damned doors!"

A lantern was lit, and a group began a poker game in the center of the car. Some of the men rolled up their jackets and lay facing the walls, pulling up collars and hunching their shoulders. Bert and Dorrit sat with their backs against the side panel, rocking with the motion of the train. After a while she ceased to be aware of the clacking; the noise subsided to a hum. Around the car, talking slowed, replaced with sounds of snoring. Bert leaned his chin on his chest and slept. Dorrit sat stiffly, now fully awake. The car smelled of men, and of grain. On her other side, Dynamite began speaking quietly. She focused on his deep, calm voice, blocking out the flashes of destruction that made her twitch.

"Now that you're riding the rails," he said, "might do you well to learn the rules, so to speak. You know the difference between a tramp and a hobo?"

"Tell me," Dorrit said, her voice barely a whisper.

"You got to speak up, on account of I don't hear so good. See, some folks see a man down on his luck, out of work, maybe a little out at the elbow, and think we're all the same. Amongst ourselves, we have a code, so to speak. A hobo's a man traveling to look for work. I, myself, am a hobo." He pointed to his chest. "Though, truth be told, I like to think of myself as a traveling adventurer. I'm always willing to do odd jobs and—don't get me wrong—I'd like a steady situation.

"A tramp—as called by us gentlemen of the road—travels too, only they're looking for handouts, not work. Then, there's bums. Bums are the poor souls who've given up, in my experience. Drinkers, most of 'em."

Dorrit raised her voice. "Dynamite?"

"Hmm?"

"The professor, which is he?"

Dynamite squinted in the dimness and pulled up his mouth on one side. "Well, the professor. He's a special case, you might say. He does favor a snort. One night in camp, he got tight and told me 'bout his life. It was right sad. Seems he lost his wife and two boys in a automobile crash. Since then he's been on the bottle, heavy. Lost his position at the college 'cause of it. Told me he don't even know why he came on the March." Dynamite was quiet for a beat, then continued with a sigh. "Says he's got nobody to go home to. I know that feeling. You wouldn't know it to look at me now, but I used to have a wife and a little house in Bell County, Kentucky. I worked at the Pioneer Mine, in Kettle Island. We got by all right, until the big explosion. That was in '30. Lost my hearing and sixteen friends that day." He was quiet for another moment. "After that, I couldn't set another charge. My hands shook too bad." He held his hands out in front of him and turned them over slowly. "My wife went to live with her sister."

Dorrit shifted to face him and asked, "How long have you been traveling?"

He leaned close to hear her, cupping his ear. "Year and a half," he said, "and I tell you what, it gets right wearying. 'Fore I came to Washington I was in Canton, Ohio. I'd been going house to house, asking polite-as-you-please did folks have some yard work needed doing. Got run off every time. Then, finally, I come upon a house. Had this mark on the fence out front." He traced a design in the air. "A nice widow lady gave me a pair of her husband's shoes and this hat." He took off his fedora, which had moth holes in the brim. He held it out. "Look inside there. See that label? From Brooks Brothers. In New York City. Can you beat that? I spent the afternoon raking leaves in that lady's yard, then she give me two bits and wrapped up a big ham sandwich for me. I b'lieve that was the best sandwich I ever had." He paused, smacking his lips. "And *that*, well, that's the hardest thing. Never have got used to being hungry—to not knowing when I'll eat next. Nobody does."

"What did you mean, about her fence being marked?"

"Well, now, this is something else you ought to know. See, if a hobo goes to a house and the folks there are kind, he'll leave a mark on the fence, like this," Dynamite traced a shape in the dust that resembled a cat. "If they'll give food there, the mark looks like a slanted *T*. If it's a cross, they'll give food, but you got to listen to some preaching first. If the people of that house'll turn you away, you leave a different mark, and a different one if they'll give money. Ha. Not many of those, b'lieve me. If I see a house is marked that they'll send us away, I just keep walking, till I find a house with a good mark. Same with hobo jungles. Some of 'em have a secret way in and out. Looks like this . . ." Using his finger, he drew more shapes on the floor, resembling sideways horseshoes. "'Cause if the bulls—that's what we call the railroad guards—find a camp, they don't ask no questions. They'll burn it out and beat anybody tries to stay."

"I don't think I can remember all those signs," Dorrit said.

"Sure, you can, once you see 'em a few times. They's about twenty different ones."

"Have you picked peaches before, Dynamite?"

"Yup. Might just stay down there again. It'd be good to be down south when the weather turns." He scratched his head beneath his hat.

Dorrit's shoulders began to bump gently against his. Someone opened one of the doors, briefly, and a hot breeze blew through. Fields of tall corn flashed by, and pastures of cows. Occasionally a farmhouse or a red barn was visible, with green mountains behind. A pair of colts romped in a paddock. A double row of gray, skeletal trees passed, then a flash of a picturesque white farmhouse with dark shutters. Dynamite continued to talk about his little house in Kentucky until Dorrit's head fell onto his shoulder and she slept again.

Seventeen
DORRIT

JULY 1932

It seemed like Dorrit had just shut her eyes when the train whistle began to blow. She woke with a jolt, disoriented, feeling as if her joints had been shaken loose. Her lips stung when she ran her tongue over them. As the train began to slow the whistle blew again and someone called, "Danville!"

Light streamed in with fresh morning air. Men swung from the door frame, hanging over the tracks as the train slowed. Dynamite winked and said, "You need to go behind the bushes, this is the place to do it. Train'll start up again in about fifteen minutes. I'll watch your tool-box, but if you're on your own, always take your belongings with you." Before the train came to a full stop, men were jumping from the car, jogging toward the underbrush. Bert helped Dorrit down. Two men climbed down from the roof of the car, windblown and deeply tanned. A line quickly formed beside a water hose as men took turns dousing their heads or filling bottles or canteens. The adjoining shed was painted with an advertisement for chewing tobacco. Near the ground beside the door a symbol was marked in white chalk: "XOX," topped with a squiggled line.

Dorrit made her way over the gravel of the sloping track bed. Pushing through a thicket, she found a man squatting, trousers around his ankles. She backed out, mortified, and continued to a gray shed farther up the track. Behind it, she lowered herself, leaning against the side of the shed, looking left then right, back and forth, prepared to yank up her drawers if anyone came.

Oh. The rust of monthly blood stained her drawers. "Damn," she said out loud. "That just beats all." At least it had not soaked through her dress. From her satchel, she took a strip of fabric. Peering around the corner, she hastily rolled a pad, wishing for a proper bathroom, or even a bucket of water. The train whistle tooted. As she put her clothes to rights, she muttered, "Hold your horses!"

Rounding the corner of the shed, the whistle tooted again with the loud grinding of gears. The wheels lurched forward and Dorrit froze for an instant, and then began to run. Dynamite leaned from the last boxcar, peering up and down the track. When Dorrit waved, he jumped down and jogged toward her, scooping her up. He passed her into the car to Bert, who knelt beside the door. As the train gained momentum, two men grabbed Dynamite's arms, swinging him inside with a whoop of triumph. He landed with a huff, then dusted his knees as he rose. He saluted the men who had pulled him in.

"Damnation, gal," he said, his breath heaving, "don't go so far next time."

Dorrit was as winded as he was. With a hand on her throat, she breathed a grateful thank you. As she settled back into her spot beside Bert, she felt a delayed flash of panic. She could have been left behind. She *would* have been left behind, save for Dynamite's kindness. In the car, there were more men than before. A pair argued over a place by the door, one indignantly claiming that it had been his spot since Baltimore. Listening to the men argue she leaned, slightly, against the professor. To Dynamite she said, "What does this mean?" She drew the mark she had seen on the pump shed.

"Means the water is clean. If the wavy line is in between two straight lines, like this," He drew another symbol. ". . . means the water's bad."

Bert opened his pack and brought out a box of saltine crackers. He unwrapped greasy brown paper from a link of sausage, sawing at it with his pocket knife, then offering chunks from the knifepoint.

"I don't have anything to contribute," Dorrit said. "My pop has our ration tickets and money. I'm sorry. But I have some things I can sell."

"Not to worry," Bert said, chewing a slab of sausage. "Not to worry. Maybe tonight we'll camp somewhere near a farm and we can acquire a few eggs, or some corn. I fancy some roasted corn."

Dorrit chewed a bite of sausage, spicier than she was used to. A peppercorn made her eyes water. Discreetly, she pried it from her teeth. Dynamite rummaged in his pocket, then tore open a candy bar. He carefully broke it into three equal pieces then said, "Help yourself, missy." The aroma of peanuts made her mouth water. He said, "Pearson's Salted Nut Roll. Good to know about. A good product and a good value." He held up the wrapper. "One of these can keep a body going the better part of the day."

Sweet and salty flavors mingled in Dorrit's mouth. She said, "Professor Purvis, would you tell me some more of *Little Dorrit*, please? What happened after they got to Italy?"

Bert waved his pocketknife in enthusiastic emphasis. "Ah, well. That's when things get interesting, and the villain Blandois makes another appearance."

Early the next morning, at Gastonia, North Carolina, the three travelers left the boxcar. Dynamite explained that the train was heading west, and they needed to wait for a southbound. They hid their belongings behind a clump of shrubs beside a creek, and Dorrit was able to wash in the cold water. The campsite was littered with empty tin cans and mason jars, but there was a nice fire circle and the fragrant grass was soft. Bert caught a dozen crayfish, then boiled them in a coffee can over the fire. Dynamite came back from a foraging expedition with corn tassels hanging from the voluminous pockets of his overcoat. He showed Dorrit how to soak the ears in the creek until the husks were saturated. As the corn steamed over the coals, they took turns describing the best meal they had ever eaten. It stayed light until after nine, and Dorrit leaned against the trunk of a tree and opened her notebook. She used a fresh page to copy out the hobo signs Dynamite taught her, then wrote until the light faded to blue-black.

A KIND LADY LIVES HERE	GOOD WATER	BAD WATER
GOOD PLACE FOR A HANDOUT	RELIGIOUS TALK HERE	THIS WAY IN
THIS WAY OUT	DANGEROUS NEIGHBORHOOD	YOU WILL GET CURSED AT HERE

July 30?

   Gastonia, North Carolina. So now, I am riding the rails with two traveling adventurers, heading south to be a peach sorter. If anyone ever asked me what I wanted to be when I grew up I would not have said a peach sorter. I suppose I could now call myself a girl hobo.

   This afternoon we found three houses in Gastonia with friendly marks on their fences. The boys hid (I've taken to calling them boys although I believe they must both be over forty years of age) while I rang the bell and asked if the lady of the house would like to buy a beaded change purse. I imagine I looked pretty pitiful. I made three dollars, and only one of the ladies actually kept the change purse! One nice woman let me use her washroom after I told her I'd been at the March. The sink was so clean and white, I let the hot water run and run . . . After I told her how pretty her little rose-shaped bars of soap were, she gave me two of them! (Well, she had a whole jarful.) I confess that I stole some of her toilet paper. Nancy Drew would have done the same thing, I feel sure.

   Now we are back at camp. I bought us a bag of cornmeal and a

*half-pound of butter, and some sanitary pads for myself. Dynamite
says that at the Methodist Church Hall they gave him a pair of trousers and an almost brand-new shirt! I hemmed the trousers for him,
as they were far too long. He is most grateful and says he believes he
looks like quite the swell gent. The Professor says he used to have sev-
enteen neckties. He has somehow got himself a full jar of moonshine.
Today I watched a hawk get a rabbit. I did not know that rabbits
could scream.*

*I believe I have gotten used to sleeping rough. I suppose a person
can get used to most anything if needs must. But I am fretting about
Pop and I imagine he is fretting about me. When I stop to think about
it, I do not know what would have become of me if I had not found
the professor. I suppose that sometimes God puts people into our paths
who will help us on our way. I miss Pop, and I miss home, and Mrs.
Coughlin and the pigeons, and Ma and even Walt. But now I am
learning to take care of myself. I have two dollars left. Tomorrow we
hope to head for Georgia. The bullfrogs are singing now.*

*PS Saw four bluebirds today. I believe I think they are the prettiest
of all.*

At seven thirty the next morning, Dorrit waited in the woods near the
tracks with the professor and Dynamite as a freight train pulled in. From
two boxcars on the end, dozens of men dropped onto the siding, dispers-
ing quickly into the trees.

"Greetings." Bert said to a passing man, "Did you come from Washington, by chance?"

The man scowled. "Men are leaving DC in droves—lots of 'em heading south. All the trains is packed. Bet there was a hunnerd men in each of
those cars, and twenty more on the roof. Spare a cigarette, friend?"

Dynamite fished his tobacco pouch from his coat, offering a hand-rolled
cigarette. "What time's it heading out? You know?" He offered a match.

The man inhaled deeply then picked a fleck of tobacco from his lip. "Engine's broke down. Putting up for repairs. No telling when the next one'll pass through. *Hell* of a—sorry little lady—" He doffed his hat toward Dorrit. "Heck of a lot of angry men on that train. Every one of us left Washington empty-handed."

Dorrit tugged the man's sleeve, saying, "Mister, did you happen to hear about any of the men who were arrested?"

"Things got right wild that last day, what with the fires, and everybody bailing out. I did hear that a baby died from the gas." He shook his head slowly. "Y'all know of a campsite 'round here?"

Late in the afternoon, word circulated through camp that a train would come through at one in the morning. When it stopped, flashlight beams began to waver down the embankment as railroad detectives with rifles and German shepherd dogs patrolled the tracks beside the steaming train, the whining dogs straining at thick leather leashes, tantalized by the scents of a hundred men hiding in the woods nearby. Not one man managed to get on the train. They all straggled back to camp in the dark, a frustrated mass.

In the crowded camp, gloom settled like a fog. The fire was rekindled and mason jars and flasks circulated. Grumbling was punctuated by the sounds of broken glass and angry shouts. When the rain started, Dorrit and Dynamite crawled beneath a thicket of flowering shrubs and held a tarp over their heads. Bert stayed, drinking with the men around the fire. The patter of the heavy drops sounded like someone hitting a tin can with a screwdriver, over and over. In blue flashes of lightning, the surrounding trees took on a spectral quality, and by morning the creek bank was a slick of clay-orange mud. As the sun rose higher, steam wafted up through loam in ghostly trails and the day promised to be hot and humid. Dirty, exhausted-looking men of all ages wrung out shirts or shaved in the creek, many with liquor-bleary eyes. Some brewed coffee, squatting on their haunches, drying their clothes on green sticks. Close by, Bert lay prone on the ground, an arm thrown over his eyes. Dynamite nudged him with the toe of his boot. "Hey, Professor."

Bert squinted with a pained expression. "Umphh?"

"Professor?" Dorrit whispered, "Are you unwell?" Her concern turned quickly to disappointment. She knew that sour smell.

Dynamite turned his head and spit. "Hungover." He prodded Bert again. "Listen, missy and me gonna head to town—try to beat this crowd and find some supplies. You coming?"

"Numph. Bilious." Bert smacked his lips, moving his hat to cover his eyes.

When a southbound train came through at midafternoon with no guards visible, Dynamite and Dorrit ferried their belongings up to the tracks, stashing them at the edge of the woods before returning for the professor, who had started back at his corn liquor while they'd been in town. Dynamite climbed into a boxcar, and with Dorrit below urging him on, two men helped push Bert up and inside. Dynamite led him, stumbling and groaning, to the rear of the car. Dorrit shouldered her satchel and went to retrieve the toolbox, as men continued to hurry toward the open car, tossing packs in ahead of them. As she neared the clump of ivy where the box was hidden, a man in a straw hat passed and looked down, then with a furtive glance left and right, snatched up the toolbox and started toward the train.

"Hey, mister!" Dorrit's voice was drowned out by the whining din of iron. "Mister, that's mine!" He tossed his bindle into the boxcar as she caught up and yanked his sleeve. "Those are my pop's tools!" She waved, trying to get Dynamite's attention. The whistle tooted twice, and the brakes hissed in anticipation of departure.

The man jerked his arm away, saying, "Get lost, kid."

The vibrating train lurched backward with a jerk, then forward. A lanky, dark-skinned man in faded overalls knelt at the doorway, reaching toward Dorrit, calling, "C'mon, miss! Give me your hand." The thief pushed Dorrit backward, then slid the toolbox into the car while the man in overalls watched, frowning in apparent consternation. As the thief pulled himself inside and gained his balance, the boxcar door began to slide closed. With a small salute to Dorrit, the man in overalls gave a shove, and the toolbox slid back out the door.

Dorrit fell backward, her legs swinging up in front of her. Helplessly, she watched the toolbox roll, opening as it tumbled, showering the embankment with its contents. She raised herself unsteadily to her elbows and watched the train grow smaller in the distance, shimmering in the heat. She wondered when Dynamite would realize she was not onboard. Despite her predicament she had to smile, thinking of her unknown accomplice, grateful for his sense of samaritan justice.

She pushed herself to stand and realized her lip was bleeding. "Well, dammit to Hell," she said, matter-of-factly. Swearing, she was finding, was really rather satisfying. "So much for sorting peaches," she said, to no one. Trudging along the embankment, she wiped her mouth as she gathered a wrench here, a screwdriver there, then finally, the battered box itself. Wedged into the bottom was a cream-colored envelope. A return address was printed in blue script: *Acme Pest Control Corporation, Columbus, Ohio.* Forgetting her lip, she unfolded the typewritten letter inside and read:

June 6, 1932

Dear Mr. Sykes,

Thank you for submitting your plan for consideration by the Acme Pest Control Corporation. After careful review, our directors feel that your trap design would be impractical to manufacture. Additionally, odor control and decontamination issues are not effectively addressed in your current design. Wishing you all the best in your future endeavors.

Sincerely,
George S. Puttworth,
Vice President

Dorrit swallowed, coloring in sympathetic disappointment for her father. His dream was ruined. The letter had arrived just before they left home. Why had he not told her? She sank down to the bank and considered first the letter, then the empty train track. She had no earthly idea of what to do next. She didn't even know which direction to walk. She began to cry, her breath heaving.

Twigs snapped behind her. Holding out a screwdriver, she turned, snuffling. A freckled boy with shaggy brown hair came out of the woods and stood in the tall weeds, rubbing his face. His brown trousers were out at the knee and far too large, secured around his thin waist with a length of rope. He wore a corduroy cap and a man's suit vest over a chambray shirt. "Train gone?" He said, "Damn. I was asleep."

Dorrit eyed him with suspicion, still holding the screwdriver, point outward. "It left," she said, only it came out sounding like, *dit deft.*

He scoffed, "You think I'm going to hurt you or something? I'm so hungry I can barely walk. How'd you get a bloody lip?" Dorrit lowered the screwdriver and wiped her mouth again.

The boy came closer. "What 'r you called, girl?"

"Dorrit."

"Clarence." He squatted on his haunches. "Got any food?"

Dorrit shook her head. "You're about the skinniest person I ever saw. How old are you?"

"Eighteen."

"*Pfft.*" Dorrit smirked. "You are not, either. Criminy." She stood, tugging her dress in place.

"Sixteen." He flushed and looked down.

"Well, Clarence, if you carry this toolbox to town for me, I might get you something to eat. Fetch that hammer up there, by the tracks. Look for bolts too."

"You ain't the boss of me."

"That's the deal. You carry the toolbox, we'll get some food. Take it or leave it. I've got to adapt to circumstances." Dorrit blew out her breath and stood, then sorted the tools in the box, keeping the screwdriver tucked into her waistband.

Clarence collected the hammer and a wrench and passed them to her. "They's some nice tools you got there."

"My pop's," Dorrit said, closing the top and latching it.

"Where's he?"

Dorrit hesitated, resting her hand on the screwdriver. "Jail. Violence and terrible short tempers run in our family. Come on, it's a walk to town."

"I can get us a ride, I bet."

"How?"

"Watch and learn. Watch and learn," Clarence said. Dorrit decided he was full of himself and had no right to be.

Outside the Gastonia station, they each took a long drink from a hose. Clarence removed his hat and scrubbed at his face with his hands, then slicked back his hair. He said, "First thing—it's important to look clean. Your mouth is still bleeding a little." As she wiped her face, he told her what to say.

They crossed the parking area and approached a well-dressed man as he was getting into a Model T Ford. Begging the man's pardon, Clarence clutched his cap to his chest, telling how he had come on the train from Birmingham with his sister, to visit their elderly aunt. Then he said that the aunt was a bit dotty, and must have forgotten that they were arriving, that they had been waiting since morning, and might he give them a ride to town?

By four o'clock Dorrit was back knocking on the front door of the kind lady with the rose-shaped soaps while Clarence stood by the gate, clutching his cap and looking earnest.

When the door opened, the woman scowled at both of them, arms crossed over her chest, with one eyebrow raised at an impressive angle. A black hairnet covered tightly wound pin curls. "What do you want, you little tramps? Come back to steal something else? Honestly, it just doesn't pay to be kind to your lot." She began to close the door.

"Ma'am?" Dorrit blushed furiously, thinking of the half-roll of toilet paper she had taken. There were two more full rolls under the chintz sink skirt, she had checked. *ScotTissue*, the wrappers said, *Petal soft. Luxury texture!* Who could resist? In desperation, Dorrit dropped her satchel heavily on the stoop and clasped her hands. "Ma'am, please, we were separated from our traveling companions and I'm in a bad way."

The woman squinted, shading her eyes with her hand to scan the street. "My foot! Those thieving hoodlums are probably hiding in my bushes right now. Took my husband's trousers and his new shirt right off the clothesline. Bold as brass, I tell you! And here I was, kind enough to invite you into my home. That's a wicked trick to play on a good Christian soul. *Wicked!* You ought to be ashamed of yourself." She flipped her hand dismissively. "Now get away from here before I telephone the sheriff. Go on!" The door slammed. As Dorrit let herself out at the gate she noticed that the charcoal mark on the fence had been rubbed out and replaced, with a row of six short vertical lines, bisected by one long diagonal one: *You'll get cursed out here.*

Eighteen
MAY

On a Thursday morning in early August, May stood in the driveway at Keswick Farm, listening to the retreating whistle of the eastbound passenger train—the train she had expected to be on at that moment. She wanted to cry in frustration, but she would not, not in front of Dennis. That would be childish and, well, she just couldn't. She cleared her throat and stood up straight. Dennis stood beside the Studebaker, looking discomfited. "So," she said, forcing a smile, "looks like I'll be getting the 11:15 now. I'd better telephone Elsie. Can we leave at eleven?"

Dennis nodded slowly, then walked toward the canning building. May blew out a slow breath. Determined not to snap at anyone, she trudged up the porch steps. She had been ready to leave on time but Hank clung to her knees, wailing, then Sister tripped over the dog, and when May picked her up, the toddler spit up down the back of her dress. By the time Delphina sponged May's back it was already past time to leave and then the car wouldn't start.

When Elsie had telephoned the week before, inviting May for a girls' trip to her family's house on the Rappahannock River, May had at first said no. The farm was in the throes of berry season, and there was no one to help Delphina with the children. Elsie said, "Listen, hon, the world will not come to a screeching halt if you get away for a couple of days. I'm talking about three little tiny days! We can go swimming, and sleep late, and stay in our pajamas drinking gin and tonics all day if we want to. And the river is so nice and breezy . . ."

May had listened and sighed, fondly remembering an autumn college weekend at the Carters' river house, Elsie's nervous mother chaperoning a gaggle of flighty girls, with raucous boys from Hampden-Sydney and the University crowded into the attic bunkroom.

Still, May said no, attempting to placate Elsie with a vague commitment to go sometime in the fall. After she'd hung up, Delphina asked about the call then encouraged—actually commanded—May to go, insisting that she could take care of Henry and the children. She would sleep on the bed in the parlor, which had somehow never been returned upstairs. It would be good for them all, Delphina had said. So May called back and said yes, she would arrive on Thursday.

At 11:10, with no further mishaps, she was at the Keswick station. Dennis carried her bag to the platform and saluted her with a grin that said, *Enjoy yourself, for a change. We'll be fine.* May bought her ticket to Richmond then made her way through the train to the last car. The conductor hefted her suitcase to the rack, and she placed her handbag on the empty seat beside hers, along with two boxes of candy for Elsie. She kept her sunglasses on and after taking her seat she opened her copy of *Delineator* magazine, holding it in front of her face, trying to project, in the universal nonvocal signals of travelers, that neither company nor chitchat were desired, because the solitude of a young mother is a precious thing.

Delphina was right. A visit with Elsie was exactly what she needed. May had packed her favorite old, ratty nightgown—the one she never let Byrd see her in—and some older, comfortable clothes, along with a bottle of applejack. Now, she would arrive hours later than she planned. *Oh well, adapt to the circumstances,* she told herself. *A delay doesn't ruin the trip.* Discreetly, she tried to sniff the fabric of her dress to see if it still smelled sour. After a few minutes, she became immersed in the sixth installment of an Edith Wharton novel that was featured in the magazine. The heroine, called Halo, seemed to May to be vapid and self-absorbed. While her long-suffering husband indulged her, begging for her return, she continued to fancy herself the irreplaceable muse of an even more self-absorbed, philandering novelist. Did this woman—this Halo—ever have to think about making payroll, or a toddler's teething? But of course, no one would want to read about the dull life of May Craig. Not when they could follow Halo Tarrant to the south of France. May closed the magazine, having lost patience with the heroine.

An abandoned newspaper on the seat beside her caught her eye. It was dated July 29.

> Reports are pouring in from Washington about the events of yes-terday and last evening. President Hoover issued a public state-ment this morning, saying 'A challenge to the authority of the United States Government has been met, swiftly and firmly.'
>
> Yesterday afternoon, backed by a battalion of light tanks, Gen-eral Douglas MacArthur led a parade of cavalry down Pennsylvania Avenue. Ahead of the parade, riding the blue motorcycle that has come to identify him, General Pelham Glassford led Washington police, canvassing the unsanitary and illegal camps, allowing the marchers twenty minutes to clear out. As the day wore on, bedlam ensued, with the military using tear gas and torches to clear the camps. There is an unconfirmed report of an infant having suc-cumbed to the gas . . .

A grainy photograph showed General MacArthur in his uniform, stand-ing on Pennsylvania Avenue. An army tank was visible behind him. Another photo showed a group of ragged-looking men covering their faces with their arms, trying to escape the tear gas grenades being thrown by mask-clad sol-diers. *How could this happen?* May wondered. *How could the President have the power to order something like this? Where would these thousands of men go? And what about the women and children?* She had heard on the radio that the army was trucking the displaced veterans out of Washington, dropping them just over the borders in Maryland and Virginia. Byrd had told her about the marchers in the city and about the vote. She had feared he might be caught up in the violence.

The train's whistle blew as it pulled into a station. Passengers departed and boarded, and May hoped no one would take the seat beside her. Her holiday mood had darkened. Outside, on the platform, a man in a dusty suit held a crate of oranges with a sign tacked to it: *No job, no prospects, four children. Buy an orange! 5¢.* At his feet, a thin little girl in a dirty dress sat, her eyes vacant as she licked the empty waxed paper wrapper of a candy bar. The whistle blew again and May rose, wrestling with the window latch. As the train pulled out, the pane finally dropped. She clasped a dollar, but it was too late to hold it out. With a pang of sympathy, she watched the man and the little girl grow smaller and smaller.

She fell back into her seat and folded the bill. *A dollar. A dollar won't go far. People need work, and food, and a feeling of purpose.* She needed to make the all-day candy bar work.

When the train pulled in to Richmond, she hurried to gather her belongings. Outside the station, she scanned the waiting automobiles for Elsie's roadster. A sad-faced man in a limp cloth cap approached, asking for a nickel. May said, "You look like you've had a hard time."

"Yes'm. Sure have. I was up in Washington, at the March."

May put down her suitcase and held out the dollar and one of the candy boxes. "Here. This isn't much."

The man's eyes lit up. "Bless you, ma'am. This'll last me all day and then some." They turned in unison toward the sound of screeching automobile tires. May wished the man a good day and hurried down the steps.

Elsie had stopped in the center of the pick-up area. She jumped out of her car and ran around the side, arms wide, while behind her another car tooted its horn. They hugged and Elsie kissed May's cheek. "Gawd, honey. So glad you're here!"

Minutes later, Elsie roared up in front of one of the largest brick houses on River Road, bumping a tire over the front walk before veering back onto the gravel. She stomped the brakes, muttering, "Dammit!" with her cigarette holder clenched between her teeth as her cocker spaniel, Pudding, slid from the front seat to the floor with a whimper.

May gasped, bracing herself against the dashboard. The dog blinked up at her with a limpid, resigned gaze, as if to say, *Believe me, toots, this is nothing.* On the walkway, May glanced back, noting dents in the car's pale-yellow paint.

Elsie bustled ahead, stopping to lean over a boxwood bush by the front steps. She rooted around then stood with a look of triumph, holding aloft a square wicker basket. Inside, something clanked heavily. She said, "Archie's bootlegger leaves the hooch behind this bush. He's also the milkman, so I leave the money with the empty bottles every week. I don't know how he does it, but he still gets the good stuff."

Inside, a petite, uniformed maid greeted May warmly, saying, "Miss May, it sure is nice to have you back. Lunch will be in ten minutes. I set the table in the sunroom, if that suits?"

"Fine, thank you, Minerva." Elsie passed Minerva the basket, saying to May, "Come on out here."

The Nelson house was furnished mostly with family antiques. From the hallway, with its nine-foot-tall grandfather's clock and sweeping staircase, they passed into a long parlor with an ebony grand piano at one end. Ignoring the Georgian architecture, Elsie had recently redecorated the room in the Modern style, with chrome-and-glass tables and geometric-patterned fabrics in shades of gray and copper. The original mantelpiece had been replaced with something industrial-looking with steel grillwork. A broad window seat behind the piano faced out onto a well-maintained garden. Beyond the parlor, the sunroom was bright, lit from a row of arched windows. There, the decor was traditional and feminine, with ruffle-skirted chintz armchairs grouped at either end. Wicker planters held begonias and a pair of bright-green parakeets lived in a wirework cage the size of a doghouse.

May took in all the details, saying, "I haven't been here since you redecorated. It's quite spectacular." Small flashes of envy twisted into silent, sour judgments: *really, she's ruined the architecture of that room. That mantel is just ostentatious.* She stepped over a miniature train set spread over the carpet, inquiring, "How are your boys?" *And honestly, do children need all of these toys?*

Elsie's tone was indulgent. "The little monsters." She tapped her ash into a crystal ashtray. "They've been following the Summer Olympics every day. Last week Bertie asked little Arch to teach him to roller skate. So Arch put him in his skates and tied him to the clothesline in the basement, then he hooked the dog's lead to the skates. Luckily, Minerva went down to start a load of wash, or poor Bertie would've been whipped against the wall and popped like a water balloon. Little Arch said they were starting a new Olympic event. And yesterday, Nanny caught Francis pissing into the third-floor laundry chute! He said Arch does it all the time and taught him how, then he confessed that Arch offered him a nickel to jump through the chute and land in a pile of sheets, three floors down. Ah, here's luncheon. I'm absolutely famished."

Minerva rolled in a wheeled tray, and Elsie and May sat at a small wicker table beneath hanging ferns. Minerva served small triangles of cucumber sandwiches. Next came delicate porcelain bowls of crab bisque with small, flaky biscuits. May spooned her soup, savoring its creaminess, determined to put aside her envy and enjoy the experience for what it was: lunch with her best friend. Below the table, Pudding's chin rested on her foot. This was so civilized. Everything polished and starched, and spotless, even the birdcage.

Elsie tapped her wristwatch as Minerva cleared. "Listen, we'd best hit the road before the monsters get back from swimming lessons. Minerva! Bring down my grip, please, and ask Britton to put the hamper in the car. Come along, Pudding." The dog's ears went back.

Elsie's gardener loaded their bags, along with a hamper of food and a wicker traveling bar. May tied on a scarf then settled the dog beside her, discreetly holding him close. As the convertible lurched off down the driveway she chided herself again, silently, for her critical thoughts. Things had always been this way for Elsie. It wasn't *her* fault. The economic downturn seemed not to have fazed her in the least.

May remembered their first meeting.

It was September 1923. May had been standing in their second-floor dormitory room at Mary Baldwin College, having just arrived for the first time. Her father had driven her in the farm truck, then left her suitcase and three fruit crates of belongings stacked in the hall outside the door. May feared it might be rude, having been the first roommate to arrive, to claim a particular bed or closet, so she waited. When a uniformed chauffeur struggled, panting, up the steps bearing a steamer trunk and then deposited it in the middle of the room's floor, May had offered him a shy smile. As he mopped his brow, she studied the trunk's fine brass fittings and leather straps and the monogram, in gilt letters: ECC. The chauffeur made four more trips, delivering two more trunks and then a train case and several hat boxes, all matching, all monogrammed. May was beginning to perspire. Who *was* this ECC? Who matched this exquisite luggage? She went to the window. Below, a sleek, sky-blue convertible with white upholstery was parked illegally in front of the dormitory doors. A tall, solid-looking young woman in dark sunglasses and a cloche gestured broadly to the chauffeur as he climbed into the driver's seat. The house mother stood nearby, hands on hips, and from what May could tell, she was chastising the man for having driven over the lawn. The young woman threw her hands into the air dramatically, as if to say, *well, it's done now, isn't it?* She waved off the house mother and tossed one end of her long scarf over her shoulder as she flounced toward the front door. A minute later, a booming, throaty voice echoed up the stairwell. May swallowed and went to stand beside the door, her clammy hands clasped in front of her. ECC strode down the hall, scowling at the numbers on each door, calling out, "Where the hell's room twenty-two, for chrissakes? And where can a gal have a smoke around here?" She stopped in front of May, studiously assessing her before raising her sunglasses and smiling broadly, displaying dimples and slightly buck teeth. Clapping May on the shoulder, she said, "Well, hiya, toots. Name's Elsie. Elsie Carter. And you're cute as a bug. I think we'll be great pals."

It was after five when they arrived at the river house. Windblown and slightly sunburned, May shook out her hair, grateful to have made it in one piece. Pudding bounded from the car and down the rolling lawn, racing toward the water. Afternoon light glinted golden across the Rappahannock River and the dog stood at the end of the long dock, barking furiously at a quartet of mallards, bobbing in the water below him.

"Help me put the top up?" Elsie said, looking skyward, "Looks like we might be in for some weather." The house was of old, pink-orange brick, with a slate roof. At the door of the English basement, Elsie wrestled an iron key in the lock. Mounted beside the door, a brass plaque said *Carter House, 1750*. Inside, low beams crossed the kitchen ceiling. The wide fireplace and brick floor smelled of old soot and damp. Upstairs, threadbare oriental rugs covered wide-planked pine floors. May pulled open the windows, pausing to look through the wavy old panes toward the water. A line of dark clouds pushed toward the river from the west and in the freshening wind cattails bowed as a rowboat rocked, tethered to the dock. Inside, dust sheets rose and fell in the breeze like sighing ghosts. *A thunderstorm would be perfect*, May thought.

From down the hall, she heard Elsie call for Pudding to come inside. Brimming with canine self-importance, he shook himself thoroughly before commencing a systematic search for mice. Elsie came in behind him, saying, "Would you look at that, it's cocktail hour! We'll unpack later. It's just us chickens, right?" She held up the traveling bar basket and the food hamper like trophies. "Tomorrow night, we'll go for oysters. I had Cook pack us a roast chicken for tonight. Hope that's all right. I sure as hell am not going to inflict my cooking on you. Gawd, remember the fire in Domestic Science class? I mean the big one—when the curtains went up?" She put down the baskets and made an explosion with her hands. "Oh, those were the days, weren't they? Highball or bubbly?"

"You have champagne?" May asked, "How on earth?" The popping cork terrified Pudding, who squeezed himself beneath an armchair, leaving only his stumpy, quivering tail visible.

With glasses and the bottle, they strolled down the long brick walkway to the dock, their skirts whipping against their legs. Settling on the weathered planks, they dangled bare feet over the water. Below, blue crabs skittered around the pilings while tiny, silvery minnows darted to the surface. Above, weeping willows bowed over the water, graceful branches tracing paths on the surface. Elsie tossed the champagne cork into the river, and they hooted, clinking glasses. The air began to feel electric—energized, and the scent of impending rain was heavy and sweet. May sipped, holding the champagne in her mouth, savoring the change in flavors as the bubbles dissipated. The taste brought memories of youth and recklessness. Being with Elsie did that to her. Why hadn't they appreciated it then, the freedom? The planks of the dock were warm beneath her legs. Overhead, clouds darkened, while the rowboat bobbed crazily on its mooring. For this moment in time, May was no one's wife, no one's mother or daughter. She was only and fully herself.

The skies opened, pelting them with pea-sized hail that bounced on the dock and pocked the roiling water. Shrieking, they grabbed up the bottle and their shoes and ran for the house with May calling behind her, laughing, "Don't you dare spill a drop!"

Pudding barked from the back door, dancing from paw to paw. Drenched and breathless, they put down their glasses long enough to close the windows, then toweled their hair and changed clothes. Elsie came from her bedroom in a pair of her husband's silk pajamas, and May wore her old nightgown, topped with one of Byrd's flannel shirts. Outside, the hail changed to rain, and May could no longer see from the window to the river. Thunder boomed, echoed by an ominously protracted shuddering *crack* as a heavy limb thudded to the lawn, torn from a massive oak.

After dinner they curled up at either end of the big sofa, sharing a garishly multicolored crocheted afghan with Pudding curled up in the valley between. On a table in the center of the room, the picked-clean carcass of the chicken lay. May poured the dregs from the bottle into Elsie's glass, feeling pleasantly and irresponsibly woozy and only slightly guilty that she wasn't with her family.

Elsie stood and stretched, saying, "Don't move. That candy you brought is calling to me." She removed the dinner tray then returned, cradling a champagne bottle while licking chocolate from the fingers of one hand. "Good *Gawd. That* has got to be the absolutely best thing, ever!" She rolled her eyes. "How on earth do you get all of those ingredients into one candy bar? I *inhaled* two, so I shouldn't have to eat for days if your claim is true. Uhm. Maybe the second was a mistake." She slouched on the sofa, passing the bottle to May. They clinked glasses, giggling, and talked long into the night about their days at college, avoiding the events surrounding May's ignominious expulsion, near the end of their first year.

Elsie reached over to grab May's forearm. "Oh, I can't believe I forgot to tell you." She slapped her forehead.

"What?" May took a swig from her glass.

"I was at Miller & Rhoads last week—you can't imagine how many socks the monsters go through—and, well, you simply won't *believe* who I saw." Elsie covered her mouth; her eyes, conspiratorial.

"Do tell."

"Bitsy *Whitman*. Amory's wife." Amory Whitman had been the cause of May's expulsion. With a "secret engagement," he convinced her to spend the weekend in a hotel with him, having neglected to tell her he was also engaged to a girl called Bitsy, who was at finishing school in Switzerland at the time.

May flicked her hand dismissively. Elsie continued, "No, no, listen. She was *working* there! In women's *foundations*."

May choked and wiped the back of her hand across her mouth. "Lord, champagne almost came out of my nose."

"But can you imagine what straits they must be in if Bitsy has to sell girdles and garters to the matrons of Richmond? *Quelle horreur!*"

May had met Bitsy once, years before. It had been after the fiasco with Amory—a total disaster—with May and Byrd losing to Amory and Bitsy in a rigged dance contest. May toyed with the dog's collar, her voice low. "That must be hard for her."

Elsie snickered. "Serves her right. She always was the most terrific snob."

May let her head fall back against the sofa cushion and studied the ceiling. "I've been working in my father's market for years. Back when I wanted to be like those Richmond debutantes, I was ashamed of that. Now I'm grateful we've got a business, as feeble as it is these days. Do you know, Elsie, that I've been chided by customers—male *and* female—telling me I ought to be home, caring for my children instead of working? One man even had the nerve to say I ought to give up my job in my own family store, so that an unemployed man could have it!" Elsie looked chagrined. May continued, sitting forward, her voice rising, "And you can bet your bottom dollar that Byrd never dreamed he'd own a rooming house. Did you hear that the railroads have fired all of their female employees, to give the jobs to men? Some of us *have* to work, Elsie. Some of us feel *lucky* to have jobs. Maybe Bitsy's grateful for the work. Did you ever think of that? And what about all of those poor people at the March, with all of their belongings burned!"

The mood in the room darkened. May had allowed herself to voice what she had been tamping down all day. Elsie rubbed Pudding's neck. She was quiet for a beat. "You're exactly right. I'm ashamed of myself. I forget sometimes, how tough things are. I'm being an ass, and you're an absolute brick." Elsie held out her glass and May refilled it. "Forgive me?"

May's voice was small, conciliatory. "Always. Listen, I'm sorry I flew off the handle. Things have been . . . things have been difficult, at home. But let's not talk about that now."

"Whatever you say. So tell me about your little business venture? How's that coming along?"

May hesitated for a moment, then said, "The most frustrating thing is that it takes so long to make each box of assorted candies. They all have to be fresh, of course, so all of the different batches have to be made about the same time. It just isn't a practical use of Blue's time. And even if we hired more workers the workspace in the market is too small to spread out. So if we could narrow it down to one or two products and make some sort of production line, we'd increase efficiency and profits. The old cannery would be the perfect space. The main problem is that it takes money to expand, and we haven't got any to spare. I don't dare mention it to Byrd. Poor man, he feels so responsible for everyone, and he's working so hard. He's lost so much, and he's afraid of losing more."

Elsie nodded slowly. "I'd like to help."

May reached out and put her hand on Elsie's arm. "Elsie, no! Lord, I hope you don't think I was *hinting* for you to . . ."

Elsie held up her hand like a crossing guard. "Hush this *instant!*" She took a slow drag from her cigarette, blowing a stream of smoke toward the ceiling, then jabbed her cigarette holder toward May. "Listen, I've got this bloody trust fund. Not many people know this, but my father put it all in my name, because—well—because he wasn't sure if Archie and I would stick. He was dead wrong, of course. Arch and I are devoted.

"So now that Dad and Mum are gone, all I have to do is sashay down to the First Commonwealth Bank and tell Mister Faulconer I need a cashier's check. He's not allowed to breathe a word to Archie and he's not allowed to ask me what I intend to do with it. Arch has his own, anyhoo." She dusted her hands together as ash floated to the rug. "So there." She grinned and winked. "We gals have got to be able to run our own lives every now and then, right?"

May smiled slowly and nodded. She said, "That's a generous offer. Can I think about it?"

The next morning, May woke in a strange bed, groaning with a dizzy headache and a dry mouth. She rubbed her eyes and listened. No baby's wail, no padding of little feet coming from across the hall. There was no clock in the room, but the light outside told her it was near seven. She crept past Elsie's closed door and down the stairs, wincing with each screech of the risers. Pudding rose from his basket beside the fireplace, stretching. May let him out the back door and squinted in the sunlight. The boxwoods still shone with moisture from the night's storm, and the leaves on the broken oak limb had begun to wilt.

Downstairs, the kitchen floor was deliciously cool against her feet. She made a pot of coffee then took a cup back to the porch. Too late, she realized that the glider seat was still wet. Pudding jumped up beside her, muddy-pawed and damp, throwing off the swing's rhythm so that coffee sloshed from cup to saucer. May didn't mind the dampness or the wet dog smell. Right now, on this fine morning, a view and a cup of coffee were enough to make her happy.

A fishing boat glided past and she watched the waking river, mulling over Elsie's offer. *A chance like this might never come along again. I wouldn't have to ask Byrd for anything. Besides, he's so distracted. He doesn't even want to hear my ideas. He doesn't believe I could turn this into a success. But Elsie does.* The offer was genuine, May knew, and it was a temptation. She ought to tell Elsie that Byrd would have to agree. That was fair, wasn't it? But that sounded so *weak*, she thought, so *acquiescent*, when she felt ready to move forward, now. The time was perfect for the all-day candy bar. It was only a matter of time before someone else had the same idea. She, May Craig, had at her disposal the wherewithal to create a product that would sell at a fair price; a product people wanted. She could create jobs for hungry men *and* women, like herself, who wanted to provide for their children. And she would pay the women a fair wage, exactly the same as men who did the same work. She said aloud, "That's only fair, isn't it?" The dog blinked up at her and she reached to scratch his back.

Nineteen
DORRIT

It was early afternoon, and on South Main Avenue in downtown Gastonia, North Carolina, the soda fountain in the Rexall Drug Store smelled of egg salad and pickles, mixed with a very slight odor of sour rag. Overhead, ceiling fans clacked quietly as Clarence took a seat on a stool. Dorrit didn't trust him, so when she went to the public telephone at the back, she carried the toolbox with her. A woman wearing a white smock with a nametag glared at her suspiciously from behind a counter. Leaving the box outside the booth, Dorrit fished a dime from her change purse. Anxiously, she dropped it into the slot and asked the operator to connect her to Boston, to Coughlin's Bakery on Blossom Street. The operator came back on, asking her to repeat the address, then reported that the line was no longer in service. Dorrit asked for Olivetti's Newsstand instead. The line rang and rang, then finally she heard the familiar Italian accent, saying, "Allo? Olivetti's."

"Mister Olivetti? Mister Olivetti, this is Dorrit Sykes? I've been trying to telephone Coughlin's, but no one answers."

"Ah. Miss Dorrit. We have been wondering, all of us in the neighborhood, what has become of you Sykeses."

A sharp longing for home constricted Dorrit's throat and she swallowed a sob. "We've had some . . . We've had some difficulties. Have you seen my father?"

"No, no. I am sorry to hear you have troubles. Everybody has troubles. The bakery, it is closed down." Mr. Olivetti's voice dropped. "Signora Coughlin, she has left. The landlord says she owes six months' rent." Dorrit's shoulders fell. She asked him to tell her father, if he saw him, that she would get herself back to Boston as soon as she could.

Dorrit hung up, then swiped her sleeve across her eyes. Sniffling, she dropped two nickels into the slot, asking for the head of military police in Washington, DC. The operator asked for an address, saying there were twelve listings. Dorrit hung up. Her nickels plinked into the coin return.

Determined that Clarence would not see her cry, she wandered the drugstore aisles, attempting to stave off despair. A mirrored display featured *Irresistible Lip Lure, leaving no paste or film . . . just soft, warm, ripe, indelible color that awakens love and makes your lips beg for kisses. Four gorgeous shades to choose from!* While the cashier in the smock continued to glare, Dorrit ran her fingers across a row of fluffy pink powder puffs. She sniffed perfumed talcum powders and a brand of soap that claimed to *ensure personal daintiness!* The stacked bars of Lux made her long for a bath, suggesting, *When you undress for bed . . . undress your face too!* And what, she wondered, was *bust food?*

At the pharmacist's counter, packets of Stanback headache powder promised she could *Snap back with Stanback!* Snap back to what? Dorrit attributed the pain that had been skulking behind her eyes to her fall. Hefting the little envelope, she wondered if it might dissolve the lump in her throat or ease the tightness in her chest. Was there medicine to calm the fidgets? She paid the white-smocked woman, then joined Clarence at the soda fountain. Prices and menu items were painted in red and black on a mirrored wall. Everything gleamed, from the chrome spigots to the pyramid stack of footed ice cream dishes. The soda jerk wore spotless white, with a black bow tie. His shirtsleeves were neatly cuffed above his elbows and his peaked cap perched at an angle that suggested swagger. Dorrit ordered two ice cream floats with Coca-Cola, at fifteen cents each.

She did not tell Clarence that she had never tasted Coca-Cola. Once, she tried root beer at Mrs. Frazier's house and nothing terrible happened, but soda pop was frowned upon by the Church, especially Coca-Cola.

Here, it was *The pause that refreshes!* Dorrit's stomach rumbled as she watched orbs of ice cream flipped into frosted glasses. A stream of soda shot in next, until cloudy bubbles rose to the rim. With a professional flourish, the soda jerk topped each glass with an impossibly red cherry. Clarence asked for an extra cherry, and crackers, and when the glass was placed before him, he hunched over it.

Dorrit took a tentative sip. The bubbly soda was wonderfully cold, burning the inside of her nose in a way that was not unpleasant. She swallowed, then burped silently, holding a paper napkin over her mouth, waiting for evil effects. With the long-handled spoon, she dipped a bit of the melting ice cream. Blending with the cola, the creamy coolness left a lovely vanilla aftertaste. She washed the bitter headache powder down, then took her time with her ice cream, trying to discern exactly what it was that made Coca-Cola an evil substance. It *was* refreshing, as it claimed to be. And the Stanback powder seemed to help her headache.

Swinging her shoes, Dorrit spun her stool slightly left, then right. Beneath glass domes, lemon meringue and apple pies sat like museum exhibits. A radio played, announcing Duke Ellington's band as the soda jerk snapped his fingers, singing along under his breath, a string of nonsensical syllables: *do-wa-do-wa . . .*

Dorrit plucked the cherry stem from her glass, idly wondering what *that swing* was. The soda jerk cut a sandwich into triangles, then enclosed it in waxed paper with precise, geometric folds while Clarence watched with the eyes of a starving dog. Dorrit decided he needed distracting and gave his shin a slight kick. "Where are you from?" she asked.

"Kentucky." Clarence licked his spoon.

Dorrit sat up straighter. "I have a friend from there," she said. "He's called Dynamite. Did you work in the coal mines?"

"Nah." Clarence's gaze moved to the lemon meringue pie. "My pa worked a horse farm. Used to, anyway."

"How come you left?"

"They's eight kids in my family." The spoon clanked in his empty glass. "When I couldn't get any work, Pa told me I needed to leave for a while, on account of I ate too much."

Dorrit's eyes widened. "That's sad. My brother left home too, only he went into the Merchant Marine."

"Yeah? Well, they don't have that in Kentucky."

"You going back?"

"Pa said I could come back in a year and check on how things are going. That was in April."

"Did you live on a farm?"

"Used to. Then we moved to a double garage, with a wood stove."

Dorrit listened, again taking a silent, interior inventory, but there still seemed to be no ill effects from the Coca-Cola, other than the burping. It was so pleasant, sitting beneath the fans when it was hot as blazes outside. By the reckoning of the clock above the mirror, she had managed to make half of her soda last for almost an hour. Her paper straw began to bend and collapse, and Clarence asked if she was going to finish hers. By the time she did, she had decided that she liked Coca-Cola very much.

"So what're you doing riding the rails?" Clarence asked. "Don't see many girls on their own."

"I need to get back home to Boston. Only things haven't gone . . . I'm adapting." She swiveled to face him and whispered, "I've got to get enough money for a train ticket home, or else ride the rails."

Clarence sat up straighter, and his ears reddened. He seemed to concentrate on tamping the bottom of his glass with his straw. "It's not a good idea—to ride on your own."

"Well, I don't have a better one. I don't have enough money for a ticket."

He swiveled on his stool to face her. "Being by yourself, you could try the Red Cross, or beg. Problem with that is, you spend the change you get just getting by, and you can't save up." He tossed down his paper napkin and spun his stool away from her and stood.

Reluctantly, Dorrit slid off her stool and asked the soda jerk if there was a Red Cross office in town. She followed him to the front window, where he pointed up the street. Dorrit thanked him and she and Clarence left.

Half a block away, Clarence paused, pulling two red-wrapped objects from his pocket. "Here," he said gruffly, offering one, "since you shared with me."

It was a chocolate bar. "How did you . . ." Dorrit stopped short, then glanced behind her, holding the candy bar like a hot coal. "Criminy! You *stole* this!"

Clarence shrugged, unwrapping his to take a big bite. He smiled, revealing chocolate on his teeth, and pulled from his other pocket two rolls of peppermint Life Savers and a small pink tin with an illustration of smiling, cherubic children on the lid. "It's provisions. You like Life Savers?"

"Yes. But why'd you get *that*?" Dorrit made a face, pointing to the pink tin.

"This is fancy candy." A doubtful look suffused his face. "Ain't it?"

Dorrit pointed to the print on the tin. "It says right here, *Doctor Hobson's Pink Worm Wafers. Formulated especially for children.*" Clarence flushed, shoving the tin into his pocket. They walked on in awkward silence. Dorrit contemplated teasing him, which was what Walt would do, but that just seemed mean. Lots of people couldn't read. She tried to match his offhandedness. "I'm going to the Red Cross to try to get a ticket home. You could pretend to be my brother again, or whatever."

"Nah." Clarence hunched his shoulders, hands deep in his pockets. "Wouldn't work. They don't give out much in there. 'Sides, they already seen me. I been asked to move on, only I been trying to start up a gang." He withdrew a hand and rubbed the back of his neck.

Dorrit hesitated, debating whether she could trust an unrepentant thief to watch her belongings. She estimated the distance to the Red Cross office and decided she could watch him from the window. She said, "Will you watch my box while I'm in there? I want to look like I don't have a thing in the world."

"All right. I'll be out here, on this bench. You see any cigarettes lying around, grab me a couple."

The reception area was dimly lit. Dorrit sat on an oak chair while a thin, nervous-looking nurse in a white uniform leaned on her elbows, listening and nodding before leaning closer. "Let me have a look at that lip. Sweetie, did someone do this to you? Did a man hit you?"

"I fell," Dorrit said. The nurse shook her head slowly, making *tsk-tsk* sounds as Dorrit tried to remember the things Clarence had told her to say. She recited, softly, "My name is Dorrit Sykes, ma'am. I was separated from my pop, in Washington—he's a veteran. Since then, I've been try—try—trying to take c-c-care of myself." She held her dirty handkerchief to her face, faking sobbing sounds as she peeked at the woman's sympathetic face. She wailed, "I just want to go home, to B-B-Boston."

"Lord-a-mighty, honey, you ain't any bigger'n a minute!" The nurse tilted her head sympathetically then patted Dorrit's arm and clucked. "Let me talk to my supervisor. You sit right there, and I'll bring you some water and we'll fix up that lip." She went into an office, closing the door behind her. Dorrit could hear murmuring through the glass. She glanced toward the front window. No one passed on the sidewalk outside. Across the street, Clarence sat on the bench, swinging his legs. Dorrit looked over the desk. *No*, she told herself, she would not steal this kind woman's fountain pen or her clean, white pad of writing paper. A packet of Lucky Strikes sat beside an ashtray. *Thou shalt not steal* . . . With a glance back at the office door, she tore three postage stamps off of a roll. From the stack of blank envelopes, she removed three, tucking them into her satchel. The voices behind the door continued. Emboldened, she shook two cigarettes from the pack and as her hand closed over them, the door handle rattled. She held her breath. *Must be that Coca-Cola*, she thought, *making me act up*. Slowly, she moved her hand across the desktop and slid the cigarettes into her satchel. *Smooth as silk*.

The nurse's expressions went through the same sequence as before: head tilt with slightly downturned mouth, a wry smile, the double arm pat, then the deep sigh with dropping shoulders. She explained that a ticket to Boston from Gastonia cost eighteen dollars. *They*, meaning the Red Cross of Gastonia, were not authorized to provide funding for transportation, but they could give out emergency rations. She handed Dorrit a clean white towel and a small bar of soap, then pointed out the washroom.

Dorrit hesitated. A chance for a proper wash meant leaving her belongings out of sight. It was a gamble. What would Nancy Drew do? She would be clean. Dorrit left the Red Cross with her split lip cleaned and salved, a fat baloney sandwich, a new toothbrush, and fifty cents the nurse had given her from her own purse.

Outside, Clarence sat on the bench in the shade, his knobby, sockless ankles visible below the fringing hem of his pants. Dorrit sat beside him. "How'd you make out?" he asked.

She passed him the cigarettes. "They gave me a sandwich and a toothbrush is all. And I cried and everything." She kept the news of the fifty cents to herself. "I s'pose I'll ride the rails back home and wait for my pop there." Sliding from the bench, she looked up and down the quiet street. The afternoon was waning. Formally, she held out her hand toward Clarence. "Nice to meet you. Good luck, yourself."

"Wait." Clarence stood and wiped his hands on his pants. "You ought not to go it alone. Hell, I bet you can't even get yourself into a boxcar." Dorrit shrugged, but it was true. Her bravado was fading. He continued, "You know, they's gangs of kids like us. They look out for each other. How about you and me start a gang? You're good at getting handouts, and lookie—" Clarence slid his hand into his pocket and withdrew a slim, wood-handled object. He pushed a small button and *snap!* a silvery blade with a menacing point unfolded. "Reckon I'd as soon go to Boston as anywhere else. Ain't ever been north before. They all talk funny like you do? *Nice ta meetcha?*"

"It's you folks down here that talk strange. We speak normally in Boston."

Clarence folded the knife and returned it to his pocket. "See that man across the street, getting into a car? Bet you could get him to ride us to the station."

Dorrit did not have to think for long. She had fifty cents and a sandwich. "All right, but you do the talking."

At the Gastonia station, they sat on a bench outside, sharing her sandwich. As Dorrit chewed, she took fleeting glances at Clarence's profile. Was she foolish to trust him? Was she foolish to trust anyone at all? Well, she told herself, she did not believe that he would hurt her. For now, that seemed to be enough. The big clock near the station door read 7:10 p.m. Beside the clock, a US mailbox was mounted to the wall. When Clarence left to look for a match and the freight schedule, Dorrit turned to a fresh page of her notebook and wrote:

POSSIBLE OPTIONS:
1. Get to Washington. Look for Pop. Stay where?
2. Ride rails to Boston
3. Sell Pop's tools? (ticket= $18.00)

At seven fifteen, when a southbound train stopped, Dorrit watched passengers depart and board. There seemed to be no way to get on top of the cars from the platform and nowhere to hide inside without a ticket. Besides, she didn't want to go south. The conductors called, "All aboard!" then the train pulled away. The station was empty, except for a bored-looking ticket agent, reading a newspaper. Dorrit began a new page.

August 3

Dear Pop,
I am writing to you from Gastonia, North Carolina. I am not sure when you will get this or even if our mail is being delivered. I wanted to let you know that I am all right and on my way home.
Your daughter,
Dorrit Marie Sykes

She addressed an envelope then affixed a stamp with a strange mixture of guilt and pride in her resourcefulness. She dropped the letter into the box and returned to the bench, sitting heavily, wondering what had become of Clarence. She returned to her notebook.

August 3

I imagine Dynamite and the professor are wondering what has become of Dorrit Sykes. I wonder if they have made it to Georgia yet.
Now Clarence and I are a gang, for better or worse, and maybe we will have more members by the time we get to Boston. Although I am picking up some unsavory habits, I do plan to shuck them as soon

as I get home. I am not looking forward to another ride in a boxcar.
It sure would be nicer to be a passenger. I'm still worried about Pop.

Dorrit returned her pencil to her bag, overcome with tiredness. Her headache was returning, and she prodded her stomach. The Coca-Cola had left her bloated and uncomfortable. Promptly at eight o'clock, the lights inside the station switched off. The night was softly warm, with a slight breeze. Occasionally, an automobile passed. In the quiet, frogs called to one another. She dozed.

"Hey!" Dorrit jolted awake, reaching for the screwdriver that had been in her waistband. "Wake up," Clarence said. Dorrit rubbed her face, finding it difficult to concentrate. "Some men at the jungle told me there's a coal train comes through after midnight most nights, heading north. Said there's no bulls on 'em, usually. So we just got to wait."

"All right." Dorrit pushed her satchel to the end of the bench and leaned on it, grateful she was not alone. With her palm propped against her cheek, she slept again.

A rumbling woke her, and Dorrit sat up, not knowing at first where she was. By the station clock, it was half past midnight. Clarence said, "C'mon. This is it." A coal train idled on the track, its long string of cars fading into the darkness ahead. In front of Dorrit was the junction of two open-topped hoppers. The ends of the cars sloped inward from top to bottom, like a chute, and a steel ladder ran up the side of each. Over the wheels, three feet above the tracks, a small metal platform jutted out about eighteen inches, with a narrow iron railing. The train chuffed, and Clarence carried their belongings to the edge of the platform. Swinging the toolbox in one hand, he grabbed the ladder with the other, pulling himself across the gap. Balancing on the thin rung, he reached back to Dorrit. "Ever ride on the outside?" Her hands turned cold as she shook her head, eyeing the drop between the cars. He continued, "Ain't enough room for two on one car, so you ride this one. I'll be across there. You can have the sheltered side this time, but next time, I get it." He leaned forward to help her over the railing, but she could not move. "C'mon," Clarence urged, "It's now or never."

Now or never. It was as if a screen rose before Dorrit's eyes, projecting her actions as she watched from outside of herself. Each muscle in her body seemed to expand with the flood of dread, then just as suddenly contract, drawing blood and heat from her face and hands, clenching her insides. The shift to disconnection was familiar, but there was no comfort to be gleaned from that. When panic was most acute, it worked as a shield of sorts, with both a heightened awareness of what was happening around her and an inner withdrawal that slowed her responses and made her bones heavy, her limbs clumsy. She allowed Clarence to hold her hand as she stepped across the gap. He jumped over the coupling to the car behind. They were four feet apart, on separate cars. Dorrit lowered herself to sit on the narrow platform, wedging her satchel between the toolbox and the car. The metal was warm, covered in a layer of soot that smelled of oil and coal. She looked down, then looked up at the sky, between the cars. Bert had told her of men losing eyes to hot cinders while riding the tops of trains. How far ahead was the engine? Would ashes and soot blow back here? *Nancy Drew would call this an adventure*, she told herself. *Nancy Drew has no damned idea.*

From the wheels upward, the train began to vibrate. Clarence leaned across the railing to shout, "Best to keep your eyes closed. If you have a bandanna, wrap it over your nose. And hold on, else you'll shake right over the side." He splatted his palms together and his next words died out in the shriek of metal as a steam whistle tooted far ahead, followed by a jolting lurch that threw Dorrit against the railing. With one hand on the rail, she rooted for her handkerchief. The vibration changed to a screeching cacophony, punctuated with *clack-clack-clacks* that quickly ran into each other as the train gained speed. Another wave of dread passed upward, from her feet, settling in her belly with the realization that there was no way off until the train stopped. Her hair whipped into her face and she squeezed her eyes shut as they hurtled forward, into the darkness. In her head, the incessant clacking ran into one phrase, repeating: *no way off, no way off, no way off.*

Time ceased. Existence became the ability to continue to grip the shaking railing. The metal platform rattled her backbone and her leg muscles cramped. Sleep was not a possibility. The whistle shrieked when they passed through crossings, and occasionally, she risked a peek, reassured to see Clarence's bandanna-covered face bobbing along behind her.

When her eyelids lit with orange, she squinted at fields of tobacco, or corn, or white puffs of cotton as they raced by like flickering cinema shots. The night was over. She had survived. She told herself, *I am here.* Gray shacks sat in dirt yards, dust blew through a rusted-out truck, while in the fields, mules stood with lowered heads as men in rough straw hats raised hoes to a rising sun that, Dorrit expected, would beat down on them without mercy, through the long summer day.

Part III
PATCHED

"Give me that life that is seamed and riven with living."

Muriel Strode,
My Little Book of Life, 1912

Twenty
DORRIT

August ?

Black smears. This page is full of black smears and fingerprints. My ears are ringing and my bones feel rattled apart. I can hardly hold this pencil. It is morning, and we are stopped at last.

I wonder if this is God testing me. I did pray last night. Not the Lord's Prayer or anything, I just talked to God, like he was there with me. I think that counts. After last night, I do not think I will ever be afraid of anything. More on this later.

Clarence has gone off to investigate. I got out to go behind the bushes, then I had a gander around. We are in a train yard. I do not know what state we are in but it is hot. I hope we are heading north.

We have sat here now for what I guess is an hour, and I suppose the train is not leaving. I wish Clarence would come back. Why on earth did I let him talk me into this?

Ten cars ahead, a man in overalls climbed down from the engine and ambled toward a shack. From the other direction, Clarence was walking back toward the train.

"C'mon," he said, pulling the toolbox off the hopper platform. When he reached to take Dorrit's arm, she swatted his hand away and climbed down by herself. Her legs felt rubbery, and although she was exhausted her muscles hummed with exhilaration and relief. She had conquered her fear. She had survived the night.

A small, open shed stood near the crossing. Beside it was a pump and, as Clarence rattled the rusty handle, Dorrit washed soot from her arms and face, inhaling the rose scent of her precious soap, grateful to smell something besides ash and hot metal. The pink slivers lathered, changing quickly to streaky gray.

"Stinks," Clarence said, sniffing, "like lady perfume."

"This is very fine soap. You'd better wash if we're going to ask for food."

"Well, ain't you Miss Bossy." Clarence stuck his head beneath the pump. He sputtered, squirting water from his mouth, then shook like a wet dog. They took turns drinking the iron-tasting water. Instead of quenching Dorrit's thirst it left metallic grit in her mouth that made her slightly queasy. The sun was higher now, and the ringing in her ears had abated enough that she noticed the songs of birds in the surrounding woods.

"What now?" she asked, overly loud, looking up and down the tracks. "I don't think I can get back on there without a rest and some food. I'm so tired I'll blow right off."

"Yeah. We can wait; see if a freight comes through with a boxcar." Clarence jerked his head to the area behind them. "We passed a depot, coming in. Reckon if there's a station, there'll be houses around. Maybe a diner."

Imagining another ice cream soda made Dorrit's mouth water and—with the heightened clarity of newfound bravery—she wondered how many ice cream sodas she had missed out on in her lifetime. Blind obedience and fear of new people and places had kept her from a simple pleasure—sharing ice cream with a friend. While Clarence washed, she watched him. Was he her ally, or simply an opportunist, waiting for a chance to take advantage? It was hard to know. Dorrit rubbed her bloated belly, wondering if perhaps Coca-Cola was something one's constitution needed to adapt to.

They followed the tracks, moving carefully between the ties. Dorrit shifted her satchel from hand to hand while Clarence carried his pack with the toolbox. Around a curve, the trees thinned out as a passenger platform came into view. Beside it, the small brick depot building appeared closed. A clock mounted on the wall outside read 6:15 a.m. Dorrit peered in the window. The waiting room had a single ticket window, two wooden benches, and a spittoon. In the faint light, she discerned from the wall calendar that the date was Thursday, August 4. Her stomach rumbled and she sniffed the air.

"Hey," she said, sniffing again, "do you smell that?"

"Yeah." Clarence's voice was sullen. "I smell like a girl."

"Not the soap. It's something sweet—like sugar-sweet."

They followed the intensifying aroma to the front of the depot, across the parking lot and onward, crossing a dirt road. A footpath wound through a patch of woods, and like Hansel and Gretel they followed, ignoring the vague odors of moldering leaves and clay soil below their feet. Like a beckoning finger, the enticement of cooking sugar and butter drew them on to where the path ended, bordering the rear parking area of a clapboard building with a green-painted tin roof. Dorrit thought it might be a filling station. Outside of the screened door were stacks of bushel baskets and two garbage cans. A black Ford truck was parked close to the building.

"Clarence," Dorrit whispered, squinting. "There's something painted on that truck door. Can you read it from here?" When he shook his head, she remembered the worm wafers. She said, "See any hobo marks on the building?"

"Uh-uh."

"The smell—it's coming from in there."

The screen obscured a view inside the door, but someone was singing in a deep baritone, accented by the clanging of pots. "Watch out for me," Dorrit said. "I'll ask for food."

She handed Clarence her satchel. He smirked, as if to say, *go right ahead, be in charge.* Crossing the graveled area, she tried to smile, in case someone might be looking outside. Closer up, she could read the lettering on the truck. *Keswick Farm Orchards, Keswick, Virginia.* No chalked markings were visible around the left side of the screened door, but the truck blocked the right side. As she came around the front of the truck a low rumbling started. Dorrit froze, as a protracted, wet-sounding animal inhalation preceded another, less tremulous growl. A small, black, wire-coated dog slunk around from the passenger side of the truck, its head low. One eye was a startling sky blue, the other brown. Its pointed, bared teeth were crooked, in a way that might be comical in another circumstance. Dorrit held out her hands slowly as she stepped back, holding her breath, praying the dog was chained.

But it wasn't.

Stalking, stiff-legged, the mutt approached slowly, winding up for another deep growl, fraught with apparent wrath and intention. Holding its ground with legs apart and tail down, it began a barking that sounded as if it belonged to a much larger animal. Behind her, Dorrit heard the thud and rattle of the toolbox hitting the ground, then Clarence's whispered, "Son of a bitch," followed by the whipping of branches and retreating footsteps crackling across twigs. She did not dare to turn her back.

Dorrit had heard somewhere that dogs could *smell* fear. "*Niiice* pooch," she whispered, dry-mouthed. She tried to make her voice light. "Go on now. You just get on home." The dog narrowed its eyes and flattened its ears, apparently having none of her courtesy. *All righty.* Dorrit thought, *Where do we go from here?*

From inside the screened door, the singing ceased, and a deep voice called, "Taffy, what are you up to?" At the sound of her name, the dog lunged closer, snapping, then backed up and hunkered lower, reconnoitering, lips curled.

"Taffy!" the voice called. "I said, get back here!" Taffy's ears shifted back briefly; her eyes flitted to the side then to Dorrit, as if weighing the consequences of disobedience. Dorrit thought Taffy might retreat, but in an instant, as if the dog *intended* a feint, she darted forward, sinking her teeth into Dorrit's ankle, with a shake for good measure.

"Aaah!" Dorrit fell, covering her head with her arms, and tried to roll into a ball.

"Damnation, Taffy! You biting again?"

Dorrit kept her eyes closed tight. A hinge whined; the screened door slapped closed, then steps shuffled through the gravel toward her.

When she opened her eyes, a gray-haired man loomed over her, scowling, haloed in a wreath of sunlight. Dorrit cut her eyes right, then left. Pain began to register. A scraped elbow, certainly, and her ankle throbbed in four distinct points—two front, two back. Four little throbbing volcanoes. The man stood up and leaned back, holding onto his suspenders. "What in the Sam Hill are you doing, sneaking through the woods this time of morning? Any mutt worth her salt'd scare you off."

Dorrit winced, pushing herself up to sitting. "Where is it?"

"Inside."

"Do I look dangerous to you, mister? Your dog attacked me!"

The man's chin jerked back in apparent consternation. "My Taffy?"

"I didn't do a thing at all. That's a vicious animal." Dorrit glanced behind her. No sign of Clarence. She brushed the grit from her palms and her voice became a whine. "I . . . I need a little bit of food."

The man shook his head. "*I need a little food.* That's what they all say. Hell, I can barely keep this place open. You need to keep on, girl, wherever it is you're headed, 'cause I got nothing for you here." He held up one hand as if taking an oath. Dorrit struggled to her feet and wiped her nose on the back of her hand. Her ankle ached. The man frowned, saying, "Humph." Turning, he said, over his shoulder, "I'll be letting Taffy out in about five minutes. She does not cotton to strangers."

Dorrit splayed her hands over her face and began to sob with dramatic volume, peeking through her fingers at the man's back as he retreated. He stopped. His shoulders rose and fell resignedly before he scratched the back of his head and faced her again. Wishing she could produce real tears, she choked out, "I'm just . . . so . . . hungry."

The man's voice was less harsh. "Wait there."

Inside the screen, Taffy barked and whined, and Dorrit wondered, with a shudder, what might have happened if the man had not been there.

She attempted to inspect her wounds through the rips in her sock. After a few minutes, the man returned, and thrust a brown paper bag toward her, along with a quart bottle of milk. "This ought to get you through a day, only don't you be telling anybody where it came from. Now, I don't know what you're doing here—ain't no concern of mine—but you need to move on. Ain't safe for a young gal to be hoboing around. Don't you have a home to go to?"

Dorrit looked him in the eye and said, honestly, "I'm doing my best to get home, mister. Thank you for this. I won't bother you again." She shuffled back down the path, painfully aware of each of the punctures in her ankle. When she stopped to retrieve the toolbox and her satchel, both seemed heavier than before.

God? She prayed silently. *This test, I was not expecting. But I got through on my own, didn't I?*

She followed the path back through the woods, indignation growing with each step, halting now and then to listen for growling behind her. The train station lights were on now; it was open for the day. Clarence sat on the edge of the platform, swinging his legs and tossing pebbles to bounce off the tracks below. Dorrit came to stand beside him, her breath heaving. She banged down the toolbox so that it rattled. When he did not look around and tossed another pebble, she raised her satchel and swatted the back of his head. It made her feel better, so she did it again, saying, "Dammit to hell, Clarence. How could you leave me like that? Look what that dog did to me." He ducked, covering his head. She pointed to her ankle, now smeared with blood. "And then, this grumpy old man came out and yelled at me and threatened to sic his watchdog on me again!" Dorrit crossed her arms over her chest. "We're supposed to be a *gang*, remember? We're supposed to look out for each other."

Clarence tossed another stone. "No sense in both of us getting bit. Figured you'd come back here." His voice was conciliatory. "Found us a place we can camp." He raised his chin toward the paper bag. "What'd you get?"

Dorrit clutched the bag to her chest, narrowing her eyes. "Damned if

I'll share it with you. Low-life coward. Honestly, who leaves a friend to get attacked by a guard dog?"

"Aw, it was only a ornery little mutt."

"Ha! That *you* ran away from." Dorrit sat gingerly, then set the milk bottle on the platform, just out of Clarence's reach. Daintily, she unrolled the top of the bag then peered inside, angling it away from him. Holding the bag to her face, she inhaled. "Ah." She closed her eyes, smiling slowly. "Smells *so* good." She closed the bag and placed it beside the milk bottle. For a long moment, she stared ahead at the tracks, her hands clasped primly in her lap. Condensation rolled down the sides of the milk bottle.

Clarence fidgeted with his cap then huffed, shifting his lower jaw; right, left, center, before he said, "All right. I'm sorry, all right?"

Dorrit did not respond but opened the bag again to pluck out a waxed-paper wrapped bar. She peeled away the covering with delicate, slow determination, revealing glossy caramel studded with nuts and dried fruit. With her pinkie finger extended, she turned the candy bar this way and that. "Looks homemade, I'd say. I do *love* pecans. Think the red things are dried cherries? Hmn?" Clarence swallowed and looked away, shrugging.

When Dorrit bit off the end of the bar, caramel stretched away in strands. "Ooh," she moaned, then continued, her mouth full, "'Ere's something fluffy inside, like marshmallow. Ooh, and they *are* cherries. 'ittle bits of cherries. It's still warm." She finished the candy bar slowly, then licked her thumb, sighing with contentment. Holding the milk bottle up, she admired the slick of heavy, pale-yellow cream at the top, then worked off the cap and said, "Clarence, you say, '*I apologize, Dorrit, for running away like a yellow-livered coward and leaving you to be chewed to pieces.*'"

Clarence's voice was resigned. "Aw, don't be so sore." He still faced forward. "I apologize."

She passed him the bag. He pulled out a second bar, identical to hers, and took a big bite. As he chewed, he reached in again and removed a roll of gauze bandaging and a small, brown glass bottle. "Lookie," he said, "what's this?"

"Iodine," Dorrit said, reading the bottle.

After Clarence finished the entire bottle of milk, he led Dorrit down another path in the woods. Through the trees, she caught glimpses of the black truck as they passed the back of the market, but there was no sign of Taffy. About a quarter-mile farther, they came to a low building surrounded by tall weeds. Gray boards showed remnants of white paint and cobwebs nearly obscured the windows, while ivy twined up the broad chimney. Clarence motioned for Dorrit to follow then pulled open a warped wooden door with rusty iron hinges shaped like snakes, with screws for eyes. The door creaked and as the sun streamed inside a scurrying noise came from the dim back of the single room. Twittering, staccato chirps echoed from the chimney. Dorrit recoiled, saying, "Are those bats?"

"Chimney swifts. Birds. They're harmless."

"What is this place?"

"A forge—least, it used to be." Clarence pulled the door fully open and stepped inside. "See? A farrier would make horseshoes here." He indicated a deep, raised brick hearth. "There was probably an anvil over there."

Dorrit would not come inside but peered around the doorway. "I bet there's snakes. You clear it out."

Clarence kicked his way through the dead leaves on the packed dirt floor. The place smelled of soot and rust. A work table stood against one wall, with racks above, all wrought in intricate ironwork. One hook was in the shape of a lizard, one a coiled snake, one a fanciful beetle. A small pile of broken, rusted horseshoes littered one corner. Clarence said, "There's a pump out back. Maybe the water's better than at the station. Looks like the houses 'round here are far off the road, but maybe when that market closes up, we can look through the trash bins."

Dorrit sputtered, "I am not going near that place again. You can go."

"All right, I will." He flicked open his switchblade. "Any damned dog wants to mess with me, it'll be sorry." He parried the knife like a musketeer. "I'm going to have a look around. Some of these places probably have chickens. We could make a fire in the forge. While I'm gone, look around for some branches—stuff we can burn."

The forge fronted onto a dirt road, and the woods that surrounded the back and sides threatened to take it over. As if the building were being reclaimed, long vines trailed from the trunks of trees, looping over to catch the roof. The tree canopy was so high and dense as to allow only small patches of blue sky to show, like an unfinished jigsaw puzzle. A lower secondary stratum contained more delicate trees—limber new pines with feathery, resinous needles, and what Dorrit did not know to call rhododendron, and dogwood, and azalea. Grass grew in clumps, and a patch of moss carpeted a small clearing near the pump.

The air became heavier; static with impending rain. Above the trees, clouds gathered into dense, billowing thunderheads. A squirrel skittered down a tree trunk and Dorrit jumped, gasping with jittery wariness, weak with the exhaustion that follows fear—that draining of the flight instinct. A prestorm smell—pleasant and strange, one that she had not known before the summer—rose from the dirt as if the earth exhaled. She had two choices: stay outside, under the trees where she could see people or animals approach, or move into the forge, where shelter could also be a trap.

Another, closer rumble of thunder sent her inside. She placed her belongings near the door, then found a balding push broom and swept the floor, warily poking at piled leaves and rubble, displacing crickets and spiders in the dim light. Beneath the workbench, a long, brittle snakeskin looped over a wide shelf. With a shudder, she used the end of the broom to fish it out. After she tossed it outside, she left the door ajar and propped open a window. Her ankle still throbbed, but less so when she placed no weight on it. Tiredness pushed down, and she laid out her quilt, then stretched out on the shelf beneath the workbench with her satchel as a pillow. Her father's heaviest wrench lay beneath it. As Dorrit closed her eyes, the first raindrops pattered on the tin roof. She remembered sitting in church in Boston, and the little rituals she went through when she felt anxious. Those dull lists and rote prayers belonged to a fearful, sheltered girl who no longer existed. She tried to concentrate on the rhythmic patter, attempting to block flashing memories of real terror, of pain. The *what-ifs* and wonderings of what she might have done differently. Her wish to be like Nancy Drew seemed so childish now. Real life was much messier. Real people got bruises and dog bites, and sometimes smelled bad. *Life isn't like a mystery book,* she thought, *a person can't just turn the page or close it up and put it aside. We have to live it, word by word and scene by scene.* She wished for a Stanback powder, and a Coca-Cola, and most of all, that she was safe in her own bed, in Boston.

When Dorrit woke, alone, in the late afternoon, the forge was quiet and hot. Clarence was not there, but she was greatly relieved to see a new stack of branches beside the door. A puddle had formed in the doorway and two wet spots on the floor showed where the roof leaked. She stuck her head outside but saw no one. Moisture dripped from the trees and the air smelled of ivy. Her mouth felt as if it were lined with wool. The water from the pump lacked the metallic flavor of the depot pump, and she drank and used her new toothbrush, wishing she had bought tooth powder in Gastonia. She peeled off her ruined sock, then washed her injured ankle. The punctures, now dark red, were rimmed in purplish bruises. Each one throbbed anew beneath the cold water. Through gritted teeth she muttered, "*Stupid dog. Damned mutt.*" She sat beneath a tree on a patch of damp moss and painted iodine over her wounds, hissing at the sting, "*Stupid, evil, mean, damned hellhound. Goddamned uglybitchcur.*" When she ran out of expletives she wrapped her ankle with gauze, cutting the roll with her sewing shears. She propped her foot on a log, then opened her notebook.

> *Thursday, August 4, continued.*
>   *My day has just gotten better and better. A dog bit me and then a mean man yelled at me (but gave me candy and milk). Clarence left me to die.*

Dorrit wanted to write "Clarence is a son of a bitch," but could not quite bring herself to *write* the curse word. Instead, she wrote:

He had better come back with some food. I believe we are getting to be
undernourished. From what I saw in the drugstore in Gastonia there
are any number of diseases caused by poor nutrition. As much as I
would dearly love to have some chicken I have never killed or plucked
one myself so I sure do hope he knows how to do that. Clarence says he
will find the northbound freight schedule.

Bored, and not inclined to explore, lest she meet another version of
Taffy, Dorrit rinsed out her extra clothes and hung them on branches
to dry. Leaving her legs bare, she tried to darn her socks, but the close
work made her eyes ache. She propped her bandaged ankle on the log
and read a few pages of Nancy Drew, but reading also seemed to strain
her eyes, so she laid the book on her chest, listening to bird calls and
the whisper of branches above. It was all so peaceful. And she was so
very, very tired.

After a few minutes, she heard whistling. She smiled, realizing
that she was able to discern that it was Clarence. He carried a lumpy
gunnysack and his faded shirt was darkened, his hair still wet from
the downpour. He said, "I watched that market for a while, from the
woods? A delivery truck came and parked in the back and unloaded
crates. After it left, that man was taking the boxes inside and the telephone rang. When he went in to answer it, I grabbed some stuff." He
pulled two cans of beans and a tin of crackers from the sack. "Then,"
Clarence smiled broadly and knelt beside her, displaying four eggs
and three fat tomatoes, wrapped in a blue gingham man's shirt. "I
found a farm, up that way." He gestured over his shoulder. "No marks
on the fence, so I went 'round through the fields. Nobody saw me,
I don't think. I'd have got us a chicken, 'cept they got to squawking
when I chased them. I was afraid somebody would come. When I was
coming back, it must've been right 'round five o'clock because that
man at the market loaded up some crates into the truck and took the
dog with him and drove off. We can go back over there and check it
out after dark."

Dorrit nodded, fuzzy-headed. When she stood, she felt dizzy. Her ankle pulsed with pain. She narrowed her eyes at him. "Now you listen to me, buster. If you leave me again, I will skin your hide."

Clarence said, "I won't, I swear."

After the sky changed from lavender to plum to moon-radiant blue, they followed the path again, back through the woods to the market. By the light from the kitchen, Clarence rooted through the garbage. Dorrit wished she had batteries for her flashlight, and she held her breath, listening for the sounds of a returning automobile or a snarling dog. They found a loaf of slightly stale bread, a can of pecan halves with burned edges, and a jar with what turned out to be mayonnaise. She took two empty soda pop bottles from a wooden crate, then packed everything into one of the empty bushel baskets stacked by the back door. Around the side of the building, a window stood partially open, the sill five feet above the ground. Inside was in darkness. Clarence jumped up to try to see inside, then pulled a crate to stand on. He peered in, whispering loudly enough for Dorrit to hear, "It's a storeroom—best I can see— canned goods and sacks of flour and such."

"Any batteries or toilet paper?"

"Too dark to see." He hopped down and replaced the crate behind the building. "If we go over there at first light, bet we can get through that window. We could get set up real good, I think."

"Criminy. You mean sneak inside like burglars?" Dorrit swatted at a mosquito. "What if that dog's in there?" She considered what they were planning to do. Stealing was wrong, but the thought of all of that merchandise lined up on the shelves was terribly seductive—*Coca-Cola, fresh bread, toilet paper!*

"Told you," Clarence said, "the dog left with the man. Listen, this place is a gold mine. We wouldn't take enough that they'd notice anything missing, and we've got a good, dry place to sleep. I have a good feeling about this place."

"You want to stay? Here, I mean? I need to get going home."

"Only a couple of nights. We can eat good and rest up. It's nice here. It's safe."

Back at the forge, Clarence made a fire, and they boiled eggs in the coffee can. He sliced bread with his knife, then they made a feast of sandwiches with thick slices of tomato and the dregs of mayonnaise, laughing as tomato seeds poured down their chins. They agreed to save two eggs for breakfast, and each ate one, juggling the hot shell as they peeled it.

Twenty-One
DORRIT

For three days, Dorrit and Clarence camped at the forge. In the heat of the afternoon, she stayed inside; bright daylight made her head ache, and she craved quiet. She had expected to feel stronger with rest, but it seemed all she wanted was sleep. Clarence managed to pilfer food and came back on Saturday, reporting that the man at the market lived in a room at the back but stayed away on certain nights. On Sundays, according to the sign on the front door, the market was closed all day. The time was perfect, he claimed, for an expedition. He bragged about how he teased Taffy—tossing pebbles at the screened door, sending her into a frenzy before he ran off into the woods with four Coca-Colas, snatched from a delivery truck.

On Sunday morning, Clarence shook Dorrit awake. Through the window, orange streaked the eastern sky. Pushing up onto her elbows, she moaned. Pain throbbed behind her eyes. Sitting up, her stomach cramped. At the pump, she rinsed her hot face, and when she bent over to prod her wrapped ankle, she felt a rushing pressure in her head. Clarence came from the forge, pulling his shirt off before sticking his head under the pump. It embarrassed Dorrit to see his pale, skinny chest and bony shoulder blades. Really, he was nothing but an overgrown boy. She looked away, wincing at a cramp, and asked, "You feeling all right this morning?"

"I'm dandy." He slicked his hair back with his fingers.

"Oh." Dorrit leaned over, clutching her stomach. "I think that mayonnaise had turned."

"Got the runs?" Clarence asked, pulling his shirt back over his head. He followed her back inside.

Dorrit felt hotter. "The trots. And a headache. And nothing tastes good, except soda pop." She did not tell him about the pink spots that had appeared on her belly.

"Is there a difference—trots or runs?" He popped the top off of a Coca-Cola and passed it to her.

"My mother said that 'trots' is more polite." Dorrit drank. Even warm, the cola tasted good to her.

Clarence said, "Bet there's some more medicine in that market. Let's get going. It's light enough to see."

Her stomach cramped and Dorrit gasped, quietly. "Clarence, I think I'm sick. You have to go." She wrapped herself in her ragged quilt then stretched out, one arm over her eyes.

"I remember some pink medicine, in a bottle," he said. "Kinda chalky. My ma used to give it to us for the grippe. Maybe they sell that. I'll see."

Dorrit closed her eyes, and heard the door squeaking as it shut, then Clarence's steps retreating. In the distance, a train whistle pealed. With a groan, she pushed herself up and grabbed her satchel, then hurried outside to the woods. After the spasms of sickness passed, she arranged her clothes and inspected the spots on her belly. Now there were twelve. In the growing daylight, she looked around the underbrush; she had learned to recognize poison ivy, but saw none. She checked the seams of her dress, finding no lice or fleas. Wincing at the sting, she dabbed iodine on the rash and attempted to take inventory of her symptoms, wishing she had Dr. Wise's Physician's handbook. Laying a palm on her forehead, she was unable to gauge if she had a fever.

Returning to the forge, the clangor of an approaching train boomed inside her throbbing head, intensifying as it neared. As the train passed Dorrit reached the edge of the woods, where another sound made her stop. She listened, then ducked behind a tree trunk.

There it was again, the familiar *scree-snap! scree-snap!* of the pump handle.

She froze, panting in short, shallow breaths, now on high alert. A slurring male voice swore. A big man in dirty overalls bent under the spigot, his bushy red beard dripping with water. On the ground beside him lay a lumpy gunny sack and a brown liquor bottle. She watched as he knelt to open her father's toolbox. As he rummaged through it Dorrit reached into her satchel and grasped the wrench.

The man tossed something aside, and looked up, right at her. He chuckled. "We-e-ell, hey there, gal. You here all by your lone?"

With her hand in her bag, Dorrit held tight to the wrench. She stepped forward, glancing behind the man, looking for Clarence. She raised her chin, saying, "There's a gang of us."

"Just passin' through, then?" For a terrible, frozen moment, the man looked her up and down.

Dorrit said, "Those tools are mine."

He chuckled again as he closed the lid and snapped it. "Finders keepers. You gonna stop me, girl?" He moved toward her. There was no laughter in his face now. "How about you and me go inside . . ."

As he reached for her, Dorrit dropped her bag, her breath heaving. With all of her strength, she swung the wrench at his head. He bellowed, raising a hand to his temple and in that instant, she left herself. He wheeled toward her, free hand open, and Dorrit felt her cheek smash against her teeth. She tasted blood. It was some other, strange, powerful Dorrit who raised the wrench again, grasping the handle with certainty. The man lifted his fist, then froze. For a split instant, amazement lit his eyes. Like a fish out of water, he made one gasp, then collapsed.

Dorrit's vision blurred; she could not draw a deep breath. Leaning over, hands on her knees, she whimpered. Marbles of pain rattled her head. She tried to focus. The forge seemed miles away. Swiping the back of her hand over her bleeding mouth, she straightened to stand. The man lay face down, his temple now purple. Blood trickled down his neck.

She would not roll him over to see his face.

Thou shalt not kill. The other Dorrit—the warrior—nudged his leg with her toe, then gave him an exploratory prod with the wrench. "Damn you," she breathed, "damn you, damn you to hell." Suddenly, she understood the power that cursing brought—the brief jolt of confidence that came from pronouncing another soul *damned*. Black spots swam in her vision as she began to nod, over and over. "*Damn* you." She looked away, finally, gasping. The cornered rabbit had fought back. A tremor began in her shoulders, then her knees began to shudder. White stars flashed in her vision. She felt filthy, as if the thick stink of the man's breath was smeared into her pores.

The clearheaded, warrior Dorrit pushed the wrench to the bottom of her satchel, knowing she had to get away. With shaking hands, she tried to lift the toolbox. It was as if it had been nailed to the ground. Strength drained from her limbs. Things went gray, then black.

Twenty-Two
MAY

AUGUST 1932

At the Richmond train station, May stood on the platform with Elsie. The late summer Sunday was already sweltering and at eleven in the morning her blouse was sticking to her back. They had not discussed again the check still tucked inside May's handbag. In the clamor of the arriving train, the friends hugged. May held on to Elsie and for a moment, did not want to let go. "Thanks for having me," she said. "This visit was heaven, really. And listen, about . . ."

Elsie held up her hand, raising one eyebrow imperiously above her sunglasses. "Pfft!" she sputtered. "None of that." She dropped her hand and grinned. "I'm excited for you, old dear. Truth be told, I'm a tad jealous. I admire your ambition. Things will work themselves out. I wish you could have stayed for the rest of the week, but having you to myself for a few days was a treat."

The conductor called, "All aboard, all aboard!"

May squeezed Elsie's hand. "I'll telephone you tonight, if I can, as soon as I talk to Byrd. Keep your fingers crossed and give my love to Archie and your boys."

"And you give that darling Hank a big hug from his Godmama."

The porter took May's bag, tipping his hat. "Morning, ma'am." She waved to Elsie through the window glass as the train pulled out.

May tried to finish the magazine story she had started on the way but kept losing her place. All she could think of was the check. She stared at her bag, pondering how best to proceed. Should she speak to her father first? His support would be important. It was his business too. Or Blue, first? Because without him there was no product. Her thoughts ran in circles, like a dog chasing its tail. *I should ask Byrd first. But then again, there's no point in broaching the subject unless Daddy and Blue agree, so . . . All right. First, Daddy. Then Blue, and if he says yes, then Byrd. So by next weekend . . . But that's a whole week. I should ask Byrd first, because if he says no, it doesn't matter what anyone else thinks.* At first, she knew, he would say no. Of course, he would. She needed to present her case in a way he could understand—as a lawyer would, laying out facts, then possible outcomes. Her father could help with projections and pricing. And then, once Byrd understood the idea, she would tell him that *(ta-da!)* the money wasn't even a loan. Elsie called it an investment in womankind, or something like that. Maybe best to leave that bit out. Anyway, it certainly sounded sensible and compelling after two bottles of champagne. Maybe she should rip up the check and toss it in the bin at the station. Why rock the boat, after all? They were getting by well enough, weren't they? May plucked the neckline of her dress, fanning herself, flushed with anxiety and anticipation.

When the train stopped at a crossing, causing a delay, May fidgeted. Another possibility crept down the aisle and took the seat beside her. For a while, it just sat there while she tried not to look over at it, but there it was, and it was not going away. The Liar. *You don't have to tell Byrd*, it whispered into her ear. *He didn't tell you about the auction, did he? You could use Elsie's money to get started and then pay it back before he even realized. It would be easy.* May chided herself, inwardly, frowning out the window, remembering what she had promised Byrd before they married. She hugged herself protectively, a visceral reaction to the shameful memory of facing him in Paris—of being forced to account for the countless, careless lies she had told, to him and to everyone she held dear. The memory turned her hands clammy with dread.

She had lied. *Why?* she wondered, *why do we lie?* It was a rhetorical question. *To make ourselves look better or more important than we are. To save face.* At the time, each lie seemed inconsequential, at first—more of an exaggeration, or a positive affirmation of what she *hoped* might happen: *She was wonderfully successful in her job as wardrobe mistress in Paris! She had met a wonderful, wealthy man who was wild about her! She was getting married, moving to a mansion on the Parc Monceau!*

But she had also told lies to protect people she loved. She lied to her father and to Delphina, shielding them from the terrible truth she unearthed in Paris, in her search for the mother who had left when May was seven. Helen Marshall had been tried and acquitted for the murder of her own infant, then later drowned herself. May had said that her mother died of the Spanish Influenza. Those lies she did not regret; she would keep those painful facts hidden always.

But the lies she told to Byrd during that time had come crashing down. May would never forget the absolute desperation—the need to bare her soul to him, to confess all—whether he forgave her or believed that she had changed. And she had changed. Afterward, he had left Paris, intent upon sorting out his own tangled life. Then, the letters began and with growing trust, they found their way back to each other. She promised Byrd that she would never willingly deceive him again. And she had meant it with all of her heart.

The train car shifted on the tracks and her handbag jostled on the seat beside her. The pale-green corner of Elsie's check peeked out. *It's enough*, the Liar whispered. The hairs on the back of May's neck prickled. The Liar, having caught her attention, continued in that silky voice she had not heard for a long time, *it's enough to get started, to buy new pans and ingredients. Maybe even enough to have a label printed or take out an advertisement in the newspaper.* But could she lie to Byrd? The rooming house was enough of an assault on his pride. This would be too much. *But aren't you partners? Didn't your father save Chestnut Grove, by instigating the penny auction? Byrd needs to realize that you have pride, too, and so does your father. Why can't a woman run a successful business? You've been working at the market for years; you understand invoices and profits.* But how, she wondered, how to bring it up under exactly the right circumstances? It was already Sunday, and he would be leaving to go back to Washington in a matter of hours. She continued to listen to the justifications: *Byrd made a momentous decision about your future, putting all of you at risk, without so much as a by-your-leave. Why aren't you entitled to do the same?*

The train whistle began to blow as the conductor made his way through the cars, calling out, "Keswick! Keswick is next. Please gather your belongings for Keswick."

At four o' clock, when the train pulled into the station, May stood in the open doorway looking up and down the platform. If Byrd left on the 4:35, she wouldn't have much time. She had memorized her points. She was ready. She wouldn't press him, though. She'd suggest they discuss it the following weekend, or on the telephone. He'd be glad to see her, after all. Being away for a few days would almost certainly have made him feel grateful for the way she cared for the children and the household. She spotted Hank, waving and dancing from foot to foot as the tails of his cowboy shirt flapped. It was difficult to convince him to wear any other, and the pearl snaps now pulled across his chest. He was growing so fast. Beside him, Dennis stood, clasping his straw hat. He took her suitcase, nodding hello, while Hank grabbed her around her legs, almost knocking her over.

"Sweetheart!" she laughed. "I think you missed me!" She leaned down to kiss the top of his head. His sweet boy smell tugged at her heart. She sniffed again and identified her own perfume.

"I did, Mama! I really did. And it was Sister who broke your bottle. I promise it was." Hank beseeched her with a worried expression, his lips pursed.

May lifted his chin. "Ah. It sounds like something terribly dramatic has been going on while I've been gone. Hello, Dennis."

Hank continued, tugging at May's hand, "And Delphie wouldn't let me listen to Orphan Annie, 'cause of the bottle, but it was Sister, Mama, not me."

May sighed and patted his shoulder. "We'll sort this out at home."

They walked toward the car and Dennis stowed May's bag in the trunk. She kept her handbag close at her side. "Everything all right at the farm?" she asked.

Dennis twisted his mouth to the side.

"Trouble?" May asked.

He cut his eyes to Hank, saying, "They'll be glad to have you home."

"Ah," May said, "I go away for a few days, and all hell breaks loose."

Dennis nodded and grinned.

Hank bounced on the back seat. "Mama, I'm so glad you're home," he almost wailed, "Daddy forgot to give me a penny to smash and I didn't ever find the one I put on there afore you left to go see Auntie Elsie and he didn't make me brush my teeth either and he can't fix Sister's diapers right and she cried and cried. Will you let me listen tomorrow? Please? Please?"

He continued his pleas, and May felt a rush of affection as the house came into view. Hank leaned over the front seat, pointing through the windshield, "See? Daddy and Blue put the sick lady on the sleeping porch and the doctor came."

"What?" May's question was directed to Dennis, but her gaze shifted to the upstairs porch.

Dennis raised his eyebrows, nodding once. "We used the outside stairs." The car stopped in front of the house.

May stared at the porch and the staircase that ran up the end of the house. "Thank you for coming to get me, Dennis. Hank, you let me talk to your daddy for a minute, all right?" She walked quickly up the front steps. Dennis deposited her case in the hallway and departed. May hurried through the hall to the kitchen, where Delphina stood at the stove, stirring a steaming pot.

"Delphie, what on earth is going on? Hank says—"

"Lordy, May. I thought you'd never get back." Delphina swiped the back of her hand over her forehead.

"Is everyone all right?" May turned toward the parlor.

"For now." The two simple words, May suspected, contained volumes. Delphina continued, wearily, "Doctor Sawyer just left."

"Who's sick? Where's Sister?"

"She's fine. She's with your father. It's that gal." Delphina scowled, pointing her spoon upward. "Byrd and Blue brought home this runaway gal from the Market, early this morning. Plumb out of her head with fever. Blue said he woke up and somebody was pounding on the back door and when he looked out, this gal was laid out on the ground. He called Byrd on the telephone and said that a few days ago Taffy bit her on the ankle, so then Byrd called Doctor Sawyer to come and they brought her here and Doc Sawyer had a look-see and says he thinks she's got typhoid, on account of the rash and the fever, and he says she ought to be in the hospital and all of us will be needing the vaccination, only nobody knows her name or where she came from. She's been ranting but she won't say her name. Might be Typhoid Mary, for all I know." Delphina paused long enough to inhale. "Lord almighty, it has been one hell of a day. I'm making some broth."

Fear clutched at May's neck; she held her hand over her throat. "What about the children?"

"Doctor says be sure to keep them away from her, on account of she's contagious. He was going over to the hobo jungle by the tracks, to see if anybody knows who she is or if any of those men have signs of typhoid. Says some of the folks from the March have got it from camping by those rivers. Then he said he'll come back by here and take her to the hospital. Ought to be any time now. And I'll tell you something else: the minute—the very minute—she leaves this house, I am boiling that bedding. She's probably crawling with cooties." Delphina tapped the spoon against the side of the pot then pointed it at May. "And typhoid is nothing to mess with."

"Hank had the vaccination when he was two. But Sister hasn't had it." May's voice was becoming frantic. "That poor girl."

"Sister hasn't been near her. Hank's been curious but I've kept him close by. The upstairs doors to the porch are locked. That gal ain't going anywhere, unless she's carried."

May walked into her father's room. He sat beside the radio, where instrumental music played, softly. He said, "Welcome home. How was your trip?"

May came closer and ran a finger over her daughter's forehead and leaned down to kiss her father's cheek. "Hi, Daddy. It was nice to get away, but I'm concerned about that girl."

Henry said, "Doc Sawyer is coming back soon."

The radio announcer came on, saying, "Stay tuned for the Ovaltine Family Hour, coming up next, at four thirty."

Her father continued, "Byrd went upstairs to get his bag. Time he left for the station, isn't it?"

Twenty-Three
DORRIT

It tracked her through dark woods—snorting, steaming breath, so close she could feel it on her neck. Huge, it was—a mass of matted black fur, clotted with blood. She tried to run but heavy, rusted iron braces were locked on her legs, weighing her down. With every step the iron screeched, giving her away. The bear followed, close behind. Hot breath chuffed; closer, stinking, illuminating the darkness. Closer.

When she fell, she opened her mouth but could not scream. Sir Galahad arrived in a pool of light. Without his helmet of armor, he was blond, with blue eyes. He carried her gently, telling her, in the kindest voice, that all would be well, soon, that he would take her home. Ma would be there, he said. All would be well, soon.

Dorrit's eyes focused slowly. Instead of Sir Galahad, a concerned-looking, older man with a graying mustache and thick spectacles bent over her. He wore a white coat, and tubes were connected to his ears. Was he an undertaker? He moved a cold metal disc to several points on her chest, then straightened, removing the earpieces while Dorrit observed, floating disembodied, above. She wanted to tell him not to touch her. Snatches of prayers and hymns flitted through her mind, but she could not string them together. Sounds slowed, slurring in her ears. There was a slight thumping on her wrist, but she had no strength to raise her hand, to show him that she was, in fact, alive. Wasn't she? Something pricked her upper arm, but it was over before she could react. Shapes were haloed in indistinct, blurred brightness. Could this be heaven? It pained her to make out individual things, so she closed her eyes again and drifted off.

Twenty-Four
MAY

Early Wednesday morning, May parked the Studebaker behind the market. Inside the screened door, Taffy barked menacingly, until she recognized May. When she opened the door, the dog bounded out, nose to the ground, sniffing, zig-zagging her way to the stack of bushel baskets against the back of the building. As if she had cornered a rat, Taffy began to growl. From inside, Blue called, "Taffy! Hush that racket!"

May was distracted, gathering her things to go inside. Wednesdays were the nights she and Byrd had their midweek telephone call. She had not been able to bring up Elsie's check before he left on Sunday and since then, she had rehearsed a hundred versions of what she might say. The telephone, she knew, was not ideal, placed as it was in the hallway with no privacy and Hank clamoring to speak to his father. Entering the market kitchen, May glanced up at the clock. Ten minutes until eight; opening time. Already, the air was redolent with vinegar and spices. Someone was making pickles.

Blue came in from the room where he slept, rolling the sleeves of his plaid shirt. "Morning," he said, going straight to the boiling kettle on the stove. He poured in a handful of sugar then stirred with a long-handled wooden spoon, squinting into the pungent steam.

"Morning," May said. "Looks like you got an early start." Five watermelons were lined up on the table, with a half-full bowl of pale-green peeled rind.

He continued to stir. "All these melons coming ripe. Got to get the pickle made."

"Blue," May sighed. "When we closed the cannery, we never meant for you to do this yourself. You have enough with keeping up the market."

"Watermelon pickle gets made in August. Wouldn't feel right if it didn't. Wouldn't feel natural." He frowned, looking down into the pot. "So what am I supposed to do with a half acre of watermelons? Leave 'em to rot?"

"Stack them right out there on the porch. Sell them. Heck, give them away to anyone who needs one. We can take a load to the soup kitchen in town."

"Don't feel right to me."

"Things will get better."

He tapped the spoon against the edge of the pot and faced her. "What makes you say that? It's so bad in Iowa, dairy farmers are dumping milk in the road."

"If Roosevelt gets elected, he's going to change things. I believe that, and I can't imagine Hoover winning another term." May saw her opening. "Anyhow, I have an idea I wanted to talk to you about. It involves you."

Blue's chin dropped and he regarded May skeptically. She continued, gaining steam. "What if . . . what if I had some money, and we could start manufacturing the all-day candy bar. I mean, in larger quantities. Lots larger. We could make a go of it, I think—buy ingredients wholesale, or find them locally. We wouldn't be dependent on our own crops, like we were with the canning business. I have some ideas for increasing sales, and we could adapt your recipe for bigger batches. Profits on candy are high." Before he could respond, she pulled a magazine from her bag and laid it on the table. "This is the *Confectioner's Gazette*. It has listings for where to buy equipment and ingredients. Did you know that there are six differ-ent kinds of molasses?" She held up one hand in a halting motion before flipping open the magazine. "The Atlas Syrup Company—it's right in Richmond—they have syrup called Silk Velvet, and one called Capitol, and Red Bird, and New Orleans Blend. And look at this," she tapped the facing page, "Burnett's Standard Color Pastes, in all the colors of the rainbow. We could use them for those fruit drops you make, and look at these adorable chocolate molds, shaped like rabbits! I think this could really work. What do you say?"

"Aw, I don't know," Blue said.

May continued to flip through the magazine, trying to appear nonchalant, but there was a thrill in knowing she had set things in motion. Now she would have to broach the subject with her father. It would have to be that very evening, before Blue had a chance to bring it up with him. Blue, she suspected, wouldn't commit without her father's approval. "Well," she said, "you think about it, and let me know. You'd be a partner, and we'd make decisions together—with Daddy, of course." The seed was planted. She needed to allow it time to germinate. She had until Friday when Byrd came home. Three days.

Taffy scratched at the screen and Blue went to let her in. May tied on her apron, asking, "Whose stuff is that, out back?"

"What stuff?" Blue said.

"A ladies' bag, with a toolbox or something—on top of the baskets. You haven't seen it?"

"I put the rubbish outside last night; there was nothing there. Taffy got to barking up a storm real early, only I didn't let her out." He scratched the back of his neck. "Toolbox, you said? That gal had some sort of box. Painted green?"

May brought the box and bag inside and made room for them on the table. Opening the well-worn satchel seemed intrusive, but why would someone leave it outside the door? Had it been stolen, then abandoned? Inside, there were sewing supplies, some ragged women's clothing and a Nancy Drew Mystery book, stamped from a library in Boston. At the bottom was a composition book with worn corners and water stains.

Leaning against the table, May opened the notebook and began to read. After a few moments, she looked up. This girl had lost her mother. *Just like me*, May thought. "Blue," she said, "this must belong to that sick girl. She's from Boston. Her father took her to the Bonus March. He got arrested. Poor thing! She's been on her own since . . ." May flipped the pages. ". . . since late July. She must have been terrified. I'm going to telephone the hospital after I open up."

Blue packed cubes of melon rind into a mason jar. "Ask them if they know what's wrong with her."

"Dr. Sawyer said it was typhoid."

"Ah. Maybe ask if they can check for rabies."

May closed the notebook. "Rabies? Blue . . ."

"Taffy did give her a nip to the ankle when she came 'round here the first time. It might've bled some. Anyhow, they might check." He tapped a measure of cloves into each jar.

"Exactly how many people has Taffy bitten?"

"That bled?" Blue cocked his head, considering. "Two? Three, maybe. She's a good watchdog. She doesn't bother customers."

"I'll tell the doctor, but honestly, you can't keep a dog here that bites."

May went to the storeroom and removed the bank bag from its hiding place then went to the front of the market, switching on lights along the way. She checked the clock above the door as she unlocked it, then began to put money into the cash register. Her thoughts were on the girl; she wanted to read the rest of her diary. How had she come to be in Keswick? Where was her father?

Through the day, between filling orders and stocking shelves, May read the story of Dorrit Sykes. From what she could discern, the girl's upbringing had been sheltered. So how had she come to be left, sick and alone, at a country market? How had she come to beg food?

May knew that there was only one answer: hunger.

This girl had a story. She had a family. And so, that afternoon when business was quiet, May drove to the hospital and found the girl's room. Shyly, she knocked and waited. A passing nurse said, "Ma'am? You can go on in. She's sleeping." The nurse consulted her clipboard and continued, "Are you a relative?"

"No," May said. "She was brought to my house. But I think I know her name."

"Ah, yes. She's a Jane Doe. A charity case. Poor little mite."

"And it's typhoid?"

"Afraid so."

"Is she any better?"

"We've been giving stipes of kerosene three times a day, and oil of cinnamon for the distention. Her fever was one-oh-four last night. All she's taken is lemonade, but today we'll try some beef tea. She had morphine this morning." The nurse held up her pencil. "You say you know her name?"

"It's Dorrit Marie Sykes. Her father's name is Roy Sykes. They're from Boston. May I go in?"

"Certainly. She hasn't had any visitors. But don't touch her, she's still contagious. The doctor said this morning that they might need to operate. We're hoping a relative will come forward."

May nodded. She stood in the doorway, afraid to approach the bed. The door clicked shut, then all was quiet, and white, and dim. The girl's chest was covered in layers of flannel and a hot water bottle, and the odor of kerosene hung in the air. The girl—*Dorrit*—May reminded herself, was very pale and her face was drawn. Splotches of rosy rash dotted her neck and stick-thin arms. *All alone*, May thought. *Imagine, being alone in a strange place, and so sick. No mother to hold your hand. No one who cares about you. Poor little thing.*

Twenty-Five
DORRIT

Light was the enemy. Each time Dorrit attempted to open her eyes, splinters of brightness pierced her pupils, boring into her head with crushing pressure. Time had become elastic. Nurses sponged her clean or spooned broth into her mouth. When she was lucid, she felt ashamed that she did not have the strength to do these things for herself.

As the day wore on she was able to keep her eyes open, so long as the shades remained down. At her bedside, someone had placed a vase of daisies mixed with leafy sprigs that smelled pleasantly of lemon, cutting the sharp pungency of rubbing alcohol and disinfectant. Dorrit swallowed, wishing for a sip of water but unable to call out for it. When the door to her room opened, she listened for the familiar, rubbery squeak of nurse's shoes on linoleum. Instead, a voice spoke softly, saying, "Hello? Pardon me?"

Dorrit squinted, trying to focus. A woman's face hovered above her, smiling warmly. A pretty, young woman. No starched nurse's cap. No thermometer. "Well," the lady said, "I'm certainly glad to see you're awake. How are you feeling? Oh, forgive me. How rude I'm being! I'm Mrs. Craig. May Craig. You've been here for twelve days. It's Thursday, August 18. You've had us worried, Dorrit. You are called Dorrit? Or is it Marie?"

Dorrit nodded toward the pitcher. How did this woman know her middle name? Mrs. Craig said, "Let me." She poured a cup of water then held it to Dorrit's mouth.

"It's Dorrit. Thank you, ma'am." Her voice was rusty. "What's wrong with me?"

"You've had typhoid fever. They had to operate, to take out your gallbladder." Mrs. Craig frowned, while still smiling. "I'm not sure what function a gallbladder serves, exactly, but the doctor says you'll have a full recovery, though it will take a while to get your strength back.

"Listen, dear," she fussed with the daisies in the vase, "I have to confess that I read your diary. I'm sorry. I know it's personal. Your things were left outside our market. It was a mystery, but then we connected who you are. My husband—his name is Byrd—with a 'y'—he brought you to our house after—well—you were brought to my house."

Vague images played through Dorrit's memory. "He carried me?"

"You've been terribly ill." Mrs. Craig continued, "Your fever went sky high, they said, and there could have been complications. You poor thing." She bit her bottom lip. A moment passed and she reached as if to pat Dorrit's shoulder then stopped and withdrew her hand slowly. With that same frowning smile she said, "I'm sorry. You're not a poor little thing at all. In fact, I believe you've been tremendously brave. I can't imagine what I'd have done in your situation."

Why was this woman being so kind? She owed Dorrit nothing in the world. Mrs. Craig continued, "I wanted to ask you, Dorrit, about your father? Do you think he's still in Washington?"

"Yes, ma'am, as far as I know. He must be awful worried." Dorrit felt tears coming. Blinking them away, she said, "I want to find my pop and go home." She tried to push herself up to sitting. The effort sent a jolt into her abdomen and she winced.

Mrs. Craig said, softly, "You lost your mother."

Dorrit looked down at her hands, willing herself to be still, to deflect emotion. To be vulnerable was to be weak. Weakness was pitiful. Dorrit swallowed, raising her eyes to meet Mrs. Craig's evenly, offering nothing. This stranger knew her secrets; she had no right to them. A long moment passed before Mrs. Craig continued, now businesslike and cheerful, "We'll get this sorted. My husband works in Washington. He can make some calls. Now, you just lie back. You have an incision, and stitches. But they'll take them out today. I'm afraid we had to dispose of your clothes, but I got you a few things at Woolworth's." She held up a brown paper bag. "The good news is that Doctor Sawyer says you're well enough to leave tomorrow. So I thought I'd bring you home with me. Would you like that? Unless you have someone else we could call."

Dorrit shook her head.

The following morning a nurse offered to help Dorrit into a stiff new housedress. Just pushing the buttons through the holes exhausted her. She pulled on the socks Mrs. Craig had brought, and their whiteness contrasted with her worn-out shoes. When the nurse wheeled her outside, the August heat was dazzling, radiating harshly up from the concrete, beating down from a near-white sky, bleaching color from everything. Dorrit shaded her eyes with her hand. Moving from the wheelchair into Mrs. Craig's car left her dizzy. She braced herself, slightly nauseated by the dusky odor of hot leather mixed with engine oil.

Mrs. Craig chattered solicitously, perhaps a little nervously. The rolling, purple-gray mountains in the distance were the Blue Ridge, she explained. She drove over a bridge with a muddy river below, which she said was the Rivanna. The scenery became rural and as they passed cornfields and pastures, she chattered on about her children and her father and their farm. She asked no more questions of Dorrit.

Dorrit observed the scenery with minimal interest. Her attention was sharply tuned on May Craig. She wore gloves, but the fingertips, Dorrit noticed, were frayed, with careful darning on the thumb. Her straw cloche had seen better days, though the grosgrain ribbon appeared to have been recently replaced. The stitches were neatly done. Her dress, a simple cotton floral, looked store-bought, not anything fancy or flounced like Mrs. Frazier would have worn.

Mrs. Craig turned in at a long driveway, saying, "Here we are!" A white farmhouse that needed a coat of paint came into view, with smaller buildings behind it. A double porch ran the length of one side, with the top part screened in. A young man came from behind the house, and Mrs. Craig said his name was Dennis.

She and Dennis each took one of Dorrit's arms and helped her inside. While they stood in the hall, an older woman in an apron stuck her head out of a swinging door, then quickly retreated, but not before Dorrit saw her scowl. At the end of the hall, the telephone stood on a table, but she could not muster the nerve to ask to use it.

From behind another partially closed door, someone called, "May?"

Mrs. Craig responded, "Be there in a minute, Daddy." By the time they reached the top of the stairs, Dorrit was winded. In the bedroom she was led to, the white iron bed had crisp sheets and the walls were papered in a fading pattern of rosebuds and ivy.

As Mrs. Craig tucked the sheet around her and smoothed it, the head of a little blond boy in a cowboy hat peeked around the doorframe. He smiled, rosy and bashful. "You're the sick lady," he announced with sudden solemnity, hooking a finger inside his lower lip. "My mama says I oughtn't go near you."

Dorrit raised her head and started to sit up, but her incision thrummed. "You must be Hank. I've heard lots of nice things about you."

Mrs. Craig held her hand out toward the boy. "Hank, darling, I've told you to take off your hat inside. Come meet Dorrit. We're going to care for her for a few days."

The boy held his hat to his chest as he came forward slowly, looking suspicious. "Did the doctor give you lots of shots and medicine?"

Dorrit smiled. "I think so, but honestly, I was too sick to remember."

"When they gave you shots, did you cry?" Dorrit shook her head. Hank looked up at his mother. "Mama, how come she talks funny?"

"She's from Boston. People up North speak a little differently than we do. Go ask Delphina to open a ginger ale, and bring it up for Dorrit, would you?" Hank nodded and left. "Well," Mrs. Craig continued, "I put your things on the bureau. We'll get you some shoes, and I have some dresses that might work for you."

Dorrit tried again to sit up, stifling a groan. "Thank you, ma'am— Mrs. Craig. Was there a box of tools? A green box?"

"Oh, yes. It's in the basement. You rest now. Hank will bring you that ginger ale. I need to see to Sister. Maybe tomorrow we can look at those dresses? Oh, and please, call me May."

When May went downstairs, Dorrit crept from the bed, feeling like an interloper. She rummaged in her satchel. Her notebook and pencil were still there. She returned to bed, then rifled the pages in an agony of self-consciousness, knowing that May Craig had read and possibly shared her most intimate thoughts. She flipped to a blank page and wrote:

Friday, August 19

I am at the Craigs' house, in a borrowed nightgown. The phone is in the hallway downstairs. Anyone might catch me using it, and that would be embarrassing, for any number of reasons, such as 1. That mean-looking woman might be on the other side of that door, listening, while I ask which jail Pop is in. She looked at me like I'm going to rob them.

A wave of guilt washed over Dorrit. She *had* intended to steal from this family.

2. Long-distance telephone calls are costly, and I have no money to offer.

3. If I talk to Pop, I will most likely cry.

Well, so much for our 'gang.' I supposed I might have become a notorious girl criminal, and maybe Clarence will turn into someone like Charles Arthur Floyd (although nobody would ever think to call Clarence 'Pretty Boy.') Ha. Mrs. Craig asked me who might have left my things behind the market and I lied and told her I did not have the least idea in the world. Not that Clarence Franklin deserves to be protected.

Mrs. Craig (May) says Mr. Craig (Byrd) will come home tonight, for the weekend. I hope he will find Pop, and that he is not sick or hurt. I miss our apartment, and the pigeons, and Mrs. Coughlin. I suppose I did not appreciate our life before. As much as I want for things to go back to the way they were I have to admit to myself that they will never be the same. I will never be the same (for reasons which are best not recorded.)

I might try going back to church when we get home. Or maybe try a different church, and here is why: I might have died of typhoid if I had not been taken to the hospital by good Samaritans. All of the doctors and nurses were so kind, and the medicine made me better, and the doctor said the operation saved my life, so is that wrong? This is confusing to me. More on this later.

Twenty-Six
MAY

Delphina said, "I know exactly what you're doing, May, being all sweet to me. Don't you have better sense than to bring that gal back here? How do you know she won't rob you and then run off in the night?"

In the kitchen, May spooned peas into Sister's mouth, saying, "All I said was, 'Dinner smells wonderful.'" Delphina cut corn kernels from the cob. The aromas of stewing tomatoes and roasting chicken wafted from the range. May continued, "She's weak as a kitten. I can't imagine how she's gotten along until now. You saw her belongings. And it's only for a few days."

Delphina tutted, muttering under her breath, "Land sakes alive, I can't turn around without folks bringing home waifs and strays and hungry mouths to feed."

May glanced up at the wall clock. "Listen, Delphina . . . I need to ask you about something."

"I've got to get supper fixed."

"I need to say something to Byrd, as soon as he gets home—something I've been putting off."

Delphina cocked her head and looked at May with an expression of beleaguered patience. "You pregnant again?"

"No, no. Not that. Elsie gave me a big check to help start the candy business, only I'm afraid to tell Byrd and I don't know if I should just cash it and not . . . not tell him." She exhaled.

"Ah." Delphina nodded.

"It's not really a lie. It's more of . . . an omission. But this is such a generous offer. I feel like it's a sign. Blue thinks it's a good idea and so does Daddy."

Delphina put her hand on her hip. "Blue thinks expanding the candy business is a good idea. That is not the same thing as going along with what you're cooking up. Folks see signs where they want to see signs, Chérie. You'd best tell Byrd. Won't bring a thing in the world but trouble if you don't. Surely you don't need me to tell you that." She waved a dish-towel dismissively. "But you know, might be best for you to wait till he's had his supper."

In the hall mirror, May smoothed her hair then stuck her head into her father's room. Hank sat across the table from his grandfather, studying the checkerboard, Bandit curled up at his feet. If she told Hank she was leaving, he would insist on coming along. And she needed Byrd alone. The weekend before, she had hoped and waited that the right time would present itself, but almost before she knew it, Sunday afternoon had come again, and Hank insisted on going to the station with them.

The train whistle blew in the near distance—a clarion call to action.

When May arrived alone at the station ten minutes later, Byrd was coming down the stairs from the platform. Weariness showed in his face, but he smiled and raised his hand. *He needs a haircut*, she thought, raising her hand in return. Even though they had been living this way for nine months now, it did not get easier, this being half of a couple from Friday to Sunday, switching back to the waiting wife on Mondays. This weekly connection and disconnection, this catching up, this conscious avoidance of conflict and unpleasantness during their brief time together—it was false, contrived. At first, she had not been conscious of the withholding—the way she gauged what to tell him on the telephone when they spoke each Wednesday against what could wait until he came home. When they had spoken last, she relayed Dorrit's progress but didn't mention her impulsive desire to bring the girl to Keswick Farm to convalesce. But Byrd was compassionate, and when May told him about the diary and all Dorrit had been through, he would surely understand.

The other thing she had not mentioned on Wednesday was the check.

Byrd kissed May and tossed his bag into the trunk. He shucked off his suit jacket before holding open the passenger side door for her. He got in and started the car, pulling his necktie out of his collar. "Whew!" He said, "I'm mighty glad to be home."

May bit her lip, then smiled. "I'm glad you're home too."

"Where's Hank?"

"Playing checkers with Dad. I sneaked out! Listen, there's something I've been meaning to talk to you about."

"Uh-oh."

"It's not *bad*." May wriggled in her seat. "Well, actually, there are two things." She smiled brightly, unable to restrain herself. "We've had a wonderful opportunity."

"Really?"

May nodded, turning on the seat to face his profile. "Yes, we have. Remember when I went to Richmond and made that sale to Miller & Rhoads? Well, Elsie was so excited about the business, about the all-day candy bar, she wanted to invest. It's her own money, and . . ."

"Are you telling me you've taken money from her?"

"Not actual money. It's a check. I wanted . . ."

Byrd shoved the gearshift with more force than was necessary. "Absolutely not."

"That's not fair. She offered it to me, not to you. Blue's worked out the recipes, and Daddy thinks . . ."

"We can't afford to take these kinds of chances. I'm getting a paycheck. Do you know how lucky I am?"

May crossed her arms and turned her face away from him, hating the pleading in her voice. "Can't you at least think it over? Please?"

"You're not going to change my mind, May."

"Why should I have to ask you about investing in my father's business? You never asked me the first thing about the auction. I understand your wanting to be careful, I do. But you need to understand that this is something I believe in. When I told you I wanted to go to work in Paris, you didn't believe in me. Why is it that men are allowed to do whatever they want, but women are expected to stay home and mind the children and do as they're told?" She breathed through her nose, collecting herself. It would not do to start a fight, not now, at the beginning of the weekend. She let the wind whip her hair, hoping the tension would blow through. She should have waited, not ambushed him the moment he stepped off the train. Bitter disappointment pressed down on her. *I should have waited until after supper.*

Byrd turned into the driveway. "What else?"

"What?" The single word overflowed with dejection and resentment.

"You said there were two things."

"Yes. I was going to tell you that I brought that girl from the market home. She's in the spare bedroom."

In bed that night, May stared at the ceiling. The six inches between herself and Byrd was a ravine, an abyss. Maybe she should reach out to him, initiate lovemaking. That crossed a line, though. Too conniving, and certainly too obvious since they had not touched each other since they arrived home. There must be a way, she thought, to present the whole thing again from a fresh perspective. It would be better to wait until tomorrow. For a few minutes she imitated sleep-breathing; a single, deep sigh then long, even breaths, knowing that Byrd was also awake. Outside, tree frogs sang while somewhere in the hills a vixen called to her mate.

There was no sleep to be had.

"Are you awake?" she asked.

"Yes."

A different angle. She rolled onto her side, facing him. "I'm sorry I didn't ask you about bringing Dorrit here. I thought you'd agree that she needs our help."

Byrd rubbed the bridge of his nose, addressing the ceiling, wearily, "Of course she needs help. A lot of people do. You can't imagine how many sad cases like her there are in Washington. A lot of the veterans have stayed on, living on the streets. I'll make some calls on Monday; try to find her father." He shifted toward May, propping his head on his palm. "But I hope you understand. We aren't in a position to help them financially. We need to be very careful. Now is not the time to be taking risks."

Twenty-Seven
DORRIT

AUGUST 1932

Through the day Dorrit slept fitfully. In late afternoon, aromas of cooking wafted up the stairs and she tried to identify them: vegetable, possibly stewing tomatoes, and something baking, buttery and sweet, a little lemony. She heard Hank greeting his father, then she tried to make out the snatches of dinner conversation floating up the stairs, picking out individual voices. Later, after Delphina took her supper tray away, the sounds of music carried from the radio along with occasional laughter. She felt like a ghost, observing these familial rituals at a remove. She ran a finger along the fraying edge of the bedsheet, worn from dozens of washings and ironings, and in the dim light, her eyes traced the placid rose vines of the wallpaper. For the first time in a long while, she knew she was safe.

Dorrit heard steps on the stairs and pretended to be sleeping. A light rap was followed by the opening of her door and May's soft call, "Dorrit?" But Dorrit stayed silent, and the door closed with a whispered click. She would not be any more trouble than she had been already. Sleepless, she listened to the settling sounds: calls goodnight and appeals from Hank for another kiss. When the house fell quiet, she ventured out furtively to use the bathroom, dreading the thought of passing Mr. Craig in the hallway. Returning to her room, the sound of voices coming from behind the door of the Craigs' room made her stop. First, murmurings, May's higher and Byrd's, deep. Then, Dorrit heard her name. She froze. The voices rose, still whispering indistinctly but angry now. Suddenly, they went quiet. Dorrit retreated back into her room and closed the door. They were talking about *her*. Arguing. He didn't want her here. Dorrit stood in the center of the room in the dark, arms crossed over her chest. Should she leave now? Slip out the back door into the night? She had nothing. Not even a dress to wear. She crawled back into the bed and stared at the ceiling for a long time.

The next morning May carried in breakfast and said, cheerfully, "Dorrit, are you up to taking a bath? I can bring you a basin if you're not. And then, if you'd like, we'll look for some clothes. I have a sewing machine if we need to hem something."

Dorrit sat up, gingerly. The pain in her side had lessened. "Is it electric—your sewing machine?"

"It is," May said. "I used to sew all of my clothes myself." She half-laughed. "Believe it or not, I once designed costumes for showgirls, in New York and Paris." May smiled at her, absently, and Dorrit could tell that her thoughts were somewhere else.

Dorrit said, "Gosh. I have a treadle machine at home. In fact, if there's anything you need mended, I'd be happy to. If Mister Craig or Mister Marshall needs, I can turn a shirt collar or cuff."

"Right now, you need to work on getting stronger. Doctor Sawyer said you're to stay in bed."

"I'm stronger than I look. I don't want to be a burden."

In the bathroom, Dorrit fitted the rubber stopper into the tub drain and turned the taps, luxuriating in the thought of water coming from a spigot, already steaming. And this bathtub was long enough to stretch out her legs, unlike the galvanized wash boiler at Blossom Street. May had given her a yellow towel and a new bar of soap. Dorrit unwrapped it and held it to her nose. The aroma was floral, but not any specific flower, as far as she could tell. Undressing, she counted sixteen dotted scars where stitches had been in her abdomen. The rash was gone, but her skin flaked in patches and her hipbones were pronounced. She washed her hair then tried to finger comb the snarls, imagining what it would be like to have May Craig's satiny dark bob or those beautiful cheekbones. As the water drained, Dorrit marveled at the convenience of merely pulling a plug instead of scooping dirty bathwater with a bucket. She wondered if she should use the yellow towel to clean the tub. Leaving it might appear slovenly, as if she expected to be waited on, or worse, didn't know any better. She wiped out the tub and then rinsed the towel, draping it squarely along the tub edge before pulling the loaned nightgown over her head.

In the steam-streaked bathroom mirror, she yanked a comb through her hair. A comb was such a personal thing, yet May had offered hers. Dorrit replaced it carefully on the glass shelf above the sink. There were three toothbrushes, and a man's razor and shaving brush. *Genuine Boar Bristle*, the handle said. She ran a finger lightly over the bristles. Gently, she swiped the shaving brush over her cheeks. It was still damp. She smelled it—a male scent, slightly spicy.

From across the hall, May called, "Dorrit? Come in here, if you've finished bathing."

In the front bedroom, May knelt on a braided rug beside an open steamer trunk. The musty scent of camphor wafted from inside. "Have a seat." She indicated the stool at the dressing table then turned to follow Dorrit's gaze toward a shelf of books with fading bindings. "Oh, if you'd like to read any of those, by all means . . . most are from my college English classes. Help yourself."

"You went to college?"

"Only for a year. What about you? Are you—were you—in school?"

"I have one year left."

"Any thoughts of college?"

Dorrit shook her head. May reached into the trunk and pulled out tissue-paper wrapped bundles then exclaimed, softly, "Oh!" as she unwrapped one. Inside was an evening coat of bottle-green velvet with a big collar of auburn fur. She ran her hand over it. "I haven't seen this in years. I bought it in New York, right before I went to Paris. That was before I married Byrd."

"It's very pretty, Mrs. Craig," Dorrit said.

"*May*. You *must* call me May. It is, isn't it? I haven't got any place to wear it now. And I suppose it's out of style." She opened another bundle. "Ah, now these might work for you. I'm afraid they're a bit dated, but if we hemmed them up . . ." She held out a dress, shaking out the creases. It was crepe, a print of white calla lilies on pale green.

"That's such a nice dress. I couldn't . . ."

"Nonsense," May said. "And here, I sewed this one myself." She held up a pink, printed cotton dress with a small white collar.

"Oh, that's so pretty. And look what a nice job you did with the piping."

"Try it on." May sounded excited. Dorrit slipped it over her head, over the nightgown. It looked ridiculous, with white muslin ballooning from the sleeves and below the hem.

"I think it will fit you fine," May said, with apparent satisfaction. "It does need to be shortened about three inches. I can pin it on you if you like."

"I can hem it myself. I have my sewing kit with my things." Dorrit smoothed the fabric, tracing the fern pattern of the print. "Thank you, ma'am."

"All right, then." May began to repack the trunk, pausing to run her hand over the evening coat once more.

Dorrit went to her room to retrieve her satchel then followed May down the hall to her sewing room. An old-fashioned, wasp-waisted dress form stood in one corner next to a door that led to the upstairs porch. Costume sketches were tacked to the walls. She picked up a pattern envelope from the ironing board. Beneath were cut lengths of three similar checked cotton fabrics and three cards of buttons. "Oh," May said, with a disparaging smile, "I've been meaning to sew some shirts for Hank. He starts first grade in a few weeks. But there simply hasn't been time . . . And, speaking of time, I'm going to run up to the market for a bit while Byrd and Hank are riding. So I'll leave you to it. Please, look around for any sewing supplies you might need, and for goodness' sake, don't over-tire yourself. Sit outside, if you like. The porch is shady. If you go down at lunchtime, Delphina will fix you something."

The sunny, quiet sewing room was like a comforting balm. Here was a place where Dorrit knew exactly what she was doing. After she measured and cut the dress hem, she stitched the raw edge, delighted to find that using an electric machine was very nearly the same as her treadle model. She measured again, then turned up a three-inch hem and pinned it before whip-stitching it into place. It felt good to have a needle in her hand again—the precision of neatly spaced stitches, the scent of cotton steaming under the iron—such *normal* things. She eyed the stack of shirt fabrics. Would May be pleased, or offended, if Dorrit tried to help?

When she finished pressing the dress, she put it on over the new drawers and slip May had bought for her. Dorrit blushed to think of May having seen her ratty old underpants in her satchel. Or worse even, than that, the unfriendly housekeeper—what was she called? Delphine? Adelphia? Had *she* inspected Dorrit's stained underclothes?

At the top of the stairs, Dorrit listened, wanting but also not wanting to go downstairs if May wasn't there. From the window in the hallway, she could see across fields, where the rail fence continued, disappearing over hill. On the bottom step, she paused to catch her breath, gripping the newel post, and listened again. From the front room, a radio serial played. Melodramatic voices rose and fell, interspersed with sound effects—tinny gunshots and clomping horse hooves.

At the other end of the hall, a swinging door was propped open, leading into a pantry. Beyond, the kitchen looked empty. She continued through to the back screened door. In the yard between a cottage and the house, the housekeeper pinned clothes to a line. In a wicker basket on the ground, the little girl sat atop a pile of dry laundry, gumming a clothespin. Bright white sheets snapped like sails in the sun. The woman stooped to collect the basket, settling it on her hip, saying, "Who wants a ride in the boat! Hang on, a wave's coming! Woo, woo!" The basket swung as Sister squealed with delight. The housekeeper came up the steps and inside. She placed the basket on the floor and lifted the girl out. Seeing Dorrit, her expression changed to blankness.

Dorrit smiled, clasping her hands in front of her. "Good morning?" she ventured.

"Thought you were supposed to stay in bed." The woman raised an eyebrow and fitted the baby into a high chair that was pulled up beside the table.

"I'm not used to being waited on."

"Well, that's a good thing, cause nobody here's got time to wait on you."

"I can do most anything that needs doing—polishing, or ironing, or sewing. I'm especially good at sewing. And Mrs. Craig has been so kind, giving me this dress and all . . ." She swayed back, holding out the sides of the dress as if for inspection. This woman's approval would be hard won, and Dorrit quashed the urge to beg forgiveness. It was as if the housekeeper could see Dorrit's transgressions written on her face.

The woman frowned, saying, "I take care of those things myself." Then she raised her chin almost imperceptibly, as if to say, *go on, keep trying, but I know what you've done.*

Dorrit said, "I could watch the baby for you, or feed her. I . . . used to babysit the neighbors," her voice dropped, "back at home."

Dorrit continued, attempting to justify herself, "I have a family. I just don't know where they are right now. My father's in Washington. You probably know that already. My older brother—he's called Walt—he joined the Merchant Marine because he got angry with our father, because in our religion we don't use doctors. My mother wouldn't have one come and she died."

The housekeeper nodded. "Umhmm." She looked Dorrit right in the eyes, saying, "Sounds like you have had a right rough time."

"Yes, ma'am."

Delphina moved to the oven to remove a pan of perfectly browned Sally Lunn bread. Setting it to cool, she said, "Maybe that's why May's taken a shine to you." She faced Dorrit then, folding the dishtowel she held. Her voice was no friendlier, but it was not hostile. "She says since they took your gallbladder out, you're not contagious. That right?"

"Yes, ma'am."

"Well, then, how about you carry Mister M's lunch in to him? He gets laid up with his back sometimes and stays downstairs. No sense in you just standing around gawking."

"Yes, ma'am. And my name is Dorrit. Dorrit Sykes. I'm not . . . I'm not sure what I ought to call you."

"Delphina Fontaine is my name." She began to arrange flatware on a tray with a glass of iced tea.

"Miss or Missus Fontaine?"

"Ain't any of your business, but it's Miss." She folded a napkin, placing it beneath the fork. Her voice was almost warm when she said, "Reckon you're wanting some lunch too."

Dorrit carried the tray through the swinging door, smiling shyly at the old man. His skin had a waxen pallor, peppered with brown spots. He cocked his head. "Thank you, young lady," he said. "How do you do?" He reached for the tray and settled it on his lap, then proffered a rope-veined hand.

Dorrit shook it, holding his gaze. His eyes were pretty, the same pale gray-green as his daughter's. "Much better now, thank you, sir."

He nodded slowly, appraisingly. "Sounds like you've had quite the adventure." Dorrit looked down, blushing, and he continued, "Get a plate for yourself and come sit with me. Tell me about the March. Unless you've got somewhere else you need to be. I'm stuck right here, myself. Bad back. I don't like to complain. I know I'm a burden, especially on May. It's my own damned fault, of course."

"Oh, no, I'm sure—" He held up a hand, and Dorrit closed her mouth.

"Now, I don't know about you," he said, "but I dearly hate being so dependent on folks to care for me. People think you can't see—but you can—when they're being patient instead of interested, and when they'd rather be doing anything than take care of a broke-down old man."

Disarmed by his candor, Dorrit was unsure how to respond. Refuting what he said with platitudes would be precisely what he was describing. They smiled at each other.

Twenty-Eight
DORRIT

After lunch, the kitchen was empty. Dorrit began to wash the plates. With Delphina, she decided, it might be best to just jump in instead of asking. She would not get back in bed, she resolved, even though being up and around had tired her. From beyond the screened door, the sounds of voices carried. A breathless shout then a child's laugh, followed by the slapping of small feet against the steps. "I beat you, Daddy!" Hank hurled himself against the door and a man trotted up the steps, catching him around the waist, swinging him up.

They burst through the door, and the man put Hank down then wiped his hands against his dungarees saying, "Well, hello there. You must be Dorrit. I'm guessing you don't recall our meeting before."

Dorrit's face burned. There, standing right in front of her, was Sir Galahad. Tongue-tied, she dried her hands quickly, offering a handshake. "Hello," she managed, then, "Yes. Yes, sir. You all are so kind to have me here."

Mr. Craig shook her hand then tousled Hank's hair. He said, "Wash your hands, buddy, and then go tell Grandpa about the snake."

Hank rubbed his hands together and announced to Dorrit, "Daddy and me saw a copperhead on a rock! And it did like this . . ." He waggled his tongue. "Peanut was scared, but I wasn't. And then, we found a arrowhead." He felt in his pocket and pulled out a gray stone. "See?"

"My, my," Dorrit said, "you've had quite a morning, haven't you? I've never seen a real arrowhead." She bent down to his eye level, skimming a finger over the stone's sharp edges. "You be careful with that, now. You could hurt yourself."

"And lookie!" He rummaged in another pocket, and pulled out a flat oval of copper, holding it out. "Guess what this is, Dort."

"I can't imagine."

"It's a lucky charm now, only it used to be a penny. My grandpa gives me them, for the train to smash. Only sometimes I can't find them, after." Dorrit nodded solemnly. Hank ran off, calling for his grandfather.

Byrd washed his hands in the sink, saying over his shoulder, "How are you today? You look a good bit better than you did the first time I saw you."

Dorrit flushed again. "I'm fine, thank you, Mister Craig."

"Well, good." There was no offer to call him Byrd. Dorrit desperately wanted to be anywhere else. He said, "I'll make some calls when I get back to Washington, about your father."

"Thank you, so much. Honestly, I—"

From the porch came a call of, "Yoo-hoo!" The screened door creaked open again, and an older, bearded man came in, struggling under the weight of a wooden crate. He smiled, nodding at Dorrit, and said, "Well, howdy, y'all."

Byrd said, "Cy, this is Dorrit Sykes. Dorrit, this is May's uncle, Cy Waddell."

Mr. Waddell nodded, releasing the crate on the kitchen table with a huff. He swiped off his cap. "Call me Cy." Looking back over his shoulder, he called, "Wipe your feet, now." The door slapped shut again, and he said, "Don't believe y'all have met our newest boarder. Been here for a couple of days, working 'round the kitchen and such."

The young man who followed Cy also carried a crate. He stopped inside the door, his Adam's apple bobbing. "Howdy, Mister Craig," he said, looking down, "miss."

"Welcome," Byrd said. "What's your name, son?"

"Clarence, sir. Clarence Franklin." He nodded toward Dorrit, then quickly left the crate and went back out the door. His ears were bright red.

Byrd said, "What's all this, Cy?"

"Found 'em, yesterday." Cy nodded toward the crates. "Clarence was washing the floors in the big front room and the mop caught on something. Turns out it was the handle of a trapdoor. Looks like your daddy had a nice collection of Kentucky bourbon and brandy from France, sacked away in a hidey-hole." He grinned. "Figure it's best to get them out of the house 'fore one of the tenants finds the stash. Couple more out in the truck. Course, if we was to be strictly legal, we'd pour it all out."

Byrd shook his head and rubbed a hand over his mouth. "I'll give you a hand." He and Cy went out as Clarence was coming back in with another crate.

The door whined shut and Dorrit was alone with him. She looked toward Mr. Marshall's door, then back at Clarence, hissing, "What are you *doing* here?"

"What are *you* doing here?"

"I had typhoid fever. I was in the hospital. The Craigs took me in."

Clarence looked abashed. "When I took you over there, I thought—"

"Took me where?"

"You don't remember?"

"I remember feeling sick."

Clarence licked his lips. "Ah . . . you were like, delirious. I carried you to the market and knocked on the door and hid. I watched, till Blue came out and found you. I was afraid he'd recognize me. You going to rat me out?"

Dorrit crossed her arms over her chest. "You mean, am I going to tell these nice people that you're a no-count, cowardly, deserting thief?"

He whispered, urgently, "Hey, I saved you. I didn't take any of your stuff, did I? Who do you think left it at the market? And look at all this hooch. It's worth a fortune to a bootlegger. I could've taken it, and no one would ever know. You going to tell?"

"I don't see the point. Anyhow, I'm only here till my pop comes to take me home."

"When will that be?"

"I don't know yet."

Clarence fiddled with one of the bottles, examining the label. Without looking at her, he asked, gruffly, "You going to be all right? I mean, with the typhoid?"

"I s'pose so. They said I nearly died."

"Well, that's good. I mean, it's not good that you almost died—it's good that you're all right. And you really don't remember?" Dorrit shook her head. "You know something?" He grinned. "I like it here."

Delphina marched in from the porch, scowling, with Sister hitched on her hip. She took one look at the crates and said, "What on earth?"

Clarence ducked his head. "Howdy, ma'am. I'm just leaving." He was out the door and away.

Byrd and Cy carried in two more crates and Delphina said, "What's this you're bringing in here? I'm not getting arrested. Get it out of here this minute!"

Byrd said, "We'll take it to the cellar. Where is May?"

"Not sure," Delphina said.

"She's at the market, isn't she?" Byrd turned toward the hall and Dorrit heard him say, under his breath, "Of course she is."

Through the weekend Dorrit tried to help around the house while also trying to stay out of the way. Hank had begun to look for her, and Sister required constant watching around the stairs, and in the kitchen. Dorrit wanted to express her gratitude, to operate in good faith. These kind people had taken in a stranger, offering shelter and safety. She debated whether she should confess her connection to Clarence. She supposed he deserved a chance to redeem himself. Who was she to judge who was or wasn't redeemable? Right and wrong were not so easily defined anymore.

At six thirty on Monday morning, Dorrit heard May going downstairs. When she heard the little girl cry from across the hall, she dressed quickly. In the children's room, Hank slept in his single bed against the wall. Dorrit took Sister from her crib, soothing her. The door creaked open and May came in, carrying a baby bottle. She smiled and whispered, "Dorrit, you're not sup-posed to lift anything! But thank you. I was getting Daddy his coffee."

Dorrit patted Sister's bottom and whispered, "Let me change her diaper and feed her. I'm all right to hold her, I promise. I won't carry her down the stairs."

The aroma of pancakes was wafting from the kitchen when Dorrit went downstairs. Squaring her shoulders, she pushed open the swinging door. Following Delphina's curt instructions, she helped to arrange break-fast. May came bustling into the kitchen with the baby, settling her in her highchair. Hank followed, still clad in pajamas, trailing his cowboy hat. May poured herself coffee, saying, "Did you sleep well? I hope you didn't run a fever again last night."

The mood in the house was lighter than it had been the day before. May seemed far more relaxed. Dorrit said, "Oh, I slept wonderfully well, thank you."

May said, "I need to get to the market before eight. I'll be home around four. You take it easy today and rest. Promise?"

"Please, tell me what I can do to help. I used to watch children, in our building—a baby, four months old."

May glanced at her wristwatch. "Little Elsie is fourteen months. She's into *every*thing. We're trying to get her to drink from a cup. You might ask Delphina if you can help in the kitchen. She'll probably say no. The im-portant thing is that you rest."

When Sister went down for her nap after lunch, Dorrit sat in the rocking chair in the children's room and read Hank one of her fairy sto-ries. Downstairs, the telephone trilled. Dorrit stopped reading and went to listen from the door.

From below, Delphina said, "Yes. We'll accept charges." Then she called upstairs, "Dorrit?"

Dorrit drew in her breath as she raised the earpiece. Delphina re-turned to the kitchen.

"Baby Doll?" She heard static, then, "Is that you?"

All Dorrit could manage was a choking breath before she began to cry. "Pop."

Roy said, "I've been worried sick about you! Mister Craig tracked me down. He says you've been ill."

"I'm . . . I'm all right now. I just want to go home."

"I do, too, Baby Doll. I do too. Only, well, there's the rub. I'm in for sixty days, no bail." There was a long pause.

"Another whole month?"

Her father continued, "It's not so bad here. They feed us three times a day. But listen, you get yourself on a train home. Soon as they let me out, I'll get up there. That Mister Craig was kind enough to offer to get you a ticket. We'll see each other real soon, all right?"

Dorrit's voice was expressionless. "All right, Pop. Goodbye." As she replaced the receiver, her face filled with heat. Her father had not asked how she had survived, nor had he apologized for leaving her alone. Now she would be further indebted. Anger and sick shame settled in her stomach. She didn't want Mr. Craig to pay for her ticket, but the thought of riding the rails again defeated her.

Twenty-Nine
MAY

This day, May thought, *can only go uphill.* At 8:40 a.m., she pulled in behind the market, having just dropped Hank off for his second day at Cismont School. The teacher had chided her for bringing him twenty minutes late, as if May herself were the first-grader. Thankfully, Dennis would pick Hank up in the afternoon and Dorrit would babysit until May returned home. Today was important.

She and Byrd had argued, but May convinced him to allow Dorrit to stay with them until her father was released from jail. The girl had insisted—May thought rather stridently—that she would only stay if she could earn her keep. Well, that worked out fine. Already, Dorrit had sewn two of Hank's little shirts without being asked. He adored her stories and her quiet, attentive patience, and she was wonderful with Sister.

While May checked off her order forms, Dennis and Blue loaded the trunk of the Studebaker with stacks of glossy white boxes, each tied with a bright blue ribbon. Inside each box were fifteen near-perfect pieces of candy. May and Blue exchanged smiles. Twenty boxes for Miller & Rhoads Department Store, fifteen for the Jefferson Hotel, and a dozen for a tearoom on Cary Street, plus six sample boxes of all-day bars, each folded neatly into waxed paper. She would deliver these orders, then take samples of the all-day bar to a dozen other places on her list.

May had charged the ingredients to the market accounts. Slowly and steadily—she felt sure—their wholesale customer list would grow. Profits would multiply, and they would start buying in bulk. All going well, she would arrive in Richmond by eleven o'clock and be back by five, after a late lunch at Elsie's club.

May looked forward to telling Elsie of this modest success. She was not, however, looking forward to returning Elsie's check to her with an explanation that she was being an obedient wife. It still stuck in her craw. She had not brought the matter up with Byrd again. She would not. Getting started would just take a little longer than she'd hoped. She envisioned a scene in her mind—holding out a stack of money to Byrd—the fruits of her own labor and ingenuity. His expression of puzzled surprise would change to dawning appreciation, then pride. She smiled to herself, and heard Delphina saying, *Don't count your chickens before they're hatched.*

She settled herself behind the wheel, saying, "Dennis, you won't forget to pick up Hank at two? Be sure he has his lunch pail." Dennis nodded.

"You got a full tank of gas?" Blue asked, leaning his forearms on the window frame, checking the gauge.

"I do. Wish me luck!" May waved goodbye, squinting into the sun as she pulled onto the road, brimming with anticipation. It was *happening.*

An hour later she was passing Oilville, where a brightly colored handbill tacked to a telegraph pole caused her to slow. With a pang of nostalgia, she recognized a poster advertising the upcoming Virginia State Fair. This would be the first year in May's memory that Keswick Farm Orchards would not have a booth there. At fifteen, May had sewn a banner to hang behind their table. When their plum chutney and spiced peaches won ribbons, Blue proudly affixed them to the banner, and for years, those ribbons increased in number. May had wanted to take a booth again, to make candy right there on the midway, but now they didn't have the help. She hadn't even brought it up to Byrd, because he would ask where the money would come from to rent the booth, and the argument would start again.

At ten thirty, as she passed Manakin-Sabot, the car began to sputter and hiss. After two jolting shudders forward, it rolled to a halt on the

Richmond Road. May steered to the shoulder, repeating, "Oh, no. Oh, no. Oh, noo . . ." She tried the starter, then banged her palms against the steering wheel. Pulling off her gloves, she got out, then took off her suit jacket and folded it carefully, laying it on the back seat. As far as she could see, tall cornfields bordered the road on the right. On the left was a peanut patch, with pine woods behind. The only building in sight was an abandoned barn with a Burma Shave advertisement painted across the side: THERE'S NO WHISKER IT WON'T SOFTEN—SHAVE 'EM CLOSE AND NOT SO OFTEN!

She dusted her palms together, then popped the hood latch. Jumping back, she shook her hand with a closed-mouth shriek, her fingers scalded. Steam billowed up into a breezeless, cloudless sky. Peering into the engine May felt impotent and foolish, not understanding what the problem was or even what, exactly, she was looking at. *Radiator?* Was that it? Heat shimmered from the engine. Dejected, she sank to sit on the running board. The black car was hot against her back. "I'll give it a few minutes," she said, inspecting her reddened palm. "Someone will come along."

An hour passed. The sun inched higher, toward midday. May fanned her face with her hat, holding her arms away from her body as sweat trickled down her sides. Finally, a horse-drawn wagon trundled over the hill from the west. The old farmer inspected the engine then scratched his head, admitting that he had never driven an automobile. He offered to take her to a telephone up the road. He didn't mention that it was ten miles up the road.

At noon, at the filling station, May described her plight to the attendant, who explained that he was there alone and could not leave until someone else came on, at two o'clock. She called Elsie, leaving a message of apology that she would miss their lunch date. Thoroughly wilted, she bought a Coca-Cola and a bag of salted peanuts, then sat on the steps to eat them, tossing shells into the gravel with a desultory aim.

Back at the car, the attendant put water in the radiator and the engine started again. He tipped his cap and drove off, and she was left with a dollar and seventy-five cents. She opened the trunk. Inside, the stacked boxes sagged. Chocolate oozed between caramels and toffees and nut brittle, soaking the paper doilies and saturating the box bottoms. Every package was ruined, and the all-day bars were nothing but warm waxed-paper-wrapped puddles. She slammed the trunk closed and got behind the wheel, wincing as hot seat leather touched her skin. She was forty miles from Richmond.

May was hot and angry—angry at the radiator, angry at herself. Should she call this a failed experiment? Should she give up? She could call her customers, she reasoned, and ask to deliver next week, instead. Was this worth it?

Shifting the car into first gear, she glanced behind her before pulling out into the road. Instead of rotating the wheel back toward home, almost of their own volition, her hands steered straight, in the direction of the filling station. When she got there, the big thermometer mounted on the porch read eighty-eight degrees. She parked in the shade and from the payphone she called her customers, asking to deliver their orders the next day instead. Thankfully, all were amenable.

She bought another cold Coca-Cola from the man who had helped her earlier. As he pulled it from the ice chest, a refreshing, frigid waft curled upward, cooling May's skin.

"Mister," she said, suddenly standing alert, "I need to buy the ice from your soda pop cooler."

"Huh?" His nose wrinkled.

"Your ice. I need to buy it."

"We don't sell ice, lady. You got to call the iceman."

"This is . . . it's sort of an ice emergency."

The man frowned but took the dollar she offered, and when he tucked it into a gray canvas bag, imprinted, *Commonwealth Bank, Richmond, Virginia*, May thought, *This is a sign!*

He carried the dripping ice block to her car, while May brushed away the bees that had begun to show interest. The attendant set the ice block in the trunk and walked away, looking as if he thought he expected a tip. *Salvage*, May thought. *Salvage what you can. Adapt.* The ribbons, she decided, could be reused if the stained sections were cut out. *A bow, glued on, instead of tying the box closed.* The nut brittle and butterscotch were still solid. *A little rinse off and air dry, and no one will be the wiser.* The melted all-day bars could be poured into muffin tins! *They'll be mix-ups, or jumbles, or fumbles. Yes, Fumbles! Chocolate Fumbles.* She slammed the trunk shut, then dusted off her hands and marched back up the steps to the payphone.

"Good afternoon Keswick Market, Blue Harris speaking."

"Blue. It's May. There's been . . . there's been a slight problem with the car. It's fine now, but how much sugar and cocoa do you have left?"

"Used it all up, except what's on the market shelves, for sale. I got it on order for next week, though. What happened?"

"We're going to have to work late tonight. I'm sorry. Get started on a batch of caramel and I'll explain later. This is my last nickel. Would you please call the farm and tell Delphina I'll be late?"

May returned to the car. She blotted her face with her handkerchief and arranged her hair in the rearview mirror before putting on more lipstick. *Crimson as Sin. Oh, yes.* She swiveled the tube closed, telling herself that the vivid color showed her to be a woman of decisiveness and nerve—a woman who wore any shade of lipstick that pleased her, men be damned. Driving to Richmond, the breeze cooled her. She pulled up in front of the imposing marble columns of the First Commonwealth Bank and pulled gloves over clammy palms, remembering her meeting with Mr. Boxley. Smoothing her skirt, she checked for chocolate stains, then squared her shoulders and marched inside. At the desk, she asked to speak to Mr. Faulconer, saying she was an associate of Elsie Nelson. Within minutes, an office door swung open and a smiling man with a shiny bald head came out to shake her hand.

"Good afternoon!" he said, jovially. "Please, come into my office, Mrs. Craig. May I offer you a cup of coffee?"

"No, thank you," May said. They sat on opposite sides of a wide desk. She met his glance squarely. There would be no ladylike mincing today. Today, she was *Crimson as Sin.*

"What brings you in to see us?"

May pulled Elsie's check from her bag. "I'd like to cash this, please." She slid it across the desk.

Mr. Faulconer's eyebrows rose and he held the check with his finger-tips. "Hmm. You say you're Mrs. Nelson's friend?"

"Friend, and also business associate."

"Well, now, isn't that interesting. I hadn't heard about this. Well, well, well." He dropped the check onto his desk and clasped his hands over his stomach, leaning back until his chair groaned. He ran a hand over his smooth scalp. "Let me explain something for you, Mrs. Craig—in a way that a lady like yourself might be able to understand. The world of banking must be somewhat . . ." He twirled his fingers toward the ceiling, indicating something hard to define. ". . . somewhat mysterious. The bank doesn't specifically keep these sorts of funds on hand, strictly speaking. It's rather complicated. But you needn't worry your pretty head about it." He shifted forward as if he might stand. As if he might dismiss her.

"Mister Faulconer," May placed her gloved palms flat on his desk, "you and I both know that Elsie Nelson's check is good. Let me try to explain this in a way that *you* might understand. I need some of that money. Today, actually." The clock on his wall read three thirty. "I need it right now." She tapped her index finger on the desk, then dropped her hands into her lap and stared across at the banker.

He smiled indulgently. "I'm afraid I can't do that, Mrs. Craig."

"Are you saying that your bank cannot honor this check? Shall we ring up Mrs. Nelson? You could explain it to her. Perhaps she could understand better than I can." May leaned toward him and dropped her voice. "You know, the way that banks have been failing left and right recently, one might become *concerned* about the security of one's funds. A patron's confidence in a particular bank might falter, mightn't it, Mister Faulconer? May I use your telephone?" She raised her eyebrows and continued to hold his gaze, unflinching. The silence grew thick between them.

Finally, the banker broke eye contact and he let out a long, exasperated breath. "Well, since you are so very insistent, here's what I can do. You deposit the check and I will open an account for you and issue you a checkbook. Will that be sufficient? Really, you ought to give a bit more notice next time."

"Why, yes. That would be entirely sufficient."

May left the bank with a stiff leather checkbook and drove immediately to the Atlas Syrup Company, where she opened a wholesale account in the name of the Orchard De-Lite Confections. She hesitated, filling out the form, then put only her own name. Taking this step had to be her own risk. She couldn't list her father or Blue without their agreement. She drove to a loading dock in back, where a pair of burly men hefted fifty-pound bags of sugar and cocoa into the back seat of her car, along with bags of shelled pecans and peanuts and jugs of molasses and corn syrup and tins of cocoa.

Driving home, May was weak with hunger, combined with the heat of the day. Her head swam with the intensely sweet aromas—cocoa and molasses combining with hopeful possibilities. *What's done is done*, she told herself. Now she could agree with that naughty inner voice—the one that sat beside her on the train and told her that it wouldn't *really* be a lie unless Byrd asked her, point-blank. Her father and Blue, however, could not be kept in the dark for long.

By the time she got back to Keswick, it was nearly seven o'clock. As she fixed herself a sandwich in the market kitchen, she wondered if she should run home to say goodnight to the children. But that would necessitate some sort of explanation. She tied on an apron and got to work. Blue worked silently alongside, and as she assembled candy boxes May blocked from her mind the enormity of what she had done that afternoon. She drank bottle after bottle of Coca-Cola, until she was jittery, and at 1:00 a.m., with Taffy curled up sleeping on gunny sacks in the corner and the sink piled with unwashed pots, May glued the last ribbon bow onto a box and untied her apron. Her ears rang with exhaustion, but there were four dozen perfect boxes of candy, ready to go.

Blue's shoulders slumped in fatigue, but he smiled, looking at the boxes. "You go on home."

"Thank you. I'll be by to get these at about eight thirty. Maybe Uncle Cy can come by tomorrow and help out behind the counter. I'll talk to him in the morning." May stood with her hands on the work table, frowning down at the last cooling pans of candy. "We have to come up with a name for the all-day bar," she said. "What do you think?"

Blue rubbed his forehead wearily. "Aw, I don't know. It's a candy bar."

"It has to be something catchy, like the candy in magazine advertisements. Something that explains why it's special. And I'll have labels printed. It'll look really professional."

Blue had his back to her, rinsing a pan. "May?" He said, "I can't help but be a mite bit curious about how it was that you lost that whole order, then came back here with a couple hundred dollars' worth of ingredients. I know how much that stuff costs. Where'd you get money like that?"

"Don't worry. I want you to be a partner in this."

"I know you went to the bank with Henry . . ."

"And Cecil Boxley told me no. It's a man's world, Blue."

He faced her, drying his hands. "No," he said. "It's a white man's world."

Holding his gaze, she said, "You're exactly right. I wish things were different. So let's prove them wrong. We can make a contract between ourselves. I'm not going to ask you to put a dime of your savings in. We need your ideas, and your art. This can't fly without you."

"So you're telling me that you've got money to do this, only it's not from the bank, and Byrd doesn't know about it?"

Here it was, the one thing she did not want to have to think about. She was too tired to come up with a story. She said, "Well, yes, that's about it. But listen, Byrd didn't . . . I didn't . . . Don't tell him, please. I figure, once we get paid for these orders we'll be in clover. So let's keep this between ourselves, for now. Can we do that?"

He shook his head, but he was grinning. "Get some sleep now. I'll see you in the morning."

The next morning, May woke up to find she had slept past seven thirty. She rolled from the bed and shrugged into her robe. Now that Hank was in school, there was a new schedule to be kept. The children's bedroom was empty. Downstairs in the kitchen May found Hank at the table beside Dorrit, spooning cornflakes into his mouth, dressed for school, his hair neatly combed. Sister sat in Dorrit's lap. Hank's lunch pail was on the counter, packed to go. The girl was a godsend.

Hank was speaking to Dorrit. "Tell me another one? Please?"

May said, "Well good morning, y'all. Is Dorrit telling you stories?"

Hank said, "About the boys who fly in the trees." Suddenly serious, he asked, "Dort, is a wood sprite like a tooth fairy?"

Dorrit bounced Sister on her knee. "Oh, they're not the same at all."

Hank looked thoughtful. "Finish telling me the other one, about the candy, please?"

May said, "I'm afraid that will have to wait until after school."

Thirty
DORRIT

September 23

I had the nightmare again.

On Tuesday, I had a letter from Pop. He should be released next week, and we will go home! I can hardly believe I have been living here for a whole month. May tried to pay me for helping, but I would never take it. She works so hard, I'm happy to help out. When Byrd is home she never talks about the business. I get the feeling he is not happy about it. On Saturday the family is going to the Virginia State Fair, and on Sunday, children from around here will come and pick apples in the orchard. Hank has been begging me to have a ride on Peanut. I am embarrassed to tell him that I am genuinely afraid of ponies (great big teeth).

He is such a dear boy. Sometimes I find myself wondering what it would have been like to have a baby brother or sister. And I wonder what became of the Sullivans. But that just makes me sad. It is not productive. Hank is learning his letters, and he's so like his father, the way he loves Bandit and his pony. One of his chores is to collect the eggs every day. I must confess here: I am also afraid of chickens (long, scaly claws, pointy beaks, yellow eyes.) And the rooster is so mean. Last week there was a blacksnake in the henhouse. Delphina just shooed it away with a broom. She thinks nothing of wringing a hen's neck and cutting its head off.

Life in the country is very different from Boston. At night, the sky is full of stars, lots more than you can see in the city. And the smells are so much nicer (except for manure, and when Bandit got sprayed by a skunk.) But still, I do miss home.

Yesterday, I mailed the Nancy Drew book back to the Boston Library. May took me to the Charlottesville Public Library. They do not have the newest Nancy Drew yet, but I did get the My Treehouse books to read to Hank. He seems to like the stories I make up more, though.

I have missed two weeks of school and I am thinking I will not go back.

Now it is time to get Sister's dinner.

Downstairs, in the late afternoon, Dorrit sat on the floor of the parlor with Sister. The toddler mouthed wooden blocks, banging them together and squealing. Hank played checkers with his grandfather. "Sister!" Hank whined, "Dort, make her hush? I can't hear Orphan Annie."

"Shh," Dorrit said, holding a finger to her lips. "Let's all be quiet and listen."

From the radio, calliope music started up as the announcer said, *"It's adventure time, with Orphan Annie! Boy, oh boy! You'll want this keen identification tag . . ."*

At the sound of a car in the driveway, Hank looked up, his mouth an O. He slid off his chair and ran to the window. "Daddy's home!"

Henry moved a king across the checkerboard. "His train doesn't get in until seven thirty."

"But it *is* Daddy!" Hank crowed, "Daddy's home early!" He tore from the room and opened the front door. Grinning, Sister pulled herself to standing.

Henry looked at his watch. "Well, I'll be. He is early."

Steps thumped up the porch stairs. Hank called "Daddy!" and opened the screened door.

Byrd hugged him, saying, "Howdy, pardner, where are my girls?" Sister held out her chubby arms and Byrd scooped her up, saying, "Where's your mama, buddy?"

"At work."

"Of course, she is. Now, hold on a minute," Byrd said, jostling Sister on his hip. "I happen to have a big surprise. It's the reason I'm early today. I have a special delivery to make." He gestured toward the door, saying, "Come on in."

Roy Sykes came through the door, swiping at his head, as if he were wearing a cap. He still wore his army jacket and had a beard. His ears went back as he bobbed his head, vaguely encompassing the entire company before his eyes rested on Dorrit. "Hello, Baby Doll." He nodded toward Henry. "Sir."

Dorrit drew in her breath, unbalanced by a surge of anger expanding in her chest, running through her veins to the tips of her fingers, turning her hands cold.

"Ah," Byrd said, "let me introduce you. Henry, this is Roy Sykes, Dorrit's father. He tells me he served in France, but he never met Jimmy. And this young man is Hank." Hank stood and solemnly held out his hand to shake. The baby buried her head shyly in her father's shoulder. "And this is little Elsie." He bounced her on his hip. "She's getting to be *so big* I can hardly hold her. Who's *so big*?" Sister cooed, holding her arms out wide.

Dorrit rose from the floor, knowing she needed to react. Everyone was watching, anticipating her joyful surprise. But she felt no joy. Her father carried no luggage, but he arrived with memories; sad, happy, and terrible. Dorrit raised her chin, regarding the man who, though still her father, was no longer a figure of authority. He had failed her. He looked, she thought, rather pathetic.

"Hey, hey, Baby Doll!" Roy started across the room, arms outstretched. How thin he was, and how ragged his clothes were. He wrapped her in a hug. Dorrit allowed herself to be crushed in his embrace, turning her face to the side. He held her out by both hands. "Now, now, none of that. No tears now," he said, grinning. She choked back the urge to push him away.

Byrd said, "Roy says the thing he wants most is a hot shower and some clean clothes. I reckon between us we can rustle up something. Eh, Henry?"

"Sure," Henry said. "Look in my closet, upstairs."

Delphina came in and was introduced, stiffly. She gave Roy a towel and took him upstairs. When she returned, she looked grim. "Best we burn his things," she said. "Mister M., is it all right if I give him these?" She held out a pair of corduroy trousers and a plaid shirt. "He needs underdrawers and suspenders, and his socks are all out at the heel."

Henry nodded. "Give him whatever he needs. Fella's been through a tough time. Find him pajamas, too—though mine are nothing to brag about. He can sleep on the sofa."

Byrd said, "I talked to him on the way down, about that. I thought I'd take him over to Chestnut Grove after supper. Cy has an empty room. He can have a little privacy. I should think that after sixty days in jail, a man might like that. I told him I'd get them tickets for Boston, for tomorrow."

Dorrit's face fell. *Tomorrow?*

Half an hour later, Roy came downstairs, shiny-faced, smelling of hair tonic. He sat with Henry, beside the radio and they began to talk about Babe Ruth. May arrived home just as Delphina called everyone to eat.

Over dinner, Roy kept rubbing his smooth cheeks and smiling. He talked about the March and about Roosevelt's Presidential campaign. Dorrit stayed quiet, hoping no one would ask her any questions. When Byrd brought up the train schedule, May said, "But Byrd, Dr. Sawyer wanted to check Dorrit one last time, on Monday. Surely, Mister Sykes wouldn't mind staying until then?" Dorrit cut her eyes to Byrd, who seemed to be concentrating on his green beans.

"Well, ma'am," Roy said, "as much as I want to get my girl home, I s'pose she'd better get all checked out before we leave. You folks are mighty hospitable."

Byrd wiped his mouth and said, "All right, then, that's decided. I'll get tickets for Monday afternoon."

Hank held up his fork like a trident. "And Dort can come to the fair with us!"

Roy looked abashed. "I surely do appreciate the care you've taken of my girl."

Delphina came to clear the plates and Dorrit rose, picking up her own and reaching for her father's, desperate to remove herself from the scene. She said, "I'll do the dishes."

May said, "Dorrit, why don't you take your father out on the porch? I'm sure you must have a lot to catch up on."

The late September evening was balmy and blue. Dorrit sat stiffly on the glider and her father sat beside her, pushing off from the floor to start a slow rocking. He squeezed her hand, saying, "Sure has been lucky, you finding these nice folks. Almost like somebody was looking out for you. Why so quiet, Baby Doll?"

She observed their intertwined hands as if they were the hands of strangers. She did not remember his with any detail. The glowing coal of anger in her chest held fast. Her response was as wooden and devoid of emotion as her inert hand. "They've all been wonderful to me."

"Ah." Roy's lips drew together. "So," he said, "tell me how you ended up here."

Dorrit took her hand from his. She traced her thumbnail over the armrest of the swing. "After the soldiers cleared the camps, I met up with the Professor and a friend of his."

"But why didn't you stay in Washington?"

She looked at him then. "You left me alone, with nothing. I tried to find you, through the police. Then I sent you a letter from North Carolina, to Blossom Street. It's probably waiting there."

"Hmm." Roy ran his fingers over his cheek. "Well," He cleared his throat. "I suppose I ought to tell you . . ."

"What? Have you heard from Walt? Is he all right?"

"No, no, I haven't heard from him. But I did make some calls when I got out." He paused. "I hate to tell you, but we've been evicted."

"*Evicted?* From Blossom Street? Pop . . ." Dorrit's feet stopped the glider, midswing.

"'Fraid so. You know we meant to be back in ten days, two weeks at the most . . . s'pose I didn't plan things too well."

"What about our things?" Pressure pushed behind her eyes. She stood, and the glider swayed.

"No telling. My plans were there, and my trap . . ."

Her voice rose, wavering. "The trap? The *trap*?" The windows behind them were open. She hissed, "I found that letter in your toolbox. They rejected your plans before we even left Boston, and you never told me. Your stupid trap isn't worth a red cent. How could you let this happen? All of Ma's things—her books and her geraniums, left out on the sidewalk like they were junk! Why did you have to throw that stupid brick in the first place?" She covered her mouth, unable to stifle a sob. "How could you leave me on my own?"

Roy's ears went back. He stared down at his hands, clasped in his lap. "I can't tell you how sorry I am, Baby Doll."

"And that's another thing," Dorrit inhaled slowly, crossing her arms over her chest. "Don't call me that anymore, not ever. I am *not* a doll."

Roy raised his eyebrows and nodded slowly. "What's come over you?"

"What's *come over* me? I've been on my own, for two months. I've learned to take care of myself. You sure as hell weren't there to help me." Roy flinched. She went back inside, letting the screen slam behind her. The family had moved to the parlor; they all laughed at something on the radio. Dorrit slipped past Delphina in the kitchen, then up the stairs to her room. She closed the door, then leaned her back against it, and let the tears come. All that she had been hanging onto was gone. She had precious little left to call her own.

Thirty-One
MAY AND DORRIT

All week, May had been planning the talk she would have with Byrd. Friday evening, on the porch. This time, she would wait, let him relax over dinner; see the children. She had rehearsed, silently, what she might say—that candy orders had increased, that she had found new vendors. She would not mention what she now thought of as *the big melt*.

But now, he'd shown up with Roy Sykes. Tomorrow morning they would leave early for the fair, then there would be Sunday's apple picking, then Byrd would be on the train. Where was the right time for her confession, for the accusations and defense she expected would follow, for the possible hours of brooding, or not speaking? How, May wondered, had she allowed two weeks to pass without telling Byrd what she had done?

At the dinner table May half-listened to Roy Sykes' stories of the Army and the March. Her father and Byrd seemed spellbound. Dorrit was quiet, but then, she often was. May watched her, trying to guess what she might be feeling. She was happy for the girl, but she would miss her. Over the past weeks, she had come to depend on Dorrit's quiet competency.

After dinner May sat downstairs with her father while Byrd put the children to bed. It was almost ten o'clock when she checked on them, then crept to her own room, leaving the door ajar, hoping Byrd was already asleep. He called quietly from the bed, "Close it," then more softly, "Lock it." May flushed, turning the key slowly to minimize the click. He held the sheet up, inviting her to bed.

From across the hall came a half-wail, a catch of breath, then a full, lusty cry. As May released the lock, footfall sounded across the floorboards of the hall, then Dorrit's voice, whispering, "Hush now, little one, hush." May stayed where she was, listening. The crying ceased.

The next morning, May arranged her father's table with a waxed-paper-covered sandwich and a pitcher of tea. "The weather looks like it will be nice all day," she said. "Won't you change your mind, come with us?"

Henry flipped his hand at her. "Y'all go on."

May said, "It feels strange, you know? Going to the fair without having a booth there. I wonder what's in our old spot." Henry rubbed his chin but did not respond. May laid her hand lightly on top of his. "Tell me the truth, Daddy. Are you staying home because you don't want to see a State Fair without the Keswick Farm concession there?"

He shook his head. "I already told you I don't have any interest, so stop asking. I'll be fine."

"Hank wants you to go, and it would do you—"

"Hush!"

May huffed, marshaling a few more moments of patience. "All right, then. We'll be back at suppertime. Is there anything you need right now?"

He shook his head and looked out the window.

In the kitchen, Dorrit was packing the diaper bag. May said, "Oh, thank you. I was going to do that. I had to see to Daddy's lunch. Sometimes he is just so"—she blew out her breath, pushing her hair off her forehead—"so stubborn and frustrating."

The girl looked like she might cry. She stuffed another diaper into the bag. May said, "Dorrit, look at me." Dorrit blinked, biting her lower lip. "You are happy he's here, aren't you?"

"Of course, I am." A tear rolled down her cheek.

May wiped the tear track from Dorrit's face, saying, "Fathers are hard, aren't they? My father and I have had a lot of rough patches, believe you me. We didn't speak for a long time, over a misunderstanding about my mother. I think it's hard for them to accept that their little girls might grow into women, with opinions, and minds of our own." May watched Dorrit's face, trying to judge if her words resonated. It was like looking at her younger self, the raw vulnerability, the hunger to be understood. She continued, "At a certain point, though, I realized that he was the only family I had left. Here, blow your nose." May passed a handkerchief. "Listen, if you want to talk about it, I'm here to listen. I want you to have a good time today. The children will be with me. You ready?" Dorrit's shaky smile and rapid nodding kept May from hugging her. She understood how close to the surface the girl's emotions were and recognized the effort she was making to keep her composure. This girl had dignity. She would work it out for herself.

Outside, Delphina was already perched stiffly in the passenger seat of the Studebaker, her straw handbag clasped in her lap. Behind the car, the truck idled with Byrd at the wheel, Roy squeezed in the middle, Blue on the other side. In the bed of the truck, surrounded by hay bales, Hank was wedged between Clarence and Dennis.

The fair awaited.

On the drive to Richmond, Dorrit enjoyed the wind on her face and the sweet weight of the warm child. Stroking the smooth, pink cheek she felt protective—or was it love she felt, already—for these children? Did love require a certain number of hours or days or weeks to be real? She wasn't sure at all. This little girl would grow up safe and loved. Dorrit wished that her own father was as dependable and responsible as Byrd Craig. But he never would be.

As the miles passed, she made a mental list of the things she might never see again—the pigeons on the roof, her books, her mother's geraniums. She thought about moving back to 23 Blossom Street, of starting over there. If given a choice, would she *choose* that place? There was certainly very little to recommend it in the way of conveniences or comforts. And with Mrs. Coughlin and her bakery gone, there were no friends.

Only memories, she reflected, and those, we carry with us everywhere and anywhere. When May spoke from the front seat, Dorrit had to lean forward and say, "I'm sorry? I didn't hear you?"

"Have you ever been to a state fair before, Dorrit?"

"Not ever," she replied. "Hank's about to bust his britches."

May smiled. "I think he's most excited about being able to ride in the back of the truck. I'd say it's probably a safe bet to skip the 4-H and livestock exhibits, unless a prize heifer is something you find interesting. The rides are fun, and the games, though I suspect they're mostly rigged. For years we had a concession stand and we'd sell out preserves and chutneys and pickles." Her smile faded and she went quiet.

When they pulled into the parking area outside the Richmond Diamond, as the fairgrounds were called, Byrd motioned for May to take the first parking spot they saw. They all met at the gates. Byrd carried Sister while Hank danced from foot to foot, his cowboy hat almost bouncing on his head. Arm in arm, couples strolled by, one pair stopping to kiss right in front of them. Dorrit looked at her shoes, coloring at the memory of the sounds she had heard from May and Byrd's room the night before. When Clarence approached the ticket seller, Byrd said, "Hold up there, Clarence. I want everyone to have ten tickets, and a wonderful time. Admission's on me. We'll meet back at this gate at five o'clock, all right?" He paid for a long roll of tickets and passed them out. Clarence and Dennis thanked him and took off. Hank pulled Byrd's sleeve, saying he wanted to see the ponies first. Delphina took Blue's arm and they strolled off together toward a banner that proclaimed, *Conklin's Magic Midway!*

Dorrit was left with her father and a long strand of tickets. They looked at each other. The hectic morning had provided cover; she had avoided being alone with him. Now, in this atmosphere of manufactured gaiety, families hurried past, laughing, carrying cheap stuffed animals and cones of cotton candy. The fair tents, so bright and inviting at a distance, were, up close, patched and dingy. The aromas of sausages and onions cooking seemed too strong, mixing unpleasantly with the sweet smell of frying doughnuts. This was supposed to be fun, but it wasn't.

For a few long moments, her father turned his cap around and around

by the brim. There was pleading in his eyes, and although he did not declare another apology, Dorrit understood that he did not know what to
say to her. He was waiting for *her* to smooth things over. She knew, but he
did not, that things between them would never be the same, and though
he seemed to sense the shift, Dorrit suspected he would not ask about her
weeks alone.

Well, those weeks were her own. She could not stop the nightmares
that plagued her sleep, but she could choose not to examine them. He had
lost everything too.

All they had was each other.

She held up her tickets, saying, "Think we can find some cotton
candy?"

Roy's ears went back and his long exhale turned to a smile. "You bet,
Ba— You bet. And I'm going to win you a prize."

They walked side by side, her father matching his stride to hers. The
space where conversation might have gone was easily filled by the sounds of
gongs, bells, and a barker's sing-song appeals to *come inside and see for yourself!* In front of the tilt-a-whirl, a hollow-cheeked father explained to four
children that they each could go on one ride. Dorrit imagined the day was,
for those fathers, a push and pull of frustration. This man might be trying
to provide his family a single day free from hunger and deprivation. There
might be a candy apple, but it would be cut into fourths. They might
watch the Ferris wheel spin but couldn't ride. The cost of the tickets might
be a week without salt pork or lard, for a chance to toss a ring over a bottle
top and bring home a trinket. At one booth a small crowd gathered, and
Dorrit stopped to watch a man shoot corks from an air rifle. Tin star targets
pinged, and wooden pins toppled, one after another, as the crowd began to
cheer him on. The carny passed a blue teddy bear across the counter, and
the marksman proudly presented it to a pigtailed, beaming little girl. When
Dorrit turned back, her father had begun a conversation with the Ferris
wheel operator. The wheel was in motion, and the man pointed out something in the mechanism to Roy, who nodded, kneeling for a closer look.

May and Byrd held hands while Hank explored the livestock tent, entranced by the exotic chickens. He tugged Byrd's sleeve, begging for a box of newly hatched chicks, but was quickly distracted by the colorful prize ribbons tacked to the stall of a huge sow with ten squealing, spotted piglets. He ran off, eager to see it all. All morning, May had felt a heightened awareness of her husband's physical presence, as well as an increasing sense of guilt. The close smell of manure began to intensify in the heat, and as they left the tent May took stock of the concessions—fried dough, hot dogs, ice cream, cotton candy, and shaved ice. She imagined a blue satin banner and crisp white tablecloths, stacked with Orchard De-Lite candies, with a long line of customers.

Hank tugged at her hand. "Can I have a hot dog, Mama? Please?"

"It's only eleven o'clock. Are you hungry already?" May shot a look to Byrd that asked, *Do we believe this?*

Byrd said, "I told him when we got here, no sweets till after lunch."

"Ah," May said, "I saw a stand back there. Speaking of sweets," she looked at Byrd. "Did you notice that there are no boxed candy concessions? I was thinking, if we could get our old spot back next year, Blue could make lollipops and caramels, right on the spot."

Byrd shifted Sister, and she reached for May. Annoyance crossed his face. Instantly, May regretted raising the subject, chastising herself. Her thoughts should be on her family today.

By four o'clock, the tops of Dorrit's shoes were covered in gray dust and her neck felt sunburned. In the heat, the smell of grease and animals was a little sickening, especially after riding the merry-go-round. She stopped at a shaded bench, telling her father to go ahead. He immediately returned to the Ferris wheel across the midway, picking up his conversation with the operator.

Dorrit sat, watching the workers who operated the rides—their thinly-veiled boredom, their wooden smiles. She had seen the row of carnival trailers and trucks with their brightly painted signboards. They traveled from town to town, she supposed, setting up and tearing down and moving, always moving. She wondered where the Professor and Dynamite were, if they had started back up north yet, or decided to stay in Georgia for the winter. She wondered if they ever even made it to Georgia, and she wondered about Nellie Burris and her little family, and about Walt.

Her father pointed at something, rubbing his chin and nodding to the Ferris wheel man. For better or worse, he was her entire family now. And soon, they would be back in Boston. She would call on her sewing clients, and maybe look for a job. Where, she wondered, would they get the money to pay rent if her sewing machine was gone, and what about furniture, and dishes? Color and heat churned around her, relentlessly. Sound and life swirled, and Dorrit felt a little lightheaded, in the middle of the whirlwind.

"Hey!" Clarence plopped down on the bench beside her. "You having fun?"

He smelled of fresh sweat. Pushing his hair out of his eyes, he leaned forward with his elbows on his knees. He continued, "I upchucked, after the tilt-a-whirl. Probably should've waited to eat that fried dough." Now that she noticed, he did look pale. He continued, "Did you watch the pig races?"

"No, but I did see the four-hundred-pound pumpkin, and I heard Margo, the Tennessee Yodeler, but I didn't stay for the whole thing."

Clarence rubbed his palms over his cheeks. "Did you go in the Temple of Terrors?"

"No," Dorrit said. "Was it scary?"

"Well," he said, "You could tell it was all fake, you know? But they surprised you—like, there would be this cardboard-looking skeleton shaking over here"—he held out his left hand, making a trembling motion—"and then, over here"—his right hand went out instead—"this black furry thing with glowing green eyes popped out and shrieked real loud." He affected a shiver. "It just surprised you, is all. What was your favorite thing?"

"I won a card of buttons, at the duck pond."

"The rubber duck pond? Haven't you done anything scary, or fun? Did you go on any rides?"

"The merry-go-round." She did not tell him that she had done it only to please her father, sitting stiffly in one of the stationary swans, freshly mortified with each rotation and her father's enthusiastic waving from behind the barriers.

"Pfft," Clarence said, "that's for babies. Got any tickets left?"

"Two."

"Well, don't let 'em go to waste, sheesh. Come on." He stood and held out his hand. Dorrit allowed him to tug her off the bench. He dropped her hand immediately, looking embarrassed. "Let's go. Ferris wheel's just stopping now."

They stood in line, and when their car stopped swinging, the attendant ushered them into the flaking, red metal seat. With a rusty shriek, the mesh gate door clicked shut. They were closed in. What if the thing broke and they crashed to the ground, Dorrit wondered, or what if it stuck, swinging, thirty feet up? Or what if it never stopped, and she was forced to go around and around forever?

She gripped the safety bar as the attendant shoved gears forward and back. The car began to swing. She squeezed her eyes shut, trapped. In the garish lights, memories flashed of the vibrating coal hopper, the hurtling speed of the train, the narrow railing. Her mouth went dry.

"It's okay," Clarence yelled, over the cacophony. "Open your eyes!"

From below, she heard, "Hey, Baby Doll!" She gritted her teeth, and when the seat swung back, she could see her father, waving from below.

Clarence said, "He calls you Baby Doll?"

Rising, she could see the buildings of Richmond in the distance—the green patches of woods, the roads. The people below grew smaller and smaller. Dorrit loosened her hands. Fear turned to exhilaration. She had never been so high. As they began to lower, back first, to the other side, Clarence clutched his stomach and groaned, "Ohh."

Dorrit scooted to the far side of their car and said, "Don't you dare get sick in here!"

He closed his eyes and rested his head, briefly, on the safety bar. She looked at the back of his neck, where his collar was pulled down; the line where his suntan stopped and the pale skin of his neck began, the way his dark hair tapered like an arrow, pointing down the back of his shirt. With a clanking of gears, they looped past the bottom and the car paused, rocking in the sudden lull, then, with a grinding sound, they started up again, facing forward.

Thirty-Two
MAY

The morning after the fair, May dressed, then went downstairs to make coffee. Her father's bed was empty, and from the back porch, she heard laughter and cups clinking on saucers. Through the screened door, she heard Roy Sykes say, "So if we get some quarter-inch cable—twelve feet should do it . . ."

Her father's voice was enthusiastic. "There're some pulleys in the barn."

May stepped outside and Roy stood up quickly, bowing slightly. "Morning, ma'am. Hope you don't mind. I strolled over, through the fields. Fine place you've got here. This and the big house both, real nice places."

May returned his greeting. Henry said, "Roy here was telling me how he's worked in candy factories, up in Massachusetts."

"You don't say?" May said, sitting on the glider.

"You betcha," Roy said. "I was at the Necco factory, in Boston—stands for New England Confectionery Company. You know Necco Wafers candy?"

"Yes, of course." May said, "We sell them at the market."

"Well," Roy said, cutting his eyes right and left, as if someone might be spying, "bet you didn't know that Admiral Byrd took Necco Wafers all the way to Antarctica, on his expedition." He nodded sagely, holding up one hand as if taking a vow. "Two-and-a-half *tons* of Necco Wafers. God's honest truth. They never go bad."

"That so?" Henry said. "What kind of dye do they use?"

"Hmm. That, I do not know, but I could make a call. Got a buddy up there." Roy winked. "And you know what? They have these custom vending machines they put around at filling stations and such. Sell a whole lot of candy that way. Big profits from those machines, let me tell you."

"We could do that," May said. "Where could we get the machines?"

"Well, I'll tell you," Roy said, "the packaged candy has to be made to fit the machine, or vice-versa. I used to repair them. Reckon I could find you one used, or have one made up special. It's not complicated, no motor or nothing, only a spring mechanism and some gears. You just fill the machine then come back and take the coins from it. Easy as pie."

"That would be something," May said. "But what about when the weather gets hot?"

"Ah," Roy said, "machines are only good with things that aren't going to melt so fast—you know, your lifesavers, your chewing gum—gum-based or starch-based candies, things like that."

Henry nodded slowly, his eyes narrowed in concentration. "So if we could put our jelly candies in a little box, they would stack in the machine?"

"Yup," Roy said. "Best if you have a couple different varieties in each machine. Increases sales that way. Now, in cooler weather you can do your chocolates and whatnot. Blue gave me some of those jelly things he makes. You might get somewhere with those. The other place you can sell them is in movie houses, on account of those places want quiet candies. I heard the Necco folks talking about that. You know, nobody wants to sit in the movie house and listen to some joker crunching away on hard candy. They want *chewy*. Am I right, Henry?"

May and Henry nodded. Her head spun with ideas. "How many flavors should be in a box?"

"Well, if I remember correctly, the Ferrara company does lemon, mint, violet, cherry, lilac, and licorice. That's in Jujyfruits, of course. They used to do a rose, if I recall correctly, back in the twenties, but they changed it to cherry." He whispered, "And I heard a rumor, that they might switch the mint to lime. So following that trend? Most likely, your fruit flavors are likely to be more popular than your flowers."

May ticked off flavors on her fingers. "Should they be shaped like fruit?"

"Maybe," Roy said, "except Farrara's already doing that. Did you ever notice that one of the Jujyfruits is shaped like a bunch of asparagus? And one like a banana, but none of them *taste* like asparagus or banana. That always was a puzzle to me."

May had not touched her coffee. "So you might know a place to have those molds made?"

"Sure. I know who makes them for Necco. Gonna cost you, though. They get paid upfront. But once you've got 'em, they last forever. The molds are shaped like the candy, see, and you press them into a pan of cornstarch so that the shape sets. Then you pipe or extrude the syrup into the impression. The good thing is, you can use the starch over and over. For a big production, extrusion is done by machines, but for something like you folks are thinking, it could be done by hand. Once you've invested in the molds, you're golden."

From across the yard, the door to Delphina's cottage swung shut and she started across the yard. At the same time, the screened kitchen door flew open and Bandit bolted out. Hank followed and stood in his pajamas, barefoot, his hair on end. He climbed to stand on a chair, then squatted, raising his fists over his head, then leaned forward, fists pushing against each other in front of his chest, his jaw jutting forward as he proclaimed, "HANK IS AS STRONG AS THE STRONG MAN AT THE FAIR! GRR!" Byrd came to the door behind him.

May stood, and said, "Hank, get down. This is all so interesting, Mister Sykes. I want to know more, but as you can see, we have an apple picking to prepare for. Two school buses from Charlottesville are bringing children and their teachers. The apples will be handed out in the schools."

"Please, call me Roy, ma'am. How can I help out today?"

"Come with us to the orchard, at eleven. I wanted to tell you, your Dorrit has been a godsend. Really, the children adore her."

That afternoon, Byrd supervised rides on Peanut, while May and

Dorrit cut cake and handed out lollipops. At three o'clock, the buses left. In the kitchen, May stacked cake plates as Byrd came inside with Sister draped over his shoulder, sound asleep. He took her upstairs, and when he returned, May poured lemonade and they went to sit on the porch. All day, she had been thinking about her conversation with Roy Sykes. She was on fire with it. Across the yard, Dorrit walked with Hank as he pulled his wagon, Bandit trotting along beside. May said, "The apple picking went well, don't you think?"

"It did," Byrd said. "If we can't make any profit on the crop, there's no sense in letting it go to waste. Hopefully, next year things will be better. People like Roy Sykes, with no steady salary or pension, need a national relief system. He was a help today, and that Dorrit was a terrific sport about riding Peanut." He laughed. "She looked terrified."

"She's wonderful."

Byrd said, "When Cy came by, he said Roy had already fixed the washing machine at Chestnut Grove and started tuning up his truck. He told Cy he's determined to work off the price of their train tickets. I don't know if he's told Dorrit yet or not, but he said on the way down here that he's been evicted, in Boston. I imagine it might be a while before he can afford another place. What do you think about asking them to stay on for a bit? There are a thousand things he could fix, between this place and Chestnut Grove."

"And the market, too," May said. "I love having Dorrit here. I asked her about school. She said she has a year left, but yesterday she told me she wouldn't go back. She says she'll have to work. It's such a shame. She's so bright."

"All right, then, I'll talk to Roy about it."

"Did he tell you that he works in candy factories? He knows all about manufacturing."

"I just hope he knows how to fix a boiler and a dripping sink."

"Right. Well. I'll bet he can. Your idea—it's a fabulous idea—makes me wonder, with Dorrit here . . ." May paused, then plunged ahead. "I could spend more time on the candy business."

Byrd gave her a long-suffering look. "We've talked about this already."

"But Blue is—"

"No, May. For God's sake, what will it take for you to understand? You ought to see some of the people in Washington—and I mean decent people, like Roy—living in alleys, begging. No man who's able to work should have to live that way. I have to be responsible for you, and the children, and your father, and for these farms. I have to be able to do what my own father couldn't. He took risks. He lost sight of what was important. And now"—Byrd rubbed his temples—"and now, he isn't here to see his grandchildren grow up."

May looked at her hands in her lap. "Byrd, I need to tell you something." She looked up at the ceiling and breathed in. "A candy order I was delivering—it melted. I had to get more ingredients. We've been doing better and better, and Dorrit had the idea to call the all-day candy bar—remember, I told you about that?—to call it the Three-Square Bar. And we're getting labels printed, only you have to order two hundred at a time and pay in advance." Byrd slowly put his glass down on the porch floor. His eyes were icy blue. May stopped talking, and realized how hunched her shoulders were, as if she were expecting a blow. He held her gaze, expressionless. She licked her lips. "So I used Elsie's money, after all."

He leaned forward, resting his arms on his knees.

"I did. I used Elsie's money, and I'm sorry I didn't tell you. But it's done. She's behind me all the way." May blew out her breath.

"You should have asked me first."

"That is exactly, *exactly* what I said to you after the auction for Chestnut Grove!" Her hands flew up from her lap like startled birds. "You expected me to trust a decision you made without me. Now I'm asking the same of you."

"How long has this been going on?"

"A few weeks." They were both silent, both looking at the floor. Finally, May reached for his hand, saying, "Every week when you come home, instead of asking me how my week has gone or how business is, you've just closed up. I *know* you work hard. I know you want to take care of us, and no one could ask for a better husband, or father. I kept waiting for the right time to tell you. But there's *never* a right time anymore."

Byrd crossed his arms over his chest. When he spoke, his voice was terribly sad. "What's happening to us, May?"

Thirty-Three
DORRIT

One month passed, then another. Fall arrived and Franklin Roosevelt was elected, promising a New Deal. Listening to the announcement on the radio, Dorrit cheered along with the assembled Craigs and Mr. Marshall. The New Deal promised hope and change for America, and a believable plan to make things better for everyone in need. A buoyant mood pervaded the household and carried them to Thanksgiving. By December Dorrit had settled into a routine.

She sat alone in the kitchen, waiting to hear Sister wake from her morning nap. Snow fell outside. The heavy, wet clumps melted as soon as they touched the ground. In the fading winter light, a goldfinch tugged at the dried seeds of a yarrow stalk while a bright cardinal flitted from the ground to explore the bare canes of a rose bush. A chickadee dropped in swooping scallops from branch to branch then perched, cocking its head with bright attention. Snow, in Virginia, seemed a novel event, different altogether from the oppressive gray piles on the sidewalks of Boston. Dorrit returned to her notebook.

December 20
> *Pop was supposed to be back yesterday. May has been working until late to get Christmas orders finished and sometimes the*

children only see her in the morning. The fruitcake balls are the most popular. I tried one and the liquor fumes made my eyes water, but there is no accounting for what these southern people like. May is very excited because they are selling for four dollars per box! This morning she asked me to write down my story about the wood sprites. She wants to have it printed on a candy box! I told her that I did not believe that the story was all that interesting, but she says this is a 'sales technique' and it will encourage customers to buy more boxes, so they can read the story a little bit at a time. I sincerely hope I can remember the parts I have thought up so far. Maybe Hank will remember them all. I will write it here, as best I can recall. I will call myself "D.M." because I think that sounds more like a genuine author.

The Wood Sprites
By D.M. Sykes

The wood sprites called Cedar and Juniper were weavers. They fashioned grass fibers into garments, sewn with pine needles and gossamer threads from spiders' webs. Indigo was a forager. Because she had one broken wing, she roamed the forest, collecting berries and seeds. One day, while she was cutting sheets of moss,

Dorrit paused and put down her pencil, chewing her lower lip. Someone knocked and she looked up to see Cy Waddell, smiling at her through the door glass. He entered, followed by Clarence. "Morning," Cy said, "Henry around? Clarence, put that down right here."

Clarence put down a box of cut holly and pine boughs. His hair, wet with snow, was plastered to his forehead, and he needed a haircut.

"I think so," Dorrit said. "He was listening to the radio a little while ago."

Cy called out, "Henry?" as he walked toward the hall. He said, over his shoulder, "Clarence, I'll be back directly."

Dorrit said, to Clarence. "How've you been?"

"Aw, I'm all right, I reckon," Clarence said. "Cy keeps me running around over there. When's your pa getting back?"

Dorrit frowned. "I'm not sure, exactly, but I expect to hear from him soon."

"Y'all moving back up there?"

"I don't know. Pop doesn't have a regular job to go back to, so he figures we'll stay here until the work runs out. But it could be he'll find something back home. How about you?"

He smiled, rubbing his hand over his mouth. "I got a letter from my ma."

Dorrit had been giving him reading lessons with Hank's primer, on Sundays. "Did she tell you to come home?"

Clarence moved to inspect the items lined up on the shelf above the sink. One by one he held them up, mouthing the printed words: *Bon Ami Soap. Ivory. Fuller Brush Company.* He put down the dish brush and said, "Nah. She said I might as well stay. They's still no work and she's got another baby on the way. Reckon I'm just as good on my own." He shrugged, but Dorrit heard the sadness behind his words. "So I'm staying. Long as they'll have me, leastways. I've been working some at the market, if you can believe that."

"What about Christmas? Don't you wish you could be with your family?"

"Christmas wasn't a real big deal for us."

Dorrit nodded. "Not for us, either. May's been talking about making eggnog, and she says they'll have a big turkey. Mister M. told me he used to go hunting with Byrd's father, and they would go up the mountain to cut a Christmas tree. I've never had a tree before."

"My pa sometimes brought one in."

"May says she has boxes of decorations in the attic, and we'll decorate the whole house on Christmas Eve." Dorrit sniffed a pine branch. "She told me that when old Mister Craig was alive, they would have a big party at Christmastime, with an orchestra and dancing and champagne, and three separate Christmas trees in the house. Do you ever wonder what that house was like, before?"

Clarence nodded slowly. "Do you think it makes him sad?"

"Who?"

"Byrd. To see his family house like it is now."

"I guess, maybe so. But can you imagine owning such a place? Growing up there?"

Clarence shook his head. "Must've been pretty swell."

From the hallway, the telephone trilled. Dorrit said, "I'd best get that."

"Marshall and Craig residence, hello? This is Dorrit speaking."

The woman's voice was abrupt. "I need to speak to Mrs. Craig, right away. It's Hazel Brownlow calling."

"I'm sorry, ma'am, but she's not here right now."

"Well, you need to tell her that the school holidays started today, for pity's sake! How could she drop little Hank off with the school locked up, and not even notice? He walked over to my house, half-frozen, told me he'd sat on the steps for a while but nobody else came. I gave him some hot milk, but she needs to come pick him up right now. Poor little mite probably caught his death."

Dorrit flushed. "I'm awfully sorry, ma'am. Thank you for taking care of him. I'll find her right away."

"You do that. And I plan to give her a piece of my mind too. If she were home where she belongs, this wouldn't have happened."

Dorrit hung up as Cy came back into the hall from Henry's room with a waft of bourbon preceding him. He pulled his hat on and said, "All righty now, Clarence, we got work to do. Enough of your jawing. Morning, missy."

Cy opened the back door and the report of a double backfire made Dorrit jump. She followed Cy and Clarence onto the porch. Her father stepped out of a faded black Model T Ford truck. He stood beside it, holding out his hands: *Ta-da!*

December 20, continued

> *My goodness, what a day it has been! Here is what happened:*

1. *May took Hank to school, only there wasn't any school today. She had accidentally written the 21st on her calendar as the day vacation*

starts. When she brought him home from Mrs. Brownlow's he was crying and she looked upset. She gave him a quarter and told him not to tell his father.

2. *Pop is back! In Boston, he bought equipment for candy making, and then he went to wherever it is they make candy molds. Then, he went to see Mr. Olivetti at the newsstand on Blossom Street. Mr. Olivetti told him where Mrs. Coughlin is living (she has moved over the river and is working in a bakery). He visited with her and she had saved some of our things and some mail! There was a picture postcard from Walt in Portugal, and also another letter from Mr. George Puttworth, Vice President of the Acme Pest Control Corporation!*

3. *Mr. Puttworth asked to buy Pop's design for a metal spring, and so he bought himself a blue suit and a necktie and took another train to Dayton, Ohio, and he had a business meeting. Mr. Puttworth paid $550.00 for the design! So then, Pop went and bought himself a truck and drove back to Boston. By then the candy molds were made, so he came back here. He even carried back Ma's geraniums in the front seat. They are on my windowsill as I write this. He used May's money, and he also used some of his own to buy some more machines. He says that now they can have an actual production line. He says he will outfit the back of his truck with an icebox so they can make deliveries in hot weather. It is all terribly exciting. I think this will be a merry Christmas after all. Pop brought back Ma's copy of* Science and Health. *When I look at it now, Christian Science does not make much sense to me. I don't know what to think about it. I like the idea of celebrating with presents and decorations. More on this at another time.*

Thirty-Four
MAY

The Christmas season proved more profitable than May could have ever imagined. Since Thanksgiving, Delphina's sausage grinder had been requisitioned to churn out the miniature fruitcake balls that were now stacked in pans and locked in the cannery, mellowing in James Craig's illegal bourbon. His legacy stash of French cognac now infused brandied cherry chocolates, so popular that the brandy ran out before they could fill the orders. These alcohol-laced "specialty" items, technically illegal, could not be sold through the market. Instead, they went out in unlabeled boxes at premium Prohibition prices. Roy's ideas opened up new possibilities—production lines, packaging machinery, route delivery.

It was tacitly agreed that May and Byrd would not discuss the candy business, and they moved through each weekend guarded and cordial, yet also disconnected. As long as business continued to improve—and it did—May felt somewhat vindicated. Eight local women had been hired to help with the onslaught of Christmas orders. Word of work got around, and more showed up every day, asking for shifts.

In mid-December, May had handed Roy an envelope with four hundred dollars in cash and taken him to the train station. He would travel to Boston to have custom candy molds made and look for vending machines and other equipment.

Now, Christmas was four days away. In the canning building beside the barn, newly outfitted as a candy factory, Blue walked down the center aisle with May, Hank, and Roy following. Until the closing, the cannery had been the site of Keswick Farm's production of jams, pickles, jellies, conserves, and chutneys. A long table ran down one side of the building and various sizes of copper pots hung from iron hooks on the wall above. On the other side stood two stoves, flanked by storage racks. In the months that the building had been unused, copper had tarnished and layers of dust coated every surface. Now, everything gleamed, and the aroma of molasses taffy filled the air. May held Hank's hand, pulling him away from the stove.

Blue stopped at the end of the long table, and over the clank of metal on metal, he said, "Look here." He turned the crank of the machine that used to be a cider press. From a newly fashioned aperture, a cylindrical extrusion the diameter of a fountain pen appeared, growing longer as he continued to crank. Roy guided the lengthening cord until it was two feet long then sliced it into sections. As it hardened, Blue rolled the individual sticks in cellophane, twirling the edges closed with a practiced flick. At the end of the table, a woman in a white apron affixed a label, centering it before smoothing it in place. Holding one up, Blue turned it this way and that, saying proudly, "How about that, Hank? Moisture-proof cellophane. This is the future we're looking at, right here. Clean and self-service. Nobody has to stop what they're doing and fetch taffy out of a jar for a customer. And the customer sees exactly what they're getting. Yes sirree, this is the future." He handed the taffy to Hank.

Thirty-Five
MAY

The train was crowded and overheated. Carefully juggling her sample boxes, May made her way through three packed cars and in the last one, a suit jacket lay folded on the single empty seat. A florid, splay-legged young man in shirt-sleeves was apparently absorbed in working, scribbling on a pad. "Pardon me," May said, "is this seat taken?" The young man shuffled his papers and stood, apologizing, then swept up his suit coat, his papers sliding off the seat. May stood patiently, balancing her boxes against the swaying of the train as it departed the station. A woman in the row ahead bent to retrieve the papers from beneath her seat, returning them along with a pained look.

The young man pushed himself upright, cheeks pink with exertion, and smoothed his hair. "Golly!" he said, offering to take May's boxes. "Sorry about that, ma'am. Allow me. Can I put those on the rack for you?"

"Yes, please. I hope it's not too hot up there."

"How far are you going?" he asked.

"Only to Richmond. I'm sorry to disturb you, but there are no other seats."

"Ah. Going up to Philadelphia myself. I was supposed to be on the earlier train—the one that was canceled? We had to wait four hours in Atlanta for this one. It's a long ride, and no dining car or anything, till Washington."

"That's hours away. When did you get on?"

"Six this morning," he said, dejectedly.

"Oh, my. That is a long trip."

"Yeah. Sure do wish I'd brought a sandwich." He fidgeted his hands then reordered his papers and began to write again, grasping his pencil childishly with his left hand. He stopped, staring out the window for a moment, and May glanced at the pad. His writing was heavily slanted and nearly illegible. His stomach growled and he put a hand over it, smiling sheepishly.

May smiled back and stood to take down one of her boxes. She opened it and held out two candy bars. "Here," she said, "These might help you get through the trip."

The young man's eyes lit up as he read the labels. "Boy oh boy! *Three-Square Bar.* I've never heard of this. And believe you, me, ma'am, I do enjoy my candy. Thanks, awfully." He unwrapped the Boo-Coo bar, inspecting it, then took a big bite. "Saaay," he said, nodding, "this is *really* swell. Where do you come by these?"

May sat up a little straighter and said, "I'm the president of Orchard De-Lite Confections. We manufacture them right here, in Virginia. The Three-Square bar has enough nutrition to get a person through the better part of a day. The Boo-Coo—that's the one you're trying now—is based on traditional French nougat. The name is a play on the French word, *beaucoup?*"

"You don't say! Don't speak French myself, but honestly, it's extraordinarily good. Are those cherries?" He licked his fingers and opened the second package. "And what about this one?"

"They are. Grown on my family's farm. We try to use locally grown ingredients and support our neighbor farmers. I'm on my way now to distribute samples. The Three-Square bar has three different fillings, one inside each square section, see? It's our first product for the mass market. We're hoping to compete with Pearson's Salted Nut Roll and the Standard Candy Company's Goo-Goo Cluster."

He nodded enthusiastically. "Yes! I like both of them—the Goo-Goo Cluster especially. But I like how you've used pecans instead of peanuts.

Peanuts tend to overpower the other flavors, don't you think?" He rubbed his hand over his belly. "Ah. Much better now. I'm Douglas Dalrymple, by the way." He held out a hand and May shook it.

"May Craig." He seemed to wish to continue the conversation, and May silently chided herself for starting it. She had planned to spend the journey with her map of Richmond. Elsie would be picking her up and driving her around, and she wanted to make as many stops as possible before she had to catch the three o'clock train back. She had counted on two hours of solitude.

"Tell me about your candy company," Mr. Dalrymple said. His pencil was poised above his pad.

"Oh, well," May said, trying to be politely dismissive, "it's just our family farm, you know. We used to be in the jam and preserve business, but with the drought and bad crops, well, we've converted to candy making. We have a new product coming out that we'll sell from machines and hopefully, before long, in movie houses." She took out a waxed paper bag from the sample box and passed it to him. "Try these. They're called Jelly Gems. Each box will have a little children's story printed on the back. See how they're shaped like jewels?"

He nodded. "*Ni-i-ce.* That's an original idea. This could go places." He hefted the bag.

May hesitated to ask her question. There were so many unemployed men these days, but Mr. Dalrymple was well dressed. "What business are you in, Mister Dalrymple?"

"I'm a journalist. I write for the *Saturday Evening Post.*"

"Really? The *Post?* My goodness! We take it every week. I've never met a reporter before." May's perception of the young man changed instantaneously. Not just anyone could write for the *Post.*

He nodded and popped a candy into his mouth. "Yup. I've been working on a series of articles about how folks are getting through these hard times. You know, how they're adapting. I've been down in Georgia to talk to peach farmers and sharecroppers. No good news there, I'll tell you." He paused, sorting through the bag, pulling out a yellow piece. "The editors send me out and say, 'Douglas, find us some uplifting stories—happy things—things folks will want to read about. Stories of triumph over hardship.' That sort of thing." He shook his head. "I'll tell you though, Mrs. Craig, in these times? Those stories are few and far between." He bit into the candy. "Gee whiz! Tastes exactly like a lemon! How do you do that?"

"Citric acid. Makes it tart and keeps it fresh longer. We have a man who works with us who helped develop the recipe. He was at the Bonus March."

"Ah. The March. I covered that too. Lots of sad tales there."

"Actually," May said, "his story has a happy ending."

"You don't say? Tell me about him. Do you mind if I take notes?"

"Why?"

"Well, I'm finding your story quite interesting. I'm thinking that folks might like to read about it. What would you say to having it published in the *Post*? I'd have to run it by my editor, of course. If Mister Larimer gives the go-ahead, I'd like to come back down with a photographer and meet you all and take some photos of your family and whatnot. What do you say? It would be darned good exposure for your business. We have over three million readers each week." He passed her a business card, smudged with chocolate.

May read, *Douglas S. Dalrymple, The Saturday Evening Post.* A tingle went up her back and she flushed, unable to contain her smile. She wanted to pinch herself. "Mister Dalrymple," she said. "That sounds wonderful."

The next evening was Friday, and May was back at the Keswick station, peering through the frosted windshield, waiting to pick up Byrd. When he got off the train, she asked, "How was your week?" She tried to infuse the question with more interest than she actually felt, because her only reason for asking it, aside from the expected wifely concern, was that she desperately wanted for Byrd to ask her the same question back.

On the short drive home, he talked with sincere earnestness about the upcoming Senate vote on the moratorium on farm foreclosures while May listened and asked appropriate questions. When Byrd said that he was hopeful, she was pleased. It boded well. They drove for a few moments in silence, and May realized that their conversation must have left him thinking about the legislation, not about the weekend. She began, "I'm happy to hear the bill's moving along well. I know you've worked hard on it." Byrd turned into the driveway. She continued, "Dear, I wanted to ask you about something before we go in." He merely raised his eyebrows. She smiled, hard. "I've had some good news too, this week. The most extraordinary thing happened! I was on the train to Richmond, and this young man beside me—the train was awfully crowded, the earlier one had been canceled, there wasn't an empty seat—anyway, this nice young man started chatting and it turns out that he writes for the *Post*. The actual *Saturday Evening Post*!" She paused for effect.

"And?" Byrd said.

"And I gave him some candy, and he liked it, and he started asking questions. Really, he seemed so interested, and *then*"—May opened her eyes wide, resting her hand on Byrd's sleeve, tugging it slightly—"and then, well, you'll never guess, so I'll just tell you, because it's so wonderful—he asked if he could write a *story* about our candy business! He wants to take photographs and everything—and publish it in the *Post*! Can you imagine?"

The car pulled up in front of the house and Byrd draped his wrists over the top of the steering wheel. He exhaled, and the windshield began to fog. May waited, hoping he would encourage her to continue, but she could tell by the way her husband's brow puckered that he was making an effort to say something positive. "May. I understand that it must have been exciting to meet this chap and talk to him."

"Oh, it was, and he was such an ordinar—"

Byrd held up one palm, saying, "Listen to me for a minute. Reporters like that are hired to find stories. I don't like the idea of having someone snoop around asking questions and taking photographs. You did tell him no, didn't you?"

"I told him I would have to speak to you about it."

"Good. Because I don't like the idea. Not a bit." Byrd opened his door and began to step out of the car.

The cords in May's neck tightened. Why did he get to decide? She had thought, *Finally, he will see that this is working. If the* Saturday Evening Post *wants to do a story on us, then it really is working.* The thrill of being singled out, of being praised, along with all of the business it would bring, was just *so* exciting. And Byrd was being a killjoy. Now he was opening her car door. She stepped out and they faced each other.

She said, "I hoped you'd be pleased about this. I think we should ask Daddy what he thinks."

"No, May. It's cheap self-promotion."

Cheap? That stung. "No, it isn't! It's a story of triumph over adversity. That's what Mister Dalrymple calls it. This could put us in clover. Don't you see?"

Byrd opened the trunk and pulled out his bag. "I don't want the story of my father's death on every newsstand. It's tawdry."

"Oh. I . . ." May paused and put her hand on his shoulder. "We'd never tell him about that."

"He's a reporter. They're paid to find salacious stories. I don't want it broadcast all over the country."

"But they have three *million* readers a week. Do you understand what that means? He can write about how we're creating jobs and adapting to the times."

Byrd exhaled noisily. "I don't want to quarrel with you about this. I'll have nothing to do with it." He looked toward the house.

May stayed where she was, addressing his sleeve. "You don't want me to work, even though I'm bringing home money and giving people jobs."

"It's a man's *responsibility* to take care of his family."

"That's old-fashioned. In these times, women *and* men need to do whatever it takes to get by. You shouldn't have to carry it all on your shoulders. You've seen how much better Daddy is, keeping busy. I'm doing this for our family."

Byrd slammed the trunk lid. His voice cracked. "All I think about is keeping our heads above water. I hate being away from you all. I hate being up there all week, alone in that awful little room. I hated missing my son's first day of school and my daughter's first steps, but it's what has to happen right now. When I see men on the streets selling apples . . . men who left their families to find work and never went back. You and the children are everything I have."

She hugged him, then, burying her face in the front of his coat. The front door swung open and Hank called, "Daddy!"

May did not venture to bring up the *Post* again that weekend. On Monday morning she telephoned Douglas Dalrymple. "Thank you for thinking of us," she said, "but I'm afraid my husband doesn't approve."

There was silence on the line, and then, in an upbeat voice, the reporter said, "Ah. Totally understandable, Mrs. Craig. Totally understandable. You know, I was telling your story to Mister Larimer—he's the president, of course, of Curtis Publishing—I told him about this wonderfully well-spoken and attractive lady I met on a train. And he was mighty impressed by your story, let me tell you. Mighty impressed. He genuinely liked the idea of a woman starting up a business, you know? And such an interesting idea too. Well, ma'am, I am sorry to have troubled you. I appreciate your time."

There was a pause. May stammered at his flattery. "Thank you, Mister Dalrymple. It was lovely to meet you."

"But honestly, ma'am," he said, "if you think there might be a possibility that your husband might change his mind, I bet I could persuade Mister Larimer to offer you a half-page advertisement—at no cost to yourself, of course—to show his gratitude. You can't imagine the effectiveness of an ad in the *Post*. A good businesswoman like yourself, well . . ."

"A half page?"

"In full color too."

"Color?"

"Yes, ma'am."

"All right, Mister Dalrymple, you're on. When would you like to come?"

"Gosh. That's terrific news! If I can get my photographer, I'd like to come down next week. I'll check the train schedule and get back to you. Thanks. You won't regret this."

Thirty-Six
DORRIT

JANUARY 27, 1933

"Dorrit, does this look too dressy?" May asked, turning a slow circle in front of the full-length mirror in her room. "Maybe I should wear my green wool instead."

"You look nice," Dorrit said, nodding from where she stood in the doorway. "Very pretty. Truly, you do." Dorrit felt flattered to be asked her opinion.

"Thanks. Oh, gosh. Here I'm all ready to walk out the door and it's still a half hour until their train arrives. If I get near the children, they'll muss me up. Maybe I should have taken Hank to school after all."

"Missing one day won't hurt."

"I'm so nervous! Please, sit and talk with me." May sank to the dressing table bench and began inspecting tubes of lipstick.

Dorrit moved to sit in a chair beside the bookcase. "I finished *Little Dorrit.*"

"Good! How did you come to be named Dorrit? Is it a family name?"

"My mother told me that her mother—my Grandmother Gertrude—had hoped that she would name me after her. My father's mother—Grandma Sykes—hoped the same thing."

"What was her name?" May frowned, swiveling a lipstick open, dabbed her lower lip, then considered the color.

"You know, I don't remember. She died, of the Spanish Influenza. I never met her."

"So what did your parents do?"

"My mother loved Dickens. And Amy Dorrit was her favorite character."

"Did you like the book?"

"Yes! I couldn't stop laughing at that Flora Finching. She reminded me a little of the postmistress here. I was happy for Amy, in the end. Her life turned out so well."

"Ha." May snorted and leaned forward to blot her lips. "Yes! She married the wealthy man and lived happily ever after, right?"

Dorrit didn't know how to respond. "That's right. How did you know that you wanted to marry Byrd?"

"Well, it didn't happen at first sight. We've known each other all our lives." May reached for a cigarette and lit it, shaking the match. "Remember I told you I lived in New York and Paris?" Dorrit nodded and May continued, "After growing up here, it was all so exciting. You know when I went to college, I thought that Richmond, Virginia, was the be-all and end-all. I mean, my world, my *entire* world, had been here, and Richmond was *the city*, and I thought the girls from there knew everything. Oh, I longed to be like them. It's funny though, once I got to New York, I realized how small my dreams had been—how small my *world* had been." She continued, "You grew up in a city. So this must be the reverse for you. You must find things dull here."

"I didn't explore much. My world was small too."

May cocked her head, her voice was concerned. "I know I asked you before, but what about college? I don't mean to pry, but it seems such a shame, a girl as bright as you . . . I had a scholarship. You could get one, I bet."

"Oh. I don't . . . I don't think that would be possible."

"Dorrit, it's girls like you—smart and hardworking, who deserve scholarships. That's not to say that you have to go to college to be successful. My friend Rocky started out as an elevator operator in a hotel, and now he owns the top hair salon in Paris. He has drive and talent. But honestly, college can open up things to you that you'd never know about otherwise. Can we look into it? I'd like to help you."

Dorrit blushed. "I never thought that would be something I could have. I . . . we . . . Pop and me—we get by day to day and week to week, you know? Tell me about how you got to Paris."

"You think over what I've said, and we'll talk about it more later. Paris. Rocky and I had grand plans. We were going to be famous. He wanted to be the *hairdresser to the stars*—that's how he described it—and I was going to be a great costume designer." May rolled her eyes. "My mother designed costumes, you know, in New Orleans. Those are her sketches, on the wall of the sewing room."

"Oh, I like the one that looks like a fountain."

"Yes. Well, I started working for a costumer in New York, then I was hired for a show going to Paris. They took American performers and musicians, because American Jazz was all the rage. Anyway, once I got there, I learned that in France, seamstresses have to be in a union and have papers, and apprenticeships. I ended up ironing, backstage. Not the least bit glamorous." She blew smoke up toward the ceiling.

"So how did Byrd—"

May sighed. "I, well." She sat forward, tapping her cigarette into an ashtray. "I fell on hard times, I suppose you'd say. Lost my job at the theater and fell in with a bad crowd. I was too embarrassed to come back home such a failure.

"You see, Byrd had proposed to me before I left New York. I turned him down. I didn't think he believed I was serious about having a career. So when things went badly, I started writing home, saying that everything was peachy—that I was terrifically successful and getting married to a wealthy man and moving to a mansion. The truth was, though, that I was flat broke, and my boyfriend was married. The house was Rocky's, and all of the furniture had been sold. I was so ashamed." She looked away, lost in thought. "The things shame will drive a person to do . . . I told so many lies, I didn't see a way back. I realized then, what a fool I'd been. Then Byrd showed up in Paris. I just had to clear the air, you know? I figured I had nothing more to lose. I confessed everything to him."

"What happened then?"

"Mm. Byrd was in a bad spot too. He had married an English girl and she ran off after three months, with an older man she'd had a fling with, before." May chuckled. "I've shocked you, haven't I?"

Dorrit shook her head slowly. She *was* scandalized, in fact, but she didn't want May to stop. She said, "And then what?"

"Byrd came to Paris to find her. Anyway, they divorced. So there we were, the two of us, both miserable. I stayed in Paris, to help my friend open his salon. After a while, Byrd started writing to me. The *most* beautiful letters. I still have them. And then—I couldn't say exactly when it started—something changed."

"That's so romantic."

"Sounds that way, doesn't it?" May smashed the cigarette into the ashtray. "Have you ever been in love, Dorrit?"

Dorrit flushed, thrilled to be asked such a question. "Not yet."

May smiled. "You've got plenty of time, for so many things. And you have such a good head on your shoulders. Oh, I'd better go now. Would you check that Sister has her pinafore on? Remind Hank that he can't go outside and he can't wear his cowboy hat. Make sure they don't go near the cannery. Do you think I ought to take them with me?"

"It's icy out. And you know Hank will want to smash a penny on the tracks."

"You're right. He'd get dirty. Now, I'll be back in fifteen minutes or so, unless they want to drive through Keswick first and see the sights. I told Delphina we'd have lunch at twelve thirty. I hope chicken croquettes are all right." She giggled, her palms on her cheeks, leaning toward the mirror. "Is this lipstick too purple? The photographs might be in color, you know."

"That shade is nice with your dress."

May pulled on a pair of sky-blue suede gloves then held out her hands. "Aren't they gorgeous?" She made a practice royal wave. "Totally impractical. Elsie gave them to me for Christmas and I haven't dared take them out of the box."

"They're beautiful. We'll all be lined up like good soldiers when you get back. And look, it's a clear day for taking photographs. Blue brought over the candy samples, and they're perfect."

"Good. Thank you, Dorrit. Wish me luck!" May hurried down the stairs.

In the children's room, Dorrit fussed with the bow on Sister's sash, mulling over what May had told her. Such an exciting life. Dorrit wondered if she regretted giving it up. But today could change everything. The week before, they had all gone through the *Saturday Evening Post*, scrutinizing ads and articles, wondering how many photographs there would be. May had taken Dorrit and Delphina aside, instructing them that they were not to speak about Chestnut Grove or the auction, or the death of Mr. Craig Sr. Those things were private family business, she said.

Hank played with the rubber band gun Roy made for him while Bandit slept, curled up on the floor beside Sister, who happily banged a wooden spoon on a pot, pleased with the noise she produced.

And there it was: the sound of the car on the gravel, the thump of feet ascending the outside steps, crossing the porch, the front door clattering open, then May's voice, higher than usual, carrying up the stairs, saying, "1825? I think. It's just an old farmhouse, really."

The murmur of voices moved into the parlor. Dorrit knew there were things she could be doing—mending or ironing—any number of things—but she was frozen in nervous anticipation. She so wanted for this day to go well for May. Through the bedroom walls, she had overheard May and Byrd arguing the weekend before. She knew she ought to plug her ears, but she wanted to know what it was that married people argued about. True love, in Dorrit's expectations, meant a perfect match, a joining of hearts, an unwavering affection, like Amy Dorrit and Arthur Clennam. Didn't it? But they had argued in hushed, emphatic voices, and on Saturday, Byrd had left the house early, with Hank. May had dark circles under her eyes that day and was very quiet. The rest of the weekend had been tense. Saturday night there had been no arguments. Dorrit didn't know whether they had made up or weren't speaking.

When May called upstairs for Dorrit to bring down the children, her voice had the affected lilt of an actress in a talking picture. The photographer posed May and the children on the stairs, each holding a box of candy, with Mr. Marshall at the bottom. In the cannery, they took pictures of May and Blue, with Blue looking stiff and proud, wearing a new suit. Hank posed, his hands full of candy. They asked Dorrit to pose making ribbon rosettes, but she declined as politely as she could, then took the children upstairs again. When May called her back a little while later, the photographer was packing up his cameras in a case and the reporter sat on a hall chair, notepad perched on his knee. "Miss Sykes?" he asked, consulting his pad.

"Yes, sir?"

"Miss Sykes, tell me about how you came to be involved in this operation."

Desperate to shift attention away from herself Dorrit's eyes darted from side to side, as if she might find the correct answer scrawled on the wall. Her palms turned clammy. "Oh, I . . . Honestly, I haven't done anything. My father has helped with the machines and Mister Harris— Blue—he comes up with the recipes, but really, it's all Mrs. Craig's ideas, the Three-Square Bar and the Boo-Coo Bar and everything. Last week she donated a hundred bars to the Mother's Club of Charlottesville, for underfed children. She sends apples and jam to all of the soup kitchens, and she's given jobs to my father and eight or nine women."

Mr. Dalrymple nodded, scribbling. "And Mister Craig, is he involved?"

"No, sir. It's all Mrs. Craig. Honestly, I don't know how she gets so much done."

The reporter flipped back several pages in his pad. "Mrs. Craig tells me that you wrote the little fairy tale on the back of the Jelly Gems box. Is that so?"

Dorrit realized she was wringing her hands and made herself stop. A prickle of apprehension crept up her back. "Oh, it isn't anything. Just a little children's story."

"Well, I think it's quite charming. I'd like to talk to you about it." He stopped writing and looked at her and smiled. "Why don't you sit down, so we can talk properly."

"Criminy." Dorrit sank to sit on the bottom step.

"Do you think you could write another story like that?" He blinked at her, expectantly. He seemed so genuinely interested, as if he had all day long to talk about *her*.

"I have had an idea. You might think it's silly." Dorrit cringed inwardly. Where was this brazen audacity coming from?

"Oh, no. Please," he said, leaning forward, "tell me about it."

"I was thinking to myself, what about a story featuring a very brave girl? I just love Nancy Drew. I wrote to Miss Keene once, but she didn't write back. I'm sure she must get thousands of letters." Dorrit trailed off, realizing, to her horror, that she must be rambling.

"Ah. Well, you know, Miss Sykes—may I call you Dorrit?" She nodded. "Carolyn Keene doesn't actually exist. The publisher—Edward Stratemeyer—he came up with the idea as a female counterpart to the Hardy Boys. He writes the outlines and then hires writers. The last one, what was it?"

"*Nancy's Mysterious Letter?*"

"Right. That was written by a man, if you can believe that. So tell me more about your idea."

Dorrit frowned, trying to take in this information. "Well, I . . . I thought of this story, of a brave girl who becomes the first female knight. In medieval times? You know, as in The Knights of the Round Table? She would do brave deeds, of course, but she might solve mysteries too." She pushed past the tightening in her throat, and took a deep breath. "I was thinking of calling it *Sir Girlahad.*"

"Hmm. That's very interesting." He tapped his pencil against the pad. "I think it could have series potential."

Thirty-Seven
MAY

FEBRUARY 11, 1933

Two weeks passed, and excitement grew as news spread about the upcoming article. On the Saturday the issue was due, May hurried inside the post office. Miss Spindle stood behind the counter, smiling expectantly. "It only just arrived," she said, hefting a stack of magazines bound in twine. She fumbled to untie the cord while May rose up and down on her toes, wanting desperately to grab the bundle and open it. But Miss Spindle took her time, saying, "You know, I met the young man myself—the interviewer. Is that what they're called these days? Journalists, I suppose, or authors? Anyhow, what a pleasant young fellow. Lovely manners, didn't you think? I was at the station, to buy a ticket to go see my Aunt Lydia. She had a fall, on the ice—can't be too careful—bruised knee. Still, it upset her. We're not as young, I always tell her—and what do you know? There he was, that young Mister Dalrumple, or it was Dalrymple? And that nice photographer! Can't recall his, but he was rather quiet, anyway. And all that equipment he has to carry around. And what about that Mister Hitler being Chancellor of Germany? I don't like the looks of him one little bit."

May half-nodded the briefest of acknowledgments until, after what seemed like hours, Miss Spindle checked the address on each copy and handed over the counter four *Saturday Evening Posts* for February 11, 1933.

May held them to her chest and inhaled the scent of paper and fresh ink. Superstitiously, she told herself she would not peek inside the cover until they were all together. All but Byrd, she reminded herself. He had stuck fast to his determination to not be involved.

May interrupted Miss Spindle's ongoing chatter. "Thank you, have a lovely day," she called as she headed out.

Behind her, she heard, "There's mail in your box, May!"

Back at the farm, everyone had assembled in the living room. Everyone except Byrd. May studied the cover artwork—an illustration of a smiling little blond boy in a sailor suit, pulling a red wagon with a pointer riding in it. The artist's signature at the bottom of the page made it all real: *J.C. Leyendecker*. He had worked from one of the photographs taken during the interview. The artist had captured Hank's curls and Bandit's mask perfectly. "See there!" Roy said, pointing to the cover, "If that ain't the spitting image of Hank, I don't know who it is." He grinned from ear to ear.

May flipped the pages and there, accompanied by an illustration of three winged fairies, was, *"The Wood Sprites," by D.M. Sykes.* At the bottom of the page was printed:

D.M. Sykes lives in Virginia and is the author of the serialized stories printed on the Orchard De-Lite Candy labels. This is her first published story.

"Will you look at that!" Roy said, pulling Dorrit toward him in a hug.

May searched the table of contents then flipped pages, reading the headline aloud, "AN AMERICAN SUCCESS STORY" and below, in slightly smaller type, "A SWEET ENDING TO HARD TIMES."

"See," she said, tapping the page, "We're the feature article!" Across from a full-page photograph of Roy and Blue at a candy machine was a smaller photo of May with Blue and Henry, and an illustration of the Three-Square bar and Jelly Gems box. As she read on, her voice grew less ebullient, then slowed, then she ceased to read aloud at all. By the third paragraph, it was clear that Mr. Dalrymple had gleaned some information that made his story of the candy business something else entirely. He had written about the loss of Chestnut Grove, and James Craig's ruin and suicide. He painted May as a heroine, saving her family farm. In the space of five minutes, May's elation turned to disbelief, then to shame, and then, to sickening guilt.

Who had talked? The household was on tenterhooks. Dorrit and Roy took Hank to have dinner at Chestnut Grove.

Frantically May searched the house for Byrd. When she found him alone on the porch and showed him the story and watched him read it, she had wanted to grovel at his feet, writhing in apology. His face was expressionless as he read, and then he put the magazine down and walked across the yard with her following behind, begging him to *talk* to her. How could things get better, she implored, if a person was not allowed to apologize? She had not mentioned James Craig, nor had anyone else at the Farm.

With apology and explanation thus thwarted, May's perturbation grew into a nasty defensiveness.

Thirty-Eight
MAY AND DORRIT

The following afternoon May leaned against the kitchen counter, arms and legs crossed. She tapped her foot in four measured beats as the grand-father clock in the hall chimed. She exhaled pointedly, but Byrd was not there to witness her agitation. *Four o'clock.* Every Sunday, Byrd took the 4:35. He could *not* miss that train today. He had left the house immedi-ately after breakfast, with Hank, telling him within May's hearing that they were going to spend the day exploring.

Now, it was getting late. She needed to work first thing in the morning, to prepare for the rush of orders she hoped the *Post* article would bring. Silently, she renewed her resolve to appear imperturbable. They could continue this silent battle, toughing it out, each convinced of the other's lack of understanding. *He's doing this to irritate me*, was what she was thinking, but another idea elbowed its way into her mind: even if he did run late, it was a good thing that he was spending the day with Hank.

The kitchen door swung open with a blast of cold air, shaking May from her reverie. Hank barreled in, beaming. From the table Dorrit said, "My gracious, Hank! Come here and let me wipe that nose. Now tell me all about your day." Bandit, panting, followed in Hank's mud tracks, stop-ping to slurp from his water bowl.

Byrd came in last, wiping his forehead with his arm. He glanced at the wall clock. "Do I have time for a shower?"

May set her lips in a tight line. She would not scold him. "Yes," she said, blinking slowly. When he went upstairs, he would see that she had not packed for him as she usually did, stacking his weeks' worth of clean clothes in his Gladstone bag: six bleached, starched handkerchiefs, five shirts, five undershirts, five pairs of socks. He could do that for himself. With an air of apparent leisure that was, she knew, intended for *her* benefit, Byrd strolled through the kitchen. She listened to his tread on the stairs and exhaled, not having been aware that she was holding her breath. Really, it did take a lot of energy to keep it up.

From upstairs, she heard a bureau drawer slam, and although she experienced a moment of shame in her pettiness, she also held it close— something she might polish and admire.

Dorrit chided Hank to wipe his muddy shoes and put the dog outside, longing to escape herself. Instead, she offered Sister another cracker. Furtively, she watched May and Byrd. A muscle twitched in his jaw. May's hands clutched at her skirt. The tension between them felt electric, poisonous. Sister began to fret. It could be the tooth she was cutting, or perhaps she sensed the friction. When Byrd went upstairs, Dorrit heard May sigh as she rummaged in her purse. When she lit a cigarette and went to stare out the back window, Dorrit knew to stay out of the way. She fed Sister another spoonful of egg. From the parlor, she could hear Hank, excitedly telling his grandfather about his pony ride up the mountain, and the spooky old graveyard they found. The radio clicked on and music played.

When Hank returned, Dorrit said, brightly, "You must be tired after your big day. Why don't you stay here with me while your folks go to the train station? Buck Rogers will be on in a little while, and we can play checkers."

"But Sister always messes up the game." Hank whined, "She chews the pieces."

Dorrit watched May smile woodenly as she smashed out her cigarette in the sink, saying, "Your sister's not even two, sweetie. You were the same when you were little. Yes, you stay here with Dorrit."

"But I want to smash my penny! Grandpa gave me a penny."

May snapped, "You're staying here, and that's final."

Byrd stood in the hall doorway, holding his bag. He said, "Buddy, it'll have to wait until next time." He looked at his watch then ruffled Hank's hair saying, "You be a good boy, and I'll see you soon."

Hank pouted. "I want to go."

"You do as your mother says," Byrd said.

Hank stomped out of the kitchen and clomped noisily up the stairs. May pulled on her coat and slowly buttoned it while Byrd fidgeted with his bag, saying, "See you, Dorrit." He crossed the kitchen and kissed the top of his daughter's head. "Bye-bye, sweet pea." Sister gurgled, "Daaa . . ." waving her arms, upsetting her cup of milk. Byrd reached for a dishtowel and began to mop the table.

May said, "Byrd . . ."

Dorrit smiled and took the towel. Byrd called up the stairs, "See you Friday, buddy!"

The front door opened and closed and Dorrit exhaled, relieved. The air turned so very thick when they were both in the house. And being in the middle of the family, she had to wade through it. All of that unspoken anger.

May strode toward the Studebaker, her irritation growing. All day, she had been available to talk. Pulling on her gloves she checked her watch again. At 4:20, it was getting dark. The driveway was slick with patches of ice and the air smelled like snow. Byrd dropped his bag into the trunk. When he slammed it, May flushed with shame at her childishness. She could have packed for him. And she had snapped at Hank. In a kinder tone she said, "I'll drive." Byrd held the door open for her but did not look at her as she got in. She glanced again at her watch as he scraped frost from the windshield. She tapped the glass, saying, "I can see well enough. We really need to go." The steering wheel was cold. She turned the key, and a grinding sound was followed by ticking. She tried again. "Oh, no," she said, "I *knew* the battery was going. Are the keys in the truck? Dammit, you're going to miss the train."

The truck was at the cannery building, and they hurried across the back field to where it was parked by the door. Now breathless, May shoved the gearshift, accelerating rapidly down the drive. She spoke, finding the necessity of looking ahead at the road a welcome distraction. "Byrd," she said, her voice conciliatory, "we have got to talk about this. I am so, so sorry this happened. You know I didn't say a word to that reporter about your father, or Chestnut Grove. It must've been Miss Spindle. She told me she met that man and talked to him. It *had* to have been her. I promised you we wouldn't discuss that, and none of us did." She glanced at him. He stared straight ahead. She had only minutes to plead her case, so she blundered on, "And as for the way he presented the story, about me being the wife who saves the family, well, everyone we know realizes that's poppycock."

Byrd's mouth twitched but he remained silent. May couldn't think of what else she should say. In the truck's cold cab, their breath steamed. As she pulled in at the station, red signal lights were already flashing, illuminating the end of the last train car as it pulled out of the station and away. A whistle shrilled over the clangor as the departing train gained speed. Byrd rubbed the bridge of his nose. "Great. I'll miss an important meeting in the morning."

May pulled the brake, blowing out her breath slowly. She switched off the engine and began again, "Listen—"

He held up a hand to silence her. "No, you listen. You took money from Elsie." The train whistle shrieked again from further down the tracks. He continued, looking away from her, out the window. "And now, against my express wishes, our dirty laundry has been displayed to the entire country. The *entire* goddamned country, May. Oh, yes, three million readers. Three million people can enjoy reading about the Craigs. What a treat. What a heartwarming story."

May pounded the steering wheel with her gloved fists. "Byrd, don't."

He spoke without turning back. "I'll get the seven o'clock from Charlottesville tomorrow morning. I think I'll be staying in Washington next weekend."

She grabbed his arm, forcing him to look at her. Tears pricked her eyes. "You can't do that. You can't do that to the children. We have *got* to talk about this."

"We've already discussed it. You knew how I felt."

"You *told* me not to do things. I decided to do something else. And as for the article . . ."

"And your father, did he go along with using her money?"

"You leave him out of this," May said, gathering herself. "How can you ask *me* if I worked out a plan with my father, when you did exactly that, before that auction! This is all about your pride, isn't it? Your family isn't the only one with pride." She was almost panting with rage. Their breath steamed like a pair of bulls, facing off. It was a relief to finally have it out. She said, "You never even wanted me to work in the market, did you? Well, you need to deal with your pride, Byrd. You need to admit to yourself that I *can* do this. We can *both* work hard. I can't stand the way things have been between us. It's so hard, during the week, without you there." He made no answer.

"All right. Fine," she whispered, her eyes blurring. "The children will be glad to have you home tonight."

Dorrit angled the highchair toward the kitchen window, saying, "Look, Sister. See the snowflakes? Maybe tomorrow we can build a snowman." She cleaned up the spilled milk and wiped Sister's hands and face. The cast-iron popover pan rattled as she slid it into the oven. Bandit scratched at the back door and Dorrit let him in. Tail wagging, the dog began to troll the floor beneath the high chair, searching for bits of egg. The aroma of warming batter filled the kitchen, canceling the odor of cigarette smoke. Dorrit loved to make dinner on Sunday nights. Having the kitchen to herself without Delphina looking over her shoulder was a relief. She took Sister from her highchair, then walked the baby through the hall to see her grandfather. Small tracks of muddy shoeprints led up the stairs. She called, "Hank? Get ready for your bath."

Over the sounds of the radio, Dorrit listened for May's return. She dampened a rag, making her way up each step holding Sister by the hand, wiping mud as she went. She called, through Hank's door, "Take those shoes off right this minute!" She juggled Sister on her hip, then changed her diaper and put her in the crib with her stuffed bear. It would be nice if May offered to bathe Hank, since he was in such a mood. He might be coming down with a cold after being out all day.

Dorrit left Sister babbling to her bear, then took a towel from the hall closet and started the tub to fill. She went into Hank's room. Bandit followed and jumped up on the bed. The dog turned two circles and collapsed with a sigh.

Back at home, May pulled the truck in beside the Studebaker and pulled the brake. Byrd got out, and she swiped her damp cheeks, stalling for time, not wanting to go inside.

Dorrit called from the porch, "Mister Craig! Is Hank with you?" May stepped out of the car to see the girl running toward them, her breath heaving.

Byrd said, "No. What's—?"

Delphina called from the door, "Is he there?"

May clutched her coat. Dorrit's eyes were wild, her voice rising, "I went to call him for his bath, and he was gone. I looked all over; thinking he was hiding. He stood on a chair and unlocked the porch door, in the sewing room. He must've gone down the outside stairs."

Delphina said, "She came and got me, thinking he was at my house. We called Cy. They're checking the barn. We looked in the cellar and attic." She clutched a flashlight. "It's getting so cold, and he doesn't have his coat or his hat."

Byrd dropped his suitcase. "He wanted to go to the station." He pulled open the back door of the Studebaker, then reached inside. He held up Hank's cowboy hat. "He was hiding under the blanket, to go with us." He looked around, frantically. "Delphina, call Blue. You stay at the house."

May leaned into the car. "Byrd!" She said, "My keys! I left them on the front seat. They're gone."

The cannery building stood across the back field, accessible by a dirt drive along the fence line. In the deepening dusk, May and Byrd ran toward it over the long grass, calling for their son. Dorrit ran behind. As they approached the darkened building, May saw the door ajar; her ring of keys in the lock. Breath heaving, Byrd ran inside and she followed, feeling for the light switch beside the door. "Hank! Hank!" her calls echoed in the space. In the seconds it took to survey the scene her mind registered, *something is missing.*

A metal storage rack had fallen forward; now it canted at a precarious angle against the edge of the work table. Its solid back blocked what was below. Byrd held up a hand, and May and Dorrit halted. He held one corner and began to raise the rack. Heavy glass canisters slid and shattered on the cement floor, broken glass glistened in a pyramid of spilled sugar, brilliant green dye splattered the floor. Byrd held the rack, panting. "Dorrit," he said, sounding unnaturally calm, "go around the other side. May, help her. Go slowly." They pulled the rack upright.

May moaned, closing her eyes for an instant. A heavy cylinder of brown paper in an iron frame had fallen on Hank. His eyes were closed, his face colorless. Blood ran over his forehead. In a flash she envisioned him climbing to reach candy on the top shelf, the rack tilting forward. She crouched behind Byrd. Hank's face was still; his eyelids, blue. May's hand went to cover her mouth.

Byrd lifted the roll of paper. He knelt over Hank and laid a hand on his neck, then his cheek. He looked up into May's face. His own was ashen. He said, "His back might be hurt, but I don't think we can wait for an ambulance." Gently, he scooped up his son. Dorrit removed her coat and laid it over Hank. "May," Byrd said, "get the truck. Dorrit, go back to the house and call Martha Jefferson hospital. Tell them we're on the way."

With one last look at Hank, May nodded, then ran, gasping, stumbling back over the field to the truck with Dorrit beside her, the flashlight beam bobbing ahead of them. Dorrit opened the truck door, her breath heaving then stood, hugging herself, tears streaming down her face.

"Go!" May commanded, "Delphina knows who to call."

May's hand shook as she turned the key in the ignition. She barreled across the field, screeching to a halt by the door of the cannery. As she jumped out, Byrd motioned to the passenger side, saying, "I'll drive, you hold him." Gently, he handed Hank into the cab, into her arms. He was as limp as a sleeping baby. "May," Byrd said, and they looked into each other's eyes, "press this on the cut." He held out his handkerchief and placed her hand, saying, "Hold here, and do not let go. Keep some pressure on it. Don't let go." She nodded, staring fixedly at her son's white face.

Don't let go. Don't let go. Don't let go. The words took on the cadence of clacking train wheels as May repeated the phrase quietly to herself. Blood soaked her glove and she tightened her grasp. Had he felt it? Had his scream been drowned out by the noise of breaking glass and metal? Byrd drove slowly over the rutted drive toward the road. She cupped Hank's cold cheek with her free hand, then held his head to her breast, inhaling the boy scent of his hair. *He must be cold,* she thought, *without his coat or gloves. You need your mittens when you go outside.* As they turned onto Route 22, Byrd accelerated. "He was hiding," May said, her voice full of wonder. "He wanted to go to the station." Snow was falling now; wet clumps slid down the windshield.

She wanted to tell her son he'd been naughty, that he knew he wasn't allowed in the cannery because it was dangerous, but he was so still. Would he ever say her name again? Was he dying right now, in her arms? Did life slip away so quietly? She had never felt such utter helplessness. All she could do was to hold on.

Dorrit hung up the telephone and said, to Delphina, "The doctors will look for them at the emergency entrance."

Delphina jiggled Sister on her hip. She put a hand on Dorrit's arm. "Call Cy again, tell whoever answers to find him and tell him what's happened. Tell him to get over here."

Mr. Marshall called from his room, his voice full of worry, "Delphina?"

Oh, dear Lord, Dorrit thought, then, *God, how could you? How could you do this to Hank? How did he get the keys? How was he strong enough to unlock the bolt at the top of the porch door?* She picked up the telephone receiver. Her cold hands were clumsy. The familiar number would not come to her. She shook her head hard, to clear it, then dialed, praying Cy would pick up. Clarence answered, and Dorrit began to speak, holding back sobs. Having to repeat the news made it more terrible. She hung up the phone, observing her hands. Her fingers were stiff, foreign. The sounds of voices from the next room retreated into a dull, faraway hum.

Dorrit covered her eyes. Images flashed; Hank on the ground, blood running from his head. Another scene lit her vision, hazy at first, then growing sharper. A bloody head. A man, on the ground.

She walked through the kitchen then out the back door, the metal knob cold as she quietly pulled it closed behind her. Snowflakes fell against the light of the kitchen window. Crossing her arms over her chest, she descended the steps, snow compacting beneath her feet with a hollow sound. She leaned over and wretched into the hedge until her stomach was empty. Still, mice ran around in her guts, prodding. Her heart beat erratically. She spit, then wiped her hand across her mouth, feeling hot and sick, unaware of the cold or the snowflakes that stuck and melted in her hair.

She had taken a life. How could she not remember that? And now, *she* had let this happen. It was *her job*, to watch the children. It was *her responsibility*. The Craigs would never forgive her.

God would never forgive her.

She was unforgivable.

Dorrit began to walk. Away from the warmly lit windows of the house, away from further news. She reached the road and as if by instinct, turned eastward. She would go to the church, she decided, and pray on her knees, all night. She would ask God her questions: *How could you take my mother, and how could this happen to Hank? Why didn't you hurt me instead of him?* The snow bathed the early evening in blue-gray shadows, and Dorrit kept walking, wondering, *what if the Craigs were Christian Scientists? What would they do?* Would Hank be lying on the kitchen table now, while they prayed over him? Would they be whispering to him that pain was an illusion?

Later, May would have no memory of the drive to the hospital. She remembered details: a white, brightly lit hallway; the insistent squeak of the gurney wheels, flying over shiny linoleum; a doctor striding alongside, taking Hank's pulse; the colorless delicacy of her son's small wrist.

When they stopped in front of a cubicle a nurse took her arm. "Ma'am?" The woman was matronly and calm, a crisp white hat pinned neatly to her head, spectacles polished. May felt as if she were underwater, her movements ponderous and heavy. She tilted her head, watching the nurse's mouth move. "Ma'am?" The nurse said, "You'll need to give us some information. Is this your little boy?" May nodded slowly.

The doctor barked out, "Ringer's Solution. Be quick about it. Is the X-ray technician ready? Two surgical nurses to standby." He looked up from Hank for the first time, his gaze moving from May to Byrd. "You're the Craigs?"

"Yes," Byrd said.

"I'm Dr. McCown. We'll do X-rays first to check for a compound skull fracture or a spicule. The scalp wound looks superficial."

Byrd said, "A spicule?"

"A splinter of bone, from the skull. Not always apparent, but the skull can be compressed—what we call a pond fracture—and sometimes an interior splinter of bone can be driven into the brain. The bleeding from the ears concerns me. Please, wait here." They wheeled Hank away, his small hand dangling off the side of the gurney.

The nurse, May realized, still held her by the arm. "Ma'am?" she said gently, "I'm Nurse Potter. Now tell me your name, and your son's name."

"May Craig. His name is Hank. Henry. James Henry Craig is his name. He's named after both of his grandfathers." Her voice caught.

The nurse took May's hand. "You can't go in the X-ray room. The doctors are doing all they can. This will take a bit of time. Is there someone you'd like to telephone?" Nurse Potter led her into a curtained cubicle, coaxing, pulling May's coat off her shoulders and down her arms. She removed May's stained gloves and began to wipe her wrists with gauze. May pushed her away. "No, take me to where he is. Please, I need to be there with him." She pushed through the curtain and ran into the hall, calling "Hank! Where is my son? Where is my son?"

Down the hall, Byrd stood outside a pair of swinging doors, watching through the glass.

When the doctor came out to the waiting room, pulling off his white cap, May and Byrd rose together. Dr. McCown said, "We've stopped the bleeding and stitched up his head. He has a skull fracture, and he's still unresponsive. He also has a broken collarbone, which we've set. The good news is that his spine is uninjured. We'll have to watch him very carefully."

Byrd said, "Will you operate?"

"Not now. His brain is concussed. We want the swelling to go down. We'll assess his prognosis then. You can see him now, but only for a moment."

May stood beside the gurney and grasped Hank's hand. It was cold; his fingernails looked bruised. She reached for Byrd's hand, connecting the three of them. Closing her eyes, she passed all of her love into her son. At that moment she would have given him her life, had the choice been offered. She prayed, with the desperate bargaining of the nonpious. After a single round of silent negotiations, she stopped. God would answer, or he wouldn't. Around her, the doctor barked instructions and nurses answered with calm assurance, instruments clanged, the bright lights above hummed with electrical force. May looked into Byrd's face. Sorrow and hope and desperation crossed between them. Guilt and regret went unspoken. She leaned over Hank, cupping his cheeks in her hands as she kissed his forehead, now crisscrossed with gauze and tape.

"Mister and Mrs. Craig?" Nurse Potter said, "I need for you to come with me now. We'll take good care of your boy." The nurse led them from the room, saying, "Now, tell me who I should telephone. Someone who can come and sit with you—bring you some fresh clothes, hmm?"

May said, "Delphina. Delphina Fontaine. The exchange is Keswick, 3880." The nurse nodded, then led May to the door of a restroom.

"Now you go on in here and wash up while I call. You'll feel better. Folks forget that they need to use the washroom when these things happen. I'll be back in a jiffy."

In a jiffy? May thought, *What does that even mean? What is a jiffy?* It took a jiffy for a roll of paper to fall on Hank. In a jiffy, he could have a brain hemorrhage. Or it could be slower—a coma lasting weeks that he would never wake from.

May wiped her face and washed her hands. Brown flakes of blood reddened as they swirled over the white porcelain and down the drain. A rapid knock sounded on the washroom door and the nurse called, "Mrs. Craig!" May turned off the tap, fumbling to open the door with wet hands. "Mrs. Craig." Nurse Potter held both of May's forearms. "Listen to me carefully. You need to come with me, right now." May followed, barely breathing. Outside the examining room doors, the nurse stopped and held her arm again. "He's having a seizure. I need for you to be calm. Do you understand?"

Inside, another nurse removed an oxygen mask, then wedged a wooden bar in Hank's mouth as Byrd stood on one side. Hank's body arched upward, and May's mouth opened as if she would scream, but she could only watch, leaning toward Byrd as he pulled her close with his free arm, resting his chin on the top of her head. Time, it seemed, shifted erratically, lurching forward without explanation, as it did in dreams. Again, she joined her hands to Hank's and Byrd's.

Hank's body ceased its bucking. With gentle hands, the nurse removed the wooden bar, then reached to his neck for a pulse. His body relaxed. His eyelids fluttered, then calmed, and May willed them to open, to move—anything to move.

Dorrit walked slowly along Route 22, blinking away snowflakes. No cars passed. The lights of the train station came into view and she drew her arms closer around her, shivering. The cold seemed purifying somehow, even though there was no absolution to be had.

The church might be another mile up the road. Why had she thought she could walk there? Morbid projections flashed through her mind. Hank, crushed by the heavy shelf. Hank, alive but never waking. Waking, but not speaking, not communicating. *Stop!* she told herself. *Stop.* She kept her gaze trained forward, to the solitary light of the market, winking through the snow. The lights of a car approached and Dorrit ducked into the woods, veering onto the path that led to the station, continuing on, tripping over roots and fallen branches. She sniffled, wiping her nose with numbed, shaking hands. The forge came into view, dark now, twined with winter-brown vines. Her hiding place.

The warped, tightly closed door bore the brunt of Dorrit's rage as she shoved against it with all her might. In the dark inside, she felt along the ledge. The box of matches was still where Clarence had left it. Fumbling, she struck one and, in its wavering flare, saw the stack of dead branches they had amassed in August. Gathering a handful of small sticks, she added them to the dry leaves in the brick furnace. A timid orange flame sputtered and crackled as she blew on it, cupping its warmth with wet hands. In the widening light, shadows shifted, and her breath steamed. It all came back in a rush. The source of her nightmares. His sunburned face. *God is punishing me, because of that man. This is his retribution.* She could not go back, nor could she go to the church. She did not *deserve* to set foot inside a church. God had laid his wrath upon her, and it was terrible and mighty. Her faith was nothing in comparison. Wind whistled through a broken window, guttering the flame. Dorrit knelt in front of the furnace, her dress dripping on the hearth as she fed larger sticks into the fire. The dirt floor radiated cold into her joints and bones and still she knelt, her face in her hands, relishing the pain, breathing prayers for Hank, beseeching God.

Sometime later—an hour, or was it two? She had no idea. An arc of light swept across the window from outside. There, again, the beam of a flashlight. She pushed herself up from the floor, stiff with cold. The fire had burned to embers. Outside, branches snapped. She held her breath. As the door swung open, snow swirled in the flashlight's beam, blinding her momentarily. Dorrit backed up, but there was no way out.

Clarence stamped his feet, leaning his head to one side. "Well, hellfire," he whispered. "Here you are." He closed the door behind him, saying, "Where's your coat?" He shrugged out of his jacket and wrapped it around her shoulders. "Your pa and Dennis are driving all over tarnation, looking for you. I figured out where you'd be, right off." His words were gruff, scolding; but in his tone, Dorrit heard relief.

"Is Hank dead?" She exhaled the words, almost inaudibly, then held her breath.

Clarence held his hands out toward the furnace. He answered, quietly, "Byrd called Cy a little while ago. He said Hank was stabilized—I think that was the word—but his brain is swelled with a . . . a . . . concussion. Yes, a concussion. That means his brain got shook and he won't wake up. He has a broken collarbone."

"But he still might die?"

"Reckon only God knows that. Now come on, we need to get you warmed up." He placed a hand on her arm.

Dorrit shook her head, backing away. "I can't. I can't go back. God is punishing me, for something I did. Something terrible."

"What? Listen, they *need* you."

"But I *can't*." Dorrit tried to pull away. "I . . . there was a man. I killed him. Here."

Clarence held her by her arms and shook her. "No. Listen to me. I *saw* him. You really don't remember, do you?"

"I do now."

"When I got back here that morning, you were on the ground, just outside. There was a big fella, out cold. You clocked him! I could see that he was breathing. You were out of your mind—sick, I mean, so I carried you to the market. After Blue found you, I came back here. That man was gone. I swear.

"At first, I thought you just didn't want to talk about it. Then I figured you truly didn't remember. I wasn't going to stir it all up."

Dorrit watched Clarence's eyes as he continued, "And what happened to Hank, that is not your fault. He hid in the car. His *parents* didn't know where he'd got to. After they left in the truck, he found those keys. Blue says he's all the time begging to watch the candy being made."

Clarence gripped her shoulders until she met his eyes. His voice was soft. "I'm good at keeping secrets. This here is our secret place, remember? You didn't do anything wrong. And you never have to talk about that man again. You were defending yourself. Hell, he might have killed you." He thrust a log into the furnace and squatted, his back to her, prodding the embers into life. Very quietly, he began to speak. "Listen. Sometimes, things like that happen, on the road. Hobo life—it doesn't follow the same set of rules and laws as for other folks. Remember, I told you we should start a gang?"

Dorrit nodded to his back. "Yes."

"I had a reason for that. I mean, I didn't think you ought to be riding the rails by yourself, but I didn't want to be on my own, neither." He held his hands toward the fire, his back still to Dorrit. "Thing is, ain't nobody can predict how they'll react to being attacked. It's like some animal part of us comes out. There's desperate folks on the road—bad men—who want to steal or do harm. Nobody who heard your story would ever blame you." He rose and tucked his jacket more tightly around her. She sobbed against his chest.

He allowed her to cry for a few minutes and then pushed her gently away, saying, "Now then, come on. If you can walk back to the market, I'll call Cy from there. You need to get warm. 'Sides, they're all worrying about you, your pa especially. They got enough to fret about. They depend on you, Dorrit."

Thirty-Nine
MAY

Somehow, five days passed.

May sat at a window by the hour, alternately studying the gray-white sterility of the hospital room and staring out at a bare oak tree. The occasional red blur of a cardinal or rusty breast of a robin caused her to start. Snow fell, outlining branches in white, and still, she sat. Shifting her gaze indoors, she concentrated on the small pale face, avoiding the bed, with its pulleys and cranks, a monument to her failure to protect her son. Once she discerned there were no changes to Hank's face, she cataloged details—flaking paint on the legs of the bed, scuffed baseboards. The white room contained dozens of shades of noncolor, and glass, she decided, wasn't actually colorless—it was blue, or green, or shades of gray, depending on how one looked at it, depending on how much focus one allowed. She worried the frayed piping on the arm of the upholstered chair, wondering, idly, how many frantic parents or spouses had waited here as she did, feeling useless and sometimes distracted, and then feeling guilty for being distracted, because she needed to concentrate *all of her energy, all of the time* on her son's recovery. A penance, she told herself. It could not be severe enough, because she needed to atone, if she was given the chance to do so. If he lived.

She knew without asking that Byrd blamed himself, too, for being so wrapped up in bickering that they had allowed this unspeakable thing to happen.

Unspeakable, she thought, *is that why we can't talk about it?*

When Byrd came to sit beside her, they whispered about what the doctors and nurses said, hoping to glean some shard of hope or reassurance, to offer these up to each other like seashells found on a beach. They were gentle with each other, overly conciliatory in their mutual avoidance of speaking about *the event.* Every day, Delphina came. Dennis drove her and waited outside while she cajoled May into changing her clothes and eating what she brought from home—soft buttered rolls, creamy soup, baked custard—comforting food.

May stood to stretch her arms. She checked the doctor's chart and noticed that it was Saturday. Not that it mattered. She replaced the chart and went to stand beside the bed, to stroke Hank's cheek and then lean down to kiss it, whispering a now-familiar litany: "We love you, darling. Mama is right here with you. You're going to be fine."

From the hallway, a booming voice reverberated. There was an assertive rap on the door before it swung open and Elsie breezed in, her big raccoon coat flapping. She carried an armload of red hothouse roses and bright yellow balloons. The sudden infusion of color into the sterile whiteness was jarring. As May rose, Elsie went to the bed, cupping Hank's cheek briefly before turning to drop the flowers into the arms of the nurse who followed her. Balloons bobbed drunkenly along the ceiling. Without a word, she enveloped May in a hug of soft, thick fur, like a mother animal. She smelled of cigarettes and perfume, and *life,* not the iodine and disinfectant and metallic, radiator-heated air of the hospital. Elsie spoke over her shoulder to the nurse. "Give us a moment, hon. And put those in some water, would you? Thanks awfully." She ignored the nurse's obvious pique. "Oh, sweetie," Elsie said in her gravelly whisper, "I came just as soon as I heard." She stroked May's hair, rocking them together, side to side. "Elsie's here, Elsie's here. Tell me, what's the news?"

May spoke into Elsie's lapel. "He woke up, once. He knew me, and he spoke a few words. They say that unless he gets an infection, he's going to live. Oh, I'm so glad to see you. It's been . . ." May put a fist over her mouth. For minutes they stood that way, as if Elsie were transfusing energy or life force, and May took it, with desperate, needy hunger.

Elsie pulled off her gloves, finger by finger, then moved toward Hank and held her palm to his brow, gently tracing one eyebrow with her thumb. "Now. I'm going to sit here with him, and you are going to go home and have a proper rest."

"Oh, no, no. I can't possibly." The mere suggestion caused a spiking anxiety, and May's voice faltered. "What if he wakes? He doesn't even understand what's happened to him. He doesn't remember. I suppose . . . I suppose that's a blessing, isn't it? When he woke up—I think it was yesterday—I explained it to him. The doctor said that when he wakes again, he might not remember being told. I'll have to explain all over again."

Elsie sighed and tutted. "Lord have mercy. You have had a time of it. Such a terrible, terrible accident."

May's voice was ragged. "How did you find out?"

"Byrd called me last night."

"He did?"

"Yes. He's worried about you." Elsie grasped May's hand. "Listen, honey, you can't blame yourself for this. Neither you nor Byrd should. These things just *happen*. Terrible things happen to good people. Now, he and I had a long talk. You'll help Hank through—both of you will.

"I stopped by the farm on my way here, to pay my respects to your dad, and I had a gander at the candy operation. That's quite a setup. I met that fellow Ray, or was it Roy? He would have gone on all day, but I told him I had to see you. They're working like ants over there! That gal, the one you told me about, what's her name?"

"Dorrit?"

"Dorrit. Anyhow, she was playing with Little Elsie, and Delphina was in the kitchen. When can Hank go home?"

"The doctor won't really say. I hope he isn't trying to shield us from bad news. I won't tell you all of the medical details, but they have to watch him."

"Gawd." Elsie looked around the room. "Where can a gal have a smoke around here? Do you just hang out the window? And look at

you, darling girl. You're thin as a rail. You need some liver, that's what
you need." Elsie raised the window a few inches and pulled a chair over
beside it. She held a package of cigarettes out to May, then flipped her
gold lighter with one hand. "Ah," Elsie exhaled, shaking her head, looking toward Hank. "You know, my darling, you're going through what
every mother fears most. Every time something *almost* happens—which,
believe you me, is pretty much of a daily occurrence at my house—we
thank our lucky stars, or God, or whatever, and then we simply go on. We
forget about the almost-tragedy. It's human nature. But sometimes terrible
things *do* happen, like that poor little Lindbergh baby. Now, don't get me
wrong. I mean, we *all* know that this could have been much worse. But
we, as mothers, have some sort of intuitive resiliency. We have to, otherwise we'd remember the horror of childbirth and refuse to have another,
and the human race would simply die out. Believe you me," Elsie pointed
from herself to May, ". . . *we* are the strong ones. We pull the rest of the
family through. And that's pre-*cise*-ly what you're doing." May exhaled
smoke toward the window, her throat tightening. Elsie patted May's arm.
"You're tough as nails." She grinned.

"But Elsie," May said, looking down at the glowing tip of her cigarette, "I'm not sure that Byrd and I will get through this—I mean, as
a couple. It—the guilt—we haven't talked about it. We'd been fighting
before it happened, and what we fought over hasn't gone away. I have to
wonder if he blames me because I deceived him by taking your money. I
think he lost trust in me. And now this." May twirled the cigarette in her
fingers, watching ash float to the floor.

"But it's nobody's *fault*. Your dad told me that Dorrit blames herself too."

"Oh, it isn't her fault at all. Poor thing, she was devastated. Byrd and
I were arguing." May took a deep drag of her cigarette. "The *Post* article
had just come out."

Elsie nodded. "Right. I saw that. When he called last night, well, of
course he told me about poor little Hank, but then we had a chat about
that money."

"You did?"

"Damned right. I told him I made you take that check. Then I told him he was behaving like an ass. Hell, I told him he ought to be *proud* of you. Anyhow, I gave him a piece of my mind. And you know, he doesn't blame you. He loves you. He's trying to be noble and provide for his family. You know how men are! I mean, for a long time, my having money bothered Archie. I told him we would live on what he brought home, but that I would buy my own clothes and things, and we were not to discuss it. Men have a hard time accepting help." Elsie glanced at her wristwatch. "Now, you listen to me. Byrd will be downstairs in five minutes." She flapped her hand toward the bathroom. "You go in there and wash your face, then go down to the lobby and talk to him. Tell him the things you've told me. I'm going to hold down the fort here and if they need you for anything at all a nurse will come and get you."

May looked toward Hank's bed with a helpless expression. Elsie said, "Listen, hon, this is part of the healing. You go on. Listen to Doctor Elsie."

May rode the elevator down the four flights to the lobby. Byrd stood alone in an alcove at one end, looking out of a picture window, his shoulders slumped, hands in his pockets. As she neared she saw that he watched her reflection approaching in the glass. He turned to face her, his face inscrutable. They had not been truly alone since the accident. For long moments, they looked at each other. She wanted to embrace him but held back. She could talk about Hank's chart or ask after Sister, but she knew this was to be a reckoning. There was a chasm between them, and she couldn't back away. She had to jump. "I'm sorry," she began, knowing the words were woefully inadequate. "You'll never know . . . I was so caught up . . ." Nothing sounded right. "I'm sorry this happened, and I'm sorry I deceived you." May looked down. "I wanted to help, at first. Then I wanted—I wanted to be a success—because I wanted to prove you wrong."

"And you did, I suppose." Byrd blew out his breath. "The telephone's been ringing off the hook—orders from all over the country. You are a success."

"But you still disapprove."

"I'm not happy with the way you went about things, no. But you were right. I was being proud. I couldn't bear the thought of not being able to take care of you all myself. I'm sorry for that."

"I understand." May inhaled, looking up at the ceiling. "Shame is supposed to teach us to do better the next time, isn't it? So many times, so *many* times I've made mistakes and felt ashamed, but then I go on and get it wrong again." She looked down, hugging herself. "I can never change what's happened to Hank."

"You should be proud of what you've accomplished. I'm proud of you."

"Proud? Proud is the last thing I'm feeling. I'm so grateful he's alive."

"I am too. But you have *got* to tell me what's going on. And I'll tell you. No more of this deception."

"I promise. I'm so sorry." She reached up to put her arms around his neck and he held her, moving his hand up and down her back. He said, "Lord, May, I can feel your backbone."

She caressed his cheek, saying, "You need a shave."

He took her hand and kissed the palm. "I want you to go home and rest. I'll stay here."

"But I can't leave him." Her voice had an edge of panic.

"You *can*. You've got to stop this vigil. It's superstitious. Hank is going to recover. I spoke with Dorrit and Roy this morning. I offered them our old cottage at Chestnut Grove. They were over the moon. Roy told me he wants to invest in your business. I told him he'd have to talk to you and Blue."

May said, "That was generous of you, offering the cottage."

"Now, you stay here, and I'm going to sit with Hank. Elsie can drive you home for a bath and a rest. Don't say no. A dose of Elsie is just what you need, and you've hardly seen Sister. I want you to stay home tonight."

"I love you, Byrd. Never forget that."

"You know I love you. I always have. I've known since I was ten years old."

Forty
DORRIT

Dorrit stood in the upstairs hall at Keswick Farm. She had heard a car drive up, then the front door, and May's voice, speaking to her father in the parlor. Her first instinct was to slip away, to hide, but she stayed rooted where she was, in the straight chair where she had been waiting since Elsie had left an hour earlier. Dorrit worried a button on the front of her dress, listening, waiting. After a few long minutes, she heard May coming up the stairs.

"Dorrit?" May looked surprised.

Dorrit rose, finding it hard to meet her gaze. May hugged her arms, leaning against the wall. She was pale, lank-haired, a desiccated shell of herself. For a long moment, they looked at each other. May said, "I haven't seen you. We need to talk."

Dorrit stepped back and held the door of her room open. May sat, tentatively, on the edge of the bed, running her palm lightly over the chenille coverlet. Dorrit licked her lips and said, very quietly, "I don't know what to say, except that I'm sorry. But that's not nearly enough." Her lower lip trembled.

May looked up for an instant. Dorrit saw anguish in her eyes before she dropped them again and began tracing the raised pattern of the bedspread. "It's not your fault," May said. "No one thinks it is. You must believe that." Her finger hovered over swirls of chenille, as if she were solving a maze. She continued, "The only one to blame is me. For a long time, I've been afraid . . . For a long time, I've been afraid that I would turn out like my own mother."

"What happened to her?"

May looked up, briefly catching Dorrit's eyes. "Do you remember, I told you that my brother died? Baby Henry. I was seven, but I remember. Delphina took care of us. My mother never seemed interested. I didn't know then, of course, that the 'tonic' she took every day was laudanum. It left her in a stupor; she was addicted. One morning, Baby Henry didn't wake up. The doctor was suspicious. I think my father was too. But no one knew for sure. He was so little . . .

"Daddy was going to send my mother to an asylum, but she ran away. I didn't know about the suspicions. Anyhow"—May paused and pushed her hair off her forehead—"she never came back."

"Did you ever find her?"

May shook her head. "No, but I did find out what happened. She drowned herself. I never told my father or Delphina the truth."

"So you hid those bad things from your father?"

"I told them she'd died of the Spanish Influenza. It seemed the kindest thing."

Dorrit frowned. *The kindest thing.* "But you would never abandon your children," she said, emphatically. "You're not like that. You're nothing like that."

"But I *am*. I am like her. Before I even knew about what she'd done, I did something awful. There was this boy I met at college, I was expelled because of him. He broke my heart. I was so ashamed, I tried to kill myself. Dying seemed easy. It was living that scared me. No one ever knew about it, but Byrd."

Dorrit's voice caught. "You're a different person now. What happened to you, it changed you."

"But I still have my mother inside me. I must."

"Your mother, she must have, she must have been very disturbed, mentally." The room grew dim, the winter light fading as they sat in silence. Dorrit tried in vain to sort what had been revealed to her. None of it fit with the May Craig she thought she knew. She had envied May. Now, she wasn't sure at all. How much shame can one person carry before they fall? Dorrit said, quietly, "Sometimes . . . sometimes people do things they never imagined, because things happen that . . . that no one could expect."

May raised her head and gazed levelly at her. "Oh, Dorrit. Please forgive me. I came up here to try to make you feel better, but I'm sitting over here . . . I'm such a mess. Such a selfish mess. Apologies seem so, so inadequate."

"Oh. I won't say a word to anyone. But please believe me. You aren't like that—like your mother."

May said, "I've laid too much on your shoulders. But I hope I can count on you, to help Hank. Things will be different around here—and I don't just mean with Hank recovering. I need to find some sort of balance, between work and home. I do trust you, Dorrit."

"Thank you," Dorrit said, quietly, "I trust you too."

Forty-One
DORRIT

APRIL 15, 1933
TWO MONTHS LATER

Dorrit held a small, rectangular box with gentle fingers, turning it to inspect each side. The surface was glossy; the front featured a colorful illustration of a treasure chest full of jewels and gold coins with small lines radiating outward to suggest sparkle. Printed in an arc across the top was, JELLY GEMS, and at the bottom, *Assorted fruit flavors!* On one long side was: *Orchard De-Lite Confection Company, Keswick, Virginia.* Turning the box over, she flushed with pleasure. There, in small print, with an illustration of a tiny fairy, was her story. Her name was not included, but it was *hers.* That was enough. Larger boxes would have a longer story, and each time they were reprinted they would feature a new chapter. How many children, all over the entire country, might read her words? She would ask Hank which should come next; the battle against the chipmunks, or the story of Indigo washing down the creek in a summer storm? She rationed the time she spent admiring it, and now slipped the box beneath her pillow. Also tucked beneath her pillow were two envelopes. She extracted them, studying again the exotic stamps and words printed in German on the smaller. She unfolded the airmail sheet and sank to the edge of the bed to read it again.

> *Dear Pop and Dor,*
> *I am in Germany at a place called Hamburg. The Merchant*

*Marine has not worked out so good after all, mainly because seasick-
ness is a problem. Most fellows got over it after a week or so, but not
yours truly. I will be on the freighter* Reliance, *docking in Baltimore
on April 13. I reckon I will get up to Boston from there. Some of
the fellows have been talking about the Civilian Conservation Corps,
and I am going to see about that.*

Walt

The second, larger envelope was from the admissions department of
William and Mary College in Williamsburg, confirming Dorrit's scholarship award. She would begin in September. May had promised that she
and Elsie Nelson would supply her books and proper clothes for college,
but Dorrit hoped to be able to do without their help. She had saved what
May paid her for her candy box stories and started sewing dresses for
herself.

She returned the letters, folding the coverlet carefully over her freshly
made bed. The room still smelled of new paint, the walls the color of butter.
There was a small desk, and Roy had moved in a dressing table from the
bedroom where he would sleep. She had never had a dressing table or desk
of her own. She smoothed the starched dresser scarf across the bureau top,
then arranged her hairbrush and comb. Next to that she placed the red,
tomato-shaped pincushion that had been her mother's. From the desk, she
took her pen and her notebook, now battered and dog-eared.

The steps to the second floor of the cottage were steep, and she held the
rope banister as she descended. In the kitchen she sat on a ladder-backed
chair, hooking her heels over the lowest rung. She opened her notebook
for the first time since the accident. She began to write.

April 15, 1933

    *Pop and I have moved to our very own cottage. I have a bed-
room all to myself. I am happy that we'll be staying here. He says we'll
eat our breakfasts and dinners at Chestnut Grove. So I reckon I will
be seeing right much of Clarence, at least until September. He has
a room of his own and plenty of work there and at the market. He*

told me that someday he's going to run that place himself, and I believe that he will.

Hank is full of beans. Aside from a scar on his forehead, which the doctor says will fade, he is back to his old self. I have written two new stories to read to him. He doesn't remember the accident, and that is a blessing. It's nice when God helps us forget. I have not been writing in here in a while. I suppose I don't need to account for everything. Some things are best . . .

Dorrit bit the end of her pencil and frowned.

~~*left*~~ *. . .* ~~*forgotten*~~ *. . . Some things are best not recorded, for several reasons, which are also best not recorded.*

She stopped to peer through the front window. When she heard her father's truck, she hurried to open the door. He jogged up the walkway, shouting, "Lookie here!"

When the reporter from the *Saturday Evening Post* had telephoned Mr. Marshall at home, a week after the article had run, Henry had told him about Hank's accident. Dorrit had listened from the kitchen. Then Mr. Marshall called her to the telephone, saying that the reporter wanted to speak to *her*.

And here it was. Dorrit stared down at her words in print, filled with pride and a feeling of accomplishment greater than anything she had ever experienced before. She shook her head, awed. Her father patted her knee and rose. "I'm about as proud of you as a father could be," he said. "I've got to get back. I'll pick you up about ten minutes before the train's due, all right?"

After he left, she went inside and folded the magazine open, placing it reverently on the table, beside her notebook. They had asked her for a photograph, and she wondered now if she should have said no. She had wanted to say no to the whole thing. May was still angry at Mr. Dalrymple. But it was Byrd who had told Dorrit that she should go ahead and send her story to him when he asked.

She took up her pencil and continued to write.

Today I touched my very own words, printed on paper in a real magazine. This time they asked for a full-page story, and the illustration is much larger! Never, ever did I expect this to happen. I cannot even describe how it feels. I get all embarrassed when I think of people actually reading it, and I wonder if they will like it or if maybe they'll think it's silly and wonder how on earth it ever deserved to be published. I wonder if this is normal for authors. That part, the doubting, is kind of awful, but at the same time kind of thrilling. I wonder if the authors who write as 'Carolyn Keene' feel excited about the Nancy Drew books, since no one knows their real names. Though I am certainly not famous and I never will be, I need to remember not to get all full of myself, because nobody likes a person who is like that at all.

Criminy. I still cannot believe that Mr. Larimer is paying me $50.00 for my little stories. He says I ought to write a whole book. That seems like an awful lot of work to me. I told him I would think about it. I would love to buy a bicycle, and one of those new tabletop radios, so we could listen to Orphan Annie and Mr. Roosevelt's Fireside Chats.

Tomorrow is Easter Sunday. I will go to church with the Craigs. I am feeling especially blessed since Walt is coming back to us. My brother, a prodigal son of sorts. I have not seen him in so long! I suppose he will be like a grown-up man by now. He will be here in two hours and stay for two nights with us before he reports at Camp Roosevelt. He is excited about joining the Civilian Conservation Corps. I am glad he has this opportunity, though it seems unfair to me that only males are allowed to sign up. He says he will be working in the National Forest in the Blue Ridge Mountains, clearing trails and building roads. I want to ask him about the places he visited in the Merchant Marine. After church we will have an Easter egg hunt for the children. The prize will be one of Blue's big chocolate rabbits.

Dorrit closed her journal and ran her hand over the cover. The composition book was almost full now. She would need to get another one.

But that would be fine. Her father could take her to Woolworth's after they went to the bank to deposit her check from the *Post*.

She rose from the table to water Augusta's geraniums, now budding on the window ledge in bright, promising whorls of red and green. She stroked the velvety leaves, wishing she could tell her mother of their good fortune. She liked to believe that her mother saw, and that she approved. The kitchen window looked out over a pasture, emerald green with new grass. Beyond the rail fence, Peanut grazed with Byrd's horse. The mountains in the distance were spotted with new growth, and the sky above was crystalline blue.

Forty-Two
DORRIT AND MAY

The next morning at church, Dorrit sat in the middle of a pew, between her father and brother. When they stood to sing, she studied the stained glass windows, the jewel hues of ruby and cobalt, visually tracing the leaded outlines and shading of the glass lilies, comparing them to the real white trumpet lilies on the altar. Grace Episcopal was far smaller than the Mother Church in Boston, but its stone walls and sturdy oak beams seemed homier, more approachable. *More forgiving*, Dorrit thought.

Each Sunday, she had asked her father to come to church with her and, though he made excuses, she prayed he might change his mind. Dorrit found solace in the services—at first, they were a small comfort in the weeks after Hank's accident. Later, she found she could pray about what had happened to her, and the things she had lost. She had prayed that she might see Walt again, and God answered that prayer. She asked God if she should tell her father about the man at the forge, but so far, nothing had happened to cause her to change her mind about keeping her own counsel. *Time*, Dorrit thought, looking over at Hank, *does heal wounds, of the body and of the heart. We go forward, even when we don't know which direction we're heading.* God had spared Hank, and for that, Dorrit felt grateful. Times were still hard, and if what Mr. Craig said was right, they would continue to be for some time. Maybe it was true, what

President Roosevelt said on the radio, *the only thing we have to fear is fear itself.* Dorrit bowed her head as the acolyte passed down the aisle carrying the brass cross, then they filed out of the church.

May poured lemonade into cups and watched out the window as children swarmed around the yard for the Easter egg hunt. Delphina bustled about the kitchen, arranging deviled eggs on a platter, while frying chicken sputtered in a big iron skillet on the stove. On the table, a vase held a riot of yellow daffodils. A pink ham sat on a platter and an angel food cake on a cut-glass stand, surrounded by pansies. Outside, Archie Nelson stood with Uncle Cy, beside her father, each holding a bottle of recently legalized beer. Elsie was smoking and calling encouragement as her four boys combed the grass for eggs. Dorrit pointed to an egg, and Sister ran for it, grasping her basket in outstretched hands. Under the ash tree, Roy and his son sat on the grass, deep in conversation with Clarence.

Today was a day of celebration. It occurred to May that if a fortune-teller had predicted what the past year would bring for her, she would never have imagined that she would be feeling grateful. But she did feel gratitude. Her heart was nearly bursting with it.

Tomorrow she would be back at work, catching up, now that all of the Easter orders were delivered. The Orchard De-Lite Company workers had been invited today, with their children. They now boasted fourteen employees, each earning competitive wages. Each had been allotted a garden plot at Keswick Farm. Tomorrow, Roy would leave to drive his son to work at the CCC camp near Luray Caverns. Hank would continue lessons at home with Dorrit and go back to school in the fall, when Dorrit started college. Byrd would leave in the morning to go back to Washington. They had talked—May with her father, Roy, and Blue, about expansion and buying a delivery van, and Byrd encouraged them.

As the children gathered around Byrd, Elsie's son Frances jumped up and down with the prize egg while his brothers tried to snatch it away. Watching them all, May wondered if a time would come when things would get back to the way they were before the financial crash. Would Roosevelt really be able to put all those men back to work? Would there ever come a time when Byrd could reopen his law practice and be at home with them every night? Might they someday be able to move into the house at Chestnut Grove, and be able to keep it up? And if there came a time when she did not need or choose to work, would Byrd understand that it was a part of her life that made her the person she was? *Yes,* she thought, *now, he would understand.*

Normal, she thought, would never be the same again. *She* would never be the same, nor would Byrd, nor Hank, nor Dorrit, nor Roy. They all had been tested. They all had come through. There would be more tests, May knew, but for now, normal was enough.

AUTHOR'S NOTE

One of my favorite parts of writing historical fiction is the research. With both of my novels I've come across historical events that I knew little or nothing about, and those events ended up shaping my plots—sometimes in a big way.

I knew I wanted to continue May's story and I had an idea of what would happen in the next chapters of her life. Dorrit's character, however, was a surprise. I've heard writers speak of having characters "come" to them. I'd always been skeptical of this, but then a teenaged girl character started knocking around in my head and wouldn't go away. I knew there was something Dickensian about her, so after a while I named her with a combination of two of Charles Dickens's characters; Amy Dorrit from *Little Dorrit*, and Bill Sykes from *Oliver Twist*. Once she had a name, so many disparate bits clicked into place that I felt I was onto something. I could tell both May's and Dorrit's stories as parallel narratives and at some point, they would meet. But how, and why?

I kept stumbling upon research that I found compelling, yet also led me away from May's story in Virginia. When I first read about the Veteran's Bonus March I knew instantly where this girl Dorrit fit in and finally, I began to listen to her voice. I knew she was from Boston, and so, with no specific agenda in mind I took a trip there in 2016 for research. By chance

I ended up taking a docent-led Art and Architecture tour of the Boston Public Library. It was fascinating, and the building ended up being a part of Dorrit's story. I visited the Gibson House Museum, most recently featured as a filming location in the latest *Little Women* movie. That ended up being Mrs. Frazier's house in the book. Also in Boston, I took a tour of the Mother Church of the Church of Christ, Scientist. Afterward, the Church library staff were very helpful with my questions. The Sykes' tenement apartment was inspired by a trip to the Tenement Museum in New York City, where educator on staff Nick Capodice was most helpful.

In Virginia, Keswick Farm is the house where I live. Chestnut Grove is not a real house, but the descriptions of it are inspired by Castle Hill, which is the home of my brother-in-law and sister-in-law. Other Keswick locations are familiar features of my neighborhood—Grace Episcopal Church, the Keswick Post Office, and the old train station (now part of a residential school). Across the road from the site of the fictitious Keswick Market is an old blacksmith's forge which has been renovated into a charming home. It really does have snake hinges on the doors. The American Silk Mill did operate in Orange, Virginia, up the road a bit. Now, the location is a restaurant.

The Great Depression is an era full of sad stories. I was inspired by the stark photographs of Dorothea Lange and Walker Evans and by the way those shots express the humanity and the suffering of this time in our history. I read about the Bonus March and the Great Depression in both non-fiction and fiction. William Kennedy's novel *Ironweed* was an inspiration, as was Woodie Guthrie's 1943 memoir of hobo life, *Bound for Glory*. *Hard Times* by Studs Terkel was also a great resource. As with my previous novel based in Virginia, I relied on a book of local history, *Albemarle, Jefferson's County, 1727–1976* by John Hammond Moore.

The Nancy Drew video games of my daughter's childhood were a far cry from the original book editions, which began publication in 1930. Through the years, Nancy has been edited, modernized, and in some ways, toned down. I doubt that the sixteen-year-old Nancy Drew of 2021 would be loaned a loaded revolver by her father when she goes to investigate a theft. In 1931, she was.

Regarding language—I use the terms hobo, tramp, and bum, since these were commonly used terms in the Depression era. I do not intend the terms as slurs.

In doing medical research for this book I wanted to be accurate to the time period. My family doctor, Daniel Sawyer, of Charlottesville, Virginia, patiently answered my specific questions and loaned me a medical text which was published in 1939. Dr. Wise's *The Modern Home Physician-Illustrated* is a real book. On eBay I was able to find an earlier original edition from 1934, and Dr. Wise became my source for medical terminology and treatments. Having dealt personally with anxiety issues for most of my life, I was fascinated by the medical opinions about it from the 1930s.

As a lifetime lover of candy, that part of research was lots of fun. I enjoyed reading *Candy, the Sweet History* by Beth Kimmerle; *Sweets: A History of Candy*, by Tim Richardson; and the *À la Mère de Famille Cookbook* by Julien Merceron. I also used my grandmother Nash's recipe for molasses taffy, which I fondly remember making as a child, with my father.

ACKNOWLEDGMENTS

I continue to be immensely grateful to Rick Bleiweiss and his stellar team at Blackstone Publishing. Also, Trident Media Group and my agent Mark Gottlieb, for being available whenever I have questions. Thanks to my editors, Jennifer Pooley and Ciera Cox, who once again made my pages better in important ways. I'm indebted to Ann-Marie Nieves of Get Red P.R. and Lauren Maturo of Blackstone, for their innovation and tenacity in launching and marketing a novel during a pandemic. Thanks again, also, to Alenka Linaschke for her beautiful cover art and book design.

Thanks to the many fellow authors who offered advice and support: Sarah McCraw Crow, Pamela Binnings Ewen, Kathleen Grissom, Alan Hlad, Francine Mathews, Nancy Thayer, James Wade, and Mary Kay Zuravleff, among others. Also, fellow workshop participants at VCFA and Sewanee Writers' Conference who critiqued these pages.

Thanks to the teachers who helped workshop these pages: At Vermont College of Fine Arts—Connie May Fowler, Abby Frucht, Douglas Glover, Brian Leung, and especially Jacqueline Mitchard, who made me read Charles Portis's *True Grit*, and Clint McCown, who checked almost every date and location and told me to read *Ironweed*. At the 2018 Sewanee Writers' Conference—Richard Bausch and Jill McCorkle gave me helpful feedback.

I'm grateful to first readers: Mary Amos, Julie Hall Cole, Dr. Stephen Geller, Brenda Hagg, Ann Potter; and to the Charlottesville WriterHouse writing group: Ron Harris, Charles Heiner, Linda Hewitt, and the late Catherine Coiner.

I am in debt to the late Mrs. Drue Heinz and the committee, as well as administrator Hamish Robinson, for granting me a Hawthornden Fellowship in 2018, where I worked on these pages and spent a glorious month with a wonderful cohort of writers: Sheena M.J. Cooke, H.S. Cross, Selina Fillinger, and T. Sean Steele.

In Charlottesville, thanks to Julia Kudravetz and her team at New Dominion Bookshop, and to Sibley Johns and WriterHouse, for supporting local readers and writers.

For assistance with research, I am grateful to the following:

Dr. Steven Geller, Dr. Daniel Sawyer.

Rich Evans and Michael Hamilton, the Mary Baker Eddy Library, Boston, for assistance with questions.

Boston Globe archives.

Jessy Wheeler, Research Services Department, Boston Public Library.

The American Presidency Project at University of California, Santa Barbara, for the text of the Franklin Roosevelt acceptance speech from July,1932. https://www.presidency.ucsb.edu.

And finally, thanks again to Rocky, for his continued loving and benevolent disinterest.